Praise for KILL ME AGAIN and for TERENCE FAHERTY

"Kill Me Again is a marvelous, meticulously crafted entertainment, recreating the cinematic era of colorful characters who spoke in razor-sharp dialog. And Faherty's notion of a sequel to *Casablanca* is great fun—even if the rest of the novel weren't so wonderful, you wouldn't want to miss it."

The Drood Review

"Alive with the music of 1947, the voices of the era, the smell of the postwar, refreshingly straightforward and evocative, *Kill Me Again* is easily one of the best of the year. Don't miss it."

Mystery Scene

"Edgar-nominated author Faherty has a feel for the way we all think Hollywood types act when the cameras aren't rolling, and he feeds our fantasies with deft characterizations and right-on dialogue."

Booklist

"The mystery packs as many curves as Betty Grable."

Kirkus Reviews

"Faherty (who writes the elegant Owen Keane mysteries about a metaphysical detective) puts together an intricately plotted thriller that is not only plausible but peopled with intriguing and very human characters. Elliott has just enough angst and anger, and he's the best Los Angeles guide since Philip Marlowe."

News & Observer

D1316881

Books by Terence Faherty:

The Scott Elliott Series
Kill Me Again (1996)
Come Back Dead (1997)
Raise the Devil (2000)

The Owen Keane Series
Deadstick (1991)
Live to Regret (1992)
The Lost Keats (1993)
Die Dreaming (1994)
Prove the Nameless (1996)
The Ordained (1997)
Orion Rising (1999)

Terence Faherty

Terence Faherty is the author of the Shamus-winning Scott Elliott private eye series set in the golden age of Hollywood. He also writes the Edgar-nominated Owen Keane series. Faherty lives in Indianapolis, Indiana, with his wife Jan.

Kill Me Again

Terence Faherty

CRUM CREEK PRESS
The Mystery Company
Carmel, Indiana

This is a work of fiction. All the characters and events portrayed in this book are fictitious, and any resemblance to real people or events is purely coincidental.

KILL ME AGAIN

Copyright © 1996 by Terence Faherty

ISBN: 1-932325-02-6

Cover art by Tim Faherty

PUBLISHING HISTORY
Simon & Schuster hardcover edition: May 1996
The Mystery Company paperback edition: October 2003

Crum Creek Press / The Mystery Company
484 East Carmel Drive #378
Carmel, IN 46032

www.droodreview.com

FOR THE CORYELL FAMILY

1

I arrived late for the screening at Warner Bros. The man who had invited me let me know how late by pointedly ignoring my entrance. He was seated alone in the last row of the little theater. The rest of the audience was grouped together up front. All six of them, by my hurried count. They also ignored me as I took my seat beside the gentleman in the back.

In place of hello, the man asked, "Do you remember where you were when you first saw *Passage to Lisbon*?"

The house lights dimmed before I could answer. I passed the few seconds of quiet darkness that followed thinking of that lost evening at the movies. The moment held a prominent place in my collection of wartime memories, not far behind the Sunday morning in Hollywood, California, when I heard that Pearl Harbor had been bombed and the afternoon in Rheims, France, when word came in that Germany had surrendered. The *Passage to Lisbon* showing fell between those two milestones, both chronologically and emotionally. The film's message was tailored for that gray, uncertain, middle period. It said, in essence, "We're up against it, but we've got the stuff to see it through."

I'd needed to hear the last part of that pep talk very badly when *Passage to Lisbon* and I, Hollywood's greatest contribution to the war effort and its most negligible one, came together. Our meeting occurred in June 1943 at the East Garrison of Camp Forrest, Tennessee, in a mess tent converted to a theater on a hot, humid Saturday night.

The smells of dinner hung on in the tent, mingling with the smells of the diners, a hundred or so of us squeezed together on backless wooden benches. The night sounds coming in through the tent's open flaps—frogs and crickets and God knows what else—almost drowned out the actors. The projector broke down in the middle of every reel. All in all, not the ideal way to see a movie, but I'd never enjoyed one more.

You remember the story. An old liner turned gambling ship with the ironic name *Joyeuse Ile* is plying the waters of the western Mediterranean in late 1941, a dangerous time for sea travel. France has fallen to the Nazis. The ship is under the protection of Vichy, and commanded by a cynical and hard drinking captain, Roland Manet. The *Joyeuse Ile* cruises between Marseille and the ports of North Africa, tolerated by British warships for the sake of the refugees it carries and protected from German U-boats by the valuable contraband it smuggles to German forces via friendly Vichy officials. Both sides share another interest in the old liner: it is a meeting ground for spies of all nations, an open market for secret information.

For the lucky refugees, the ones whose papers are in order, the ship is a relatively safe way of escaping Europe. For the unlucky majority, a passage on the *Joyeuse Ile* represents one last gamble. More than information can be bought on board. The black market also does a brisk business in passports, visas, and identification papers. Despairing refugees gamble in the ship's casino—run by a mysterious American expatriate named Steven Laird—hoping to win enough to buy their way to freedom.

All that background was passed along in a couple of quick scenes that were over almost before I'd grown numb to my wooden seat. The story really started with the *Joyeuse Ile* making ready to leave Marseille. Two rumors have electrified the ship's company. The first is that the liner will make an unprecedented stop in the neutral port of Lisbon. The stated reason is the delivery of a German diplomatic delegation led by a professor named Benz. He and his companions are correctly assumed to be Nazi spies by everyone from Captain Manet to the cabin boys. The second rumor is that someone aboard the ship has obtained two Geneva Exemptions, diplomatic passports issued under the authority of the Geneva convention. Designed to facilitate the movements of convention inspectors and diplomats, the Exemptions are the bureaucratic equivalent of the ruby slippers from *The Wizard of Oz*. Anyone possessing them can tap their heels together and escape the *Joyeuse Ile* forever.

Because of its tantalizing destination, the ship is well stocked with refugees. Among them is Franz Wojcik, a one-time concert pianist turned Polish resistance leader who has been fleeing the Nazis since his escape from a concentration camp. He is traveling with his beautiful cousin Maura.

Wojcik and his cousin make the acquaintance of Steven Laird. Wojcik is desperate to obtain the Geneva Exemptions, which have come into Laird's possession as security for a gambling debt. The unlucky gambler, a black marketeer named Tursi, is lost overboard under mysterious circumstances prior to the ship's stop in Oran. Laird and Maura fall in love at first sight. For them, the voyage becomes a cruise out of time, an interlude in which the horror of the war is replaced by moonlit strolls on the deck, cocktails in the ship's lounge, and endless dances to an old Tin Pan Alley gem, "Love Me Again."

The action heats up as the *Joyeuse Ile* nears its final port of call, Lisbon. Laird discovers that Maura is really Wojcik's wife. He decides that their brief affair has been nothing more than an attempt to obtain the Geneva Exemptions. Maura will say only that she loves Laird. In anger, he pretends to burn one of the passports and offers the other to Wojcik. The patriot can save himself and leave Maura with Laird or send Maura to safety and face certain arrest when the ship returns to Marseille. Either way, Laird will be rid of him. Wojcik surprises him by choosing Maura's safety over his own.

To redeem himself, Laird gives both the Exemptions to Wojcik and sees the couple off the ship and onto the pilot boat at the mouth of Lisbon harbor. Then, to prevent Benz from interfering with the Wojciks ashore, Steve frees members of the crew imprisoned at the insistence of Benz because of Free French sympathies. He leads the men in an attempt to take the ship, intending to sail it to England. Benz is killed in the fighting, but the mutiny fails. All seems lost until Captain Manet, sickened by the sight of Frenchmen killing Frenchmen, decides to take the ship and its refugee passengers to England himself and join the fight against the Nazis. Fade out as the *Joyeuse Ile* slips into the fog.

Not Ibsen on a good day, but the movie had struck me as something special at that first showing. Art maybe, or, if not, something as close to it as the Hollywood movie factory could turn out. A lie told by liars so accomplished that it constituted a high order of truth. Between the shots of toy ships that opened and closed the picture, there was a stretch of pure Hollywood, a place I'd longed after in that Tennessee camp the way a blinded man longs for a sunrise. Hidden in the picture's patriotic public message, there seemed to be a love note direct from Hollywood to me. "I'm behind you," it said. "I'll be waiting." More lies, as it turned out.

A projector came to life through a peephole just above my head, dragging me back to the present, to August 1947. I settled in to watch a scene from the sequel to *Passage to Lisbon*. It had a hopeful title, borrowed from the original's theme song: *Love Me Again*.

The air in the screening room was heavy with smoke, making the projector's beam appear as a solid shaft above me. The beam lit a small screen painfully until the film began, a dark long shot of a stretch of black sea littered with floating wreckage and obscured now and then by drifting smoke. The movie smoke blended seamlessly with the smoke floating over my head, drawing me into the scene against my will. In place of cigarettes and cigars, I began to smell spent explosive, a smell that was also a sensation, a stinging, a burning. This trick of memory had my palms moistening the plush arms of my chair.

In the background of the shot was a burning bit of wreckage that moved up and down slowly on the oily swell. I tried to distract myself with thoughts of the technicians who had set the prop afloat in the studio tank after rigging it to burn gently, like a fire in a grate. During the shooting, there would have been a man with a fire extinguisher just out of the range of the camera. I tried to move my eyes from the screen to the point in the darkness where he would have stood, but I found I couldn't manage it.

In the foreground of the shot was a wooden raft and on it were two men. Two sailors, I mean, wearing the gray, tattered uniforms of war. Any war. One man was lying on his back, his right hand pressed against a wet, black wound in his chest. The second figure supported the first. His head was bent toward the wounded sailor and his face was obscured by some craftsman's careful placement of the lights.

I knew the name of the gentleman playing the wounded man. It was Nigel Clay, one of the top character actors in Hollywood. He was too old in 1947 to be passing himself off as a combatant, but the makeup men had done their best for him. They'd darkened his gray hair and—to balance things—they'd lightened his face, which both simulated a loss of blood and disguised the furrows on his brow and the bags under his eyes. The disguise was far from perfect, but that didn't matter. Dying men tend to have old men's faces, so Clay was exactly right for his part.

As the camera moved slowly in on the pair, the face of the second actor was revealed. It was Torrance Beaumont, a one-time crooner turned movie gangster turned romantic star. His short, dishevelled hair was black, as were his eyes and the shadows in his sunken cheeks. The effect should have been sepulchral, but somehow wasn't. Beaumont looked as fully alive as Clay looked nearly dead.

The scene was a rough cut, an intermediate step between raw rushes and a finished film. The long opening shot was designed to play out against the closing bars of the film's title music, music that was still unwritten. The shot ended with a close-up of Clay's ravaged face. When the camera got as close as it was going to get, the actor smiled, weakly.

"It's all up for me, Steven," Clay said in the sweet, husky voice that was his meal ticket. "I wonder if that mine was one of theirs or ours. Theirs, I hope."

"They haven't made the one yet that's gonna get you, Captain," Beaumont's off-camera voice said.

Clay barely moved his head, but his rejection of the lie came off the screen like a shout.

The next shot showed both actors, Clay in right profile and Beaumont full face. They'd adjusted the lighting for this setup. You could clearly see Beaumont's eyes now and his slightly twisted mouth.

"Not much time," Clay said. "I must tell you. Something about the old days."

"Save your strength, Rollie."

Clay's close-up came back on the screen. There was a trickle of blood at the left side of his mouth. It was black, of course, but that limitation of the film stock was accidentally right.

"It's about Franz Wojcik … and Maura … and Professor Benz … and the Geneva Exemptions." Clay narrowed his eyes slightly, as though he were straining to remember some lost moment from his childhood. "It's about our voyage to Lisbon."

Back then to the two shot as Beaumont spoke. "What about it?"

Clay's gravelly voice grew more honeyed as his eyes began to lose focus. I found I was leaning forward in my seat.

"It was all an act, Steven. A melodrama worked out by Professor Benz."

"Then he gave himself a bad part. He left the stage feet first, remember?" Beaumont was keeping pace with Clay now, affecting a light delivery but undercutting it with a dead look in his eyes. Was he worried about Clay or frightened by what the dying man was trying to say? I couldn't tell.

Clay laughed at Beaumont's joke. It was the kind of laugh that ends in a cough, a Hollywood convention that tells the audience the lights are about to dim.

11

"Benz did overplay a little," Clay said. "He hated you, Steven. He wanted to kill you, even though he needed you to complete his mission."

"What mission?" Beaumont demanded, a little panicked now, his hand gathering up the bloody front of Clay's uniform.

"Forgive me, Steven. I was blind then or I would never have been a party to it. Forgive me for that and for this, for taking away the great moment of your life. I thought there still might be …"

Cut to a close-up of Beaumont as Clay's out-of-focus head slowly tilted away in the foreground. Beaumont's eyes remained dead, but his mouth bent down in a familiar sneer as he asked the dead man, "What might there be?"

2

When the indirect lighting came on in the screening room, the half dozen men in the rows before me got to their feet amid the happy sounds of self-congratulation. I stayed in my seat in the last row, as did Paddy Maguire. Together we watched the audience make their way out. They shook each other's hands and patted each other's backs and generally treated Paddy and me like two extra items of furniture.

After the little theater's upholstered door had swung shut, Paddy spoke without turning toward me. His big voice filled the room, bouncing back at me from the blank white screen. "The money men seemed pleased, Scotty. What did you think of *Love Me Again*?"

"It was a little short," I said.

Paddy chuckled. "They'll fix that soon enough. They just rushed this bit together to scare up some more backers."

He stood up to stretch and then parked himself against the

12

next row of seats so he could face me. He was just under six feet tall, but big for his height, his waistline running a close second to his barrel chest. His face was broad, with features that were regular but generously doled out, and his jaw was heavy enough to gracefully support its original chin and a healthy spare. Although he was only the age of the century, he had gray hair that stuck up in front in the style made famous by his former coworker Stan Laurel. Paddy still dressed more like the old vaudeville hand he'd once been than the successful businessman he now was. Today's outfit was a double-breasted suit of the same unsubtle stripe as his vest. His silk shirt was the color of an egg yolk, and his tie and handkerchief shared blue polka dots.

This fashion plate operated a company called the Hollywood Security Agency. It provided discreet security services for the studios, which most often meant cleaning up the messes left by their stars. Paddy hadn't set out to be a watchdog for spoiled actors. He'd come west in the last years of the silents, hoping, like thousands before and since, to become a spoiled actor himself. The best he'd done were a few turns as a heavy in Hal Roach comedies. He should have been a natural for talking pictures, as he had a deep voice with no sharp edges or accents. Not even an Irish one, though I could hear an echo of his immigrant parents in the way he formed his sentences. Instead of prospering, Paddy had gotten lost in the sea of new faces the talkies ushered in. He'd drifted into security work for Paramount, where I'd met him shortly before the war.

Not long after that, Paddy's eye for the main chance had spotted a business opportunity. The big studios had seen the outbreak of war as a good excuse for cutting off the protection money they'd always paid the local police. Like Paddy, the payola dated from the silent days, and it had kept many a star out of the drunk tank and off the front pages. One result of the decision to stop the payoffs had been Errol Flynn's celebrated 1942 trial for statutory rape, a message to the studios on the dangers of not playing ball. Another, quieter by-product had been the founding that same year of the Hollywood Security Agency by the enterprising Patrick J. Maguire.

"I noticed you were watching that screen pretty intensely," Paddy said. "Bother you, did it?"

I shrugged and changed the subject. "Why a sequel? Sequels are for Frankenstein movies. Not for A pictures."

"*Passage to Lisbon* wasn't just any A picture," Paddy said. "It was the surprise hit of 1942." Then he added, "I meant the war angle. Did that get to you?"

I let the question beat itself to death against the soundproof walls. "Why didn't they shoot this thing in '43? Why did they wait four years?"

Paddy took out a cigar case and selected a six-inch corona. In his hand the big cigar looked like a brown cigarette. He bit off the end and spat it onto the carpet.

"Dirty habit, smoking," he said. "They thought of a sequel right away, as a matter of fact. Something named *Return Voyage*, I'm told. They had a scenario worked up, but they never filmed it. It was too much of the Rover Boys meet the Nazis, with Tory Beaumont, Steve Laird I should say, sailing around blowing up things and escaping by the skin of his teeth. Not the same thing as *Passage to Lisbon* at all, you see. No love story. No human being story, for that matter."

Paddy paused to light his cigar, rolling it over and over in the flame of a wooden match. "So nothing much happens for years, except that Beaumont becomes a big star on the strength of *Passage to Lisbon* and makes half a dozen movies that vaguely resemble it. Then out of nowhere one Bert Kramer comes up with a script for an actual sequel, and it's a dandy. He's a Warners screenwriter with mostly B pictures to his credit, but he's a big fan of *Passage to Lisbon*. Kramer's timing couldn't have been better, what with Beaumont launching his own production company. Siren Productions it's called. Tory needs a big hit to set himself on his feet, and this thing has box office written all over it."

14

I dug out my pack of Luckies and tapped one free. Paddy had another kitchen match going before I had the cigarette in my mouth. I leaned toward the flame. "If the script's so good, why are they scrambling for money?"

Paddy shook the match out with a single quick flip of his wrist. "You've never understood the business side of this business. There's no such thing as enough money in Hollywood. The cast alone on this one could soak up a swimming pool full."

"I heard Nigel Clay got a hundred thousand for a single day's shooting."

"That moonshine is straight out of a still in the publicity department. Not that Mr. Clay donated his services, mind you. But he's not the only one at the trough. There's also Ella Larsen. She's not the greenhorn she was in '42."

"She's signed though, hasn't she?"

"Yes. So has the colored dance team, the Clausen Brothers, Eddie and Joe in the movie. The only holdout is that foreign fellow, Hans Breem. From what I hear, he's not crazy about having the great Franz Wojcik, hero of the resistance, turned into a villain."

I wasn't sure how I felt about that myself. "So what are we supposed to do?" I asked. "Find Hans Breem and break his fingers one by one?"

Paddy laughed regretfully. "No. Casting is someone else's lookout. We're here to see about this." He reached into his breast pocket and removed a folded piece of paper. He opened the sheet ceremoniously and handed it to me.

On it was typed a single sentence: "Why are you using a Communist writer on *Love Me Again*?"

I whistled, softly.

"Exactly," Paddy said. "What you're holding is a typescript of the actual note, which, incidentally, was also typed and unsigned. The original was sent to no less a personage than Jack Warner himself. It put the wind up his holiness in no small way."

That was easy to believe. Hollywood was currently buzzing about its latest Red scare. Representatives of something called the House Un-American Activities Committee were in town, sniffing around in people's underwear drawers.

"Warner is scheduled to appear before the HUA Committee, isn't he?" I asked.

Paddy glanced up to the projection room behind me. It must have been empty, because he said, "That's just for show. He's already testified. In secret, last spring. That doesn't leave this room, by the way."

I would have asked Paddy how he'd learned of Warner's secret testimony if there was the slightest chance he'd tell me. Instead I asked, "Is Kramer a Communist?"

"Or was he, in his dewy youth?" Paddy countered. "That's what we have to find out. Also, who sent the note? And can they be bought off or scared off or no? That's the jackpot question. There are some influential parties at this studio who share your low opinion of sequels. They also wouldn't mind seeing Beaumont's production company fail. A hint of scandal, and they'll be pushing to scrap the whole project."

Paddy brushed some cigar ash from his vest, knowing without looking that there'd be some there to brush. "Warner Bros. is particularly sensitive about the charge of Communist sympathies on account of having made those pro-Soviet films during the war. What was that big one with Walter Huston? Something about Moscow."

"*Mission to Moscow*," I said. "With Ann Harding and Oscar Homolka."

"Right," Paddy said, smiling as he always did when my studied indifference to the movie business slipped. "Those pictures were the subject of Mr. Warner's secret chat with the committee."

"The Russians were our allies when those movies were made."

Paddy nodded. "But now they head the list of all-time

16

bogeymen. And the same Congressmen who shoveled arms and money to Stalin five years ago are today searching for his minions in the national basement. Politics is a strange business. Almost as screwy as motion pictures. When Hollywood and Washington get together, it's best to be somewhere else entirely."

"Sounds like the cue for an exit to me," I said.

"Actually, it's Scott Elliott's entrance music. I've a feeling you're just the man for this job."

Finding the job I was just the man for was something of a preoccupation with Paddy. He'd taken me in after my discharge from the army, a move that spoke more of kindness than business sense. Like my boss, I was a former actor. To be precise, I'd been a contract player with Paramount for a couple of heady years before the war. I'd worked my way up to small parts in B pictures and an occasional walk-on in A's before I'd won a little lottery called the draft. That had taken care of my open dates between 1942 and V-E Day. After that, I'd had all the free time in the world. Hollywood had changed while I'd been away, or I had changed. Probably we both had. I was as much in demand after the war as oleo margarine and meatless Tuesdays.

I should have packed up and moved back to Indiana, but somehow I hadn't been able to. I might have ended up selling cars or leading tours of the movie stars' homes, if Paddy hadn't found me. He'd decided that, as I was an ex-soldier, I was tailor-made for security work. It was an understandable mistake, but my boss was not a man to admit a mistake, however understandable.

Paddy wore a golden chain across the front of his vest. He pulled at it now, reeling in a pocket watch the size of a demi-hubcap. "We've just time to make our appointment," he said.

"Our appointment with whom?"

Paddy used his cigar to gesture toward the screen behind him. "Steven Laird, no less," he said.

3

The Southern California morning was, as usual, severely overlit. I thought about putting on my sunglasses, but I knew they'd inspire some wry observation from Paddy. Something about the cheaters being a legacy from my salad days. I made do with pulling my hat brim down toward my nose. Paddy's own hat, a homburg, sat on the back of his head, and he marched along, puffing on his cigar, like a prosperous baker taking the air on a Sunday afternoon. As we walked, Paddy nodded to people he knew. It was a steady process, Paddy's circle of friends being only slightly smaller than Eleanor Roosevelt's. At one point, he stopped to shoot the breeze with Jack Carson, a former bit player who'd made it big while I'd been away. Carson didn't know me or seem interested in filling that void in his life, so I took in the scenery.

You've probably seen shots of Hollywood studios in a dozen different movies. A typical one might show groups of chorines in plumed hats, African natives also plumed, foreign legionaries, and men in top hat and tails all parading back and forth like they were using the soundstages for a giant game of musical chairs. Not exactly a true image, like every image out of Hollywood, and not an entirely false one either. On this particular morning the Warners lot looked less to me like Ringling Brothers Circus than the swing shift at Lockheed. It looked like a factory, in other words, running full bore, whose product just happened to be fairy dust.

When Paddy finished buttonholing Carson, he led me to soundstage number seven. The guard at the door greeted Paddy like an old lodge brother, which he was, in a way. Then he waved us through into an enclosed space that rivaled an aircraft hangar for size. It was largely wasted space on this particular day. I could see only two sets, neither very large. The one farthest from our door was lit with work lights. It was a cabaret of some sort and it was empty, except for a small chorus line in street clothes stepping through some blocking.

Next to the cabaret was a smaller, busier set. It was a single, shabby room—a dressing room for the cabaret probably—with a theatrical poster in French on one wall. There were two men in the pretend room, one seated at a dressing table and the other standing over the first in a menacing pose. The two stand-ins remained frozen in place like mannequins in a shop window, while half a dozen lighting technicians fussed over them. The process was supervised by a small, black-haired man in a silk shirt, jodhpurs, and riding boots.

"You recognize him, of course," Paddy said, nodding toward the dark man.

"Cecil B. DeMille, I presume," I said, tired by then of Paddy's name dropping.

"Max Froy, you mean. The old pro who directed *Passage to Lisbon*. Beaumont's leaving nothing to chance on this one."

That judgment seemed unduly optimistic, given our current errand. It reminded me of a line in *Passage to Lisbon*, and I quoted it, loosely. "Fate's already dealt itself in."

Paddy missed the allusion. "It's early days yet," he said.

He led me to the quiet corner of the stage where Beaumont's mobile dressing room stood. As we neared the trailer, its door opened and a harried looking man stepped out. He had a thin, pale face, hair that needed trimming, and oversize horn-rims. He carried a bundle of papers, and the collar of his jacket was turned up on one side. Central casting's idea of a tyro college don, I thought, late for his first day of class.

The professor smiled and said hello to Paddy without breaking stride. For once, my boss had to be prompted for a name.

"Bert Kramer?" I asked.

"No," Paddy said. "Fred Wilner, assistant to the coproducer, Vincent Mediate."

Paddy reached the trailer door before it swung shut. The

great man himself called to us to come inside. The trailer was the size of a blue-collar living room, and its interior was hazy with cigarette smoke. At the center of the cloud sat Torrance Beaumont, resplendent in a red silk dressing gown over a frayed shirt and cheap gray suit pants.

The internal contradictions of his outfit reminded me of the Hollywood insiders' take on Beaumont: he was a sensitive, intelligent man who happened to make his living playing gangsters and grifters. At least he had before the war, when I'd almost been a Hollywood insider. Since then things had changed. Beaumont was another example of a supporting player who had risen to stardom since Pearl Harbor. He was the premier example, in fact, as there were few stars bigger than Beaumont in 1947. It was a case of the times catching up with the screen image, the times having been shifted into overdrive by the war. People no longer saw their heroes as godlike or even particularly pure. They'd seen too much or heard too much of the heroism of ordinary, imperfect men. They'd also learned the basic lesson of war: that good men with noble intentions do truly horrible things.

Beaumont had come to personify the new hero. His characters typically had shady, even criminal, pasts. They'd had their early idealism beaten out of them, and they wore the resulting disillusionment very much on their sleeves. Their cynicism took in everything from political systems to sexual relations. On this last point, however, the irresistible force of the new realism met the immovable object of Hollywood cliché, the cliché being that love was the ultimate transforming, ennobling force. For love, the Beaumonts of the world would rise up in the last reel and do whatever nasty, heroic work had to be done, often losing everything in the process.

Beaumont remained in his chair. Paddy stepped over to shake his hand and then turned to me. "This is Scott Elliott," he said. "One of my top operatives."

Instead of extending his hand, Beaumont ran a thumb along

the edge of his jaw. "We've met before, haven't we?" he asked.

"Yes," I said. "Before the war. At the Brown Derby. I slugged you."

"Damn," Paddy said.

I'd been at the Derby that night with some starlet I'd never met before, paired with her by a studio publicity genius and sent out with orders to see and be seen. The starlet had known someone at Beaumont's table, and we'd stopped by to say hello. Beaumont, who'd had a few, had taken an unaccountable interest in me, nicknaming me "Handsome" and then "Hoosier" after he'd forced me to trot out a thumbnail autobiography.

I hadn't met Beaumont before that night, but I'd heard about the game he liked to play. He would pick out some innocent party and goad him until said party was about to throw a punch. Then Beaumont would back down in such a way that the injured innocent would have no excuse to belt him. The challenge for Beaumont was seeing how far he could push the mark and get away with it, how much insult he could deliver with impunity. The goal was to leave his victim standing there as red and helpless as a fireplug after the dog has moved along.

I'd realized belatedly that Beaumont had selected me for the treatment. I'd seen only one way out.

"So you were in *Second Chorus*, huh?" Beaumont had asked, showing too many teeth as he smiled up at me. "Is it true what they say about chorus boys?"

The front of his dress shirt hadn't given my left hand much purchase, but I'd still managed to lift him to his feet before I socked him. I hadn't hit him hard—I didn't known how to in those days—but it had been hard enough to rock his padded chair when he landed.

"No," I'd said, as evenly as I could. "It isn't true."

End of flashback. On my walk to the trailer with Paddy, I'd worked out the odds of Beaumont remembering me as roughly slim to none. Seven years had passed since that night, and he'd been soused. But maybe not so soused as I'd thought. Or maybe his ribbing game didn't often backfire quite that badly.

Beaumont smiled at me now the way he had at the Derby, showing only his upper teeth, but showing every bit of those. "Oh yeah," he said. "I remember now. Scott Elliott. Two T's followed by two more T's. Must not have been a shortage of them in your family. You were an actor back then, or trying to be."

"Trying to be," I said.

He looked me up and down, taking in the quality of my suit. It was easy to take in, as I'd stupidly left my red silk dressing gown at home.

"Army?" he asked.

"Yes."

"Overseas?"

"Yes."

"Rugged, was it?" His toothy grin had faded into nothing more than a solicitous smile.

"Every now and again," I said.

"Have a seat."

Paddy gave me a black look as we sat down, but said nothing. He took up most of a divan that rested against the same wall as the trailer's door. I sat in a club chair on the opposite side of a small table from Beaumont. He pushed a box of cigarettes across the table to me.

To Paddy, Beaumont said, "Care for anything? Or is it too early in the day?"

Paddy glanced briefly toward the glass at Beaumont's elbow, which contained water, neat. "A trifle early, I'm afraid," Paddy said.

Beaumont studied us while he hunted for a loose piece of tobacco on his tongue. He was made up for the day's work. His hairpiece was in place, and a phony five o'clock shadow had been painted on his cheeks. He'd aged visibly since the *Passage to Lisbon* days—his thin face thinner and his prominent eyes more prominent—but then the world had aged, too. Every new line on Beaumont's face only made him more fitted for the role he'd been born to play, the weary, knowing fighter, struggling out of his corner for one last round.

"You know the layout, I guess," he finally said.

"I've met with your Vincent Mediate," Paddy said. "He explained the problem."

"Mediate's not my anything, pal," Beaumont said. "He's Jack Warner's man. Ever since Hal Wallis jumped ship, Warner's been looking for a new goose to lay his golden eggs for him. Mediate's the latest goose in training. He worked on Broadway before the war, which makes him an automatic genius as far as the deep thinkers in this town are concerned. He's supposed to be the liaison between Siren Productions and the studio, but he's really the studio's watchdog. I know that, and Mediate knows I know it, so we get along."

"How does the studio feel about you and Siren?" I asked.

"The same way the British feel about Mahatma Gandhi. I'm an upstart, an ingrate, a lousy dresser, you name it. They're hoping I'll fail the way Cagney did and come back to them with my hat in my hand. That's okay. All I want is a fair shot at the big money, and the big money's in production. That's been true since Theda Bara vamped her first parson. I've got just so many more years as a heartthrob left in me. After that, I'll be living off my war bonds. That's okay, too. Nobody lasts forever in this business. I just don't want to end up one of those sorry old goats who've watched it all run through their fingers."

He paused to light another cigarette. "That's enough of my life story," he said. "Let's get down to cases. What are we to do about the note and how are we to do it?"

Paddy leaned forward slightly, his hands resting on his knees. "Tell us what you know about Kramer."

"Practically nothing," Beaumont said. "Except that he's been kicking around the studio since '40 or '41."

"Ever work with him before?" I asked.

"I heard he did some rewrites on one of my pictures. *We Die at Dawn*, I think. I've never met him. You don't often meet the writers on a picture unless you make a point of it or there's trouble."

He meant script problems, but his comment gave Paddy an opening for the big question. "On the subject of trouble, is Kramer a Red?"

Beaumont shrugged. "He says no. Mediate went to talk with him yesterday. I wanted him to wait until you boys were on board, but that wasn't fast enough for the big brass. Kramer denied everything in triplicate. Mediate seemed convinced."

"What do you think?" I asked.

"That none of this amounts to a piss in the ocean." Beaumont leaned forward in his chair now, as Paddy had done. We three would have formed a huddle if I'd joined the movement. I stayed where I was.

"I don't give a damn about Kramer's politics or yours or Joe DiMaggio's," Beaumont said. "Politics don't matter. It's whether you can deliver the goods that counts. Kramer's delivered, and if we want to make a picture, we've got to see him through this. We can't whitewash the guy or undo any mistakes he made twenty years ago. So we've got to keep this quiet. *You* have to keep this quiet."

"Did Kramer have any ideas on who the author of the note might be?" Paddy asked.

"If he did, he didn't share them with Mediate."

Paddy turned to me. "A talk with Mr. Kramer is on your agenda, then."

Our client addressed me next. "After that, you can dust off your tuxedo. Mediate's throwing a reception at the Stratford Hotel tonight. He and his wife are renting a suite there while the paint is drying on their new house out in the hills. They could have stayed on their yacht—also new—but Vince gets seasick. This reception's for *Love Me Again*. Mediate's wining and dining some of the money men from back East, and maybe getting some free ink out of the columnists, if he can pique their interest."

"What's supposed to be piquing my interest?" I asked.

Beaumont leaned back in his chair, smiling his mirthless smile again. "The original of the anonymous note was an interesting document," he said. "It was typed on hotel stationery. Stratford Hotel stationery."

4

While Beaumont was still savoring my reaction, a knock sounded on the trailer door. "Yes?" he said, without taking his eyes from me.

The reply wafted in through the trailer's tin foil wall. "They're ready for you, Mr. Beaumont."

"Thanks, Willie. Be right there."

Beaumont stood up, so Paddy and I did, too. The actor traded his dressing gown for a gray suit jacket that matched his worn pants. "Stay and watch the show if you want," he said to Paddy. "We're doing a master shot, so it should be easy enough to follow." To me, he added, "You can hang around, too, if reliving the old days doesn't poke a wound."

There was another knock, and a large woman whose clothes were protected by a smock came in to touch up Beaumont's makeup. She and Paddy went a long way toward filling the inside of the trailer. They waltzed around for a few bars getting out of each other's way, and then Paddy made his exit, the trailer rocking slightly as he stepped down onto the soundstage. I followed him.

Paddy walked us to a lonely spot and then turned to face me, his hands in his pants pockets and his weight on his heels. "Why didn't you tell me that your fist had made the acquaintance of Mr. Beaumont's jaw?"

I thought of saying that it was his own damn fault for being so coy about the details of our assignment, for feeding me facts no faster than Gypsy Rose Lee dropped lingerie. But I'd never won an argument with Paddy.

"Sorry," I said. "I'll go home and make up a list of everyone I've pasted."

He surprised me by smiling at that. "You're a man of unsuspected qualities, Scotty," he said. "And that's a fact."

He glanced toward the trailer, and I turned in time to see Beaumont step down from it, more lightly than Paddy had. We watched as he walked toward the waiting set.

Toscanini, walking out to the podium with the orchestra in place and the audience settled in, never got more attention than Beaumont commanded as he strode toward the set. It was an island of candlepower in the gloom of the soundstage. An individual's ranking in the hierarchy of the proceedings was indicated by his position relative to the light. The actor supporting Beaumont in the scene was in the bright set itself, just one side of center. The cameraman was on the edge of the glow, flanked by Froy and his flunkies. The outer rings were formed by the sound people and the lighting technicians. Beyond them, in the full darkness, were the set hands and other hangers-on, whose only job during shooting was to stand still and keep quiet. The whole tableau reminded me of the Nativity scenes they used to set up outside the Catholic churches back home, with plaster angels and wise men and shepherds arranged in order of importance around the manger. This soundstage crèche lacked a Jesus, but Beaumont supplied that deficiency when he arrived at the center of the light.

"Isn't that Fritz Taber on the set?" I asked.

"Yes," Paddy said. "They wanted as many of the old hands from *Passage to Lisbon* as they could get. Besides which, Taber is something of a good-luck charm for Beaumont."

"But his character died in *Passage to Lisbon*. Or did I dream that part?"

"He was lost overboard under mysterious circumstances," Paddy said, nodding. "At least that's what Steve was told. It's pretty clever the way Kramer worked it out. I should tell you first that this scene they're about to shoot takes place after the war. Steve has drifted to Paris, where he joins up again with Eddie and Joe, his tap dancing sidekicks from the *Joyeuse Ile*.

"Steve is drinking too much and wallowing in memories of his happy prewar days with Ella Larsen. What was her character called again?"

"Maura Wojcik," I said.

"Ah, yes," Paddy sighed. "Anyway, through American newspapers, Steve is keeping tabs on the career of Maura's husband, Franz Wojcik. Wojcik has stayed on in America and become a leading figure in the new United Nations."

"That's slick. But what about Nigel Clay's dying confession? Captain Manet's, I mean. About Wojcik's escape being a phony?"

"That's what Steve is drinking to forget. But, of course, there isn't enough liquor in Paris to work that miracle."

Things were getting serious on the set. Beaumont had suggested a final lighting adjustment, one that benefited Taber, and the technicians were scrambling to get it done. Taber was seated at the set's shabby dressing table. He was already in character, slumped over and hollow-eyed, as though he were being blamed for the entire miserable war and half-believed the charge.

The already quiet set downshifted to a new level of stillness. Paddy dropped his narrative to a whisper. "One night Steve is drinking in a club where Eddie and Joe are performing. Who should walk in but the drowned Fritz Taber."

"Tursi," I said, naming Taber's character from the film.

"Tursi, right. Risen from his watery grave in the western Mediterranean. When Tursi recognizes the dancers as his old shipmates, he looks around nervously and tries to blow the joint. Steve heads him off and forces him into a back room."

Paddy pointed toward the set. "This very one. There follows some of the lapel yanking and face slapping that passes for rough-house work in pictures. That brings us up to date, I think."

Froy had been addressing the actors in a voice too low for me to hear. Now he called for quiet, his voice echoing across the perfectly noiseless stage. Beaumont was standing over the seated Taber, his left profile to the camera. Taber almost faced it, which told me that he would have most of the lines in the scene. Beaumont had called it a master shot, which meant they'd run through the scene from beginning to end without cuts. The resulting take, if successful, would provide the framework on which the edited scene would be built. Froy would order close-ups and reaction shots for certain lines, and the film's editor would cut and splice these into the master shot to create the final scene.

The cameraman announced that the camera was running at speed. The kid with the clapboard stepped into the quality lighting and called out the scene and take numbers. Beaumont reached over and took hold of Taber's jacket. Then Froy barked out, "Action!"

Beaumont released his hold, pushing Taber away from him at the same time. "Talk then," Beaumont said. "While you've still got teeth."

"Please don't make me, Steve," Taber said.

"Talk, or I'll name you as a collaborator. You know what they've been doing to collaborators."

Taber added genuine fear to his hunted expression. He looked up at Beaumont's face as though searching for something. Friendship? Respect? That's what the old Tursi had wanted from Steve on the *Joyeuse Ile*, the reason he'd shown him the Geneva Exemptions in the first place. That gambit hadn't bought him anything, so he'd know better than to look for respect. Compassion then. Or humanity. Tursi might have expected to find those traits in the old Steve. His expression told me that whatever he'd expected to find was no longer there.

"All right. I'll tell you," Tursi said. "But you won't thank me for it. You'll hate me." He shrugged resignedly, as though Steve's hatred would make the world's opinion unanimous.

"Franz Wojcik's passage on the *Joyeuse Ile* was engineered by the Nazis. They arranged everything. His escape from the concentration camp. His flight across Europe."

Steve interrupted him. "Franz Wojcik was a patriot. A hero of the Polish resistance."

Tursi nodded. "He was. Until the Germans got him inside a concentration camp and tortured him." He looked around the room, inviting a comparison between the beating Steve had given him and the Nazi torture.

"Have you ever been tortured, Steve? It's worse than killing. The man lives on, but the spirit inside dies. The nobler the spirit, the worse the dying is. The emptier the man left behind is."

"Meaning a cheap parasite like you wouldn't notice the difference."

Tursi smiled in sad agreement. "No. I wouldn't. But Franz Wojcik did. After the Germans had broken him and learned everything he knew, there wasn't enough spirit left inside him to fight them or even to take his own life. So he went to work for them. They arranged his escape from the camp, and then a whole series of more and more brilliant escapes as they moved him across Europe."

"Why?" Steve asked. "To finger the local resistance leaders?"

"As he did on the ship," Tursi said, his big head bobbing up and down. "Captain Manet happened to raid their meeting on the very night they took Wojcik in, you remember. But that was just part of the plan. The real reason for that two-year game of hide-and-seek was to build his reputation. To make the name Franz Wojcik known throughout the world. So that when the time came to move him *to America*, so that he could spy for the Nazis *in America*, he would be welcomed with open arms."

Tursi's reluctant confession became a torrent of self-reproach mixed with anger at the gullibility of Steve and the world he represented. "There were no Geneva inspectors murdered in Marseille. No real Geneva Exemptions even. My death was staged. Franz Wojcik's every move aboard the *Joyeuse Ile* was staged. And *you* never suspected. The great Steven Laird. You fell for everything. You packed Wojcik off to that fat, stupid country of yours and yelled 'bon voyage' to him as he went!"

Tursi turned toward the dressing table and buried his face in his arms, sobbing. After a moment's dazed hesitation, Steve grabbed Tursi's shoulder and yanked him upright.

"What about Maura Wojcik?"

"Who?" Tursi asked in a small voice.

"Wojcik's wife. Was she in on it? Did she know about Wojcik and the Germans?"

Tursi looked confused and frightened again. "I don't know. I never heard. I never even saw her. I was smuggled ashore at Oran. I swear I don't know."

He raised his hand to ward off another blow, but Steve was almost calm now. "Are you still in your old business, Tursi? Black-market identification papers and exit visas, I mean."

"Yes, Steve," Tursi whimpered.

"Good. You're going to get me some papers and a visa. Everything I need for a visit to America."

Tursi nodded happily. "I'll do it, Steve. Of course, I'll do it. Anything for you, Steve. Just tell me what name to use."

Steve looked into the empty air over Tursi's head. "The name is Captain Roland Manet. Late of the Free French Navy."

5

Paddy and I and the other onlookers thought so much of Taber and Beaumont's performances that we gave them a hand. Mr.

Froy was less impressed, or perhaps he was just the cautious kind of director. He ordered another take. While the director and his star were talking it over, Paddy and I slipped back out into the sunlight.

"Remind you of your old stand?" Paddy asked me after passing the soundstage guard a cigar and biting the end off another for himself.

I dug out my dark glasses. I had nothing to lose now by wearing them, as Paddy was already thinking about my previous incarnation. "Paramount was a lot classier," I said. "They'd lower us onto the set with wires while a trumpet fanfare played."

Paddy lit a match on the side of a stuccoed building. "In my day we had to help put up the set before we acted in front of it. And do our own makeup and take our own falls."

"Did you work for Hal Roach or Mack Sennett? Next you'll be telling me that you had to crank the camera and bake your own custard pies. Or was that Mabel Norman's department?"

Paddy laughed his deep, slow laugh. "Maybe I am remembering back too far. It's a fault we old hands have. You'll find out about that one of these days. You'll catch yourself telling people how you recommended Jolson for *The Jazz Singer*."

"I recommended Eddie Cantor," I said. "Story of my life."

"Go ahead, wise guy, laugh away. The thirties are going to seem like the Garden of Eden to you someday, a perfect place you can never get back to."

"They seem that way already."

My true confession shut Paddy up for as long as it took us to walk to a spot of shade outside the studio commissary. He paused there and tossed cigar ash back in the direction we'd come. "What do you think of Mr. Kramer's work?"

"He seems to have a lot of good ideas, but he uses them up pretty quickly. He put a load-and-a-half of exposition in that one little scene."

"That's Warner Bros.' style. MGM would make four movies out of the plot these jokers cram into a single reel. Making Franz Wojcik a broken man turned Nazi spy, though, think your relations back in the corn belt will buy that?"

"I think with Fritz Taber selling it they could get away with making Wojcik a nun turned fan dancer."

Paddy checked his watch. We must have been early for whatever was next on the agenda, because he continued to rock on his heels. "They've got more than Taber's salesmanship working for them. They've also got Hans Breem's performance from the original film. I've always thought it was the only off note. Too passionless. Too uninspired. I could never picture anyone following that iceberg onto the barricades."

"Not even when he was playing Chopin?" In that famous scene, Wojcik had disrupted a Nazi songfest by commandeering a piano and banging out the *Heroic Polonaise*, which had become a wartime theme song for the Polish resistance.

"Not even then," Paddy said. "Remember how the piano player waited to get Beaumont's permission before he gave Wojcik his bench? Even a musician wouldn't follow Wojcik, and they're natural anarchists. No, there was always something missing in that bird, but now that negative will seem like a positive. After people see *Love Me Again*, they'll think back on Breem's performance in *Passage to Lisbon* and decide it was right on the money."

"Assuming anyone gets to see *Love Me Again*," I said.

"That's what makes Hollywood Security great, positive thinking. Hop over now and see how far Bert Kramer is actually leaning to the left. I'm going to find Vincent Mediate and get the lowdown on this little soiree he's throwing tonight. I'll find my own way back to the office."

Paddy didn't know where the writers were hidden away. The first passerby I asked, who was either a carpenter or an actor made up to play one, directed me to a small building behind the administrative offices. It was called the Writers Building, originally enough, and it was painted white, like every building Warners owned. This one was in serious need of touching up, though. Something told me that the roof leaked when it rained, too. Each of the building's three stories was broken up with the kind of windows that crank outward. I judged from the windows standing open that roughly half the offices were occupied, which made my chances of finding Kramer no better than even money.

The receptionist was a Maria Montez type with dark, wavy hair and even darker eyes. She was a little over fighting weight, but then so was Maria Montez these days. She had no idea whether Bert Kramer was in, but she gave me his office number—317—and the run of the building.

Someone was at home on the third floor. From the stairwell I picked up the sound of a ball being bounced against a wall, music being played on a phonograph with an old needle, and voices arguing about the Yankees' chances in the current pennant race. I could even hear the sound of a typewriter being pecked at in a tentative, pessimistic way. The third floor had a central hallway lit only by dusty sunlight escaping from the offices whose doors were standing open. Office 317 was not contributing to this effort. I knocked on its door and then tried the knob. The door was locked, but it didn't have the kind of hardware that would keep anyone but small children and clergymen out. Paddy Maguire could have opened it with a deep breath.

I was looking around for witnesses when a voice called "hello" from the next office. It was a woman's voice, and the woman it belonged to was seated at a desk. The desk wasn't big, but it almost filled the office. There was just enough room left over for me, a filling cabinet, and the pair of pictures that graced the walls. They were framed lobby cards from *Each Dawn I Die*, an old Cagney epic.

"Help me out," the woman at the desk said. She was small and slender and pushing fifty with both hands. Her brown hair had a red tint and permanent waves that were crisper than the crease in my trousers. "What's another word for eschew? A simpler one, I mean."

"You've got it backwards," I said. "You end up with words like eschew. You don't start with them. You start with shun or avoid and work your way up."

"Not when you've been writing for pictures as long as I have, honey. Old scribblers like me just naturally write prismatic when we mean colorful and ethereal when we're trying to say thin. It's a fight every day to get back to the language of the living. You looking for Bert?"

She pointed to an open connecting door with her pencil. Through it, I could see Kramer's office, which was dark and empty.

"I was."

"He's home hiding, letting his baby bride massage his tired brow. Some altercation or wrangle, I mean, or …"

"Dustup?"

"Thanks. A dustup with that kid producer Mediate. For years, Kramer's been the kind of dedicated professional, by which I mean hack, that you couldn't poison with a barrel of red ink. But since he wrote that *Passage to Lisbon* reprise, he's developed artistic pretensions in the battleship class. I guess I don't blame him. It's the best thing he's done or is likely to do and he can't stand the thought of it being marred or ravaged or…"

"Fouled up," I said.

"Exactly. God knows it happens often enough. The scripts that go out of here are works of pure genius. And you've seen the finished products. It's shameful."

"Ignominious, you mean."

She smiled, showing teeth that looked a little yellow against the white of her face powder. "You're a quick study. My name's Hanks. Florence Hanks. What's yours, kid?"

I told her my name, and she repeated it a few times until she

34

got the rhythm down. "Paramount had a youngster named Scott Elliott kicking around before the war. I don't know what happened to him."

"Me either," I said. "How well do you know Kramer?"

"What's your interest?"

"It's confidential."

"You a federal agent or something?"

"Insurance agent."

"Uh huh. Bert Kramer and I have been answering each other's phones here in the kennel for donkey's years. But I wouldn't say I really know him. Most writers, even glorified scribblers like us, are basically selling bits and pieces of their autobiographies, hashing and rehashing the one plot they've actually lived. Not Bert Kramer. If there's a story in his past, he's saving it for Broadway. But he's a pro. Give him some magazine filler by Edna Ferber and a couple of weeks and he'll bang out a treatment. It'll end up playing the bottom half of double bills, maybe, but second features make money, too."

"*Love Me Again* is no second feature," I said. "Not from what I've seen of it."

"That's why Bert is suddenly having fainting spells. When you've only got one pass at the brass ring, you want to make the most of it."

"How about politics? A lot of writers wear their politics on their sleeves. Does Kramer?"

Florence frosted over ever so slightly. "No," she said. "Quite the opposite. He's not much of a one for current affairs. I'd be surprised if Bert knows that Roosevelt is dead. He would have missed the whole war, if Warners hadn't sent him to Washington to work on some movie for the War Department. The studios rotated writers back and forth all through the fighting. I think Bert's contribution was a short subject on trench foot.

"Well," she added pointedly, "I'd better get back to work."

Breaking and entering was out with Florence on guard, so I scrapped my plan to search Kramer's office for copies of

Bolsheviks' Home Companion. That left talking to the man himself. "Do you happen to know Kramer's home address?" I asked from the doorway.

"Theresa, down at the front desk, can give it to you. Flash those baby blues of yours at her and she'll throw her own address in for good measure." She gave me a last narrow-eyed examination. "I suppose you've never even heard of Paramount."

"Sure I have. They make the Popeye cartoons. I'm a sucker for Olive Oyl."

6

Theresa gave me Bert Kramer's address, but didn't volunteer her own. My baby blues weren't what they used to be, I guess. I hiked back out through the main gate and retrieved my car from the rental lot where I'd parked it. The lot attendant, a skinny kid in overalls, gave my bus a professional examination as he handed me my keys.

"LaSalle," the attendant said, reading the scrollwork on the narrow grille. "Don't see too many of these."

"Before your time, kid," I said, sounding to myself like one Patrick J. Maguire.

"Thirty-nine?" the kid asked.

"1940," I said. A bad year for isolationists and London real estate prices, but a great one for LaSalles. The last one, in fact.

To be specific, my car was a LaSalle Series 52 Special Coupé, cream colored with as much chrome as a showroom full of Chevrolets, not that you could find a full showroom in 1947. It was the latest thing in prewar styling, with headlights that were almost blended into the rounded front fenders, which in turn were almost blended into the sleek body. I'd bought the coupé during my flush time at Paramount. It hadn't been Gary

Cooper's Duesenberg by any stretch of the imagination, or even as classy as LaSalle's big sister marque, the Cadillac. But I'd felt as though I'd genuinely arrived the day I'd driven it home.

Little did I know that I'd shortly be in the army and the whole LaSalle line would be in the history books. I'd thought about selling the car when my number came up, but that had seemed a little too much like settling my estate. So I'd stored it on blocks in a friend's garage in Pasadena. It was there waiting for me in 1945, looking just as I'd left it, except for a protective coating of greasy dust and four empty wheel rims, my friend having generously donated my whitewalls to the war effort.

I'd paid a lot of money for a set of blackwalls that didn't last a year, but it had been worth it to have one small piece of my civilian life back. Any car was worth having in those days, but even after production started to catch up with demand, I kept the LaSalle. A little too flashy, a little out of date, the car and I seemed made for each other.

I tried to gauge the parking lot jockey's age and decided that his high school graduation was a recent memory, if by chance he'd stuck around for the ceremony. My guess was he hadn't. He had a rawboned, rangy look that seemed out of place in prosperous, complacent Burbank, California.

"Where you from?" I asked him.

"Normal," the kid said, adding "Illinois" as an afterthought.

"I'm from the Midwest myself," I said. "Indiana, that is."

"Sure you are," he said. He lifted one overalled leg. "Pull the other one."

"Have it your way," I said.

As I settled in behind the wheel of the LaSalle, the young skeptic stepped up to its open window. "I saw a picture of the new Packard Clipper today. The '48. It's gonna make this tub of yours look like a Model T."

"Have fun parking them."

I drove off wondering what had brought the kid from Normal, Illinois, to Unnormal, California, or greater Los

Angeles, as the locals were starting to call it. It hadn't been movie fever, a disease I'd experienced firsthand. The kid had lacked the classic symptom, a dazed glow. What then? I'd noticed the trend before Pearl Harbor, but it had greatly accelerated since, perhaps due to the thorough shaking the war had given the country: people with no particular ambition were gravitating toward Los Angeles. The movement wasn't the frenzied stampede of a gold rush or an oil strike. It was more like a mass wandering that happened to end in a single spot, the common end of rainbows connected to every small town in America. Whatever its cause, the migration was making Southern California one interesting place to live.

Kramer's address was in West Hollywood, just off Santa Monica. It was a nice enough older neighborhood, but a little too close to the burgeoning commercial development along the boulevard. The actual house was a twenties bungalow on a burned out half acre. The grass was dead, but the tecoma bushes that bordered the front porch were thriving. So much so that they almost blocked the front steps. I pushed branches aside like Randolph Scott parting the swinging doors of a saloon and stepped up into the cool quiet of the porch. The quiet turned out to be a passing phase. My finger was an inch from the electric bell when a storm broke inside the house.

"Damn it, Violet," a man's voice said. "Can't you even keep ice in the goddamn house? What are you good for? Huh? Will you tell me that? You're not functional. And you're sure as hell not ornamental. Is there a category I'm missing? Give me a goddamn clue. While you're at it, tell me what's eating up your free time. Are you working on the side for J. Edgar Hoover? Are you doing polio research? Or is the problem your afternoons at the motel with Ronald goddamn Colman? Tell me anything that explains why I come home day after day and find you sitting around reading movie magazines with dust on everything deep enough to plow. And no ice in the house!"

That was where I'd come in. I leaned on the doorbell for a

long ten count. When I took a breather, I heard blissful silence followed by the sound of footsteps shuffling my way.

The door was opened by a woman who had the look of a spaniel left out in the rain. Her brown eyes were round and huge and wet and her small, pointed features were unnaturally pale. That detail seemed wrong to me. If she'd been standing up under the grilling I'd overheard, she should have been red to the roots of her frazzled hair, which was the color of old carpet matting and almost as lustrous. Florence Hanks had described her as Kramer's baby bride, and she probably wasn't thirty, but she was nobody's baby. Something had beaten the spirit out of her, if she'd had any to begin with. Or someone had, namely Bert Kramer.

All of which assumed that the man I'd been listening to was the missing screenwriter and the woman before me was his wife. The last assumption was easy enough to verify. I touched the brim of my hat. "Mrs. Kramer?"

She dropped her eyes to the doorsill, which I took for a yes. "I'm from the studio," I said, more or less truthfully. "I'd like to speak with your husband."

She moved aside without a word. I stepped past her into a room overdecorated in dated florals. There were flowers in the rug, flowers in the curtains and the wallpaper. Even the paper shade of the standing lamp had a fringe of faded roses. No need to garden in the hot California sun when you could do it in the comfort of your parlor.

Bert Kramer didn't rise to greet me. He was busy filling a leather armchair that sat like a throne against the room's far wall. He was the right man for the job of filling armchairs, as he was fat from the earlobes down. He wore his black hair short and slicked back, like a shiny skull cap. His broad face was also shiny in the heat of the afternoon, and his small eyes were red rimmed. He was overdressed for a day away from the office, in a white shirt and striped tie and the vest and pants of a worn blue suit. His only concessions to the heat were his shoes, which were missing. Or perhaps he just wanted to show off his socks, snazzy ones with a zigzag pattern in yellow and green. There was a radio cabinet on one side of his chair and a jumbo ashtray with legs on the other. On the edge of this smoking table was a tumbler of light brown liquid, sans ice cubes.

"Who the hell are you?" Kramer demanded. "And don't hand me that line about being from the studio. I know every flunky in that sorry place."

"You're right," I said. "I'm not from the studio. I'm from the bowling alley down the block. We'd like you to cut out the racket. We can't hear the pins falling."

Kramer grunted. "Every bum in this sorry town is a genius with dialogue. Or thinks he is. Where I come from, even the stutterers could top you."

"Where would that be?" I asked, although Kramer's clipped delivery had already told me.

"Brooklyn, New York," he said. "Now answer my question. Who are you?"

For some reason I didn't feel like answering him. I dug out one of the fancy cards Paddy liked his employees to carry. Kramer leaned forward in his chair to pluck the card from my hand.

"Hollywood Security Agency," Kramer read. "I've heard of you guys. You nursemaid ham actors through their tantrums and deliver starlets from the clutches of evil producers. Or is it deliver them to the producers?"

"Depends on our mood," I said.

"Well, I'm not the nervous type and I've got no starlets hidden under my bed, so I don't need any Hollywood operatives following me around."

"Torrance Beaumont and Vincent Mediate think differently," I said. "As for who's hiding under your bed, someone seems to think it's Joseph Stalin."

That shut Kramer up for a few ticks of the hall clock. Then he moved his head in the direction of his wife, who was still standing by the front door. The small eyes stayed on me, though.

"That ice isn't going to make itself," Kramer said.

Violet shuffled past me and out through a doorway toward the sound of the ticking clock. Kramer waited until her dancing footsteps had faded away. Then he said, "I told Mediate that letter was the bunk. I'm telling you the same thing. I am not a member of the Communist Party or any of its front organizations or any other kind of organization for that matter. Not even the damn Screen Writers' Guild. I never have been a member of any Commie group. Anybody who says I have been is a damn liar."

"Any idea who this particular liar might be?"

Kramer gave that one some serious thought, probably the latest in a long line of serious thoughts on the same question. "No," he finally said.

"Since you're not a Communist and never have been, what motive would anyone have for accusing you?"

Kramer gave that question no thought at all, serious or otherwise. "Jealousy," he said. "It's the lifeblood of Hollywood. I'm about to make the big time, and somebody can't stand it."

"Another writer?"

"No," Kramer said. "I don't think so. Not that we're above some mild backstabbing over at the Writers Building. A lot of that stems from the way the producers cover their bets at Warners. It isn't uncommon to have two or three writers working on the same project and none of them wise to the others. Divide and conquer, that's Jack Warner's favorite strategy. It makes for some pretty fierce scrambling for screen credit, let me tell you.

"But that can't be what's going on here. Nobody else has been working on *Love Me Again* for the very good reason that no one else knew about it until I had it finished and perfect. So there can't be any back-room fighting over who wrote what. Besides which, no writer outside of a rubber room would encourage a witch hunt. Nobody's safe when something like that gets started. No, it can't be a writer."

"Who else but a writer would be jealous of a writer?"

Kramer's sweaty face became a study in incredulity. "Are you kidding me? What freight train did you get in on? Everybody in this town is jealous of the writers. It's the reason the writers are the serfs in this kingdom. We should be leading the damn circus parade. Instead, we're following along behind it with shovels and buckets. You know why that is?"

"You mix your metaphors?"

"We have too much talent, wiseass. In the beginning was the word. It was true at the start of the world and it's true in this travesty of creation we call Hollywood. The words come first. If they're no good, nothing that any set designer or director or ham actor does will matter a damn. If the words are perfect, the best you can hope is that the studio won't screw them up too badly on the way to the screen."

I recognized a rephrasing of Florence Hanks's lament. Kramer shook his head at the inequity of the world. "I should write novels," he said. "You don't collaborate with a novel. You don't compromise."

"With your luck, they'd probably misspell your name on the dust jacket."

Kramer had been addressing the ceiling. Now he fixed his little eyes on me. "You don't like me very much, do you?"

That stopped me cold. I *had* taken a dislike to Kramer, and I didn't know why. He was a client, after all, not my blind date. I should have been deferential. Or, at worst, indifferent. Instead, I was riding him. It could have been his socks or the gentle way he'd spoken to his wife. Or it could have been the idea of him tampering with a certain movie.

"How did you come to write *Love Me Again*?" I asked.

The change of subject relaxed Kramer visibly. He settled a little lower in his chair and reached for his iceless drink. "Just too sentimental by half, that's me," he said. "Most writers are, under our stony facades. Hollywood writers, anyway. We get sentimental about our characters. Hell, we spend enough time with some of them. More than we do with real people."

He glanced briefly toward the exit Violet had used before continuing. "I'm sentimental like that. I hate to kill a character off or leave one standing around unhappy. I hate to plain leave them hanging. The end of *Passage to Lisbon* left a busload of them hanging."

"But they weren't your characters," I said.

"Hell," Kramer said. "They're everybody's. That's what I think. You could say they're Lester Ferrell's. He's the kid who wrote "Port of Call," the short story *Passage to Lisbon* was based on."

"Never heard of it," I said.

"Not too surprising, seeing how it was never published. It came to Warners' story department as an unsolicited submission. Or you could say that the characters belong to the Tierney brothers, Charlie and Bill, who wrote the first draft of the script, or Clark Gray, who rewrote it. Hell, you might as well throw in Tory Beaumont. Steve Laird was tailored to the screen character Beaumont had been building up for years. Then, though, you'd have to credit all the writers and directors who pointed Beaumont that way."

"I see what you mean," I said.

"No you don't," Kramer said in his charming way. "When I say the *Passage to Lisbon* characters belong to everybody, I'm not talking about who wrote what. I'm talking about the way the movie went over. The way people still feel about it. The way they feel about Steve and Maura, like they're family. People want those two to be happy. Which is what a sentimental writer like me wants for his characters."

Kramer took a long, sentimental drink, nearly emptying his glass. "Come on, admit it. Haven't you ever wanted Rhett Butler and Scarlett O'Hara to get back together?"

"How about Romeo and Juliet?" I asked. "Maybe they were just holding their breath."

"We're not talking about Shakespeare here, pally. Not that I couldn't have improved a few of his fade-outs. We're talking about standard Hollywood issue. What's wrong with a happy ending?"

"Nothing," I said, "If that's the way it happens to work out. A lot of times, it doesn't."

"So that's it, is it?" Kramer looked me over as though I'd just walked into the scene. I thought he was going to ask me about the war, about the men I'd killed or seen killed, about all the unhappy endings I'd been forced to sit through.

Instead, he said, "You're that kind of fan. The goddamn purist. You don't think anybody should be tampering with *Passage to Lisbon* because it's a goddamn work of art. It's the one the studio system accidentally got right. You don't think any hack like me should be tampering with the ending. You think I'm painting a moustache on the goddamn Mona Lisa."

Kramer was closer to the mark than he knew. I felt the truth of his insight in the moist heat rising upward from my collar. But I wasn't about to let on.

"It's Bert Kramer's ending you should be worried about," I said. "You could be close to a fade-out yourself if this charge sticks."

Kramer smiled and finished the last swallow of his drink. "Don't worry about my ending, pally. It'll be a happy one. Something straight out of Frank Capra."

"That's if you're writing it," I said. "Suppose Vincent Mediate is at the typewriter."

"Our wonder-boy producer? Listen, just between you and me, Mediate couldn't type his name. But don't you worry about old Vince. He's a war hero, isn't he? Carried his whole crew off the beach at Normandy while filming away with a camera clamped in his teeth. Old Vince will carry me, too. Wait and see."

7

I thanked Kramer for his hospitality and left the way I'd come, through tecoma pass and across the alkaline desert of the bungalow's front yard. Then I drove to a drug store on Santa Monica Boulevard and called the Hollywood Security Agency. The fan in the drug store's phone booth was broken, so I left the folding door open and stretched my legs. Other legs were being rested nearby. Long, slender ones that belonged to a couple of bobby-soxers who were seated at the fountain, practicing their eyelash batting on a lucky soda jerk. I enjoyed the show while I listened to the ringing on the other end of the line.

Her nibs answered the phone herself, to use Paddy's favorite nickname for his wife, Peggy. She had been his partner on the stage once upon a time, and now she was his business partner. She was the actual businessman of the pair, although her attitude toward Paddy's lost-sheep employees leaned a little toward the maternal. I was poor little lamb number one.

"Scotty," she said, "have you eaten anything?"

I smiled at the phone. "Not yet, Peg." One of the kids at the counter turned toward the sound of my voice. She caught my eye and looked away quickly. Then she slowly glanced back, her long brown hair masking one side of her face, Veronica Lake style.

"You must be famished," Peggy said.

"Wasting away," I said. Veronica smiled and looked back to her friends.

"It figures. Paddy lets you do the legwork while he talks some big shot out of a fancy lunch."

"Vincent Mediate," I said.

"That's the sucker. His lordship is sleeping it off right now."

"I'll call back, then."

"Oh no. I've been waiting for an excuse to sound reveille. You just hold the line."

45

After a minute or so, Paddy came on, alert and unabashed. "Scotty. I've just been turning this business over in my mind."

"So I was told."

I heard the sound of a match being struck, perhaps on one of Paddy's chins. "You first," he said. "What did you learn from Kramer?"

"That he's a sentimental slob, though you wouldn't guess the sentimental part by looking at him. He wasn't at his office. I thought about searching it, but he'd left a neighbor on guard. I tracked him to his castle. He's holed up there."

"Too bad about the office. What did you learn on the subject of his political leanings?"

I eased my legs into the booth and shut the door. "Hasn't any. Or so he says. Couldn't tell a Red from a redcap."

"What about the sender of the note?"

"He suspects everybody between Santa Barbara and San Diego. Except other writers."

"Huh," Paddy said. "They must be a tight-knit crew. Not much there to work on. Maybe you'll have better luck tonight at Mediate's little fund-raiser. The layout is just the way Beaumont described it. You're to be there at eight. Your contact is Mediate's assistant, Fred Wilner. You almost met him this morning."

"I remember. What am I supposed to be doing there? Besides frisking everyone for hotel stationery, I mean."

"Meeting Mr. Mediate mostly. He wants to size you up. Feel free to pump him while he's giving you the once over. A very close man is Mr. Mediate. I've met with him twice now, and I know more about the plot of his blooming movie than I do about him."

The operator came on at that point to ask for another nickel. I gave her one. It was a nickel wasted, as Paddy was anxious to get back to his meditation.

"Take the rest of the day off," he said. "You'll kill most of it getting out to that log cabin of yours anyway. Go home and lay out your best bib and tucker."

"Shouldn't I be doing some more poking around?"

"Into what? Kramer's background? I've been giving that a lot of thought. We could never prove he isn't a Red. Not when an inclination is enough to get a person branded. The only concrete thing we could do is prove he is one, and nobody wants that.

"No, Scotty. At the moment, this is a hand-holding job, pure and simple. Show up on time tonight and hold whatever hand is offered."

"You're the boss," I said.

The thing to buy and hold on to in prewar Los Angeles had been land, so naturally, I hadn't bought an acre. That oversight kept me from making my fortune when the value of orange groves skyrocketed during the fighting. Worse, it meant I'd end up caught in the postwar housing squeeze.

In '47, I was living outside of the city in the foothills of the Santa Monica mountains. An old friend from my Paramount days had an estate there, and she was nice enough to rent me a cottage on a quiet corner of her land. The rent was nominal, due to a services clause in my verbal lease. It required me to shoot any mountain lions I saw. As I never saw any and I didn't own a gun, this provision was no problem at all.

The cottage was set down in a little wash of scrub oak and pine, out of sight of the main house. It was reached by a rickety flight of wooden steps. I left the LaSalle in its sandy spot by the side of the road and made the descent, causing the usual panic among the ground squirrel population.

The front door was unlocked, as I'd left it. I opened the one or two windows that weren't already open and hung my hat and suit coat and tie on the various door knobs I passed on my way to the single bedroom's single closet. I took my tuxedo out and laid it on the bed, as Paddy had instructed. It didn't look any better on the bed—any more stylish or any less tired—but

47

orders were orders. With that out of the way, I was a free man. I put one of my newer Duke Ellington records, "I'm Just a Lucky So and So," on my portable player and then moved into the combination kitchen and bar.

One of the ways the men in my old unit had gotten through their time in the field was by imagining themselves doing perfectly ordinary things. Soldiers everywhere knew the same trick, I'm sure, but it had become a mild obsession with us. In quiet moments, we'd told each other in great detail how we would someday perform again some absolutely routine civilian task, making coffee, say, or changing the spark plugs on a car. As most of the men in my outfit had hailed from Tennessee, some of our recitals had been on the secrets of skinning a squirrel or curing a frying pan.

The subject of my own contribution to this lecture series had been "Mixing a Gibson." I'd mixed dozens of them verbally for my captive audience, discussing as I mixed the virtues of various gins and vermouths, the characteristics of pearl onions, the advantages of stirring over shaking.

Later, after the fighting had ended, five of us had found ourselves in a tiny hotel bar on the outskirts of Paris. There, under the curious gaze of the bartender, I'd mixed five Gibsons, one at a time, with hands that had actually trembled. We'd raised them in a toast to nothing in particular or maybe to everything.

The faces of those farm boys had been as alive with light as the cocktails themselves as we'd stood staring at our glasses. Then we'd drunk, and the lights had blinked out, one by one. The magic of the moment had disappeared, trampled by a chorus of orders for beer chasers. The real Gibsons had failed to live up to the expectations created by months of imaginary ones, even for me. It had been a foretaste of my return to civilian life, though I hadn't recognized that nuance at the time.

Despite that notable failure, I'd stuck to Gibsons. I still reveled in the silliness of mixing one as though it were the most important operation of my life. I made a shakerful now, measuring the ingredients with a precision that would have lit a smile under William Powell's pencil-line moustache. Then I took the shaker and a long-stemmed glass and a phial of onions and left the cottage.

I climbed the rickety stairs and followed the road until it intersected a roughly cut firebreak. I left the road, climbing the hill the break had scarred until I came to its summit. There I sat down on a slab of rock awash in dry, spiky weeds.

To my right was Douglas Fairbanks, Jr.'s house, though I couldn't see it for the trees. I wasn't looking for it anyway. The view I was after was the one that stretched out before me, the gray blue blur of Los Angeles. At night, with a million lights burning, it was a more impressive sight. But this late afternoon version was worth the walk. Worth all the walks I'd taken, in fact.

Once I'd actually dreamt of conquering a small, select part of Los Angeles. That vague and naive ambition had been replaced by a simpler one during the war: staying alive, existing, being. It was an imperative that hadn't faded with the end of the fighting. I still just wanted to occupy a quiet place somewhere. The closest I'd come to a return to my old, silly dream had been to define the quiet place more narrowly. I just wanted to be here, in greater Hollywood.

I coaxed one onion from its jar and into the bottom of my glass, where I drowned it in gin and vermouth. Then I raised the cocktail in a toast to the hazy horizon.

"It's still good to be back," I said.

8

The Stratford was a big old pile on the edge of Beverly Hills.
The hotel made me think of a back-lot set, one that had stood in
for so many different countries it no longer had a single,
recognizable identity. The name was vaguely English, while
the facade quoted classical Greece. The lobby was from a later
flowering of civilization, namely the silent movie period. Some
more recent redecorators had tried to mute its original Arabian
Nights motif, but it was still possible to imagine Rudolph
Valentino and Agnes Ayers stamping out a tango through its
arched passageways.

The orchestra I could hear as I crossed the lobby was more
up-to-date. And more restful. When I entered the first-floor
room the studio had rented, the string section was crooning
"Something to Remember You By" in tones muted enough for
a wake. A wake is what the gathering resembled at that moment.
It was just after eight, but there were only a dozen guests
assembled, none of whom were straying very far from the bar.

The orchestra was too good for its small, inattentive audience.
I recognized the leader as a trumpet virtuoso named Tony
Ardici who'd played with some of the bigger West Coast bands
before the war. A gang of us had driven down to Long Beach to
hear him play on a soft summer night that now seemed farther
away than the moon.

Fred Wilner was easy to spot among Ardici's current listeners.
He was standing in a quiet corner, cleaning his glasses with a
huge handkerchief. Without them, he looked like an
undergraduate. A nearsighted one. He put the glasses back on
as I walked up.

"Hello," he said. "Elliott, isn't it?" He spoke with a Southern
accent I hadn't noted when he'd greeted Paddy earlier in the
day.

As we shook hands, I asked, "You're Mr. Mediate's

50

assistant?"

"That's right. I'd worked my way up to better things before the war. Now I'm working my way up all over again. But at least I'm around to do it. You were in the field artillery, I hear."

It had become a ritual since the war for men of our generation to compare service records upon meeting. "Yes," I said.

"In France?"

"And points east."

"How was that line of work?"

I glanced around the ballroom. Its motif was Egyptian. I took in the plaster-of-Paris pillars ending in a flourish of reeds and supporting plaster-of-Paris ceiling beams on which were painted slaves and pharaohs and the odd Cleopatra. The carpet was a huge secret message written in hieroglyphics, and the green curtains behind the orchestra featured Ra, the sun god, done in faded gold. "It lacked glamour," I said. "How about you?"

"Infantry. New Guinea. We were a little short of atmosphere ourselves."

I gave Wilner a closer examination. He seemed as ordinary as a Wednesday morning, which was how most real infantrymen looked. But with his polished horn-rims in place, it was hard to picture him slogging along in the mud.

"Officer?" I asked.

"Yes, but don't hold it against me. I was only a lieutenant."

"How about your boss? I hear Mediate was a regular Audie Murphy."

"Who told you that?"

"Bert Kramer."

Wilner chuckled. "All Bert knows about war he learned from reading his own scripts."

"Is he here yet?"

"Kramer? God no. He isn't going to be here, either. Wasn't invited. Wasn't even notified. Until this business about the letter is cleared up, we're keeping him under wraps. If things get too bad, we might have to use someone else's name for the

51

screenwriter credit."

"Kramer would love that," I said. "He thinks the whole town is after him as it is."

Wilner sighed. "Don't I know it. We'll end up throwing more money at him. That's how you deal with the Bert Kramers of this world."

"What's the story on Mediate?"

"He's up in his suite having cocktails with the New York big shots. Once they're sufficiently fortified, they'll come down here and face the press." He nodded toward the little crowd by the bar.

"I meant Mediate's war record. Kramer said something about Normandy."

Wilner pushed his glasses back up his nose for the fourth or fifth time. "Right. He was there heading up a combat film crew."

"Like those directors they drafted? George Stevens and John Ford?"

"Nothing as grand as that. At least it wasn't supposed to be. Stevens and Ford and John Huston were overseas to make films. Vincent Mediate was just supposed to be exposing film. There were units like Vince's in every theater of the war. They were there to film combat and send their stuff back to the States for editing. Sergeant Mediate exceeded his orders."

"How?"

"First I should tell you about Normandy. Vince and two of his men landed on Omaha Beach with one of the first waves. His cameraman was hit right off the bat. Vince took over the filming himself. Some time later, his other assistant caught shrapnel in both legs. Vince carried him to what passed for an aid station in that hellhole. Then he went back to filming."

"He wasn't hit himself?"

"Not a scratch. After the breakout, some colonel who'd seen the film crew in action told Vince he was recommending him for a medal. Vince asked to be allowed to edit his footage into a film instead. This colonel happened to report to a general who had advanced ideas on publicity. They set it up for Mediate to do the work back in England, at Teddington Studios, which are owned by Warner Bros. That's how Vince first came to Jack Warner's attention, through the studio grapevine.

"Anyway, the short he put together, *Sunrise at Normandy*, caused a sensation when it was finally shown over here."

"I've seen it," I said. "It's great. I didn't know it was Mediate's."

Wilner gave his glasses another shove. "Put him on the map. That one and *Death Camp*, which he shot at Buchenwald. For my money, that thirty minutes of film is worth all the features Warners will make this year."

"Including *Love Me Again*?"

The assistant producer looked around. "Yes, but don't quote me. Even a lousy job is better than no job at all."

"It sounds as though Mediate should be directing, not producing."

"I don't think directing is a grand enough job for Vince. Why start anywhere on the ladder when you can take the elevator?"

We stood side by side, surveying the room. After a time, Wilner said, "If Vince and company don't get down here soon, none of these newshounds will be sober enough to put pen to paper."

I didn't comment. My attention had been drawn to a woman standing near the bar. She was either a very light brunette or a borderline blond, and she was listening to the animated conversation of a couple of the bar's best customers. The drunks were sporting tuxedos that made mine look respectable. Their audience was wearing a very striking dress of electric blue. It had padded shoulders, a plunging neckline, and sleeves that covered the tops of her hands. The skirt was full and long enough to hide everything but her very slender ankles. Her almost blond hair was shoulder length and straight, except for a slight curl in her bangs. That was all I could tell at a range of

53

thirty feet, even squinting.

When I looked back to Wilner, he was smiling at me. "I'd lend you my field glasses, but I left them at home."

"Some pal you are," I said.

"Would you settle for an introduction?"

"You know her?"

"I work with her. So do you, in a manner of speaking. She's our publicist on *Love Me Again*."

The publicist couldn't have heard Wilner's quiet voice, so it must have been clairvoyance that made her glance our way. Or perhaps the Elliott charm was finally coming out of mothballs. Before we could move, she made her excuses to her drinking buddies and started across the room to us. We met her halfway.

"Miss Englehart," the well-bred Wilner said, "I'd like to present Mr. Scott Elliott. Mr. Elliott, Miss Englehart."

Miss Englehart had a firm, businesslike handshake that was just a degree or two above room temperature. "How do you do?" she asked.

In close-up, she was still striking, if no longer perfect. Her wide mouth was a little too wide and her pale blue eyes a shade too pale. Her nose took the slightest leftward jog south of the bridge, which, in combination with a merry look in her eyes, gave her an unbusinesslike air, not at all in keeping with her handshake.

"I do fine, thanks," I said.

Wilner put a hand on my shoulder. "You might as well have a drink and relax while you wait. I'm going to see what's holding up the parade." He started to leave and then turned back to me. "No need to observe any vows of silence around Miss Englehart," he said. "She knows everything."

When the assistant producer had finally gone away, I asked, "Is that true?"

"Literally," Miss Englehart said.

"Care for a drink?"

"Yes, but not in here. I'm on duty when I'm around newspaper people. The hotel bar is right across the hall."

"You do know everything."

She led me out through an archway shaped like the tip of a minaret and across a quiet hallway. On the other side was a heavy, ornately carved door that might have once graced a castle in Spain. The publicist paused to let me open it for her. As I reached past her to the door's wrought-iron handle, I said, "Wilner didn't mention your first name."

"Freddy was just being gallant. You can call me Pidgin."

"Excuse me?"

"Pidgin. As in Pidgin English. You know, the kind of English Tarzan uses. The guys who broke me in at the studio dubbed me that as a tribute to the way I wrote back then. I've gotten a lot better since."

"Why hang on to Pidgin then?"

"Because my real name is Eloise."

"Oh," I said.

The Stratford bar was built along English lines, with the bartender stationed inside a box of mahogany and brass set against one wall. There were booths along the opposite wall, but Pidgin ignored them, selecting instead a tall stool on an unoccupied side of the bar. She addressed the bartender by his Christian name, which was Art, and ordered a gimlet. I sat beside her and ordered a Gibson, for a change of pace. The change would be watching someone else make it.

"How about you?" Pidgin asked. "Is Scott Elliott your real name or a professional one?"

"Professional," I said. "My real name is Samuel Spade, but that created exaggerated expectations in clients."

"Cute. I happen to know you used to be an actor. Freddy told me. So I've been wondering if Scott Elliott is some studio's idea of what would look good on a marquee."

"It's my real name," I said. "But not all of it. It's my middle and last name, I mean. The studio didn't like my first name."

"Eloise?" Pidgin asked.

55

"Thomas."

Art brought Pidgin her gimlet and then went on his dinner break.

"Thomas Scott Elliott," Pidgin said. "T.S. Elliott. Any relation?"

"No. He's shy a T."

"Or you have one too many."

"Two too many, according to Mr. Beaumont."

"Maybe you should drop a couple then. Tory isn't wrong very often these days."

"I'll think about it." Someday. At the moment, I had other things on my mind. Pidgin guessed one of them, clairvoyant that she was.

"It was football," she said. "A touch football game with my brother Bill. He accidentally hit me a shot on the nose with his elbow. It's been leading me into left turns ever since."

"Why not have it fixed? After all, you're in the face work capital of the world."

"That's why I haven't done it. The women around this town are so perfect, so unnaturally perfect, that I'd never make the grade. It's better to be different. Men like different. I like it for that matter."

"Do you?" I touched the tip of my nose. "Maybe I'll see if your brother's elbow is available."

"It isn't. Billy is buried in France."

"Sorry."

Art returned with my Gibson, and Pidgin and I drank in silence. Then she said, "Anyway, in your line of work it's only a matter of time before some thug gives that pan of yours a little character."

"You've got me mixed up with the parts your pal Beaumont plays. I'm just a professional handholder."

"No heater under that rented tux?"

"Not gat one. And the tux isn't rented. We've both just seen better days."

"Don't feel bad. I'm wearing a loaner myself." She sat up and squared her shoulders so I could admire her dress. I admired it all over again. "I've got a pal in the wardrobe department. Janis Paige wore this last year in *The Time, the Place, and the Girl.*"

"It's easy to tell which one Janis played," I said.

"Shame on you."

I was feeling a little ashamed at that moment, but not over my repartee. I decided that I'd spent enough time playing hookey. "What do you know about Bert Kramer?"

"Only what I read in anonymous notes. I never met him before I was assigned to this picture. He made a pass at me before we'd gotten beyond hello, so I've been sidestepping him ever since."

"Kramer makes passes? He doesn't seem the type."

"Take my word for it. You don't have to be tall, dark, and handsome to figure yourself a ladies' man. All you need is an ego, and ego is the lifeblood of this town."

"Kramer thinks jealousy is. The lifeblood of this town, I mean."

Pidgin shrugged. "Ego. Jealousy. Those two are pretty closely tied, wouldn't you say?"

I never got a chance to say, one way or the other. The Castilian door to the bar opened, and Fred Wilner stuck his nondescript head in.

"Show time, kids," he said. "The royal barge approaches."

9

Miss Englehart wasted no time deserting me. She was off her stool and gone before her "See you later, shamus" had completely faded away. That saved me the trouble of coming up with a tag line of my own. Art, the bartender, didn't seem to be expecting one. At least not from me. He was standing nearby, gazing toward the exit Pidgin had used. I finished my drink and pushed the empty glass across to him.

"I'll put in a good word for you," I said.

"Sure you will," Art replied.

I was a few steps short of the minaret archway when Ardici and the boys stopped playing "Moonlight Becomes You" and struck up "Love Me Again." The abrupt transition reminded me of a wedding, with the church organist shifting from "Oh Promise Me" to "The Wedding March" when the bride and her entourage finally decide to show up.

I reentered the Egyptian room, still playing with the idea that the wake I'd left there had somehow become a wedding. A wedding reception, anyway. The guests, Pidgin's journalist charges, were still gathered near the bar, but they'd turned respectfully toward the room's main door. The wedding party was just now making its entrance, led by the bride and groom.

I guessed the happy couple to be Mr. and Mrs. Vincent Mediate. The dark fullback with the hawksbill profile and the heavy jaw was the only man in the group young enough to be a boy-wonder anything. The woman on his arm was a good three inches taller than her escort and as blond as he was dark. Blonder. Blond enough to drop Pidgin Englehart to brunette second class. Her round face was pale, which made her Chinese-red lipstick show up across the room like a moist, new wound. She was wearing a long dress of what looked like white silk under a shimmering white jacket whose broad diagonal stripes matched her lipstick exactly.

The rest of the party were the money men I'd been hearing so much about. I recognized them from the screening Paddy and I had attended that morning. Each one looked tough enough to call in his own grandmother's note and liquored up enough at the moment to invest the same dough in imaginary oil wells, which was basically what they were out west to do. Mixed in with them was a sprinkling of studio heavyweights, including *Love Me Again*'s director, Max Froy. Even in his impeccable tuxedo, Froy looked like a high-priced riding instructor.

Fred Wilner left his position on the flank of the advancing column and joined me. We watched as Pidgin introduced a lady columnist in a silly hat to the Mediates.

"What do you think?" Wilner asked. "So far so good?"

"Where are the actors?" I asked back. "Shouldn't you have Beaumont and Ella Larsen jumping through hoops or something?"

"Too early for that. In the shooting schedule, I mean. We're just trying to get the picture's name in print at this point. If we use our big guns this early, the press will be sick of us by the time we get around to releasing the damn thing."

"You guys run a pretty elaborate campaign."

"You're telling me. MacArthur wasn't this organized." He looked at me over the tops of his slipping glasses. Then he asked a question that reminded me of Paddy's lectures. "This is a whole new side of the movie business for you, isn't it?"

"Movies never were a business for me, pal."

Almost an hour passed before Wilner decided the moment was right to introduce me to our host. Mediate had lost his wife sometime during the evening. As Wilner and I walked up, the producer was patting a soused reporter's shoulder with his left hand and easing him in the direction of the bar with his right.

"Have fun," Mediate called to the drunk's retreating back. To Wilner, he said, "That one will never spell the name right. If he even remembers it. Who do we have here?"

"Scott Elliott," Wilner said. "Of the Hollywood Security Agency."

"Right," Mediate said, easing the charm down several notches as he shook my hand. The firm handshake was consistent with the broad shoulders and the lifeguard's tan. Mediate had intense, slightly protruding eyes under an extremely protruding brow and the dark jawline of a man who has to shave before every

59

meal.

"That boss of yours is quite a character," Mediate said. "He's forgotten more about Hollywood than the three of us will ever know. I could listen to his stories for hours."

Everyone who knew Paddy could, I thought. It wasn't as though any of us had a choice. Out loud I said, "About this hotel stationery …"

Mediate cut me off. "You came by the set today, I hear. What do you think of our little production?"

"It's a license to print money."

Wilner said, a touch too brightly, "You should have had Mr. Elliott with you in the suite."

Mediate ignored him. "How about the film's artistic merit?" he asked, showing me some very white teeth. "You're qualified to judge them, from what I've been told."

"If you have box office, you don't need artistic merit."

"I need it," Mediate said, almost to himself.

I didn't ask why. It was common enough for people who had achieved commercial success in Hollywood to change their goal to artistic affirmation. Mediate was rushing the process a little, but that seemed to be the way he did things. I shrugged. "I haven't seen the script. From what I have seen, Kramer has bitten off a good deal."

Mediate started scanning the small crowd. "Opened Pandora's box, you mean, by resurrecting characters who were neatly disposed of in the first film? Running the risk of disappointing a lot of diehard fans?"

It was the charge Kramer had thrown at me, restated by Mediate in a breezy way that dismissed its importance. Or maybe he only meant to dismiss the importance of my answer.

I gave him one anyway. "I meant that Kramer has bitten off a lot by taking up Steven Laird's story again. Steve is a redeemed man at the end of *Passage to Lisbon*. He's done the one great thing he's ever likely to do."

"So what's the problem?" Wilner asked.

Mediate answered for me. "The problem is living the rest of your life with the knowledge that you've had your best day." He fixed me with one very intense, though not unfriendly, gaze.

I returned it. "Like I said, a lot to bite off."

Mediate was still giving me the X ray when someone stepped up next to Wilner. With an effort, I broke eye contact with the producer and turned toward the newcomer. I recognized Mrs. Mediate and then someone else, someone I hadn't seen in years. That is, I finally realized that I knew Mrs. Mediate. Or had known her, before the war. She'd been a starlet then, one of the troop of starlets Goldwyn always had under contract. Her name then had been Carole Leslie, and we'd been acquainted, socially.

I knew by the way her very red lips parted that she recognized me, too, and I knew it wasn't the highlight of her evening. Her husband said, "Darling, I'd like you to meet a business associate, Mr. Elliott. Mr. Elliott, my wife, Carole."

I waited for Carole to tell her husband that we were way past formal introductions, but she let the opportunity slip by. "I'm pleased to meet you, Mr. Elliott," she said, extending her hand. I managed to brush her red-tipped fingers just before they were withdrawn.

Then Mrs. Mediate addressed her husband. "How about asking me to dance?"

We all turned toward the room's tiny dance floor. Only two couples had been tempted onto it by the orchestra's rendition of "Embraceable You." One of the investors was shouldering around a respectable looking stack of masonry who could only have been his wife. Max Froy had done better for himself. He was dancing with Pidgin Englehart.

"I'm still working the room," Mediate said. "But Fred here would be happy to do the honors."

"Charmed," Wilner said.

"He's lighter on his feet anyway," Mediate added.

It was an old straight line, and Carole Mediate came through with the old punch line. "Lighter on mine, you mean."

We all smiled. Then the lady and her dancing partner left me alone with Svengali junior. I watched her go, wondering if I should have felt offended by her snub and then wondering if I still could feel that way.

Mediate drew me back with a cough. He was holding a conspicuously unlit cigarette and waiting. The cigarette got me out of neutral as far as my delicate feelings were concerned. I had been given the air by an old friend, and now the friend's husband wanted me to play valet.

"Forget your lighter?" I asked.

"Yes," Mediate said. "Do you mind?"

"Not at all." I dug out a pack of matches I'd palmed in the Stratford's bar and tossed them to him. He caught the pack without taking his eyes from mine.

I managed to get a Lucky into my mouth before Mediate had shaken out his match. "Do you mind?" I asked.

"Not at all," Mediate said, his bemused delivery of the line conveying the same sense as "touché."

I expected a dismissal after that. Instead, Mediate said, "The dilemma you mentioned with the script, about a man trying to follow up the greatest deed of his life, really isn't a problem, you know."

"Because Bert Kramer's undone Steve's great moment by making Wojcik a Nazi spy?"

Mediate waved his cigarette. "That's the way the script deals with it. I meant that it shouldn't be a problem for any man. The trap is telling yourself you've seen your best day, you've done your best work. As long as you don't admit that, as long as you keep looking for new challenges, the dilemma doesn't exist."

"I see," I said.

"The secret, if you've shot your bolt in one thing, is to move on to something new. Find something so important that it makes everything you've done to date seem like a warm-up."

"That's like saying the secret to jumping off tall buildings without getting hurt is being careful never to hit the ground. It's a small point, but tough to work out."

A waitress came by with a tray of bubbling champagne glasses. Mediate smiled at her and shook his head. "Tough or not, you have to make the change. Otherwise, you might as well pick yourself a comfortable rocking chair. Look, Elliott, our whole generation just climbed out of uniform. A lot of those ex-soldiers are looking for nothing more from the rest of their lives than a quiet place to sit and listen to baseball games on the radio. With maybe a wife in the kitchen and a Ford in the driveway and a couple of kids playing in the backyard."

"Doesn't sound too bad," I said.

"It's a cage," Mediate said. "One that's going to seem awfully small ten years from now when the memories of the glory days start to fade. I want my best years ahead of me, not in some scrapbook. My best years *are* ahead of me."

I didn't feel up to arguing with Mediate's positive attitude. He'd found new worlds to conquer and he was conquering them. I hadn't worked that little trick, which put me at a sizeable disadvantage. I might maneuver him into lighting my cigarette, but he could afford to do it gracefully, knowing, as Wilner had put it, that his elevator was going up while mine was stuck between floors.

I decided to get back to business. "What about the Kramer note being typed on Stratford stationery?"

"What about it?" Mediate asked a little wearily. "Anyone could get that paper. You can walk out of here right now and into the sitting room off the hotel lobby and pick up a ream of it, if you don't believe me. The idea that anyone connected with the picture wrote that letter is ridiculous."

"Anyone connected with the picture? Don't tell me the cast and crew live here, too."

"Not at these prices. But I maintain an office as well as a residence here. It's taken them forever to find me something suitable at Warners. A lot of the preproduction work on *Love Me Again* was done right here. Half the people connected with the picture have been through this place at one time or another. But as far as any of them writing that note ..."

"I know," I said. "It's ridiculous. I wasn't thinking of the stationery as a way of narrowing the field of suspects. I agree, it's useless for that."

"What is the paper good for, then, if it doesn't point to the writer?"

"It could point to the writer's target. His real target."

Mediate took a long drag on his cigarette. "Me, you mean."

The idea wasn't new to him, but it was fairly new to me. I played around with it out loud. "The note wasn't sent to you or Beaumont, and it easily could have been, as you two are the producers. It was sent over your head to Jack Warner. And it's written on paper from your hotel."

"Which tells you what?" Mediate asked patiently.

"That the writer could be trying to imply a connection between your operation and the charge against Kramer."

The producer almost laughed, but when he spoke he kept his voice low. "Mr. X is hinting that I'm a Communist?"

"Or that you've known the truth about Kramer all along and kept it quiet."

Mediate started to drop his cigarette stub onto the plush carpet but thought better of it. He handed it to a waitress who carried it off like a souvenir.

"I do know the truth about Bert Kramer," he said, "and the truth is he is not a Communist. The letter was sent to Warner because the idiot who wrote it doesn't know how a studio works and figures Jack Warner is the man to talk to about a Warner Bros. picture. The fact that it was written on stationery from this hotel is a coincidence and nothing more. Now, go find yourself a drink. I should be seeing to my guests."

That was his plan anyway. Just as he finished laying it out for me, there was a disturbance at the far end of the room. Mediate and I turned in time to see Bert Kramer make his entrance.

10

Kramer was at least dressed for the party he was crashing. His white dinner jacket didn't look like it would actually button, but a natty black vest had his fat stomach held somewhat in check. His tie was a little askew and his face was flushed, but his line of march as he crossed the room to us was as straight as a new pool cue. He'd evidently bumped into someone at the door, which explained the ruckus we'd heard. The injured party—the dowager duchess I'd seen earlier on the dance floor—was staring after Kramer with a look that was the facial equivalent of a fist being shaken in the air. Kramer's own expression was cherubic. I didn't like it.

Neither did Vincent Mediate. "Don't go too far, Elliott," he said. "We may be requiring your services."

Not going too far implied going as a first step, which I now did. Kramer was calling out Mediate's first name in greeting—yelling it, actually—and his performance was causing the small crowd to rearrange itself. I took cover in a knot of people who had turned toward Mediate in expectation of a scene. Carole Mediate showed her loyalty by rejoining her husband. Fred Wilner was also nearby, but out of the line of fire.

Just before Kramer reached center stage, Pidgin sidled up beside me. She took hold of my right arm and addressed my right ear. "Bring your brass knuckles, Lone Wolf?"

"Vince," Kramer said for perhaps the tenth time. "It's good to see you."

"And you, Bert," Mediate replied.

I had to admire the producer's poise. His tone was calm and polite, but his bulgy eyes were giving Kramer the same sunlamp treatment I'd recently enjoyed.

Kramer noticed Carole Mediate. With a single leer, he more than confirmed Pidgin's assessment of him. "Mrs. Mediate,"

Kramer said, "you're, ah …"

"Looking well?" Mediate suggested.

"I'm the writer, Vince," Kramer said for the benefit of the entire room. "And I'd say she's looking a damn sight better than 'well.' I'd say she's looking … incandescent."

"Oh brother," Pidgin whispered. The distraction of her breath on my ear almost made me miss the next line.

It was Kramer's. He was defining the word "incandescent" for Mediate's benefit. "Luminous, you know. Glowing. Radiant. Hot."

Mediate opened his mouth to reply, but his wife beat him to it. "You, on the other hand, are looking drunk, Mr. Kramer. You know, tight, soused, pie-eyed."

Kramer's laughter spread to the surrounding eavesdroppers, lowering the tension a hair. "The funny thing is," he said, "I haven't had a drink yet. Not on the studio, anyway. I only just got here. I was late on account of only getting my invitation an hour ago."

"The bar is right over there, Bert," Mediate said. "Let me show you."

"Don't bother," Kramer said. "This will do me fine." He waved at one of the roving champagne distributors, and she reported on the double.

Kramer helped himself to a glass and told the waitress, "Don't be a stranger." To Mediate, he said, "I thought you'd want Bert Kramer here, Vince, seeing as how this movie you're making is his brain-child. *Love Me Again* started right here," he said, pointing to the bony part of his head. Then he moved his fat finger down to the stiff front of his shirt. "Or maybe I should say right here, because it was a labor of love."

If Mediate was moved by that admission, he kept it to himself. "You're welcome here, Bert, of course. But you can see this is just a small get-together. We didn't impose upon Mr. Beaumont or Miss Larsen. Or you. Later though …"

"Later it will be Mr. Beaumont's picture, Vince. We both

know that. A Tory Beaumont movie. Nobody will think of it any other way. They won't want to interview the guy who produced it or the guy who directed it or even the poor slob who thought it up.

"Nope, Vince. This is my moment to crow. Right now. By the time the thing comes out, nobody will give a damn who wrote it." He leaned toward Mediate, his fat chin hanging out in the air. "Why, you'd be able to slap any name you wanted to under the screenwriter credit. Nobody would even notice."

"We wouldn't do that, Bert," Mediate said.

Kramer raised his empty wineglass over his head like a distress signal. "I know you won't. Now."

The waitress arrived during a lull in the dialogue. Kramer set his empty on her tray, took two full glasses from it, and tossed one back like a shot of bubbling whiskey.

Pidgin tickled my ear again. "Five will get you ten that's the last one he finishes."

I didn't take the bet.

One of the reporters stepped up to Kramer and asked him how he'd come to write the movie. It was the question I'd put to him earlier in the day. The answer Kramer gave now was identical to the one he'd trotted out for me, complete with the preamble describing how sentimental writers were. The only variation was a slight slurring of the words.

Pidgin might have heard the story already herself. She squirmed a little, but didn't release my arm. "How about a dance?"

I looked over at the Mediates. They hadn't taken advantage of the opportunity to get away from Kramer, which meant I couldn't either. "Later," I said.

"Oops," Pidgin said.

She'd said it in reference to Bert Kramer. He was repeating the word "fulfillment" over and over again without quite getting it right. He was standing with his left profile toward us, and the eye I could see didn't seem to be focusing on anything in particular. His once flushed face was pale, and he was sprinkling the carpet with wine from his neglected glass.

Pidgin released me. It was the closest thing to a cue I was likely to get. I walked over to Kramer and put my arm around his shoulders.

"Bert, old buddy," I said. "Where have you been hiding yourself?"

Kramer was still wrestling with his tongue. "Fulment," he said.

"What do you say we get a breath of fresh air?"

"Fillfent."

I interpreted that as "yes" and turned him toward the nearest exit, the one Pidgin and I had used earlier. Mediate stepped up at that point, smiling and shaking his head like an indulgent parent whose pride and joy had just broken another window.

"I think an escort home is called for," he said.

"Okay," I said.

"Not you," Mediate said. "Fred will see to it."

Wilner, who was hovering at Mediate's elbow, rolled his eyes toward the ceiling. "Of course," he said.

Kramer was still able to walk, luckily for us. With one of us on each arm, Wilner and I guided him into the hallway. I started to turn him toward the lobby.

Wilner pulled the other way. "The parking lot's out back," he said.

The hallway ended at a door marked "Fire Exit Only," which opened readily when Kramer's stomach hit the crash bar. Then the night air hit Kramer, turning him into dead weight.

"Be sick," he said.

We were on a sidewalk behind the hotel. As Wilner had indicated, the hotel's parking lot stretched out before us. We managed to drag Kramer to the curb at the edge of the walk before he made good on his promise. He made good in spades.

"What were you saying earlier about glamour?" Wilner asked. "Damn. It took a whole bottle of courage to get Bert ready for that scene."

"Several bottles," I said.

The screenwriter was kneeling between us, more or less upright. His stiff shirt front was less stiff and his vest was no longer natty.

Wilner pulled out his handkerchief and handed it to me. "See what you can do," he said. "I'll get my nice clean car."

I made a few tentative swipes at Kramer's shirt before he surprised me by grabbing the handkerchief. "Lemme," he said.

"Feeling better?" I asked.

"Little."

I was still wondering why Wilner had drawn the Kramer detail instead of me. My best thought to date was that Mediate didn't want me questioning Kramer in his current pliable condition. That made it important to try.

"Vince Mediate backed up your story about not being a Commie, Bert," I said to get us started.

"Better have," Kramer said.

"And he was pretty patient with you tonight."

"Better be," Kramer replied.

"Why is that?"

Kramer was more resilient than the average drunk. His little eyes regained their ability to focus as he looked me over. Then Wilner's headlights found us, changing the lighting of our scene and its mood. Kramer almost smiled. "We're pals, Vince and me."

I tried another approach as he struggled to his feet. "Who called you tonight to tell you about the party?"

"Dunno," Kramer said. That line didn't satisfy him, maybe because he came off sounding less than clever. He rewrote it. "A little bird told me."

Wilner's Plymouth pulled up at the curb. He opened the passenger door from the inside, and I manhandled Kramer into the front seat.

So far, I'd struck out with my interrogation. I decided I

needed another at bat. "Slide out of there," I said to Wilner, "and go back to the party. I'll drive Mr. Kramer home."

The assistant producer shook his head. "Mr. Mediate wouldn't like us deviating from our orders. He'd give me hell if I showed up inside."

His smile was almost as slow as his speech. "So would a certain lady publicist, I suspect."

11

The lady publicist was waiting for me when I got back inside. "Did you get Dumbo into his pen?" she asked.

"He's on his way."

"How about a drink?"

I shuddered. "I may never drink again."

"Dance with me, then."

The orchestra was starting to wilt. They were playing "Good Night Sweetheart" as a broad hint to Mediate's guests. There weren't many guests left, Kramer's sudden deflation having made the rest of the evening an anticlimax. Pidgin and I had the toy dance floor to ourselves.

She was light in my arms, but not—as Florence Hanks might have put it—ethereal. Nor was she distant. She pressed against me as though we'd been dancing together all our lives.

"You're good," she said. "A good dancer, I mean."

"I used to do it for a living," I said.

"I like you, Thomas Scott Elliott." As she practically had her head on my shoulder, that wasn't exactly news. I was beginning to wish I'd taken her up on the drink.

"You remind me of the war," she added.

"That's an odd thing to say."

"I say odd things when I feel comfortable."

Perhaps inspired by our dancing, Tony Ardici deigned to give us a muted trumpet solo. He still had the same dreamy, liquid way with a horn. The evening took on a soft-focus quality that made the Kramer incident seem like a reel the projectionist had mounted by mistake.

"Why do I remind you of the war?"

"You remind me of the soldiers I met. You've got the same 'How the hell did I get into this?' look on your face. You're not exactly sure what's going to happen, and you hate not being sure. Call it a creeping foreboding."

"You like that quality in a man?"

"Let's just say it arouses my sympathies."

We made the last few turns without speaking. When the number ended, Pidgin gave the musicians a hand. Ardici bowed from the waist. Another Englehart conquest.

"Mr. and Mrs. Big-Shot Producer have flown this coop," Pidgin said, "which means that we working stiffs are off the clock. How about giving me a lift home?"

"My pleasure," I said.

I now knew where the parking lot was kept, but I'd surrendered my keys to a car hop when I'd arrived, so we crossed the lobby to the hotel's main entrance. While the hop was off in search of the LaSalle, Pidgin and I stood admiring Beverly Hills' expensive peace and quiet. She stood a foot or two away from me on the Stratford's stone steps, but the distance felt like a mile or two after the intimacy of our dance.

We seemed to have stepped back into our professional roles, so I tried a professional question. "How did you come to read the Kramer note?"

"How did it work its way down to my humble level, you mean?"

She was smiling, but her question still embarrassed me. "I would have expected the studio brass to have kept it as quiet as possible," I said.

"They probably think they have, the poor saps. The truth is

too many people know about it already. It will be a miracle if Kramer gets to hang his name on his labor of love, even with that grandstand play he pulled tonight. To answer your question, I was let in on the secret so I could be ready to issue a statement in the event the great ax falls."

"What kind of statement?"

"There's some disagreement on that point. Messrs. Mediate and Beaumont want something that says the studio is standing behind Kramer, the First Amendment, motherhood, and General Motors.

"Jack Warner's version is an exercise in hand washing. While not acknowledging Kramer's guilt, the studio will publicly wish he'd never been born."

"If Warner dumps Kramer, can *Love Me Again* survive?"

"There's the rub," Pidgin said.

The LaSalle ghosted up at that moment, its eight cylinders murmuring like a chorus of English butlers.

"Nice," Pidgin said. "A souvenir of your former life?"

"All we saved when the Yankees burned the plantation."

The Stratford's doorman tucked Pidgin in for me. I tipped him and the car hop and then slid in beside her. Before I could put the car into gear, she leaned over and kissed me. The kiss was long and smooth enough to make Tony Ardici's work on the horn seem like a jackhammer solo.

"Surprised?" Pidgin asked.

"I didn't think you were the kind of girl who kissed on the first date."

"I've got news for you, brother. We haven't even made it to our first date."

This time I kissed her. When we came up for air, she said, "Don't tell me, I know. You used to do it for a living."

The doorman was ready to start selling tickets, so I eased us into the light, well-to-do traffic. "Where do you live?" I asked.

"I have a little place in Burbank, not far from the studio. How about you?"

I told her about the country estate I shared with the ground squirrels.

"I've always wanted to see squirrels by moonlight," she said.

"Doing anything tonight?"

"I don't know. Am I?"

I checked the rearview mirror before wheeling the LaSalle into a sweeping U-turn. The maneuver must have made me dizzy, because I followed it up by asking, "Does the hard-to-get routine always work for you?"

For once, Pidgin didn't crack wise. "I'd appreciate it if you'd think of yourself as out of the ordinary," she said. "Then maybe I wouldn't feel quite so ordinary myself. Or is the word I want 'common'?"

"Sorry," I said. "I'm still a little out of step with civilian life. Do you want me to take you home?"

"Not unless you want to."

"I don't," I said.

"If you're feeling delinquent, you can pass the time by giving me the third degree. Maybe I sent Jack Warner that note."

"Why would you do that?"

"I don't know. Maybe I don't like the charming Vincent Mediate. Maybe I resent him coming in from nowhere and landing a seat at the head table. Maybe I don't like him because my brother was killed in the same fight Mediate got a medal for filming. Maybe I think the medals should have been saved for the guys carrying the guns."

They were good enough reasons, but I wasn't buying them. I looked over at Pidgin. She was curled up on the far side of the seat with her head resting against the door. The passing street lights turned her hair from brown to gold with the regular rhythm of a neon sign.

"I don't think you're the least bit ordinary," I said.

"Thanks."

We drove for a while in silence. When we'd traded the quiet suburbs for a dark stretch of highway, I asked, "Have you read

Kramer's script?"

"Cover to cover. It's good. Bert's right about that much."

"Mind if I ask you a question about it?"

"Not at all. It will keep me from boring you with the story of my life."

I filed the critique. "Why wasn't Steve able to return to America? What was the dark secret in his past? It was never explained in *Passage to Lisbon*."

"You mean, did he rob a bank or steal an election or just break someone's heart?" Pidgin asked, expertly reeling off the three guesses Captain Manet had made in the original film. Saying she wasn't ordinary was underrating her.

"Right," I said. "Which was it?"

"None of them. Steve couldn't go back because the mob was after him."

"Huh?"

"They told you about organized crime during your detective training classes, didn't they?"

"First day."

"Well, Steve could never go back to America because he'd crossed those guys. Back in the thirties, he'd been a crusading reporter in New York City. He'd exposed a mob takeover of a local union, and, in the process, he'd fallen for a gangster's girl. What do you call them in the trade?"

"Gun molls."

"Right. In retaliation, the gangster killed the girl and put a price on Steve's head. That's why he had to leave the country."

Despite the vivid memory of Bert Kramer teetering on the edge of a gutter, I found myself admiring the guy. "Kramer's a screwball pitcher who manages to cross the plate every time," I said.

Pidgin had moved from her neutral corner and was now very close to me. I felt her hair brush across my shoulder as she nodded in agreement. "The way he worked it out explains Steve's idealism and his death wish both," she said. "Explains why he ran an antifascist newspaper in Paris before the war, I mean. One high-risk occupation."

"It also explains why no amount of war service could buy him a reprieve."

"Exactly. It's a well-tied package. If our friend Mr. Kramer had voted Republican all his life, his future would be rosy."

We were finally on the winding tract to the cabin. The air coming in to us from the blackness beyond the headlights was cooler and scented with pine. When I shut the LaSalle down for the night, the sounds of the forest flooded into the void: miscellaneous insects and, after a moment, the hooting of an owl.

"Nice touch," Pidgin said.

There actually was a moon out, but no ground squirrels. At the sight of my rickety stairs, Pidgin took my arm long enough to remove her high heels. Then she took off down the steps without me, her blue, shimmering dress appearing and disappearing as she moved from moonlight to shadow and back again. I followed her circumspectly, like a man walking into a certain ambush.

When I got to the bottom of the stairs, she was waiting for me, her back pressed against the cabin, her arms stretched out against the wall as though she were holding the place up. It was a self-conscious pose, one inspired by countless, forgotten movies, but that was just one more reason for me to like it. If I needed another reason.

"Sorry for playing the wounded innocent in the car," Pidgin said, with a shadow of her old smile. "I'm not entitled to. Haven't been for years."

"That's no business of mine," I said.

"I'm making it your business. During the war I told myself I liked being nice to servicemen. I've turned out to be pretty fond of civilians, too."

"Let this civilian buy you a drink," I said.

"A Gibson?"

75

"If you twist my arm."

On the way to the kitchen, I stopped by the record player long enough to enlist Duke Ellington's aid. The number I selected was "Clarinet Lament."

"That's an old one," Pidgin said after Barney Bigard's clarinet had set the mood of the piece. She hadn't put her heels back on. Without them, she looked almost petite. I had an impulse to lift her onto the kitchen counter, but I mastered it and reached for my cocktail shaker.

"It wasn't an old one when I bought it," I said.

"Since we've broached the subject, what were you like in the old days?"

"Lighter," I said. "Generally speaking."

"Weren't we all. So, when are you going to tell me how you won the war?"

"That was some other guy."

"Ah," Pidgin said.

"Ah what?"

"I have a theory that there are two kinds of veterans: the ones who won't talk about the war and the ones who won't stop talking about it. Now I know which kind you are."

While I measured and poured, Pidgin told me about her family's farm near Sacramento. In exchange, I passed on a little about growing up in Indiana, how I'd divided my time between watching movies and dreaming of them. I told her about a friend whose father had run a little theater in the late days of the silents, the Rialto, and how the friend and I would sneak in and watch the movies from the wrong side of the screen.

"Not unlike your current situation," Pidgin said.

I handed her a Gibson. "Very like it."

"You were going to be the next who back then? Douglas Fairbanks? John Gilbert? Charles Farrell?"

"All of the above."

She tasted her drink and set it down. "What's next on the agenda?"

I thought for a moment that she'd picked up where Vincent Mediate had left off, that she wanted to hear my new goal, my plan for the future. Then she wandered into my arms, and I realized that her "What's next?" referred to the here and now.

"A discreet fade to black, usually," I said.

"You're not at the Rialto now, kiddo," Pidgin said.

I dreamt that a phone was ringing for a long time before I realized that it wasn't a dream. The sun was up, but not up all that far. There was just enough light for me to see the furniture I was tripping over as I ran to the phone in the cabin's front room. I needn't have hurried. The party on the other end was going to let the phone ring till doomsday, if that's what it took.

The determined caller turned out to be Paddy Maguire. "Scotty," he said, "thank God. I was beginning to think I had two murders on my hands."

"Who's been murdered?"

"Bert Kramer, sometime last night. It happened at his place in West Hollywood. Meet me there as soon as you can. Sooner, if possible."

12

I offered to drive Pidgin to her apartment, but she asked instead to be dropped at the Stratford. At the Stratford's parking lot specifically, where she'd left her coupé. She called the studio before we set out, but whoever answered their phone knew no more of Kramer's end than Paddy had.

It was a quiet drive. Without makeup or moonlight, Pidgin looked surprisingly young in her borrowed gown. She caught me glancing her way at a light outside of Bel Air and read my mind again.

"Cinderella the morning after," she said.

"Wishing you'd gone home last night?"

"Hell no. I've got the best alibi in town. How about you? Disappointed with anything?"

"Just this finish."

"You're not half as let down as Bert Kramer," Pidgin said. Then she added, "Poor Bert," sounding as though she meant it.

That took me back to the war. My battery hadn't had many casualties, but, when we had lost a man, he'd always been remembered fondly by the rest of us. No matter how big a loser he'd been.

When we pulled up next to Pidgin's car, I started to open my door. Pidgin held me in place with a hand on my arm.

"I can manage," she said. She drew me closer and kissed me, getting the job done without really working at it, as she had me thoroughly broken in by then.

"You do that well," I said.

"You know what we Engleharts say: If you don't have a good kisser, be one."

It was a natural exit line, and she used it for that. She crossed to her car and then turned back toward my open window.

"I told you last night you reminded me of a soldier. Now I have the silly feeling I'm sending you off to war."

"I'll be back."

"That's what they all said."

Paddy Maguire was enjoying a morning cigar on the Kramers' front walk. He looked like a man standing in the middle of main street during a parade, as there was a steady flow of traffic washing around him. Paddy had chosen an appropriately somber charcoal-gray suit, but he'd ruined the funereal effect with a bright yellow vest. The boy cop stationed at the front steps was watching Paddy's back with a puckered look that told me he wanted to hustle him along but didn't like his chances of getting it done.

"It's about time," Paddy said to me in greeting. "If it wasn't for them holding things up so some bigwig from the DA's office could have his picture taken with the corpse, you'd have missed Mr. Kramer altogether."

"Must be my lucky day," I said.

The patrolman sentry was squaring himself up for the challenge of turning us away. Before he could settle on a plan, a plainclothesman came out onto the porch and called to us. I recognized this newcomer as a member of the secret fraternity to which Paddy belonged, a society whose initiates were bound together by countless reciprocal favors and the common memories of men who had seen it all.

Paddy introduced the cop as Sergeant Dempsey. He was my height—six foot even—but more solidly built, and he'd been busted up pretty badly sometime in the recent past. His left eyelid drooped, and a shiny, fan-shaped scar ran from the corner of the eye back toward his ear. He carried his left hand in the pocket of his suit coat and, when he led us into the house, he limped.

Dempsey stopped in the flowered front room where I'd interviewed Kramer. "I'll let you in on the setup before I take you back," he said. "It'll save time."

There was no trace now of Paddy's impatience. "Good idea," he said.

"Your pal was shot twice in the chest with a gun we haven't located yet. It could have been his own gun, which he kept in his desk, according to his wife. The shooting happened sometime after eleven last night. Probably shortly after."

"Is that time official?" Paddy asked.

"No," Dempsey said, "best guess. We're figuring the time this way. Just before eleven the victim was brought home drunk as a lord by a business associate, name of Wilner. Two steps inside the door, Kramer, the victim, starts to read his wife the riot act. She decides to spend the night with her mother. She asks Wilner, who hasn't managed to sneak away, for a ride. He drives her to the old lady's place in Pasadena."

"Where else?" Paddy asked, rhetorically.

"They left Kramer alive and drinking just after eleven. The wife remembers locking the front door behind her. She came back by cab before dawn and noticed that the front door was unlocked. She found her husband on the study floor. He was still wearing the evening clothes she last saw him in, including his shoes. The wife says he never wore his shoes in the house for very long. So we figure he was past untying them sometime very shortly after eleven."

"Nobody heard the shots?" I asked.

Dempsey gave me a long, lopsided look. I thought he was going to ask Paddy to repeat the introductions, but he didn't. "We're still canvassing the neighbors," he said, "but, so far, nobody's given us much. The neighbor on the study side of the house turned in about ten. She was awakened sometime during the night by the sound of a radio blaring. She couldn't read her alarm clock without her glasses, and, before she found them, the music stopped. It could have been meant to cover the sound of the shots. What this place lacks in decorating, it makes up for in radios. There's a cabinet job in here and a table model in the study."

Paddy glanced toward the foot traffic moving through the room behind us, noticing, as I had, that the tide seemed to be going out. "Let's see the radio in the murder room," he said.

Kramer's study was a left past the easy chair where he'd sat during my visit. It was a large room with three tall windows facing the side yard. We stood across from the windows in the room's only doorway, Paddy and I shoulder to shoulder and Dempsey behind us. Like the front room of the Kramers' house, the study seemed underfurnished. A desk and a chair were aligned with the center window. A table against the wall to our left held the radio Dempsey had mentioned. On the opposite wall was a bookcase with glass doors. The desk, the radio, and the bookcase had already been dusted by the fingerprint boys, and they now looked like castoffs from a haunted house. The hardwood floor was covered by a plain brown rug and the walls with the inevitable souvenirs of a career in Hollywood, autographed photos.

"Those windows were shut when we got here," Dempsey said.

They were open now, but a trio of overgrown hibiscus bushes cut off the flow of air. It might still have been possible to smell burnt powder, if there hadn't been other, more aggressive odors.

The source of the competition—Bert Kramer—lay facedown on the brown carpet at the foot of the desk. A dark stain had spread out from him across the rug like a permanent shadow. His left arm was stretched out to break his last fall, and his right arm was tucked beneath his chest. But for a rough chalk line sketched around the body, it would have been possible to believe that the screenwriter's remains had been completely overlooked by the technicians who had worked the room. They were gone, and Kramer was still here, one very large, unpleasant clue they'd stepped around in the process of collecting minutiae. For company, Kramer now had two attendants in white. They were standing next to a stretcher, speaking in low tones about some wrestling match.

A third man—another plainclothesman—had been guarding the radio table when we walked up. He crossed to us now. He had wavy hair thick with oil and a dark, pitted complexion. He looked as wet behind the ears as Dempsey was seasoned.

"When's Phillips getting here, Sarge?" he asked Dempsey.

"When it suits him," Dempsey said. "And it's Sergeant, Detective Grove, not Sarge. We're not in the goddamn army, thank Christ."

Detective Grove smiled and turned to Paddy. "Who do we have here?"

"Visiting celebrities," Dempsey said. "That's Babe Ruth and his young friend is Dizzy Dean. They're interested in the workings of a first-class homicide squad. Run through your assessment of the crime scene for them."

Grove smiled and went along with the gag. He walked over to where Kramer lay. "This is what we call the victim. He's pretty much the way we found him. Except that the lab boys took away his reading material."

"Reading material?" I prompted.

"Movie script. This guy wrote for the movies."

"What was the name of the script?" Paddy asked casually.

The kid tried to remember, snapping his fingers to help himself think. "Name of an old song," he said.

"*Love Me Again*," Dempsey said.

"Right. He was holding it like this." Grove lifted his right arm across his chest. "There were no bullet holes in the script, so he must have raised it to his chest after he was shot."

Paddy addressed me in his booming stage whisper. "Basil Rathbone should be so sharp." Grove looked up quickly, and Paddy pointed to the carpet in front of us with the toe of his shoe. "What about these blood stains over here?"

"That's where we figure he got it. Standing near the doorway, looking out toward the hall. He dragged himself to the desk before he died. Maybe to get to the phone."

"Maybe to get what he got," I said. "The script."

Grove laughed. "It made one lousy bandage."

I started to reply, but Paddy stopped me by squeezing the life out of my forearm.

"Thanks for your help, son," he said.

"Any time, pop," Grove said.

Sergeant Dempsey seemed anxious for Paddy and me to be somewhere else. He led us back through the front room and then down the hallway Violet Kramer had used for her shuffling exit during my previous visit. I caught a glimpse of a large bedroom furnished in dark, heavy pieces. The technicians who had forsaken Kramer were giving the room a once over. We passed a dining room and then squeezed through a narrow butler's pantry.

Our tour ended in the kitchen. Everything in the room was white, except for the phony blue marble of the linoleum floor. The stove, refrigerator, and sink were all white enamel, each piece given a matte finish by years of service. In one corner of the room, two white chairs flanked a white metal table with a leaf folded down on each side. Given the room's antiseptic quality, it was hard for me to imagine anyone ever eating there.

A bottle was balanced on the corrugated drain board next to the sink. It was a bottle of twelve-year-old bourbon, down by two-thirds.

"Join me?" Dempsey asked. "This room's already been thoroughly checked, I'm told."

"Has the liquor been checked?" Paddy asked. "For cyanide and the like?"

"It's been checked so carefully we're lucky there's any left."

Using only his right hand, the sergeant took three glasses from a white metal cabinet and rinsed them in the sink. Neither the cabinet nor the glasses looked like they'd been carefully checked by anybody. While he worked at the sink, Dempsey summarized things for us.

"If Mrs. Kramer's story is backed up by this Wilner guy, it figures that the shooter was someone else Kramer knew, somebody he'd let into the house when it was going on midnight."

"It could just have easily been a stranger who stuck a gun in Kramer's face when he opened the door," Paddy said. "A well-maintained gun will get you an entree into the best of homes."

"Or so you've been told," Dempsey said affably. He handed us each a glass with a finger or two of liquor in the bottom. When he turned back to the counter to collect his own ration, Paddy gave me a nod of encouragement.

"Happy days," Paddy said, and we drank. The bourbon echoed in my breakfastless insides like a shotgun fired down a well.

"Now," Dempsey said, "while I have some time on my hands, is there anything you wanted to tell me?"

It was payback time. I stole a glance at my boss, wondering how he would satisfy the plainclothesman without giving too much away. Paddy was holding the last of his drink up to the light and rolling the previous swallow around on his tongue.

"You were engaged by the studio in connection with Mr. Kramer's latest effort, is that right?" Dempsey asked.

"Yes," Paddy said.

"Why was that exactly? Some trouble?"

Paddy gave the cop some innocent, featureless background stuff about the movie being a joint venture between Torrance Beaumont's production company and Warners. "Because studio security reports to Mr. Warner, Mr. Beaumont brought us in to represent his interests, as it were."

"I see," Dempsey said.

It was a plausible explanation, delivered in Paddy's best offhand manner. I was mentally congratulating him on avoiding Dempsey's trap, when Paddy did an about-face.

"There is one thing you should know, Sergeant. The studio has kept this quiet, as you'll well understand, but that's no excuse for holding out on you. You've been more than square with us, and I know you're a man who can respect a confidence."

"What do you have, Maguire?"

Paddy reached into his suit coat and produced a folded piece of paper that looked very like the one he'd shown me in the screening room the day before. I knew it couldn't be that particular piece of paper. It couldn't be the typescript of the anonymous note.

But it was. "The studio received the original of this— unsigned—a few days ago," Paddy said, handing it over.

"Jesus," Dempsey said after reading the note. "So Kramer was a Red?"

"We don't know," Paddy said. "Nobody he worked for had any inkling of it before that note arrived. That's certain. The

84

whole thing may be hot air. The note may just have been meant to make trouble for Kramer."

"It might have done just that," Dempsey said, looking down the hallway toward the murder room. "We'll need the original of this, Maguire."

"You'll have it. I only ask that you keep a lid on it while you're untangling this business. It could turn out that the note has nothing whatever to do with the murder. The studio could get a black eye over nothing."

"Not to mention a certain ritzy security agency," Dempsey said. "I'll do my best for you, Maguire. You've played straight with me. Who knows? It could be you'll solve this one for us."

"Stranger things have happened," Paddy said.

13

Detective Grove stuck his head through the kitchen doorway and added his smile to the general whiteness. "Phillips is here, Sarge, all ready to say 'cheese.'"

Dempsey's ravaged face briefly became homogenous in color, his sunless cheeks taking on the same pink cast as his scar. I couldn't tell if it was a reaction to Grove or Phillips or the world in general. When the glow faded, Dempsey said to us, "Come by the station when this is over if you want to listen to the Widow Kramer's story. Bring the original of the item we've been discussing."

"I'll do that," Paddy said. Then he led me out the back door of the house and into the warm stillness of the morning. The dead grass motif of the front yard was continued in the back. Just beyond the steps of the house, a twelve-by-twenty rectangle of earth had been cut out of the brown lawn at some time in the past. It was now a solid stand of dried weeds.

"Looks like the Kramers had a victory garden," Paddy said. "Miracle we still won."

I was in no mood to discuss gardening. "What exactly is going on here? Why did you give Dempsey that note?"

My employer saw nearly every situation as a chance to instruct me. Even a mutiny. "I had two reasons for doing it," he said mildly. "The first is that it's better to cooperate with the police when possible. You'll want your back scratched from time to time in this business, and you'll find that often means scratching someone else's."

"Is reason number two any better?"

Paddy smiled. "It's a pip. You see, Sergeant Dempsey already knew about the charge against Kramer." He nodded with satisfaction at my double take. "It's a fact. When the somewhat hysterical Violet Kramer finally got around to calling the studio people this morning, she told them she'd let that little detail slip out during her initial interview with the police."

"I'll bet Mediate hit the roof."

"Not yet he hasn't. No one's been able to contact him so far."

"Wait a minute. Dempsey was surprised when you told him about the note."

"He acted surprised, you mean. That old war-horse could leave your average Academy Award winner standing in the starting gate. Remember that, if you should ever play poker with him."

"Why would he pretend he didn't know?"

"To see where he stood with us. If we'd held that note back, the kid gloves would have come off in one big hurry. As it is, the good sergeant thinks we're regular joes. He'll do his best to keep the note quiet if by some slim chance it has nothing to do with the murder. Oh well, a slim chance is better than none, which is what we had after Violet Kramer sang her aria."

Having wrapped up the latest installment of my training, Paddy became all business. "We've got to get a move on now. We've a busy day ahead of us. First stop is the Warners lot. I want to report to Mr. Beaumont and collect the original of that letter. We won't get past the door of the Homicide Bureau without it."

"What am I doing, besides chauffeuring you around?"

"Following through on that bright idea you had yesterday by tossing Bert Kramer's office. If we're lucky, no more than a dozen other people will have beaten you to it."

We managed to reach the LaSalle without being collared for trespassing. A few blocks north of Santa Monica, Paddy interrupted the lighting of another corona to ask me a question.

"What do you think of Dempsey's thumbnail sketch of the murder?"

"I don't like the timing," I said. "No one could have known that Kramer was going to be alone last night, just asking to be murdered. Kramer didn't know it himself until his wife walked out on him."

"Maybe Kramer deliberately drove her out so he could be alone. Maybe he had a meeting all worked out in advance."

I thought of the glassy-eyed drunk Wilner and I had all but dragged out of the Stratford. "He was too soused for any fancy footwork."

"Okay. Suppose someone was following Kramer last night. Or watching his house. The watcher would have seen Violet run off to her mother. This party could have been ringing Kramer's doorbell before Wilner's taillights were out of sight."

"Who is this guy, and why was he watching Kramer?"

Paddy used his homburg to herd some stray cigar smoke toward his open window. "Who is something we'll have to work out. Why might be easier. There are a couple of things about this business I don't like. One is the famous anonymous note. Why was it written in the first place? Was it to make trouble for Kramer? Or to undermine Siren Productions? Or, since it was written on stationery from a very specific hotel, was it intended to give Vincent Mediate a black eye?"

That last idea was my pride and joy, and it bothered me that

Paddy had come up with it unaided. "It could have been any of the three," I said.

"And it could have been none of them. If an honest person knew something damning about Kramer's past, this man or woman could have come right out and told the studio or, better still, the Un-American Activities people. If a dishonest person had the same information, said person could have made better use of it than giving it away for free in anonymous notes."

"He could have blackmailed Kramer with it," I said.

"Exactly."

"So why didn't he?"

"How do we know he didn't? Or she didn't? That brings us to item number two on the list of things that don't seem right to yours truly. Namely, Kramer's house. Anything strike you about that place?"

"It's pretty modest," I said.

"A dump, in the vernacular. The late Mr. Kramer had been a Hollywood writer at a major studio since before you were drafted. Through all those years, he made what passes for serious money anywhere else in this country. Six-fifty, say, or seven hundred a week. Yet his standard of living was only slightly higher than—you'll pardon me for saying so—your own."

"You think someone may have been bleeding him?"

"Let's put our two surmises together. Bert Kramer had something in his past that made him a prime target for blackmail. He also seems to have had an unidentified hole in his wallet. Suppose the two are connected. Suppose he's been paying out the nose to some blackmailer. Now the anonymous note starts to make sense. It could have been a spur set to the late Mr. Kramer's ample rump. Maybe he was slow with a payment or maybe he'd stopped paying altogether. The note was on the order of a dunning letter from a collection agency. Pay up or next time I'll make real trouble."

It hung together, as near as I could tell in my weakened

condition. I'd had Gibsons for dinner and bourbon for breakfast. In between there'd been too much Pidgin Englehart and not enough sleep. I felt myself sinking steadily into the LaSalle's soft upholstery.

I spotted a diner dead ahead that looked like it had been built specifically to handle my current emergency. A twenty-foot-tall coffeepot sat on top of the little building. Every few seconds, a puff of steam was released from the pot's enormous spout. The message was subtle by California standards, but it got though my mental haze.

"How about stopping for a cup of coffee? I'll buy the donuts."

"Drive on, MacDuff," Paddy said. "Hollywood Security is bringing up the rear on this case as it is. I'm not going to lose any more time just so you can put on weight."

That was a hard crack to take, coming from a man as painstakingly put together as Patrick J. Maguire. I knew better than to reply in kind, though, so I attacked his latest brainstorm.

"Why would this blackmailer of yours kill his meal ticket? In the movies, it's always the blackmailer who gets bumped off, not the mailee."

"That might have been exactly the way Bert Kramer saw it playing out. He was liquored up enough last night for desperate acts. You told me that yourself. And his gun is missing. If you care to bet against it being the murder weapon, you'll get a lot of takers down at police headquarters."

Paddy held his cigar out the car's window and the loose ash disappeared in the slipstream. "As long as we're woolgathering, let's say it happened this way. Bert Kramer has a meeting set up with the blackmailer. He arranges for his wife to be elsewhere by bawling her out in front of poor Fred Wilner. You say he was too drunk for that kind of playacting, but maybe abusing her was second nature to him."

I thought back on the little domestic scene I'd overheard through the Kramer's front door. "Maybe it was," I said.

"When the blackmailer shows up, Kramer pulls a gun on him. Maybe intending to scare him or maybe intending to kill him. Kramer turns the radio up to cover the noise of the shot. While he's about it, the blackmailer grabs the gun and takes it away from him."

"There was no sign of a fight."

"None left for us to see, anyway. But let's not get sidetracked. The blackmailer shoots Kramer and goes off, taking the gun with him. It's probably scaring the fish at the bottom of Santa Monica Bay right now."

"You still have the blackmailer killing off the source of his income."

"Ah well, in the heat of battle, a man can lose sight of his own best course. Torrance Beaumont himself said that, I think. In *The Crusaders' Cross*."

"Fritz Taber's character said it."

"There, you see? You didn't need that coffee after all. Your brain is working fine without it."

14

As a further sign of the hurry he was in, my fare had me drive him right onto the Warners lot. The guard at the gate was a youngster, even younger than Detective Grove, but unlike the plainclothesman, he'd been on the job long enough to know Paddy. He waved us past with a broad grin. Paddy had had a cigar ready to use as our entrance fee. Instead of handing it over, he waved back with it. "No point in corrupting a minor," he told me.

It was still early everywhere in the city except dairies and bakeries and movie studios. The little parking lot between the administrative offices and the Writers Building was all but full.

We pulled into a space reserved for a producer named Lord.

"It's all right," Paddy said, adding unnecessarily, "Bob owes me a favor or two. You've got ten minutes to turn over every grain of dust in Kramer's office." He leaned over and tapped the LaSalle's horn. "I'll give you three blasts on that when I want you."

"Anything in particular you'd like me to find?"

"Correspondence that ends in 'or else.'"

The writers kept better hours than the actors. Their building was even quieter than it had been the day before. Even Theresa, the exotic and particular receptionist, had found somewhere else to be. She was off enjoying bacon and eggs, I decided jealously, as I climbed the stairs to the third floor.

I was quiet as I made my way down the twilight hallway, but not because I had a premonition of trouble. The building itself was so still that anything but a stealthy tread would have sounded like Oliver Hardy in tap shoes.

A few steps from Kramer's door, I heard something that made me even quieter: the sound of a desk drawer being shut in the murdered writer's office. It was the way the drawer was shut that got me up on the balls of my feet. The sound was as soft as Miss Englehart's parting kiss. No one authorized to search the dead man's desk would have been half so reverent.

I was certain that the sound had come from Kramer's room, but when I actually arrived at the paneled door, all was stillness behind it. I listened for a moment and then reached for the knob. My movement was answered by the faint rustle of papers being fanned.

I drew my hand back and did some quick calculations, the major factor of which was Kramer's missing gun. It seemed to eliminate picking the lock, kicking the door down, and all options in between. Then I remembered the connecting door between Kramer's cell and Florence Hanks's. I decided it just might be possible to spring her lock and get a look at whoever was at Kramer's desk without making myself a target.

I moved over to Hanks's door and tried the knob. The door was unlocked. I took that for a piece of luck, as opposed to a warning, and opened the door as slowly as Paddy's ten-minute deadline allowed.

The lady screenwriter's office was revealed to me inch by inch as I eased the door open. I saw the cover on her typewriter and her empty desk chair. By then, the opening was wide enough for me to slip my head inside. The connecting door to Kramer's room was also open, but not completely. It blocked my view of the office beyond, but also blocked the office's view of me.

I stepped across the threshold onto the thin carpeting and slipped over to the angle formed by the connecting door and the wall. I took off my hat and leaned forward until I had one eye up against the gap between the door and the frame.

Through this crack, I saw Kramer's desk and, seated behind it, Florence Hanks. She was leafing through a stack of papers balanced on her lap. Her powdered face was drawn up in a grimace of concentration, and she was chewing on one well-rouged lip.

I'd started to relax at the first glimpse of her. Then I told myself that she was as qualified for the role of blackmailer as anyone else. And she could have any number of guns out of sight behind the desk.

My next move was inspired by the hat I still held in my hand. I looked around Hanks's office for a noisy target and selected the wooden blinds that hung across her only window. I flipped my hat in the direction of the blinds and then leaned back toward my peephole. The sound of the slats hitting the glass wasn't exactly a Gene Krupa solo, but it was loud enough to bring both of Hanks's hands up to her skinny chest. Neither hand held a gun.

I stepped out from behind the door and marched into Kramer's office, irritated by the idea that I'd been playing a game of cat and mouse without a cat. "Lose something?" I asked.

"A year off my life," Hanks replied weakly. She leaned backward, almost upsetting her chair. "You scared me half to death, Mr. Elliott."

"By an odd coincidence, the same thing happened to Bert Kramer last night. Only there was nothing halfway about it."

"You *are* a policeman, then," Hanks said. "I thought so."

I would have scowled and pulled my hat brim down to encourage her mistake, if I'd still been wearing my hat. I took out a Lucky and lit it instead. I needed one just then. "So you know about Kramer."

Hanks nodded. "A friend of mine at the *Times* woke me up with the news."

"And you decided to come in and straighten up his papers. Nice of you."

The blood was coming back into Florence's face. And into her muscle-bound vocabulary. "I wasn't straightening his papers, I was scrutinizing them."

"For what?"

"Bert's magic lamp. It's sure as hell he doesn't need it now."

By magic lamp, I knew she could only mean the last screenplay he'd written, the one he'd died clutching. "You're looking for a copy of *Love Me Again*?"

"Actually for the early drafts of it and his notes and research. But none of that material is here. The only things I've found are some memos that mention it. Bert must have cached it all somewhere else."

"There probably," I said, pointing to a metal waste can that hugged one side of the desk.

Florence managed to smile. "It's safely stowed somewhere. If you were a writer, you'd be sure of that, Detective or Sergeant or Inspector or whatever you are."

My most recent rank had been corporal, but that hadn't even impressed the privates. "What good are Kramer's notes and drafts to you?"

"They're a chance to pass myself off with the studio brass as

something I'm not. Namely a confidante of Bert Kramer's."
She gestured toward my cigarette. "You wouldn't happen to
have another of those, would you?"

I shook a spare one out of my pack and lit it for her. "Why
pretend to be Kramer's soulmate?"

"Bert is dead, which leaves his movie without a writer. No
one to do the million-and-one rewrites a script goes through
while it's being shot."

"Assuming *Love Me Again* needs rewrites."

This time her smile was genuine. "As long as there are
producers and directors and actors, there'll be rewrites. They
were rewriting *Passage to Lisbon* up until the last day of
shooting. After the last day of shooting, in fact. They had to pull
Tory off another picture to record that 'friends for a lifetime'
line."

"I'll concede the point."

"All right then. Some lucky writer in this building is going
to be picked to do those rewrites. It will probably mean screen
credit on what could be the biggest picture of the year."

Her fear of me had left the building while she talked. She
repeated her narrow-eyed examination of the day before. "How
about you flash me a badge?"

I dealt a business card onto the desktop. "Will that do?"

Florence examined it briefly. I expected a show of temper,
but she was too relieved for that. "Private dick, huh?"

"If I pass my exam. We were hired by the studio to handle a
little security problem."

She nodded. "Bert Kramer's politics, right? The rumors
were flying around here yesterday. Nasty ones. I wouldn't have
told you this if you'd turned out to be the law, but those rumors
make landing the rewrite job a very important move."

"Now that Kramer's dead, his name may not show up in the
credits?"

"It won't show up. Take my word for it. It's easy enough to
scam a breathing writer. A dead one—especially a dead one

with a skeleton in his closet—doesn't have a prayer."

"Which brings us back to you rifling this dead writer's desk."

Hanks looked like a schoolmarm all painted up for a trip into town. As she patiently explained her scheme to me, she even sounded like one. "I'm trying to get a line on the development of the script so I can play the part of Bert's sounding board. If I can convince the powers that be that I was the one Bert bounced his ideas off, I'll be the front runner for the plum job of the decade."

"But now you've been found out."

"Only by you." It was the perfect line on which to draw a gun, if Florence had had one to draw. What she yanked out instead was another scheme. "If you'll forget you saw me in here, I'll help you."

"Help me how?"

"You need someone on the inside, someone tied into the grapevine. I'm that someone."

I let Paddy's recent lecture on mutual back-scratching persuade me. I'd had my fill of being an outsider at Warners, and I was also growing tired of my role as permanent juvenile with the Hollywood Security stock company. If I was ever going to be more than Paddy's straight man, I needed my own contacts, and Florence Hanks looked gilt-edged.

"Let's try you out," I said. "What can you tell me about Kramer's income?"

"He drew a decent check but not a huge one. Seven fifty a week for the last year or so. Of course the salary's not the whole story. To collect it, you have to have your options picked up. If your contract runs out when you're between assignments, out you go. You can end up cooling your heels for weeks before they call you back. Or you could just be out for the weekend. However long you're off the lot, you're not being paid, which improves the studio's almighty bottom line."

"Did that happen often to Kramer?"

"Almost never. Bert was a past master at beating the option

game. The way to do it is to pace your projects so you're always in the middle of one when your option comes up. Bert could rush a job or stretch one out forever, whatever the situation called for. A slob he may have been, but Bert Kramer was the hack writers' hack."

"If he worked steady, why did he live so badly?"

"Ah. There were a lot of reasons for that, and they all had four legs and a taste for hay."

"Come again?"

"Equines. Horses, I mean. Bert liked to play them. He thought he was the world's greatest expert, in fact. The truth was, he was so bad at it that he made Bing Crosby look like a tout. There isn't a writer working on this lot who isn't out the price of one of Bert's sure things. Or a bookmaker in town who isn't going to be crying at Bert's funeral."

So much for Paddy's blackmail idea. I decided to switch us back onto the main line. "Have you found anything in those papers to support the rumors about Kramer being a Red?"

Florence lifted the pile of paper from her lap and let it fall with a thud on the desktop. "No," she said. "Not that I expected to find anything like that. What I told you yesterday was on the level. Bert had even fewer political notions than social graces. Whoever started that rumor was just out to smear him."

"As a way of latching onto his work?"

"Don't look at me, brother. I don't stoop that low."

"Could someone connected with the picture have wanted Kramer out of the limelight enough to send that note?"

Florence had ground her cigarette out in Kramer's ashtray. She suddenly noticed it there with its conspicuous smear of red lip rouge. She scooped the stub up and held it in a very small fist.

"Sure," she said. "Anybody on the movie might have wanted there to be one fewer person to share the glory. But would that anybody have picked a way to do it that threatened the whole picture? Bert sweating it out in front of the HUAC boys would have been the worst publicity any movie ever got."

"Bert will never testify now," I said. "And his movie goes marching on."

"That's true." She thought about it for a moment, then roused herself with a shake of her permanent waves. "I've got to be going. It's time I was whispering my name into the right ears. Are you out of questions?"

I had one left. "Any thoughts on who shot Kramer?"

"If I were writing this, the killer would be an egotistical producer. But then, I'm prejudiced."

15

It took Paddy a lot longer than ten minutes to shake the original of the Kramer note out of Jack Warner or Beaumont or whoever had it. After my showdown with Florence Hanks, I still had time to duplicate her search of the murdered writer's office. The room was a twin of Florence's own or at least the mirror image of hers, as the connecting door they shared was on the left as you faced Kramer's standard-issue wooden desk. In place of Florence's movie posters, Kramer had more of the signed photographs that hung in the room where he'd died. Kramer and Ann Sheridan. Kramer and Olivia de Havilland. Kramer and Joan Blondell.

There was even a picture of Kramer and Vincent Mediate. It might have been taken at the Stratford the evening before, except that neither man was wearing a tux. The contrasting moods of the photo's subjects were the link: Kramer cocksure and smiling, Mediate tight-lipped and grim. Mediate had his hands buried in the pockets of his jacket, but the jovial Kramer was waving at the camera, his right arm stretched straight out from his shoulder, his fat palm raised toward the lens. The photograph wasn't signed "Best wishes, Vince," or any other way.

The desk and matching filing cabinet were both loaded with paper, no sheet of which happened to be Communist Party letterhead. As Florence had told me, references to *Love Me Again* were almost as scarce. The picture was only mentioned in memos. A sheaf of those were carbons of ones sent by Kramer to Mediate. They contained detailed suggestions on everything from the costumes to the score. If Mediate had sent replies, Kramer hadn't kept them.

My meditation on that was interrupted by the sound of a car horn. I recognized the LaSalle's dulcet tone, but instead of the three-blast signal Paddy had promised me, the horn was sustaining a single note. From old habit I thought first of an air raid. Then I heard what sounded like a platoon of infantry coming toward me down the hall.

I got out of Kramer's chair in a hurry and slipped into Florence's empty office, shutting the connecting door behind me. For good measure, I slid home the bolt on my side of the door before I collected my hat.

A second later I heard the sound of Kramer's door being unlocked. Then a voice said, "Do you smell cigarette smoke?" It was Detective Grove's nasal delivery.

A voice I didn't recognize, a gruff, disinterested monotone, replied. "The last of Kramer's probably. The room's been shut up."

By that time, I was easing myself out into the hallway. The back stairs were only a few steps from Hanks's office. I reached them without drawing fire.

Paddy Maguire was waiting for me on the front steps of the Writers Building. "Good man," he said. "I was afraid you'd gotten yourself an escort to the police station. Let's clear out of here."

When we were safely inside the LaSalle and rolling, I said, "Thanks for sounding the alarm. Lucky thing you spotted Grove."

"Luck had nothing to do with it. The arrogant puppy wanted none other than the head of Warners' private police force to usher him around. The gentleman in question was closeted with Beaumont and me, but that didn't keep Grove from barging in on us.

"Never mind that mosquito. What did you learn in there?"

"Not to smoke while trespassing." It didn't take me long to describe what I'd found in Kramer's office because I omitted the only interesting item, Florence Hanks. I did pass on the information she'd given me, though, letting Paddy guess where I'd run into her.

He took the news about Kramer's gambling stoically, even though it deep-sixed his theory that Kramer had been blackmailed. "We'll pass the betting angle on to Sergeant Dempsey," Paddy said. "Maybe it will distract him long enough for us to get on top of things. That would make for a nice change."

I asked Paddy if he'd picked up anything interesting in his conference with Beaumont.

"Only that Vincent Mediate is still among the missing. He and his wife left their hotel after last night's party and haven't been seen since."

The Homicide Bureau was downtown in the City Hall building, a limestone tower that was a skyscraper by Los Angeles standards. Next door to the edifice, on Temple Street, was a little lunch wagon. I gazed at it longingly as we exited the LaSalle.

"Rise above it," Paddy said.

Just inside the hall, we ran into the unlucky Fred Wilner. If he hadn't traded in his tuxedo for a seersucker suit, I would have sworn the assistant producer had been on his feet since the Stratford reception. He looked that tired. He carried his suit coat over one shoulder, revealing a white dress shirt that was limp with perspiration. Wilner's chin was resting on his chest, so he didn't spot us in the lobby traffic. When Paddy called his name, he raised his head slowly and forced a smile.

"Hello," he said. "Know anyone who's hiring assistant producers?"

"It hasn't come to that, has it?" I asked.

"Not yet. Be prepared is my motto. At least it used to be. Some things you just can't prepare for."

"Give you a thorough going over, did they?" Paddy asked.

"Nothing like what I'll get at the studio. It'll do for a start, though. Take my word for it, fellows. Never be the last one to see a murder victim alive."

"Finding the body's worse," Paddy said. "It's Violet Kramer needs the alibi."

Wilner nodded. "That was why the gentlemen in Homicide lavished so much time on me. They wanted me to tell them I hadn't driven Mrs. Kramer to her mother's. I wish to God I could have. Right now it would be worth serious money to me to have never heard of the Kramers."

Paddy tapped Wilner's shoulder with his fist. "What you need is something in your stomach. Take care of the inner man first, that's what I always say."

He turned to me before I'd raised my jaw completely and said, "Take Mr. Wilner to that hash house next door and set him up right." He treated me to a wink as broad as his yellow vest. "Follow me when you're through."

Wilner lacked my enthusiasm for the plan, but he was too worn out to argue. He didn't say a word until we were seated at the lunch wagon's counter. Then, while he stirred his coffee too slowly to do any good, he said, "I should have taken you up on your offer last night. To drive Kramer home. But then you'd be the one pounding the bricks."

I pushed my empty cup across the counter for a refill. "Nobody's going to blame you," I said.

"You don't know Vince Mediate. He wanted Bert tucked in nice and quiet last night, out of harm's way and most especially out of the public eye. I did one crackerjack job of that."

I would have tried to console Wilner, but that wasn't the play Paddy had called. I knew my boss was only interested in the Southerner's breakfast as an opportunity for me to pump him. After my second cup of coffee, I felt up to listening.

"Tell me what happened."

Wilner took his first sip of coffee and then pushed his cup away. "I drove Kramer straight home from the Stratford," he said, his words lollygagging even more than usual. "My first worry was him getting sick in my car, but that didn't happen. Concern number two was getting him into the house. That turned out not to be a problem either. He wasn't as far gone as I'd thought, or else he had more stamina than Joe Louis.

"I should have rung the doorbell and run, but I stayed to see him in. Mediate expected that much at least. Mrs. Kramer answered the door. She said something pretty mild to him. 'Oh, Bert,' I think it was. Not much of a rebuke to make to a drunkard who was wearing his dinner on his shirt, but it was enough to set him off. He laid into that poor woman harder than any drill sergeant ever chewed out a draftee."

The memory had the gallant Wilner bristling. "Mrs. Kramer looked like she'd already had a lifetime of that abuse, but last night's portion made it a full load. Maybe having me there as a witness embarrassed her. Or maybe my car and I just gave her a way out. She told Kramer she was leaving and asked me for a ride."

"What did Kramer say to that?"

"He never missed a beat. He yelled something at her, 'Fine,' or, 'Good for you,' then started banging around in search of a bottle."

"Was he ever out of your sight?"

"Not until Mrs. Kramer came back into the room wearing her Sunday hat. She hadn't bothered to pack a bag. When she came back in, Bert turned on his heel and walked out on her. She said, 'I'll be back in the morning,' and he yelled, 'Suit yourself.' That was the last thing I heard him say."

The ham and eggs I'd ordered for us arrived at that juncture. Wilner's first bite took longer than my whole meal. Between mouthfuls, I asked him whether Violet had locked the front door behind her.

"Like Jack Benny closing up his vault," Wilner said.

"She found it unlocked this morning."

"So that cop with the battle damage told me."

"Sergeant Dempsey."

"That's the one. What's the big deal about the door being unlocked?"

"Dempsey thinks it could mean that Kramer knew his killer. My boss has an even cuter theory. He thinks that Kramer had an appointment with someone last night. According to Paddy, the whole fight with Violet was just a way of getting rid of her."

Wilner shared my opinion of Paddy's inspiration. "Bert was awfully drunk for that grade of clever."

"What happened after you left the house?"

"I drove us to Pasadena, where the mother lives. Mrs. Kramer didn't say anything to me en route. I expected her to start in crying, but she just sat there, all closed in on herself. Living with Kramer had wrung it all out of her, I guess.

"It took us a while to get her mother to answer the door. She lives in a little frame house that makes the Kramer bungalow seem like San Simeon. Maybe Mrs. Kramer had saved all her crying to do on her mother's shoulder. They were wrapped up in each other's arms the last time I saw them.

"I went back to my apartment and tried to get some sleep. There's just my word for that, as I live alone. I was a long time getting settled. Bert's performance at the reception had me on edge. I was sure he was going to do us all in. Do in the picture, I mean."

"Might have been the other way around," I said.

Wilner ignored my attempt at a bon mot. "It seemed like I'd just dropped off when the phone rang. It was the police. They asked me to come downtown on the double. Then they kept me cooling my heels all morning."

"Hurry up and wait," I said.

"Right. Just like in the army. The whole morning's been like the army. I know I haven't sweated this much since New Guinea. But that wasn't the cops' doing. I've been beating myself up by imagining the dressing down I'm going to get from General Mediate."

He broke a piece of dry toast in half and chewed on the crust. When he'd choked down a swallow of that, he asked, "How was your evening?"

"Fine," I said, briefly.

Wilner seemed to approve of my discretion. He was the kind of stuffed-shirt-in-training who would approve.

"Don't get the wrong idea about Miss Englehart," he told me. "She's good people. The war was harder on her than she lets on. Harder than she may even know. You and I aren't the same boys who went into the service. Folks accept that. But the people who stayed behind aren't the same either. The whole country's not the same.

"Pidgin was really shattered by her brother's death. It changed her. That and the way this whole town carried on during the war, which was like one continuous USO dance." He took off his glasses and began cleaning them with a paper napkin. "I guess what I'm trying to say is, ah …"

"That she's no tramp. I know she's not."

Wilner actually blushed. "Good," he said. "Well, I'd better be going. I've kept the firing squad waiting long enough."

16

I found Paddy standing in the busy bullpen at the center of the Homicide Bureau, posing, as he often did, for his commemorative statue. He probably would have called it thinking. While hard cases with guns under their arms circulated around us, I summarized Wilner's story in a low voice.

"Dempsey evidently believes him," Paddy said. "He's treating Violet Kramer like a genuine grieving widow. Her mother's statement was the clincher. Seems Violet and the old lady sat up half the night comparing sorrows."

Violet now sat without her mother in an office whose walls were glass from waist height up. Sergeant Dempsey was handing her a cup of something, coffee or tea or, perhaps, bourbon.

"Looks like intermission is over," Paddy said. "Dempsey's going to quiz her now about her husband's extracurricular activities, armed as he is with the fruit of our labors. Come along and listen to how a professional gets the job done."

We slipped into the office at the end of a parade that included a police matron, a stenographer, and a distinguished-looking gentleman with features so finely honed they made the wire rims of his eyeglasses look indelicate.

Violet's chair was in front of the room's only desk, which was doubling as a bench for Dempsey. He'd taken off his suit coat, depriving his left hand of its usual hiding place. At the moment, the hand was resting in his lap, balled into a fist and covered by his right.

Dempsey started the session by introducing Violet to the swell in the glasses. That gentleman turned out to be Phillips, the assistant district attorney whose late arrival at the murder house had given me a chance to say good-bye to Bert Kramer.

Phillips was more interested in Paddy and me than he was in the woman being questioned. "And these gentlemen are?"

"Representatives of the studio," Dempsey said, briskly and inaccurately. "They brought us that item of evidence I mentioned earlier."

And then invited themselves to dinner, Phillips's expression seemed to say. "Of course," he murmured as he seated himself behind the desk. "We appreciate your cooperation."

Paddy was his expansive self. "No more than our duty," he said.

Dempsey got us out of the spotlight by addressing Violet. "We've just a few more questions for today. The first one concerns your husband's politics. Do you know whether at the time of his death or at any time in the past your husband was a member of the Communist Party?"

Violet blinked a few times in the silence that followed. She looked as undernourished as she had the day before, although she'd traded in her housecoat and slippers for an unseasonable black dress and a matching hat. Her big brown eyes were as dry and flat as the hair escaping from beneath her black pillbox. The expression those eyes held now was not so much grief as bewilderment.

"I have no idea," she finally said.

It was the first time I'd heard her voice. I would have bet on a whine, a squeak, and a mumble to win, place, and show, and lost on all three. Her voice was deep and husky, the kind of rumble starlets had been affecting ever since Lauren Bacall hit town.

"I can't believe Bert was a member of any party. He thought politics was for the people he called suckers. That was most people, I'm afraid."

"But he told you that he'd been accused of being a Communist," Dempsey reminded her.

"Only recently. Yesterday, it was. When that man came to the house." She pointed to me, and I was treated to a moment of attention from everyone in the room, including the stenographer. I was suddenly grateful for my own alibi.

"I knew before yesterday that something was bothering Bert," Violet continued, "but he wouldn't tell me what. He wouldn't talk to me about work, good or bad. Not lately. Our marriage hasn't been what it was once. I used to always know what Bert was working on. I love the movies, so I was always interested. That's why Bert stopped telling me about the studio: he knew I enjoyed it."

That little insight into the Kramers' home life silenced the room for a moment. Then Dempsey said, "There's just one more area to cover, before we let you get some rest. The financial side of your marriage, who handled that?"

"Bert did. Except for the household allowance he gave me, he handled everything."

"Was your husband a frugal man?"

Violet started to smile and then stopped, suggesting that Dempsey's question amused her but the answer did not. "We don't have much put away, if that's what you mean. Some war bonds. Not much else."

"And yet your husband made a good salary. Where did the money go?"

"My husband had a weakness, Sergeant. He gambled."

Paddy nudged me in the ribs to prevent the finer points of Dempsey's technique from sailing over my head. The damaged detective had led Violet to the subject of gambling without ever mentioning it, which made her confirmation of our tip that much more reliable.

"Tell us about it," Dempsey said.

"He bet on the horses mostly. And he lost. Almost all the time. You'd think he would have won sometimes, just by accident. He used to say that himself, that the odds should have been in his favor after so much losing. It never worked out that way.

"He promised me he'd quit. I've forgotten how many times. The gambling finished our marriage. The real marriage. Everything Bert made went into the same hole. Everything we had. Everything we dreamt of having."

"Any idea who he gambled with? I'm referring to bookmakers now."

"No. There were several. I don't know any names."

"Was your husband threatened by any of them?"

"I don't know. It wasn't something he'd talk to me about. Not if he could avoid it."

Dempsey was thinking over his next line when he was distracted by the sound of a voice being raised in the bullpen beyond the glass wall. The voice belonged to Vincent Mediate, and he was demanding to see the ranking officer.

Still gazing out at Mediate, Dempsey said, "I think that will be all for today, Mrs. Kramer. You're going to stay with your mother tonight, I understand. We'll see you get a ride over there. Thanks for your time." He held his right hand out to help her from her chair. The left one, which remained in his lap, looked perfectly normal.

Violet left in the company of the matron. The rest of us held our places. All except Paddy. Without moving his lips, Paddy whispered to me, "Here's where a whole morning's work gets shot to hell." Then he eased himself over to the doorway and blocked it.

Mediate had paused to say a word to Violet Kramer. Her back was to us, but I could see that she was bobbing her head to the rhythm of his condolences. The producer was dressed for his golf club—assuming he'd found one grand enough to suit him—in a checked sports coat with aggressively padded shoulders, a polo shirt, and flannel trousers. When he finished with Bert Kramer's widow, Mediate marched up to Paddy.

"A word with you, Mr. Mediate," Paddy said softly.

"Later, Maguire," Mediate said unsoftly. "I've got bigger fish to fry."

Paddy stood stock-still for a moment. Then he shrugged and backed out of the doorway.

"Who's in charge here?" Mediate demanded of Dempsey.

Dempsey waited a moment before replying. "Whoever it is," he said, "it most certainly isn't you."

The producer's tongue sputtered and then caught. "I'm Vincent Mediate."

"I thought as much. My name is Dempsey. I'm conducting the preliminary interrogations. The gentleman seated behind me is representing the district attorney's office." Phillips interrupted his examination of his right thumbnail to glance up at Mediate. His expression suggested that he found the exchange of scenery disappointing.

Dempsey turned to address the stenographer, who was seated at the far end of the desk. "Start a new page for Mr. Mediate's statement, Mary."

"Wait just one minute," Mediate said, "I didn't come down here to make a statement. I'm here to see that the studio isn't involved in this tragedy. Bert Kramer was working on an important film for us. The wrong kind of publicity could, ah ..." He hesitated at the sight of the stenographer taking down his every word. Mary paused with her pencil above her pad, which disconcerted Mediate even more. "Damage it," he finally concluded.

"Are you aware that we've been trying to contact you?" Dempsey asked.

"Yes," Mediate said. "That is, I didn't know until I returned to my hotel less than an hour ago. I came here directly, thinking you wanted to brief me on your investigation."

"An understandable mistake," Dempsey said dryly. "Perhaps you'll begin by telling us where you've been since you left the reception at your hotel last night."

"My wife and I are building a home near Hobart Lake. We drove out there last night to check on things and ended up staying. The phones aren't in yet, so no one could reach me. We drove back in this morning and learned what had happened."

"What time did you leave last night?"

"Eleven or eleven-thirty."

Dempsey referred to a note on his desk. "You called for your car at five past eleven."

"All right, eleven then. What's the meaning of these questions?"

"Eleven is a pretty late hour to undertake an inspection tour, wouldn't you say?"

"I'm a busy man," Mediate said, the statement a small echo of his original bluster. "I have to take my free time when I find it. Besides, I felt like a drive last night. I needed to unwind."

"Because of the reception?" Dempsey asked.

"Yes, you could say that."

"Didn't go as well as you'd hoped?"

"Not exactly as I'd planned, no," Mediate said.

I was familiar enough now with Dempsey's technique to know that he was leading Mediate. They'd almost arrived at their destination. "What happened that was unplanned, sir?"

"Nothing really. Bert Kramer showed up. He'd had a little to drink."

Dempsey looked down at his notes again. "He showed up drunk and confronted you, isn't that what happened? You two had an argument on the subject of the film you're working on together. On the screenwriting credit for the film, to be more precise."

Paddy had overestimated Dempsey's dependence on the Hollywood Security Agency. The sergeant conveyed that message with a sidelong glance at us. Then he asked Mediate, "Isn't that how it was?"

Mediate's tan had taken on a milky quality. "I wouldn't call what passed between us an argument. You don't argue with a drunk. You try to pacify him. I didn't want a scene in front of my guests, so I tried to quiet him."

"I see. Why exactly was he concerned about receiving credit for his work?"

Mediate was being backed into a corner, and he knew it. "He was overreacting to a situation at the studio. An internal situation strictly, one that has no bearing on Bert's death."

"This, you mean?" Dempsey opened a folder on his desk and produced Hollywood Security's special delivery: the original of the anonymous note.

Mediate shot Paddy a look that was tantamount to walking papers. I began to take Fred Wilner's worries seriously.

Dempsey, meanwhile, was reading to us. "'Why are you using a Communist writer on *Love Me Again*?' Is this the internal situation you were referring to?"

"Yes," Mediate said.

"Let's get back to your little discussion with Kramer at the Stratford reception. *Love Me Again* was the subject of the argument you say wasn't an argument. Isn't that so?"

"Yes."

"It might interest you to know, then, that Bert Kramer died holding a copy of the movie's script. See any significance in that?"

Mediate finally demonstrated the quickness of foot that had kept him whole on D-Day. "That can't have been a reference to me. The last thing I told Bert at the reception was that I intended to stand by him. His mind was settled on that count."

"This was after he'd all but spit in your face?"

"Bert Kramer wasn't the easiest man to work with, but that's beside the point. I would have stood by him, whether I liked him or not. He was a member of my team. I depended on him and he depended on me."

Sergeant Dempsey had been holding up the Stratford note like a magician displaying a volunteer's card. He returned it now to its folder. "If Kramer was also a Red, that was all right with you?"

"Bert Kramer was no Communist. He never was one as far as I knew. But even if he'd had some leanings that way when he was younger, well, I don't think a mistake like that should haunt a person forever. Not in America."

"Give the soapbox a rest," Dempsey said. "Kramer's mistakes

aren't haunting him anymore. If anything, he's haunting them. Any witnesses besides Mrs. Mediate for this trip to Hobart Lake?"

"No, but my wife will verify everything I've told you."

"I'm sure she will. I'll send a man around to take her statement. That concludes our business for the time being, I think. Unless you've got more weight you'd like to throw around."

Mediate's padded shoulders had drooped noticeably. "I apologize for the way I came in. And for not being totally frank about the note. You can understand my motives."

Phillips stood up and spoke for the first time since Mediate's entrance. "We were more sympathetic with your studio's dilemma when its representatives dealt honestly with us. Luckily for you, we're no fonder of this Un-American Activities circus than you are. The Federals have been stepping on toes all over town for months now. The upshot being that we're cooperating with them on a very selective basis."

"I won't forget that," Mediate said. Beside me, Paddy bunched his hands into fists.

"Don't forget this," Phillips fired back. "We can and will feed you and your whole studio to those wolves any time it pleases us. Remember that in your future dealings with this department. All three of you."

17

Mediate, Paddy, and I marched single file out of Dempsey's office and stayed in formation until we reached the hallway outside the Homicide Bureau. Then Mediate turned to face us. I expected a taste of what Fred Wilner had coming, but the producer didn't have that much air left in him. He mopped his face with his handkerchief and then shook it out like a flag of surrender.

"I certainly made a hash of that," he said.

"He took you by surprise," Paddy said diplomatically. He gently explained how Mrs. Kramer had tipped the police to the existence of the anonymous note and the course we'd taken to minimize the damage.

"You'd better come along to the studio and fill me in properly so I'll know where not to step next time," Mediate said.

"I'll be along directly, if you don't mind. I've some fences to mend here first."

Mediate nodded and left us. As he stepped into an elevator, Sergeant Dempsey took his place in our little circle.

"How about it, Maguire? Is his majesty still employing your services?"

"Only so he can have the satisfaction of chewing me out a few more times. My ears are still ringing."

I looked down at my shoes.

"You two have my sympathy, having to work for that tin god. I got a lifetime supply of his type during the war. Ninety-day-wonders so full of themselves it was coming out their ears."

"Mediate saw a little action himself," I said.

Dempsey shook his head. "He may have been there, chum, but he didn't see anything. He couldn't have and still think the sun rises and sets in this crackpot town."

"Don't let his deficiencies of character cloud your professional judgment," Paddy said.

"That will depend on his alibi. Anyway, I'm sorry about making trouble for you. If there's anything I can do …"

Paddy wasted no time sticking his broad foot inside that open door. "What do you hear from your medical people?"

"Just some preliminaries. Kramer was shot with a thirty-eight. His missing pistol was also a thirty-eight, which we determined from a box of ammo he kept in his desk.

"You'll ask me next what the lab boys have to report, so I'll save you the trouble. They gave the script Kramer was holding a once-over. It looks to be Kramer's own copy, since it has his name written in his own hand on the inside cover. That was the only handwriting in it. No notes, no insertions, no deletions. No secret messages written backwards in invisible ink."

"Sounds like you're making progress," Paddy said.

"We haven't even started yet. Thanks to your tip, we have to canvass all the bookmakers in town to find out how much Kramer owed and who he owed it to. That's in addition to the legwork we were already looking at, namely finding out whether Kramer was a Commie."

"Any chance of doing that last bit quietly?" Paddy asked.

Dempsey scowled in the general direction of Mediate's elevator. "As a matter of fact, there is, although I'm suddenly less inclined to give a damn. When the Un-American Activities geniuses hit town, they hired some local talent to do their spade work. One of the beneficiaries is a former cop. We'll contact him first to get the lay of the land."

"There's a question or two you could ask him for me," Paddy said.

"Come back to my office and let's hear them."

"Just let me give my man here something to keep him occupied and I'll be right with you."

"Your man?" I asked after Dempsey had left us.

Paddy took my elbow and started me toward the elevators. "My right-hand man, I should have said. That's what I need you to be today. Get over to the Stratford as fast as that circus wagon of yours will carry you. Get in to see Mrs. Mediate. Find out what really went on last night."

"Is Mr. Mediate going to like us double-checking him?"

"I'm no longer interested in Mr. Mediate's likes and dislikes. We've got to get ahead of the police on this thing, so we'll know which way to jump. Call in to the office when you're through."

"There's something I haven't told you about last night. I found out that I know Carole Mediate. I knew her before the war, I mean."

"Don't tell me you flattened her, too."

"It was more or less the other way around."

Paddy pushed the elevators' call button for the fourth time. "If you once courted the lady, it will be that much easier for you to get an audience."

"I'm saying it might be better to send somebody else."

"Look, Scotty, it's long past time you were seeing these old associations of yours as assets. I didn't hire you because you can do a time step. If this woman likes and trusts you, so much the better for us."

"Suppose she hates the sight of me?"

"Then you've nothing to lose, have you?" He pounded the down button again. "You may have to take the stairs."

"There's something else I found out last night."

"Which is what?"

"Steven Laird couldn't come back to America because of the mob."

Paddy pushed his homburg back and tugged at a tuft of gray hair. "What has that to do with the price of apples?"

"It was in Kramer's script. He had to get the idea for it somewhere. Maybe Kramer was being threatened by the mob for owing too much to his bookies. Maybe that's what he was trying to tell us when he grabbed for the script after he'd been shot."

My audience yanked his hat brim down decisively. "I'll pass that on to the sergeant if I think he's starting to take us too seriously."

An elevator finally arrived, and Paddy saw me into it with a parting pat on the back. "Get your mind off the *Joyeuse Ile* and back to Los Angeles," he said. "And leave the brain work to your elders."

The elevator's pilot—another of my elders—started to shut the door, but I blocked it with a question. "Just so I'll know, are you planning to blow the lid on this murder or cover it up?"

Paddy shot the operator a weary smile. To me, he said, "Ask me again when we know who did it."

I was halfway across the busy lobby when someone grabbed my arm who knew something about arm grabbing. Detective Grove had either caught an early lunch or he'd seasoned his Wheaties with garlic. "Where are you off to in such a goddamn hurry, pretty boy? Your boss forget his hip flask?"

I pulled my arm free and checked my coat sleeve for grease spots. "Speaking of bosses," I said. "Yours has been whistling for you."

"Let him whistle. As he's fond of saying, this isn't the army. And I'm nobody's gofer."

He leaned into me on that line to give me the full benefit of his insult and his breath. I drew my cigarettes in self-defense. Grove helped himself to one and stuck it behind his ear. I lit mine, wondering as I did if the detective was bloodhound enough to identify the brand he'd sniffed in Kramer's office. To help him along, I blew a little smoke in the general direction of his face. He waved it away ungratefully, his open hand passing very close to my chin.

"Here's some free advice for you, hotshot. I don't know why Dempsey is letting you con artists on the inside of this and I don't like it. Don't let me catch you following us around."

"I'll do my best not to follow you anywhere," I said.

18

Making good on my promise to Grove meant making time. I drove like a cabbie between Burbank and Beverly Hills. Or at least I drove the way cabbies did in the movies, a distinction Paddy might have drawn to my attention after our most recent conversation. I parked the LaSalle a block from the hotel on the off chance that Grove had spotted it during his visit to Warners.

The day shift doorman was on duty at the Stratford, so I was spared any winks or grins from the night man over my torrid scene with Pidgin. The front desk clerk was a not-so-young man with a shirt as white as Sun Valley snow. He looked overqualified for the job of fielding rented detectives. Yet another career interrupted by the Axis, I decided.

I told the clerk I was there to see Carole Mediate, and he asked if he could announce me. That sounded like a pretty good idea. It would give the lady a chance to turn me down flat, which would be a valuable lesson to my boss on the wisdom of trusting my judgment.

It would have been, too, except that the clerk said, "Mrs. Mediate asks that you go right up."

Up, as I should have known, meant all the way up. The air on the hotel's top floor was rarefied, which is to say cool and thin. The hallway carpet was plush enough to remind me of walks on the beach.

I was expecting Arthur Treacher to answer the Mediate's door in a frock coat and striped trousers, but Carole Mediate did the job herself. In place of morning attire, she'd chosen a simple lime-green dress and sandals, their flat soles giving me back my advantage in the height department. Her blonder-than-thou hair was drawn back severely. If she was wearing any makeup, it was subtle enough to have been a waste of her time.

"Scotty," she said and took my hand. "I'm so glad to see you."

Still holding my hand, she led me into a room whose furniture had been pushed into the corners to accommodate a baby grand piano. I dropped my hat on its lacquered lid as we stepped around it on our way to the sofa.

"Vince had that brought in so Erich Kohler—that Austrian composer gentleman—could play some ideas he's had for the score of *Love Me Again*. For the entertainment of our distinguished guests last night. Now I suppose we're stuck with

116

it." She still spoke with the accent that had always reminded me of the late Jean Harlow, the never-never-land patrician tones that Hollywood elocution teachers inflict on the particularly unwary.

I waited for her to release my hand after we'd sat down, but she didn't oblige. "I'm so happy you got back from the fighting in one piece," she said. "I hope you believe that."

"I do," I said. It was easy enough to believe. Millions of people felt that way about total strangers.

"I was hoping you'd come by today or call. I wanted to explain about last night."

I started to say something polite that would have let her off the hook, but a little voice told me to play her for a while.

"It was a shock seeing you again," she said. "How long has it been?"

I was tempted to borrow a famous line from *Passage to Lisbon*, "since the Germans outlawed dreaming," but Paddy had told me to stay off the *Joyeuse Ile*. I settled for, "A long time."

"I didn't even know whether you'd come back to Hollywood."

"In some respects, I haven't," I said. "I'm doing security work now, as you may have heard."

Carole nodded. "Vince told me. I was sorry to hear you'd had to give up acting. If it's any consolation, my own career didn't last much longer than yours. If you can call being part of the background in other people's movies a career. I was getting a little old for modeling swimsuits anyway."

Not from where I sat, which was close enough to see every furrow on her porcelain brow, if there had been any to see. Even dressed as she was, like Edith Head's idea of a Kansas farm wife, she was worth a good long look.

While I looked, she let a more plausible reason for her retirement slip out. "Vince and I have been married now a little less than a year. He's only been in town a few months longer than that. A lot less time than I've been kicking around here.

117

He's good and tired of me knowing more people than he does."

"Is that why you didn't recognize me last night?"

Carole gave penitent a try. "In part. Vince is especially sensitive about the number of men I seem to know. You can understand that. But I also wasn't sure how you'd feel about me glad-handing you after years of being out of touch. As I recall, I let you down pretty hard."

That was the way I remembered it, now that I came to think about it. Bert Kramer, taking his last fall, hadn't hit the carpet any harder than I had after Carole had "let me down." The difference was that Kramer hadn't gotten up again and I had. Carole Mediate, née Leslie, now seemed like all the other people and things I'd worked myself up over in the old days— the contracts, the parts, the parties, the connections—nice enough worries to have as worries went, but as far away from me now as Los Angeles was from Berlin and Tokyo. As far away, in fact, as a glorified gofer should have been from a big-shot producer's wife. And yet here we were, sitting close enough together on her expensive sofa to balance a Ouija board on our knees.

"Did you recognize the bandleader last night?" Carole asked.

"Tony Ardici," I said.

"And did you remember the time the old crowd went down to Long Beach to hear him play?"

I'd remembered the ride but not Carole being along on it, which told me a lot about where I'd filed our brief affair. There had to be even less of a tug left for her.

But that wasn't the way she was playing it. "I picked out last night's orchestra myself," she said.

"Good choice," I said. Then, before she could throw in something about the reception's cocktail napkins matching the color of my eyes, I said, "Something happened last night after Ardici packed up his horn. Something unpleasant."

"I know. Somebody shot that horrible Bert Kramer. We had

118

messages waiting for us when we got in this morning. Vince went off to try and straighten out the police."

Custer had had more luck straightening out the Sioux. "Have you spoken with him since?"

"Only very briefly. He called to say he was on his way to the studio."

"The police will be dropping in shortly to talk with you. That's why I'm here. I have to know what you're going to say."

"The police? Why would the police want to question me? What could I possibly tell them?"

That short speech demonstrated why Carole had spent her movie career modeling bathing suits in the background of other people's shots: she couldn't deliver her lines convincingly. I suddenly understood the thinking behind her understated outfit. She was dressed to play the credible, innocent witness.

"If you've spoken to your husband this morning, you know the police are interested in his movements last night. And don't ask why. You were standing close enough to Kramer during his big scene to get tipsy from his breath. He and your husband sparred around a little and then he left. Let's get to what happened next."

Carole finally released my hand, her timing making the small gesture dramatic. "Vince didn't say anything to me about talking to you. Why should I tell you anything?"

"Because I'm working to protect your husband's interests."

She'd been around too long to believe that. "You were hired to protect the studio's interests. To protect their silly movie. You're not looking out for us."

"Then think of me as your dialogue coach. Run through the story you're going to feed the cops, and I'll let you know which lines need work." She didn't have a comeback ready for that, so I plowed ahead. "When I got back from seeing Kramer out last night, you and your husband were gone. Where to?"

"This suite. Vince didn't want to answer a lot of questions about Kramer. Questions from the press or our guests. So I

119

developed a splitting headache, and we called it an evening."

"Then what?"

"We'd no sooner gotten up here than Vince told me he wanted to drive out to the house. The maid hadn't cleared away the remains of the little party we'd given, and the mess reminded Vince of what had gone on downstairs. So we changed clothes and hopped into the Lincoln and left."

"Any side trips?" To West Hollywood, for instance.

"No. We were out at the lake by a quarter to twelve. We spent an hour or two arranging some of the furniture I'd picked out, and it got to be so late that we decided to stay. It was our first night in the house."

Thanks to Bert Kramer, it had been one inauspicious beginning. Carole's smooth brow wrinkled for a moment, perhaps with the same thought.

She shook it off. "We don't have our phones in yet, so we didn't hear the news about the murder until we arrived back here this morning."

That last part sounded underrehearsed, but I let it go. The telephone situation at Hobart Lake would be easy enough for the police to check, and the Mediates knew it.

"How did your husband feel about Bert Kramer?"

"He didn't understand the need for him. Since he came out here, Vince's biggest adjustment has been getting comfortable with the idea that he has to work through other people. He was used to doing everything himself in his little army unit. Or overseeing everything, anyway. He still tries to do too much. Out here, everything is a collaboration, which, to Vince, is another way of saying it's a compromise."

She stood up and began to pace back and forth across the patch of carpet the piano wasn't shading. "It's more than just having to work through other people. It's the people themselves. I think Vince came out here expecting the people to be as large as the movies they made. Instead, he found hypocrisy, pettiness, ordinariness. Bert Kramer was the premier example of that. A man who could write a beautiful, sensitive story, but was himself an insensitive bore from Brooklyn."

That knock was probably a direct quote from Mediate, and it rubbed me the wrong way. "Did your husband bring his own pedestal, or did he have the prop department at Warners whip one up?"

Carole's almost white eyebrows were nearly invisible against her pale skin, but they rose high enough now to get her reaction across. "I thought you'd understand," she said. "You were overseas."

"What has that to do with Bert Kramer's breeding?"

"Vince always says it was the war that made him so impatient with little men and little ideas. Especially the little men out here. They have the opportunity to make films that will touch people's lives, and they're only concerned with how much money they can grab and how many possessions they can pile up."

"Lincolns and yachts and lakefront mansions, for example?"

Carole stopped in midstride and treated me to a look that was a memory of days gone by. The bygone day she'd told me to lose her phone number, to be precise.

"I think I've given you enough of my time," she said.

I stood up and retrieved my hat. "Here's a suggestion. If the police should happen to ask you whether your husband liked Bert Kramer, leave out that bit about Kramer being unnecessary. They might not understand it, being insensitive bores themselves. Just say that Vince and Bert were members of the same happy team. That's the story your husband's using today."

Carole crossed to me and put an arm on my sleeve. By an unhappy coincidence, it was the sleeve on which I'd once worn my heart.

"I'm sorry, Scotty. I didn't mean to be short with you. Now that we've finally gotten back together, I don't want to drive you off again."

"My fault. I should know better than to talk a man down in

front of his wife."

"I wish you could like Vince for himself and not just because he's my husband. He's going places, Scotty. He could do a lot for you, if he thought you were in his corner. You could get back on the inside of this business."

Here was the new goal Mediate had told me to find, wrapped up in tissue paper and ribbon and held out to me by Mediate's own wife. Actually it was an old goal, the ambition of the movie-soaked kid I'd told Pidgin about, the kid who hadn't survived the war. He would have grabbed at this chance with both hands. I was too busy looking for trip wires.

"I don't think I've carved that kind of niche in your husband's heart," I said.

Carole came a little closer, close enough to press against the crown of the hat I held between us. "I could tip things your way."

Before I had time to explore her offer or even figure it out, there was a knock on the door. It was the kind of knock the landlord uses when you're behind in your rent. That wasn't likely to be among the Mediates' problems, so I decided that Detective Grove had finally shown up.

"Is there another way out of here?"

Carole led me down a short hallway to a door that opened onto a tiny utility room. The remains of her breakfast resided there on a silver tray. Another door stood on the far end of the closet.

"The service stairs," Carole whispered.

She leaned close to me to whisper it and then stayed close, her eyes half closed. I went along with the gag and kissed her. For old times' sake.

19

The way I left the Mediate suite, sneaking down the back stairs like a boyfriend after the husband shows up, put me in a guilty frame of mind. Or maybe my exit had nothing to do with it. Maybe I was feeling guilty about the kiss I'd stolen from Carole Mediate, having only recently given my fraternity pin to Pidgin Englehart. Then again, when I'd kissed Carole, I might actually have been two-timing Paddy Maguire. I'd received what amounted to a bribe from the producer's wife and I'd failed to register a protest. Only I wasn't entirely certain that what she'd been offering me was a bribe. The more I thought about her parting kiss, the more it reminded me of the way her husband had lit my cigarette the evening before. Both had been gestures so brimful of noblesse oblige as to be damn near insults.

To ease my conscience, I changed a quarter into nickels at the lobby desk and checked into a phone booth that had beveled glass in its door and a seat upholstered in leather. First I called Hollywood Security. Peggy, after inquiring about the lunch I'd yet to have, told me that her business partner was tied up with the Warners brain trust. She gave me the number of the studio switchboard and told me to ask for Vincent Mediate's office.

I followed the first half of Peggy's instructions. But when the switchboard operator had finished saying the studio's name, I asked to be connected with Pidgin Englehart.

I'd whistled most of my own arrangement of "Take the A Train" before Pidgin picked up her phone.

"Hello again," I said.

"Scotty, I've been looking for roses from you all morning, but none have come. Is there a problem?"

"Yes. The bank turned down my GI loan. Would you settle for lunch? I have a yearning for something on a bun with mustard and sauerkraut."

She bargained me up to a hamburger, and I told her to pick a place and I'd call her back. Before I could hang up, she said, "Hold on a minute, Scotty. Have you caught the killer yet?"

"Our dragnet is tightening."

On my next trip through the switchboard, I asked for Mediate and then gave his secretary Paddy's name. He came on the line at a canter, skipping hello and going right to his first question: "How was the reunion with your old flame?"

"Confusing," I said. "She's backing her husband's story. He may or may not have coached her on it."

"Will she convince Detective Grove?"

"If he listens with his eyes, she'll get by."

"So what has you confused?"

"Mrs. Mediate promised me plenty if I'd sign on to help her husband. My name in lights again, that sort of thing."

"When was your name ever in lights?" Paddy asked politely.

"The point is, why would she be trying to buy my loyalty if her husband's story is on the level?"

"Just playing the percentages probably. There's no such thing as safe enough in this town. Not with careers popping like soap bubbles every day. You refused her offer, I trust."

"No. I like to play the percentages myself." Paddy's soap-bubble simile reminded me of something. "Has Fred Wilner been fired?"

"Not yet. Mediate hasn't fully recovered from his own sorry performance. When he gets around to looking for a scapegoat, Hollywood Security could squeeze Mr. Wilner out of the top spot. Luckily, we've gotten a genuine break. Sergeant Dempsey dropped the name of his HUAC connection. The committee's retired policeman is a character named Dunne. He and I have had dealings before. I'm pretty sure he'll sell me a preview of any information he'll share with Dempsey. That is, he will if I get to him first. I've left messages for him in half a dozen likely places."

I checked my supply of nickels and decided to wrap things

up. "What would you like me to do after lunch?"

"I haven't decided yet about after lunch. Before lunch, I want you to get a line on Kramer's bookies. That's the safest territory for the police to be exploring, so it behooves us to break the trail for them."

"I have a date."

"Change it to dinner, but don't make it a firm commitment. And keep Peggy posted on your whereabouts. I may want you along when I go to tackle Dunne. And one thing more: I want you to pick up an item of equipment."

"If it's that gun you've been trying to sell me, I'll pass."

Paddy made a familiar snorting sound that the phone reproduced imperfectly. "I didn't think soldiers were afraid of guns."

"Generals aren't. Everyone from colonel on down has a healthy respect for them."

"Look, Scotty, there's a killer out there somewhere who's demonstrated a proficiency with firearms. You yourself think the mob may be involved. I'd feel better if you were able to defend yourself."

I thought back on my faint-hearted approach to Florence Hanks earlier in the day, when the fear that she might have a gun tucked in her corset had had me tiptoeing around like a ballerina. "I'll pick it up," I said.

"Good man," he said and hung up.

Florence Hanks had told me that every bookie in town would be crying at Kramer's funeral, and I wondered now if she'd be able to name the chief mourners. Unfortunately, Florence didn't answer her phone. The Warners operator and I were becoming old friends. I had her switch my call to the publicity department so I could cancel my luncheon date. Pidgin took the news quietly. By way of an excuse, I told her about the assignment Paddy had given me.

"You can do that and have lunch, too," Pidgin said. "I happen to know the name of the bookmaker who services the studio and the restaurant where the party in question usually eats lunch."

"Should I hock my spare tire?"

"Hock a couple. The restaurant is Romanoff's. I'll meet you there in twenty minutes."

I made one last call—to Peggy to tell her where I'd be—and then set out. As I was already in Beverly Hills, I made it to Romanoff's well before Pidgin. I hadn't been near the place since my discharge pay had run out, but the doorman—suffering in the August heat in his ersatz Cossack hat—gave me a regular's greeting. The headwaiter was nowhere near as chummy. He took my name but made no promises. I thought about slipping into the kitchen to wash a few dishes on account, but instead I wandered into the bar in search of a lonely Gibson.

I was also looking for a place to hide. I had reasons for avoiding Romanoff's other than a shortage of funds. The restaurant—which was owned and operated by a former con artist who fancied himself a Russian nobleman—was the place where the most successful people in Hollywood came to parade their success. It was a parade that made me uncomfortable, all the more so because I knew so many of the privileged class. I'd spent much of my last visit to Romanoff's wondering who bothered me more, the old friends who were solicitous and comforting or the ones who looked right through me. I'd left without an answer.

The bar was as dark as a cave after the high noon sunlight of the street. From my padded stool, I watched the entrances of the high and mighty. And they definitely were entrances. It was a peculiarity of the place that the patrons had to pass through the bar to get to the dining room. Each group or couple stepping from the darkness in which I sat into the halo of light surrounding the headwaiter would pause as though they expected that worthy to announce them. I wondered how often Vincent and Carole Mediate had posed in that same spotlight. I could easily picture Mediate there, looking down his Roman nose at the hypocrisy of the whole operation and loving every minute of it.

When Pidgin finally appeared, the sight of her was as cheering as mail call. She was wearing a vest and skirt of light blue and a cream-colored blouse with baggy sleeves. The pointed shoulders of the vest were wider than Pidgin's own and they bent downward at the ends like the wings of a Christmas pageant angel. The skirt was long and full, as skirts had tended to be since wartime fabric shortages had eased. She'd topped off her ensemble with a blue beret.

Pidgin was past my bar stool before I could get her attention. I caught up with her just as she reached the entrance to the main room. "This could take a while," I told her.

It was my eighth or ninth misjudgment of the day. When the headwaiter returned, he addressed Pidgin as "Miss Englehart," and she called him "Gustave." My name was mud, evidently, as I was excluded from the conversation. Gustave led us to a table for two near the buzzing center of the dining room, for which service Pidgin tipped him with a smile. He didn't get that much from me.

When we were seated, I asked her, "In addition to knowing everything, do you also know everybody?"

"Knowing everybody is actually more important, at least in this business. You haven't told me yet how nice I look."

"You look swell. Is that another Janis Paige castoff?"

"No. This is a Pidgin Englehart original."

"I thought you might be wearing black."

Her smile dimmed ever so slightly. "I considered something muted, but I decided it would just be for show and I didn't want to do it just for show."

A waiter appeared from out of nowhere and Pidgin ordered a gin and tonic. I sent him away disappointed.

"This morning you seemed genuinely sorry that Kramer was dead," I said.

"I was. I still am, I guess, but not in the same kind of personal, direct way. The trouble is, I've written about Kramer's death since this morning. I slapped together a press release on his career for the studio to send out."

"Writing about something distances you from it?"

"That's how it works for Hemingway and company. For serious writers, putting something down on paper is a way of getting rid of it. It's different for me. In my job I tell so many damn lies that when I occasionally write the truth it comes out sounding unlikely. I summed up Bert Kramer's life and times this morning, and now it seems like one more phony story."

"Any outright lies?"

"Mostly half-truths. For example, I described Kramer as one of a team of writers currently working on an unnamed Torrance Beaumont vehicle. I wouldn't have mentioned the movie at all if Kramer hadn't put on a show in front of those reporters last night. The word has come down from on high that he won't be named in any future press releases for *Love Me Again.*"

Florence Hanks had been right. I quoted her now: "Dead writers don't stand a chance."

Pidgin shrugged, the wings of her vest emphasizing the gesture. "They have that in common with dead butchers and bakers and candlestick makers."

Our waiter returned with Pidgin's drink. She asked for a chef salad and I ordered a club steak, which was as light as the bill of fare got.

When the waiter had whisked himself away, Pidgin said, "Perfect timing. She'll be alone in a minute."

"Who will be?"

"The bookmaker you're here to see, Maria Cassel. She's in the booth behind you."

I twisted in my chair and looked upward at the booths occupying a terrace that ran around the perimeter of the dining room. A woman was seated in the booth directly behind me. She was shaking hands with a man who was holding a balled-up napkin. He tossed the napkin onto the table as he left her.

I turned back to Pidgin. "A female bookie?"

"Why not? We had female everything during the war.

Haven't you heard of Rosie the Riveter?"

"I didn't know she took bets on the side. Did the mob have a manpower shortage, too?"

"Not exactly. The story I've heard is that Maria's husband, Mickey Cassel, was a bookmaker before the war. Cassel joined up after the fighting started, and Maria took over his territory. The arrangement became permanent when he was killed at Guadalcanal."

"Who breaks kneecaps for her, Mickey Junior?"

"Play it safe and assume she does it herself. Now get over there or you'll miss her."

I knew a direct order when I heard one. I got up and crossed the dining room to the terrace stairs, doing a good job of not gawking at any of the stars I passed. They did an even better job of not gawking at me. Maria Cassel was pondering her luncheon bill when I arrived at her table.

"Yes?" she said when she got around to noticing me.

I had one of my business cards out and ready. I handed it to her and introduced myself.

She was a large woman, big framed and heavy both. The shoulders of her navy suit were broad and not conspicuously padded. Her face was also broad, but her dark features seemed crowded together near its center. This impression was accentuated by round horn-rimmed eye glasses whose arms squeezed the fleshy sides of her head. Her hair was dark and elaborately curled, and the hand she held out to me was as large as my own.

"Have we a client in common, Mr. Elliott?" Her voice had a worn, raspy quality, but it was friendly enough. "Someone you're wanting to get off my hook?"

"He's already shaken your hook, the hard way." I wondered as I made that crack if death was an excuse someone in Maria Cassel's business would accept. "I'm looking into the murder of Bert Kramer."

"I see. Have a seat and tell me how I can help you."

129

I slid in beside her, trying to think of a question that didn't sound like a rephrasing of "Did you shoot the poor bastard?" I finally hit on, "Did you know Kramer?"

"Yes. I've known Bert for years. He was one of my better customers."

"Meaning he lost a lot."

"Almost all the time. When I heard about the murder on the radio this morning, I thought to myself, 'Poor Bert loses again.'"

"How was he about paying?"

"Only a few weeks ago, that would have been an embarrassing question, given the way Bert checked out. It used to be like childbirth getting him to pay. The steady losers are always a problem. They stop expecting to win, so they don't care about staying on the good side of the person paying out."

"Why would they gamble if they don't expect to win?"

"Because they want to lose, of course. That's a theory of mine, anyway. It's a phenomenon that may be unique to the movie business. I think a high number of the leading lights of this burg are uncomfortable with all the adulation and money heaped on them because they know they don't really deserve it. They deal with the money part by throwing it away on silly houses and yachts and parties. Or they give it to people like me."

"That doesn't sound like Bert Kramer. His ego was pretty iron-clad."

"You're right. That category of loser mostly contains actors. With writers, the guilt usually comes from having compromised their principles for money. 'Sold my soul to the devil' is a phrase you hear a lot. So they try to unload the devil's dirty money."

"On you."

Maria smoothed the white tablecloth before her. "If you provide a service people really want, you're going to do all right in this world. You can quote me on that."

"Why aren't Kramer's gambling debts an embarrassment to

130

you now?"

"Because they no longer exist. A few weeks back, Bert paid me everything he owed me. He paid off every bookie in town, from what I hear. Since then, it's been strictly cash-and-carry as far as Bert was concerned."

"That's pretty convenient for you, seeing as how the police are scratching around for a motive for Kramer's murder."

"They really are scratching if they think a bookmaker had anything to do with it."

"You don't threaten deadbeats?"

"Sure we threaten them." She waved a hand as airily as a grand duchess admitting to an occasional pinch of snuff. "I'm only fair at it myself, and I could threaten the roses out of your cheeks. But you don't kill the goose that's laying your golden eggs, if only for fear of scaring off the other geese."

"How big was Kramer's last egg?"

"You mean, how much did he owe me? I'll deny this in front of witnesses, but it was five grand."

"Serious money."

"But not worth killing over. I know there are places in this world where you can get killed for less than this lunch set me back, but this neighborhood isn't one of them. Not in sunny 1947."

"Suppose he was into every bookie in town for that much."

"What are you saying, we all chipped in and had him killed? Maybe to teach our other customers a lesson? We're nowhere near that close. Even so, I'd be careful where I trotted out that idea if I were you. Not everyone in this business is as easygoing as I am."

"Thanks for the tip."

"Here's another one for you. If I were in your shoes and I heard that Bert was paying off five-grand notes like they were parking tickets, I would be asking myself an entirely new question."

She paused to let me work it out. "Where did he get the

money?"

Maria leaned toward me slightly. "Did anyone ever tell you that you're dreamy when your wheels are turning?"

20

Pidgin was nibbling on lettuce when I got back to our table. Between nibbles, she asked, "How are those cute kneecaps of yours?"

"Intact. Which is more than I can say for my theory that Bert Kramer was rubbed out by the mob. According to Mrs. Cassel, he paid off all his debts a few weeks back."

"Using what?" Pidgin asked without the benefit of Maria's prompting.

"The lady's point exactly. How was Kramer paid for *Love Me Again*?"

"There was a flap over that, from what I've been told. Kramer claimed to have written the script on his own time and he wanted extra money for it. Jack Warner said that Kramer's contract made everything he wrote the studio's property, even if he wrote it at two in the morning in the john. I think Warner really believed that Kramer had written it at his desk in the Writers Building when he was supposed to be working on something else. A lot of goofing off goes on over there."

"So I've noticed," I said. "If Kramer wrote *Love Me Again* in his office, he cleaned up after himself. There's no trace of his notes or rough drafts in his desk."

"Huh. Anyway, in the end, they agreed on a payment they called a bonus. But it was no fortune. Only three or four thousand."

"Not enough to have paid off Cassel," I said. "Never mind all her competitors."

I ate some of my expensive steak while we thought it over. After a while, Pidgin asked, "What are your plans for the rest of the day?"

"I haven't been told yet. I'm supposed to stay near a telephone."

"By an odd coincidence, I have a phone in my apartment."

"That's handy."

"Yes, it is. I thought if you weren't actually scheduled to take the murderer this afternoon, we might run up your roses tab."

I tried to stare a blush out of her, but that was a bigger job than one man could handle. Before I'd entirely given up, our waiter reappeared, carrying a telephone that matched his white jacket. He set the phone on our table and plugged its cord into a jack near my feet. "A call for you, sir," he said.

Pidgin settled back in her chair with folded arms. "It's no challenge to stay near a phone when they follow you around."

The party with the bad timing was Paddy Maguire. "I thought I told you to cancel your date," he said, a little louder than the distance between our phones required. "What the hell are you doing at Romanoff's?"

"Just now I was thinking of asking you for a raise," I said. "But I actually came here to interview Kramer's bookie, Maria Cassel."

"Mickey Cassel's widow," Paddy said, somewhat mollified. "She must be expanding her territory. I didn't know it took in Burbank."

"Only the better neighborhoods. She put the kibosh on the idea that Kramer was killed over his gambling debts. It seems he paid them all off a few weeks back. Where he got the money is another mystery."

"It'll have to wait for the moment. I've an important job for you. Dunne called the office and set up a meeting. You're to go in my place."

"Why?"

"A slight snag has developed at the studio. Jack Warner's

taken personal charge of the Kramer business, which is like having the bull running the china shop. He's fired Hollywood Security twice in the last hour. Mediate's behind him, but Beaumont is on our side. So far, I've been able to talk our way back in, but if I leave now, we're probably out for good. Dunne can't put off the cops for very long. If we're to talk with him first, it has to be now."

"Where am I meeting him?"

"Her nibs will give you the details when you stop by the office. She'll have something for you to slip to Dunne if he comes across with anything useful. Now get a move on."

"Wait a second. There's something you can do for me before they toss you off the lot. I'd like to get a copy of the script for *Love Me Again.*"

"Still on that hobbyhorse, are you? I thought you'd given up on the mob angle."

"Kramer had to have a reason for grabbing that script. He could have been trying to say that the killer was connected in some way with the movie. Or the clue could be subtler than that. It may be a detail of the plot itself. If not the mob connection, then something else. I won't know until I've read the thing."

"Or even after," Paddy said. "You're looking for too many wheels within the wheels. A dying man's mind doesn't work like that. Kramer probably grabbed the script because it was the best work of his career. Another man seeing his life slip away might grab for a picture of his children."

"Humor me," I said, "and when my time comes I'll grab for a picture of you."

Paddy chuckled. "I'll see what I can do."

Pidgin was ready for the bad news, so I gave it to her. "Looks like the florists and I are out of luck. Seems I have an appointment to bribe someone."

"What an interesting job you have. Speaking of bribes, how about letting this lunch be my treat? Or better still, the studio's? I should be able to pass you off as a business expense."

"Linking yourself with Hollywood Security could be a bad career move," I said. "The bill's no problem." Eating until my next paycheck would be though.

I signaled our waiter with a raised hand. A raised eyebrow would probably have done the trick. I asked this omnipresence for our bill.

"There is no bill, sir," the waiter said. "Mr. Romanoff asks that you consider yourself his guest today. He recently heard of your gallant service during the late war. He himself once had the honor of serving in the Imperial artillery."

"Against Napoleon, probably," Pidgin whispered.

I thanked the waiter, and he dematerialized.

"I'm impressed," Pidgin said. "You'd better break down and tell me your story."

"Some other time."

On our way out of the restaurant, I spotted Mike Romanoff in one of the booths at the back of the cavernous bar. He was a distinctive if not a particularly distinguished-looking man who sported the dated combination of a clipped military moustache and a bristly crew cut. Romanoff's table was crowded with courtiers, which made me reluctant to approach him. While I was trying to make up my mind, he looked up and caught my eye. I bowed from the waist. Romanoff inclined his head, slightly but imperially.

Pidgin was chatting up the Cossack doorman when I got outside. His accent was pure bluegrass Kentucky. Before I could cut in, another retainer drove Pidgin's coupé up to the curb. Her good-bye kiss was a peck on the cheek, but she made up for it by saying, "Let me know if you need to use a phone anytime soon."

Hollywood Security had its own building, a white stucco one-story with a roof of bright orange tile. It was on a little side street called Roe, almost in the shadow of the 20th Century–Fox lot. The front door opened onto a plush reception area that doubled as Peggy Maguire's office. Her desk, which stood to a visitor's right, guarded the entry to Paddy's more private quarters. A second doorway, stage left, led to a large, unplush room where we members of the rank-and-file hung our hats when we weren't out on assignment. Even though, in 1947, Hollywood Security had a record six operatives on the payroll, the frugal Maguires saw to it that this room was seldom used.

I certainly wasn't given a chance to put my feet up when I stopped by to get directions for my meeting with Dunne. I was barely through the front door before Peggy Maguire was hurrying to meet me. She and her husband partner were a teaming of opposites, physically and temperamentally. That had held them in good stead both in vaudeville and now in the business portion of their joint career. Peggy was a short, thin woman with sharp features that were dark in coloring and expression. This stern front was a bluff, I'd come to learn, a defense against the same hard world her husband battled with smoke rings.

"And here you are finally," Peggy said. "You've just time to make it." She was carrying a canvas bag the size of a lunch sack and using both hands to do it.

"What are we paying Dunne in?" I asked. "Gold bullion?"

"What? No. This is the pistol Paddy wanted you to have. It's loaded, so be careful."

I took the bag from her and untwisted the top. The gun inside was a Colt Model 1911A1 forty-five-caliber automatic, a hot surplus item since the war. Paddy had thoughtfully provided a shoulder holster.

"You do know how to use it, don't you?" Peggy asked.

"I'm better with a howitzer."

"Don't tell Paddy that, or one will be showing up COD." She'd had a white business envelope hidden under her arm. She held it out to me now. I noted that it was sealed and unmarked. "Put that in the inside breast pocket of your coat," she said.

"Should I pin the pocket shut, maw?"

That finally produced a smile, a thin, dark one, appropriately. "Pin that mouth of yours and get moving. Here's the setup."

"Let me guess. I'm supposed to stand at the corner of Hollywood and Vine whistling 'Somewhere I'll Find You.'"

I was fanning Peggy's ember smile too hard. It went out, abruptly. "You're to go to a bar called the Black Rose," she said sternly. "It's on Vernon, near Exposition Park."

"How will I know Mr. Dunne?"

"He'll be wearing a black hat. He must like them. Paddy says he's never seen Dunne without one."

21

Once I was out of the range of Peggy's sharp eye, I was tempted to open the white envelope, but I knew it would only spoil future pay days. The canvas sack didn't tempt me at all. I wrapped it tightly around the holstered automatic and slipped the bundle into the glove compartment of the LaSalle. I asked myself why the sight of the gun bothered me so much. I'd used guns since I was ten, first to shoot Indiana rabbits and squirrels and later to shoot German soldiers. The one break had been my short career as an actor. Maybe that was it. Maybe the physical presence of the gun threatened the illusion that I was safely back in the old Hollywood. Threatened that part of the illusion that hadn't died with Bert Kramer, that is.

I might have guessed, given enough guesses, that Paddy and the mysterious Dunne would pick a bar for their rendezvous. But I never would have come up with the specific bar. The Black Rose was more than a new one on me. It was something I wouldn't have believed without seeing, a bar as out of place in modern Los Angeles as a horse-drawn carriage, although a delivery wagon would have been a better comparison. The tavern was tucked into a block of tiny, respectable businesses—a typewriter repair shop, a used-book store, an accountant's office, a florist—and it somehow managed to be the dowdiest storefront of the lot. There was no neon visible on the brick facade, just a black wooden sign with the name of the bar lettered in weathered gold. The small front window was dusty, and its lace curtains had aged to the color of ripened wheat.

The inside of the bar was well-lit compared to the one at Romanoff's, which meant it was only moderately dim. I stood in the entry while my eyes adjusted. A wooden bar began near my left elbow and ran all the way to the back of the room. Behind the bar were bottles of all sizes and shapes arranged around a large mirror that needed resilvering badly. Its current backing had deteriorated into large irregular patches that looked like lily pads caught in the frozen surface of a rectangular pond.

Standing in front of the mirror was a bartender in a collarless white shirt. The sprinkling of hair left on his head was combed straight back, and it arched above his pink scalp like the skeleton of a long-dead pompadour. Across from him, on one of the bar's tall wooden stools, sat a man holding a newspaper. Dunne.

There were a couple of other candidates for the honor—one farther down the bar and another at a shadowy table in a distant corner—but I knew that the man whose reading had been interrupted by my entrance was Dunne. For one thing, he looked like an old-time policeman in his dark three-piece and his tightly knotted tie. And he was the right age, his face as wrinkled as his suit and his hair nearly white. The clincher, though, was the black hat. It was a venerable trilby, one of those high-crowned, flat-brimmed models that were fixtures in thirties gangster pictures. Unlike the rest of his attire, the black trilby was impeccably maintained. It gave Dunne the air of a man with an interesting, incongruous past, like a preacher with a patch over one eye.

A short beer occupied the stretch of bar in front of Dunne. I sat down next to him and ordered a beer of my own. The bartender and Pidgin Englehart would have had a basis for a conversation; his nose had also been broken, often and well. He and I lacked that common ground. He set my beer in front of me and went away without a word.

"Nice day," I said to Dunne.

"This is Southern California, bub," Dunne said. "It's always a goddamn nice day."

I had one of the Hollywood Security pasteboards out of my pocket by then. I slid it across the bar until it rested between Dunne's nose and his beer.

He folded his paper. "Where's Maguire?"

"Unavoidably detained. He sent me in his place."

"He should have sent two of you," Dunne said in his friendly way.

He picked up the business card and rubbed it between his thumb and forefinger like a tailor rating a sample of cloth. "Hollywood Security," he read. "What a racket. If the studio bosses had it to do over again, I wonder if they'd be so quick to sever their financial ties with the police. All they did was add a few middlemen like Maguire to the equation, operators who get rich paying off all the people who always got paid off. What a sweet racket."

"Speaking of rackets," I said. "I hear you're passing off Roosevelt liberals to the House Un-American Activities Committee as Commie spies."

Dunne did a slow burn that would have turned Edgar Kennedy green with envy. Then, before he could think of the right name to call me, he smiled. "I may have misjudged you," he said. "You're not the hothouse plant you look to be.

"As for my job with the HUAC, I'll admit it isn't the hardest time I've ever clocked. But it's honest. I'm not passing anybody off as anything to anyone. That was all done before I hired on."

"What exactly are you doing?"

Dunne moved a weary hand over his weary face, the gesture

finishing up with a yank at his chin. "I'm verifying allegations made against members of the Hollywood community. When Parnell Thomas and the other big hitters on the committee were out here last spring, they met over at the Biltmore Hotel in executive session, which is to say secretly."

I nodded as though I knew all about it. In a way, I did, since Paddy had told me about Jack Warner's secret testimony.

"Anyone could stop in and denounce anyone else," Dunne said, "and there was some serious denouncing going on, let me tell you. It's taken us working stiffs all summer to winnow down the list. But we did it. The subpoenas will be going out soon. Probably in the next couple of weeks."

"Subpoenas for what?"

"Full committee hearings to be held in Washington this fall. They're going to be whatchamacallits, trials where the verdict is in at the get go, the kind Joe Stalin likes to hold."

"Show trials?"

"Right, show trials. The gentlemen I work for have selected the invitees very carefully. I think the list stands at nineteen now, and they're all pretty solid cases. They have three important things in common. Almost all of them are current or former Communist Party members. My job was verifying that, which wasn't hard, given how open people were about that sort of thing during the war."

Dunne took a sip of beer without noticeably lowering the level in his glass. "Party membership or sympathy is the only common denominator my bosses will discuss openly. I came across the other two while I was poking around in the files. They're subtler. And more interesting."

"I'll bite," I said. "What else do these guys have in common? Are they all subversives or spies or what?"

"They're not spies," Dunne said, still stalling. "Patsies maybe. Pawns surely. But not spies or even really serious troublemakers."

He finished off his beer with a movement so quick it startled me. Then he gave the bartender a come hither wave. "Another, Joe, and a shot of Bushmills. My friend here is buying."

When Joe had gone away again, Dunne said, "The Federals have been out here sniffing around for Reds before. The first visit was way back in the twenties, believe it or not. Those other expeditions never came to anything. The reason they failed is that the big studios closed ranks and protected their people. Common denominator number two is going to prevent that from happening again."

"And it is?"

We touched hat brims as Dunne leaned toward me. "The nineteen are almost all involved with local unions or guilds."

So was Steve Laird, I thought illogically. Or maybe not so illogically. I didn't have a chance to work it out, as Dunne was moving on.

"That hook is guaranteed to pull the studio heads into the government camp. There's been a lot of labor unrest out here since the war ended. One of my first freelance jobs was in the big Warners strike back in '45. Both sides played rough in that one, and it hasn't been forgotten. Hell, the idea that Commies are running the labor unions has knees knocking all over the country. It's one of the things that's driving the current scare. And it's the reason the studio bosses will throw their people to the HUAC wolves this time."

The detective hadn't shown his high card yet. I could tell that from the way his little eyes were twinkling. "What's the third common denominator?"

Dunne had been watching his shot of whiskey as though he expected it to make a break for the door. He grabbed it and tossed it down now like a gunslinger beating a tenderfoot to the draw. "The real reason these nineteen suckers were selected, the big link, is that they're almost all of them writers. Idea men. The people who write the words that get shouted from movie screens into every unsuspecting melon in the country. That's the battleground of the coming fight, the space between your rosy ears. It's Hollywood's territory now, which means it belongs in part to these Commie writers, and the jokers in Washington want it back. Even the studio bosses haven't cottoned onto that angle. The dumb, fat, and happy of this town aren't going to know what hit them. This dream factory is Poland, and 1939 is just around the corner."

Dunne's apocalyptic vision quieted us both for a time. The passing of Bert Kramer didn't seem to amount to much in comparison. I sat looking at the bar's ruined mirror. My own reflection appeared in a relatively solid section of the glass, but Dunne's was distorted, his face a puzzle with too many missing pieces. His trilby, floating above the jumble, was its crisp, black self.

I roused myself with an effort. "It's a writer I've come to ask you about," I said. "Bert Kramer. Is he one of the nineteen?"

"Kramer? No. Wait a minute. Isn't he the joker who got shot last night? Is that why my old friends on the force have suddenly remembered my phone number?"

"Yes. They're looking for a motive for his murder. So are we. The difference is, we'd like to find one that doesn't involve Warner Bros."

"Why come to me?"

I tried my hand at coy. "There's a rumor floating around that Kramer might have been a Communist."

Dunne gave his chin another yank. "If the Communist tag was on the level, you'd expect Kramer to be the gunman, not the victim. To silence his accuser, so to speak."

"You just said that Kramer wasn't a Communist."

"You were only listening with one ear. I said he wasn't one of the nineteen selected for the show trial. The committee's original list was much more comprehensive."

Getting information from Dunne was reminding me more and more of the tooth-pulling I had to do with Paddy. "Was Kramer on the original list?"

"I don't think so. Not as I recall. If he had been, he surely would have made the final cut, him being a writer and all."

"He wasn't active in any unions," I said, remembering Kramer's sincere contempt for the Screen Writers Guild. Again a few frames of plot from *Love Me Again* came back to me. Steve Laird had been a union supporter. His fidelity to the cause had gotten him in trouble with the mob. Kramer had dreamt that up to explain why Steve couldn't return to America. While I chewed on this difference between the writer and his character, Dunne was speculating in a new direction.

"Kramer could have been involved with the HUAC in another way. He could have been a friendly witness. An informer. I haven't been allowed to see a full list of the locals who testified against their neighbors. This Kramer could easily have been one of them. Maybe he was killed to shut him up."

"What point would there be in shutting him up now if he already testified last spring?"

"To keep him from giving a repeat performance in Washington in front of the newsreel cameras."

The old cop clearly found our murder more interesting than his government work. He was yanking on his chin with gusto now. "Or how's this? Say Kramer didn't testify last spring. But suddenly there are these rumors floating around about him being a Commie. Maybe he had the goods on a real Commie. One we didn't know about. He could have been planning to spill it to keep his own skirts clean."

Dunne's guesses were dragging me into deep left field, but his rambling had given me an idea. Other people besides the HUAC's flunkies could tell me whether Kramer had been a Communist. Namely, the Communists themselves. But I wanted a very specific Communist. The trade union link between *Love Me Again* and the HUAC's list of nineteen was still dancing around in my head. Not a hunch exactly. Not yet. Just the seed of one.

"You said the writers being subpoenaed are all active in the labor movement. Is there one who's especially active?"

Dunne didn't need to tug his chin this time. "That would be a Mr. Potts over at Columbia. Carl W. Potts. He was one of the founders of the Screen Writers Guild. President of it at least once. And he was an advisor to the Conference of Studio Unions, the umbrella organization that was behind the '45 strikes. Hell, Potts marched in their picket line."

I tossed some money onto the bar, and the crumpled bills reminded me of Dunne's bribe. I tapped the bulge in my coat caused by his pay packet. "How do we do this?" I asked in a low voice. "Should I slip it inside your newspaper or leave it on the bar or drop it on the floor as I go?"

Dunne's answer was another of his lightning moves. He reached inside my jacket and yanked the envelope out. "Hollywood," he said with disgust.

22

I came out of the Black Rose half expecting to find that the broad, sunny streets of Los Angeles had been transformed into the dark alleyways of a nightmare. But Vernon Street at least was as bright and placid as I'd left it. Dunne's story hadn't affected anything but my fading sense of well-being.

I didn't call the office. I was tired of the short leash I'd been on all day. The Carl W. Potts angle was a lead of my very own, and I wanted to hold on to it for a while. Besides which, there was an excellent chance that Hollywood Security had been fired by Jack Warner for the third and final time since Paddy and I had last talked. I was far from ready to be taken off the Kramer case.

Columbia Pictures was located at Gower and Sunset. The actual grounds were the least picturesque of any of the major studios. Even the no-nonsense Warners lot was parklike in comparison. "Termite terrace," one of the nicer nicknames for the studio, came to mind as I parked the LaSalle in the gravel lot next to the building where Columbia kept its writers. It was a long, frame, two-story reminiscent of the barracks that had sprung up on army camps all over the country. I deduced that the building lacked a central hallway from the fact that every office had an outside door. The doors on the second floor were accessible by a balcony that was serviced by four open stairways, one at each corner of the building. The stairs I chose felt as though the studio termites had been working on them for some time.

The guard who had let me pass through the main gate on the strength of the LaSalle's chrome had given me the number of Potts's office: 205. That office was guarded by a screen door. It had been patched in one corner with a scrap of paper on which was typed, "Western Union man enters." I could see 205's occupant through the tattered screen. He was seated at a desk and he appeared to be asleep.

I knocked on the door frame, and the sleeper started. "Who is it?"

"Western Union," I said. I tried the door. Its catch wasn't fastened, so I opened it and stepped inside. The creak of the warped framework shutting behind me was like a postcard from Indiana.

The office was decorated in books. Bookshelves lined the three interior walls, and I couldn't see a gap in any of them. Overflow piles stood in the corners, some rising as high as the desk.

"I don't remember telling you to come in," Potts said. He was a small, thin man with wet eyes, a large red nose, and scarred, sunken cheeks. His tie and vest were undone, and his shirt was damp from the heat of the afternoon. His voice reminded me of the dead Bert Kramer's; Potts was another displaced New Yorker. A second reminder of Kramer stood on the desk at Potts's elbow: an open bottle of liquor.

"Since you obviously don't work *for* Western Union," Potts continued, "am I to conclude that your name *is* Western Union? That would make your parents two pretty cruel people."

"Just my dad," I said. "My mother wanted to name me Bell Telephone."

"And me without a pencil," Potts said, patting the pockets of his unbuttoned vest. "Please don't be witty again till I've found one."

What he found was his empty glass. He splashed a little whiskey into it.

"Did anyone ever tell you writers you drink too much?" I asked.

He smiled. "The Sinclair Lewis syndrome we call it. Care to join me?"

"No, thanks. Are you drinking for any particular reason?"

Potts thought about it for a moment, his sad eyes checking each corner of the room in turn. "For two particular reasons. Nicola Sacco and Bartolomeo Vanzetti. You've heard of them, surely."

"The anarchists?"

"The martyrs. Executed on August 23, 1927. Twenty years ago this week. Twenty years." Potts held up his glass and looked at me through the brown liquor. "It's way too pat. I'd never get away with putting it in a script."

"What's too pat?"

"The symmetry. The coincidence of the ending falling on the anniversary of the beginning. Or so close to it as to be the same thing. The Sacco-Vanzetti executions woke me up politically. It was the beginning for me."

"What's the ending?"

Potts's eyes did another furtive dance around the room. "You're asking me? Your bosses didn't brief you very well."

"What bosses would those be?"

"Parnell Thomas and the other fascists on the House Un-American Activities Committee. I've heard that I can expect an invitation from them shortly."

"You've mistaken me for another flunky," I said. "I work for a company called Hollywood Security. We're looking into a little matter for Warner Bros."

"Got a name? And don't tell me Wells Fargo."

I'd wasted my last business card on Dunne. "Elliott. Scott Elliott."

"A nice gimcracky name for this gimcrack town. Couldn't be anything plain like Smith or Brown or ..."

"Potts?"

"Right. Like Potts. A good, common-as-dirt name, Potts. Wait a minute. Scott Elliott. I've heard that name recently. Somebody was talking about Hollywood war vets who can't get their calls returned. Guys sent off with a brass band and welcomed back with brass knuckles. Your name was on the list. Way down the list, of course."

"Of course," I said.

His sympathy took the form of a bubbly chuckle. "So you're working security, huh? For Warner Bros., no less. Those fascists. Too bad you weren't with them in '45. You could have been on the crew that turned the fire hose on the CSU pickets. Or you could have been one of the sharpshooters they had stationed on the soundstage roofs."

It was a shame Dunne hadn't come along with me. He and Potts could have reminisced together. Or slugged it out. "I've heard the strike was nasty," I said.

"Criminal," Potts countered. "Warners was trying to shove out the legitimate unions to make room for scabs from the IBSE."

"Could you spell that for me?"

"The International Brotherhood of Studio Employees, a so-called union that's been in the producers' pay for years. Not to mention the fact that it's been infiltrated by the mob."

"There's a coincidence," I said.

"What is?"

147

"Nothing. You were saying?"

Potts waved me away. "I forgot you used to be an actor. You probably never heard of a union. Or a class struggle. A pampered aristocrat like you."

"Right now I'm late for a manicure," I said. "Suppose we get down to business."

"What exactly is our business?"

"I'm looking into the murder of Bert Kramer. Happen to hear about it?"

Potts gave me a very brief nod.

"Happen to know him?"

"I knew of him. Apolitical guy. The kind of mindless know-nothing the producers love."

"Not a union man?"

"No."

"Or a Communist Party member?"

"Are you kidding? Kramer probably thought Karl Marx was Zeppo's real name. Why are you asking?"

"Late in his life, Bert got himself accused of being a Red. It could even have had something to do with his getting shot."

"That's crazy." Potts had been holding his glass for some time, but he'd yet to take a drink. Now he set the tumbler back on his desk. "Kramer was no Communist."

"You'd have to say that even if he was. You guys don't name names."

"We don't inform on our own people. We've got no problem with disowning a parasite like Bert Kramer."

"Ever hear the one about not speaking ill of the dead?"

"Sorry. I call 'em as I see 'em. Bert Kramer was as self-centered and self-important as this whole town."

"A good writer, though."

"Was he?" Potts asked without interest.

"I think so. The last thing he worked on was top notch. You might have heard about it. It was a sequel to *Passage to Lisbon*."

"Sure I've heard about it. Everybody in the business has." I

148

was boring him.

"Not a *Passage to Lisbon* fan?"

He shrugged. "As sentimental, bourgeois pap goes, it was okay. At least it was antifascist. Of course, everything was in '42, even the cartoons. It's a terrible thing to say, but I miss the war years. They were the only time I ever felt at home in this town. The only time I ever felt we were all pulling together. That unity's long gone."

"Look on the bright side," I said. "The fascists are long gone, too."

"Think so, huh? I have reason to believe otherwise, given my current situation. I think the fascists on this side of the pond just pulled their ears in during the war. They minded their manners and did their jobs. They maybe even worked their way up the chain of command. Now the war's over, and they're still around. Leaderless maybe but not gone. Forgotten even but not gone."

"There's another coincidence," I said.

This time, Potts didn't bother to ask me what I meant. He appeared to have lost interest in me. We listened to a persistent fly battering away at the screen door behind me. Then I asked, "What do you intend to do?"

"About what?"

"The HUA Committee. You're right about them. They've got your number."

"It'll blow over," Potts said without conviction. "It always has."

"Suppose it doesn't. Suppose there's a blacklist."

"Then I'll do something else. I'll write novels or build houses or dig ditches. There's a big wide world outside of Hollywood, you know. Or do you?"

He looked up at me for the first time since I'd mentioned Bert Kramer. "Maybe you don't remember the real world, Elliott. Or everyday life. You've been deprived in that area, haven't you? You cut your teeth in Hollywood and you came of age on the

149

battlefield. Neither one of those nasty places has much to do with ordinary, day-to-day life. They're both too extreme in their opposite ways. War is concentrated reality, one hundred proof, uncut. Hollywood is pure fantasy, wishes and buts becoming candy and nuts before your eyes. Everyday life is reality and fantasy mixed up in ways you'd never expect."

"I wasn't a child actor," I said. "I did a long stretch in the real world before I came out here. I have a hometown. And a family."

"Why haven't you gone back to them then? Why hang around where you're not wanted?"

I didn't have an answer handy, which seemed to give Potts a lift. "Until you've worked that out, don't look down your nose at me and my troubles. And speaking of being where you're not wanted, why don't you trade places with that fly who's knocking on my door. I'd prefer his company."

By the time I left Potts, my seedling hunch had definitely taken root. On the strength of it, I stopped again at Columbia's main gate. The dress extra who had admitted me was still on duty.

"I couldn't find Potts," I told him. "His car wasn't there either. He still drives that red Chrysler, doesn't he?"

"No," the guard said. "He's got a big black Packard. Looks like Eisenhower's staff car."

So much for worker solidarity.

I parked the LaSalle on Sunset, in a spot shaded by a chamber-of-commerce palm tree. My vantage point was halfway between two Columbia gates, the main one I'd just exited and a smaller one used by studio employees. I had my hood ornament pointed toward the employee entrance, as I considered it the better bet.

It turned out to be a sure thing. Ten minutes after I'd taken up my watch, a black Packard as long as a doubleheader slid out of the employee gate. The driver was wearing a slouch hat and dark glasses just like mine, but I had no trouble recognizing

Potts.

The Packard headed east on Sunset. I gave the car a block's head start and pulled into the late afternoon traffic behind it. Potts drove well for a man who had been drinking the day away. I figured the effort was using up a fair amount of his concentration, so I wasn't worried about being spotted. I was careful to keep a car or two between us. Other than that, I just enjoyed the ride.

Potts stayed on Sunset until it crossed Alameda Street. Then he took Alameda south. We crossed Vernon, coming within a few blocks of the Black Rose, where Dunne might still have been straining to read his paper in the half light. For a crazy moment, I thought Dunne might be the one Potts and I were hurrying to meet. But that would have been too cute, one wheel too many within the wheels, as Paddy might have said.

As we continued south, I wondered what my employer would have made of the clues I was piling up. I had labor unions infiltrated by the mob, leaderless fascists hanging on to positions of power, and a writer who looked down his nose at sentimental, bourgeois movies but still cried in his whiskey over two anarchists, dead twenty years. Or maybe Sacco and Vanzetti really weren't the subjects of Potts's private wake. Maybe the death that had shaken him was slightly more contemporary.

We stayed on Alameda all the way to Anaheim Street in Long Beach, the destination of my long-lost summer odyssey with Carole Mediate. I didn't recognize the place. The shipyard had boomed during the war, and business still looked good. Blocks of what I remembered as space for let had been transformed to accommodate the yard's workers and their pleasures. As we travelled east, things improved, by which I mean they started to look poky, prewar, and familiar. Just shy of the Long Beach Marina, Potts pulled into one of the old places, the Cove Inn. He parked his battleship himself in the Cove's gravel lot. Then he went inside.

I drove on past the inn, turned around, and headed back, parking where I could see the Packard and the entrance. I wasted a little time wondering whether Potts and I had been the first to arrive. In the end I decided it didn't matter one way or the other. If I'd been too late to see the writer's date go in, I'd surely see him or her come out.

As it happened, I wasn't late at all. I was just getting down to my last drag on my first Lucky when a Lincoln convertible pulled into the lot. Its top was down, which made it no job at all to identify the driver. Vincent Mediate's dark hair was a little worse for the wind, but he was otherwise unruffled. He passed the Lincoln off to the inn's parking attendant and went inside.

It was then up to me to call the play. I could wait around for someone else to show up. Walt Disney, say, or Thomas Dewey. Or I could dig out the automatic from its glove compartment hiding place, chamber a round, and kick the Cove's door in. I picked a third option. I tossed my cigarette into the street, fired up the LaSalle, and drove off.

23

Peggy's post in Hollywood Security's front office was deserted. I approached the inner sanctum unobserved, getting close enough to hear Paddy's voice through the fancy double doors. There was a second voice to overhear, one as familiar as Paddy's, although I'd only met its owner a couple of times.

I knocked on the door as I opened it. Smoke filled the upper third of the room. The fancy damask curtains were drawn against the late afternoon sun, and the resulting gloom made the little lamp on the half-acre desk look like a lighthouse on a foggy shore. Paddy, in shirtsleeves, reclined behind the desk, using his file drawer as a foot rest. His visitor still wore both his coat and his hat, and he sat with his back to me.

The presence of a client softened Paddy's greeting. "Where

the hell have you been?"

I pulled an empty chair toward the curtained window, choosing a spot that gave me a view of both men. "I've been fishing," I said.

Torrance Beaumont sat slouched with his legs crossed before him. His right elbow was propped on the arm of his chair so he could hold his cigarette above the level of his sleepy eyes. Without the makeup he'd been wearing the last time we met, the ex-crooner looked ancient and tired.

"Catch anything?" he asked.

"My limit, I think. Is Mr. Warner still employing us?"

Paddy, on the other side of the lighthouse lamp, looked far away but sounded very close. "For the moment. What did Dunne have to say?"

"What everyone else has said: Kramer was no Communist. The HUA Committee's never heard of him or from him, as far as Dunne knows."

"Then the note was a hoax all along," Beaumont said.

"No, it wasn't."

I saw the tip of Paddy's corona glow bright red through the haze. "Let's have it," he said.

"The note didn't mention Kramer by name. It turns out, it didn't refer to him at all. The writer of *Love Me Again* is one Carl W. Potts. He works at Columbia and he's redder than Santa's underwear."

Neither man stirred, which could have been a sign that my revelation had shocked them. For the moment, I accepted that possibility.

"The tie-in with Potts is the labor movement. Unions figure in *Love Me Again*, at least in the background. But the guy who supposedly wrote it, Bert Kramer, was too tight to join one. According to Dunne, anti-union feeling is one of the things driving the current Red scare. I asked him for the name of the Red most active in the local labor fracas, and he served up Potts. I went to Columbia to talk with him."

I paused to give Paddy a chance to ask who had authorized the move, but he didn't speak. "I learned that Potts is as sentimental as Kramer claimed to be. Sentimental enough to miss a time when everyone in Hollywood was on the same antifascist bandwagon. Sentimental enough to revive the time by writing a sequel to *Passage to Lisbon*, the movie that embodied those good old days. A sequel, incidentally, that features a hidden fascist in a position of power. That's a breed of hound Bert Kramer wouldn't have known if it bit him. Potts sees one behind every tree."

"Did Potts admit any of this?" Paddy asked.

"I never put it to him. He was shaken up when I found him. Over Sacco and Vanzetti, he said. I think it was really over Kramer being dead and the scheme to sell *Love Me Again* maybe dead with him.

"If I'm guessing right, the scam went this way. Potts wrote *Love Me Again* because he's sentimental, like I said, or because he had an idea of how the plot might work out and he couldn't keep it bottled up. The trouble was, the script was no good to him. *Passage to Lisbon* belongs to Warner Bros., not Columbia, and Potts is one unpopular guy at Warners. He participated in the big CSU strike of '45 as a volunteer on the picket line. He's still wet from the fire hose they used on him, so the bad feelings are mutual.

"And Potts has bigger problems than being unpopular. He knows about the digging the HUAC people have been doing, and he smells a blacklist in the making. This afternoon, he tried to laugh the idea off, but it was a pretty hollow laugh. There's one sure way for a writer to beat a blacklist."

Beaumont knew it, too. "He hires a front, an innocent who can pass himself off as the author of the blacklisted writer's work. Smooth."

I didn't know if he was complimenting Potts for thinking of it or me for figuring it out, so I didn't take a bow. "A front would solve Potts's problems with Warners and the HUAC both, which is where Bert Kramer comes in. As I said, Potts was shaken up when I found him. I shook him up some more by asking about Kramer."

"Did he admit knowing him?" Beaumont asked.

"Barely. He said Kramer was politically illiterate. It's a quality that would have made Kramer perfect for the job of fronting for a Red. He was also an ex-New Yorker, like Potts. Could have been they knew each other in the old days."

"There are a lot of us kicking around out here," Beaumont said as he leaned forward to use Paddy's ashtray.

I wondered again how much of my story was news to him. And to Hollywood Security.

Paddy knew I was still holding out. "What was the point of shaking up Mr. Potts if you didn't intend to ask him whether he'd written the script?"

"I wanted to get him moving so I could see which direction he'd take. I wanted to know if anyone else was involved."

"Me, for instance?" Beaumont asked. His face was illuminated briefly as he lit another cigarette. He looked amused.

"For instance," I said. I thought about lighting up myself, but I was already breathing in all the smoke my lungs could handle.

Paddy and I had traded roles. He was after information now, and I was playing the bashful bride. "So what happened?" he demanded.

"Potts ran and I followed. To Long Beach. The Cove Inn. A little while later he was joined by our friend Vincent Mediate."

Beaumont's only comment was a long, low whistle. Paddy was still digging with both hands. "What did you do next?"

"I came back here for orders."

"At long last," Beaumont said.

Paddy only had eyes for me. "Orders?"

We were back to the question I'd put to Paddy as he'd shoved me into the elevator down at City Hall. "Do we turn Mediate and Potts over to the police or start looking for a rug big enough to sweep them under?"

"Turn them over for what?" Paddy asked.

Paddy's question made me realize just how long the day had been. The bloody morning now seemed like a detached piece of memory floating around loose, like a fragment of my senior prom or a day in boot camp. I made an effort to grasp the image of the shapeless body on the carpet and pull it into context. "For shooting Bert Kramer."

Beaumont ground out the cigarette he'd just lit. "I think we'd better have that drink you offered me earlier," he said to Paddy. "All this storytelling is making my throat dry."

The fancy office should have had glass decanters with tops cut like diamonds and little silver bibs to identify the liquor they contained. A setup like that would have been right for the office, but not for its owner. Paddy eased his feet off the open file drawer and turned to reach into the dark corner behind him. He retrieved a brown bottle and three jigger-size glasses. He pulled the cork from the bottle and tossed it backward into the darkness. "We won't be needing that again, I think," he said.

He set two full glasses on Beaumont's side of the desk. The actor handed me one and raised the other in a salute. "You've done a fair day's work, soldier."

"The day's not over yet," I said.

Beaumont set his empty glass back on the desk, and Paddy leaned forward to refill it. To me, Paddy said, "Suppose you tell us how Potts and Mediate getting together in Long Beach makes either one of them a murderer."

I tasted my drink. It was Irish whiskey, not as medicinal as Scotch or as bland as Canadian. "Mediate getting together with Potts means that Mediate knew that Kramer was a front. And I learned from a local bookie, Maria Cassel, that Kramer recently paid off all his gambling debts."

"How is Maria?" Beaumont asked.

"Substantial. Kramer didn't get his money from Warners. A front can't have expected more than a percentage of the bonus Warners paid for the script, and the whole bonus wasn't enough to pay off Kramer's losses. So we're talking about something else."

"Blackmail again," Paddy said. "This time with Kramer as the blackmailer."

"That was your pal Dunne's guess. He thought Kramer might have been killed by a Hollywood Communist to keep him from testifying at the big hearings in Washington. I think Kramer was bleeding the Communist pink. I think that's why he was killed."

"Just how much did you spill to this Dunne character?" Beaumont asked.

"Not much. Yet."

Paddy leaned into the light to fill Beaumont's glass for the third time. "What's that 'yet' supposed to mean?"

"Even if everything I've guessed is right, it doesn't add up to a good reason for Mediate to be involved. Potts and Kramer didn't need him to work their little scam. Another conspirator is just extra overhead."

"Leading you to deduce what?" Paddy asked.

"That we may be dealing with more than one Communist. Maybe Potts didn't know Kramer in New York in the old days. Maybe Potts's connection to Warners is Mediate. Maybe they've been getting together ever since Vince hit town to read Marx by candlelight."

"That's pretty thin," Paddy said. "In fact, the whole idea that Mediate was in on the connection between Potts and Kramer from the start is thin. You said yourself that they didn't need Mediate to make the scheme work. Listen to this scenario. Kramer gets himself shot by persons unknown. Potts is in a panic because his pipeline to the Warners pay office has been cut off. He takes a chance and calls Mediate. He says, 'You don't know me, but I'm the guy who wrote your movie. Meet me in Long Beach or I talk to the newspapers.' Mediate would have gone on the double."

"I would have," Beaumont said.

"You're forgetting the money Kramer was shaking out of somebody."

Paddy grunted. "It could have come from Potts."

"Why would he have paid out? To protect what secret? He wears his Communist Party card pinned to his chest. Only a secret Communist would have been a mark for a blackmailer. Maybe a former Communist. Mediate was pretty passionate in Dempsey's office on the subject of forgiving youthful mistakes."

"I would have given the same speech if I'd been there," Beaumont said. "I've half a mind to testify before that goddamn committee myself. I'd give them an earful, too. Those windbags forget we were in a depression for the better part of a decade. People were open to any way out of that. The kids especially. They swallowed ideas even more boneheaded than Communism. Look at what happened in Germany."

We all three drank in silence for a time. It occurred to me that I'd made the break I'd hoped for earlier in the day. I was no longer Paddy's errand boy. I felt a new distance between us, and it made the morning seem like yet another lost time.

"Let's get back to cases," Paddy said. "It's way too soon to pass this on to the police. We're none of us interested in covering up a murder. But we don't have definite information yet. We need to do more checking."

"It will take months to finish the picture," I said. "We can't stall that long."

"To hell with the blooming picture," Paddy shot back. "I'm not talking about stalling. I'm talking about being sure of our ground. If we hand Mediate over to Dempsey and Phillips on the strength of your whimsies, we'll lose control of the whole situation."

I had my answer all ready. "That's where Dunne comes in. We go to talk with him again, armed with another of your long, white envelopes. He can tell us whether Mediate's been named to the HUA Committee."

"Nix, pal, nix," Beaumont said, getting up from his chair.

The whiskey or the mood of the moment was making him sound like a character from one of his pictures. He even looked like one as he paced the room with his thumbs tucked in his belt. "If you mention Mediate's name to Dunne, the committee will reel him in, Red or no. Then he and the movie will both be finished. I've got a better way to check him out. A quieter way."

"We're listening," Paddy said.

"If the answer is in Mediate's past, his prewar past, it's gotta be in New York. He worked on Broadway before the war. I still have plenty of contacts back there, people who can put us in touch with people who knew Mediate. I'm proposing that we send young Sherlock Holmes here east to talk with them. There's still time to get him a seat on the red-eye to La Guardia. He can be there early tomorrow morning."

"You're calling the shots," Paddy said. "If you hadn't stood up to Jack Warner today, we'd be on the street right now."

Beaumont rubbed his thin hands together as he warmed to the plan. "I'll have the studio make the arrangements with the airline. Can I use your phone?"

"Use my better half's." Paddy waved his cigar toward the reception area. "I want to have a word with my operative."

The actor nodded and left us, closing the door behind him.

I stood up myself then. It seemed like the right moment to stand. "This trip idea is another stall," I said. "The solution to the murder is here, not in New York."

"Tory thinks differently, and the customer is always right."

"Since when have your customers even gotten a vote?"

Paddy broke his cigar in two grinding it out. "Since you became one more part of this business I can't keep track of. I've all the balls in the air I can juggle right now. I don't need anyone tossing me new ones. Especially someone on my own payroll."

"Are you sore because I upstaged you or are you worried that I won't go along with a cover-up?"

"You can take your pick," Paddy said, "since you've already made up your mind that I'm an accessory after the fact in this murder. Either way, get this much straight. You're following orders from now on or you're walking."

Beaumont came back in before my next line reported for duty. "It's all set," he said to Paddy. "He's just got time to pack a toothbrush. That is, if he's going."

"I'm still awaiting his decision," Paddy said.

"I'm going," I said.

Paddy picked up a bound manuscript from his desk and held it out to me. "Here's something for you to read on the plane." It was the script I'd asked him for, *Love Me Again*. "Where's your part of the bargain?"

"The gun, you mean? It's in my car."

"A fine lot of good it's doing there."

"Leave it be," Beaumont said. "New York's a civilized place. They have laws against those things."

24

There should have been a trace of Pidgin in the air inside my little house. There would have been a trace, if my return to the cabin had been a scene in a movie. The screenwriter would have had me find a long, almost-blond hair on my sofa and the émigré who composed the score would have had the orchestra play her theme as I looked around the empty rooms.

The schedule Mr. Beaumont had laid out for me didn't include a lot of time for gazing around wistfully, but I gazed anyway. I was that indifferent about catching my flight. I'd made up my mind that the trip to New York was just an expensive way of getting rid of me, that Paddy and Beaumont wanted me safely filed away while they worked out how best to use or not use the information I'd brought them. If I'd really been the hero of my own movie instead of a bit player in

Paddy's, I would have quit my job and stuck with the case until I'd dragged Kramer's killer into police headquarters bound and gagged. Paddy would then have given me back my job, and we all would have lived happily ever after.

A better ending would have had Jack Warner offering me the lead in a western. That fantasy reminded me of Carole Mediate's vague promises from earlier in my long day. She'd said her husband would get me back into my old profession, and maybe cap my teeth while he was at it. Had the offer been Carole's idea or had Mediate been speaking through his wife? That would have been on my list of questions, if I'd had time to make one. Paddy had given me a list of his own, a list of orders. Item number one involved packing my toothbrush.

I opened my old calfskin case and then pointedly ignored it. As a second meaningless act of rebellion, I took a long, increasingly tepid shower. Afterward I dressed in my suit with the least shiny pants, a conservative navy blue one that had an East Coast look to my West Coast eye. As I tightened the knot in a low-key necktie, the phone began to ring.

I had my ear tuned for Pidgin's laughing soprano, which meant it was open far too wide for what I got. "You're a hard man to reach," Florence Hanks barked at me.

"The maid's day at the beach," I said.

"Lucky girl. Some of us have been running our tails off."

I made an effort to block that mental picture. "You were whispering your name in producers' ears when I last saw you."

"Yes, and the campaign paid off. You're talking with the new writer on *Love Me Again*."

"Congratulations."

"You could sound more celebratory."

"Sorry. Events have been too alacritous for me today."

"You're not kidding, brother. If I had slept in this morning I would have missed the whole deal. By the way, you're wrong about the script not needing rewrites. Requests are already piling up."

"Did you call to rub that in?"

"In part. I also wanted to keep my half of our deal and pass along some information. They've cleaned out Kramer's office."

"Already?" Things did move fast at Warners.

"Desk and file cabinet emptied, pictures off the walls, the works. I've never seen the like. It usually takes them weeks to free up an office after somebody gets canned or runs off to write the Great American Novel. So I did some poking around. Guess who gave the order to box Kramer up and ship him out."

"Vincent Mediate."

"Damn. You're not just another pretty face."

"Thanks, I think."

"Poor Bert. It's like he was never here."

Florence was trying to work up to a sniffle, but she couldn't quite make it. Her good fortune had more than cancelled out Kramer's bad break. "Have fun with the rewrites," I said.

My contact hung up, but I held on to the handset. I was still hoping to hear Pidgin's voice over the dead wire. It was an irrational dilemma, but it had a practical solution. I dialed information and asked for all the E. Engleharts in Burbank. They only had one, and she answered her phone herself.

"All through bribing people for the day?" she asked after my hello.

"I ran out of unmarked bills."

"Any plans for this evening?" Her voice was almost a physical presence in the room. I began to miss my nice, cold shower. "I'd like to come over and look for something valuable I may have left there," she added.

"Your tiara?"

"My nylons."

And I'd been squinting around for a loose hair. "Sorry," I said. "I do have plans for the evening. I'm flying to New York."

"You and Howard Hughes."

"I'm serious."

"Oh," Pidgin said. "Anything you can talk about?"

162

"What you don't know won't hurt you."

"Assuming the murderer knows that I don't know. I'll be sure to wear an especially blank look until you get back. Which will be when?"

"Soon."

"Did you call to not tell me anything else?"

I almost said that I'd only called to hear her voice, but that line seemed too antebellum. All my lines did. I did have something else on my mind, though. A warning I felt I should leave with someone.

"I talked with a guy today who's working with the HUA Committee. He said that Hollywood isn't going to know what hit it when the Washington hearings get going. He said the whole industry's being targeted, not just some Red writers. The studios won't be calling the shots when it's over."

"You sound worried."

"Why shouldn't I?"

"Scotty, this is the town that turned its back on you. You're working as a freelance janitor for the studios, never mind the fancy title that shady boss of yours probably gave you. You're called in to sweep up what the real janitors won't touch. Why do you care what happens to Hollywood?"

"I'm hoping for a part in a western."

Pidgin did a fair imitation of Paddy's snort. "You're like a guy who's been thrown over by a girl and then spends the rest of his life looking out for her from the wings."

"Joseph Coffin, *The Imperial Albertsons*, RKO, 1942. My hair's not that wavy."

"I'll see what I can do next time I get my hands on you. Till then, take care of yourself."

"I will," I said. Now that I had something to look forward to.

25

I'd never been inside a Lockheed Constellation before, and I'd really been missing something. The plane was a ballroom with wings compared to the prewar airliners. A long, narrow ballroom certainly, but at least a level one. Boarding a tail-dragging DC-3 meant climbing a steep slope to a tiny seat. The Connie sat level, thanks to a nosewheel, its strut as long and elegant as one of Vera Ellen's legs. To enter the plane I had to first ascend a wind-swept flight of aluminum steps. But once inside, a smiling stewardess led me down a flat, carpeted aisle to a soft, reclining armchair. Each seat had a reading light and its own spotless ashtray. The plane was even quiet. Until they started the engines.

The Connie that carried me east that night was all but full. The seat next to me was especially so, as it was occupied by a machine-tool salesman named Gunderson. The way he filled the gap between the armrests reminded me of the late, unlamented Bert Kramer. Gunderson had yet to meet his first stranger. He told me I looked familiar and asked if I was in pictures. When I unwisely told him I had been, he pumped me for stories on Linda Darnell, Abbott and Costello, and Oscar Levant. A very eclectic fan was Harry Gunderson.

He made a big impression on our stewardess, too, but she was trooper enough to still bring us dinner. The meal was served early in the flight, right after the captain's ritual goodwill tour of the cabin. That wasn't soon enough for some passengers, who had settled in to sleep the moment we'd left the ground. I hadn't eaten since Romanoff's, so I chewed my little airline lamb chops with gusto. So did Gunderson, but only after some interesting preparations. First he spread his napkin across the burial mound that passed for his lap. Then he took the long cellophane wrapper his silverware had come in and slipped it up over the bottom half of his tie. It hung there like a flat, inadequate prophylactic.

"In case of rough air," Gunderson told me. "This trick has saved me from many a grease spot. You'd better try it."

I'd never had a tie I liked that much. It turned out to be an unnecessary precaution in any case. The night air we passed through was as smooth as Paddy's Irish whiskey.

After the stewardess had reclaimed our trays, my neighbor switched off his light and reclined his seat. A minute later, the engines had serious competition in the droning department. I decided it was time to watch a movie, or at least to read one.

There was no longer any reason to bother with the script for *Love Me Again*. I was pretty sure that I'd deciphered Kramer's dying message. He hadn't grabbed for the script because it was the best work of his career, as Paddy had believed, but because it wasn't his work at all. Pretending the script was his had somehow gotten him killed. I knew Kramer's secret, but I couldn't follow it up. I was flying to New York, getting farther and farther from the murderer with every snore out of Gunderson.

And still I held the script as tenderly as if it were a first folio or a lost book of the New Testament. I asked myself why. I was certainly curious about the sequel to a movie that meant as much to me as it did to Carl W. Potts. But it was more than that. I couldn't shake the feeling that my only chance to see *Love Me Again* would be this private showing inside my head. I didn't believe that Paddy and Beaumont could rescue the movie. Not with its writer booked for a show trial and its producer up to his neck in a murder case. That was why I handled the script reverently. It was a fragile, doomed thing, a dream dying in my arms.

The picture would start with the Warner Bros. shield on the screen and the fanfare that Max Steiner had written to accompany it blaring away like God's entrance music. Then Steiner would pass the baton to Erich Kohler, the composer of the *Passage to Lisbon* score and, according to Carole Mediate, the man tapped for *Love Me Again*. Kohler would surely segue into the title song, even though, according to Hollywood legend, he thought so little of the piece that he'd tried to have it yanked from *Passage to Lisbon*. After mixing up some variations on "Love Me Again" with a theme or two of his own, Kohler might finish up with a few bars of Chopin's *Heroic Polonaise*. It had been lucky for him and Warners before.

Passage to Lisbon's titles had scrolled across a map of the western Mediterranean. I imagined the sequel starting with the same shot. The camera draws closer and closer to the map until it focuses, not on Marseilles where the first picture had begun, but on the unmarked stretch of water where Torrance Beaumont and the dying Nigel Clay float on their raft. As the credits continue to roll and the *Polonaise* pounds itself out, a slow dissolve replaces the map with the long shot that Paddy and I had seen in the projection room. The burning wreckage and the two as yet anonymous survivors on their anonymous raft form a background for the last credit: "Directed by Max Froy."

Only the name should have been "Scott Elliott." I was directing the movie now. At least the parts Froy hadn't beaten me to. I was also casting the minor roles, selecting the locations, and designing the sets and the costumes. I knew enough about the movies to flesh out Potts's shorthand, the dialogue and the little, respectful cues on setting and camera movement he'd passed on to the director. Suggestions Froy and I would use or discard as we saw fit.

I watched again while Captain Manet made his cryptic confession to Steve. I heard him say, "It was all an act, Steven," watched him cough blood, then listened again while Laird intoned, "What might there be?"

After Manet's showy death, the action jumps forward to Paris after the war. Potts suggested a montage of newsreel clips to convey the passage of years, shots of the Normandy invasion, the fighting after the breakout, the liberation of Paris. I supplied those from my own library of stock footage. A shot of a boulevard of flag-waving Parisians would fade into a view of the same street in peacetime, ablaze with peacetime lights.

That transition set things up for a nightclub scene and a musical number that Potts and I could only sketch in. It features the Clausen Brothers, dancing to an up-tempo piece like *Passage to Lisbon*'s "Count Me In."

After they take their bows, Eddie and Joe are approached by a formally dressed French woman of some maturity who asks to be introduced to the brothers' brooding friend, Steven Laird. The man in question is sitting at a quiet table, a cigarette in his mouth and a drink at his elbow. A newspaper is spread out before him. As the camera arrives for a close-up, Steve's dull eyes come to life. He's found an article about the new United Nations and its temporary headquarters at Lake Success on Long Island. The camera pans the article in a dizzying sweep, stopping abruptly at a mention of a recently appointed undersecretary, Franz Wojcik. Wojcik's wife Maura is also mentioned. She, too, is working at the UN, with the bureau for refugee children.

Steve carefully tears the story from the paper and adds it to a collection of clippings he carries in a long, battered wallet.

Back at the dance floor, Eddie is trying to persuade the woman not to bother Steve. The personage rudely dismisses the warning. She sweeps over to Steve's table with a man in tow, a little, wizened man who seems no more than an accessory to her ensemble. He glances longingly at the bar as they pass it, suggesting that he looks forward to being cuckolded as an excuse to return to his drinking.

The woman introduces herself to Steve as the Countess de Moncordiae and asks if he is the American who received the Croix de Guerre from de Gaulle himself.

"Yes," Steve says. "I'm sorry I can't show it to you. I hocked it yesterday."

The countess is only momentarily taken aback. She asks Steve if he would care to join their little party for a late supper.

Steve looks her up and down before replying. "That would depend on what your daughter looks like. Or are you planning to set me up with your granddaughter?"

The countess draws herself up like a rearing horse before turning to march away. The little count takes her place at the table and raises an indignant forefinger. Before he can challenge Steve to a duel, his wife grabs him by his stiff collar and drags him after her. Steve and the camera follow the couple's stormy exit. At the door, they nearly knock down a small man with large, dark eyes and a bemused smile. Steve's own eyes grow wide as he recognizes Tursi, a ghost from the *Joyeuse Ile*.

Tursi belatedly spots Eddie and Joe and realizes the danger he is in. He tries to escape, but Steve cuts him off and forces him into a back room. There Steve beats the secret from him. Tursi tells Steve that Franz Wojcik's escape to Lisbon was stage-managed by the Nazis. The once-heroic Wojcik was really a Nazi spy, and, with Steve's unwitting help, he was moved to the place where he could best serve the Reich: America.

Steve demands a passport and a visa for a visit to New York. When Tursi asks what name he should use, Steve smiles sardonically. "The name is Captain Roland Manet, late of the Free French Navy."

The action then leaps ahead to the tramp steamer carrying Steve and Eddie and Joe to America. Here Potts suggested another montage, this one made up of clips from the original film. As Steve paces the steamer's deck, we see excerpts from *Passage to Lisbon*'s happy middle reels, the beginnings of Steve and Maura's hopeless love affair. Steve then beats himself up with memories of their last moments together, his drunken reaction to the discovery that she is really Franz Wojcik's wife, their secret reconciliation, and, finally, their parting on the fog-shrouded gangway of the old liner.

A shot of Steve against a background of swirling fog ends the flashback. He is watching the Lisbon pilot boat carry Maura and Wojcik away. When the camera pulls back, we realize that

Steve is watching the Wojciks' escape in memory only. Flanked by Eddie and Joe, he is standing at the rail of the tramp steamer, not the *Joyeuse Ile*.

The tramp is a rusted old ship, but a proud one. Near the three men is the remains of a gun emplacement. Two swastikas are stenciled on its paint, representing planes shot down by the gun crew during the war. As he leans against the ship's railing, Steve stares intently at the swastikas. The paint beneath one of them is peeling away, and the Nazi emblem flutters slightly as Steve watches. The movement symbolizes the question Tursi couldn't answer for him. Was Maura Wojcik a party to her husband's masquerade? Will Steve find one Nazi in America or two?

Eddie and Joe take turns playing the voice of reason. They try to talk their friend into heading west when they land, hoping to get Steve away from New York City, where he is known. Here Potts first mentions the reason Steve could never go home. "The mob is in New York," Eddie says. "They won't have forgotten how you crossed them up. You won't be safe."

"Where have we ever been safe?" Steve asks him. "Where have we run where we haven't found gangsters, most of them in uniform?"

On that cue, the fog parts, revealing New York harbor. Center stage is the Statue of Liberty, caught in a shaft of sunlight. The three expatriates give the statue a long look as the camera pans from one man to another. Despite their apprehension, Eddie and Joe are smiling. Steve is grim.

"Anyway," he says, "it's time we did our fighting on our home ground."

Cut to stock footage of New York City. An aerial shot features tall buildings with taxi cabs scurrying between them like herds of warring, two-tone mice. In an establishing shot, a cab drops Steve and Eddie and Joe in front of a fashionable hotel. Inside, a sleek and well-stuffed desk clerk watches Steve register. He addresses Steve as Captain Manet and engages him in a dialogue that was Carl Potts at the top of his socially conscious form.

"Is this your first visit to America, Captain?"

"My first in many years," Steve replies.

"Do you find it changed?"

"Very much."

The clerk then notices Eddie and Joe and informs them that the hotel has no vacancies.

"They're staying with me," Steve says.

"Excuse me, Captain," the clerk replies. "We may have a problem accommodating you after all."

Steve tears up his registration card. "Come to think of it," he says, "things haven't changed at all."

The clerk signals to a house detective, but before he can arrive, Eddie and Joe persuade the angry Steve to leave the hotel. Their exit is carefully watched by the detective, a horse-faced man with a comfortable paunch who stares after Steve and scratches his chin.

The three travel to a Harlem night spot, the Club 88, which is owned by a man named Rawley, an old friend of Eddie and Joe's. Rawley greets the dancers with open arms and invites them to perform at the club. Eddie tells Rawley that they need a place to stay and warns that there might be trouble.

"What kind of trouble?"

"Could be the mob," Eddie says.

"Could be Nazis," Joe adds.

"Man, when it comes to enemies, you guys sure live big."

In spite of the danger, Rawley takes them in. Steve leaves his friends at the club and journeys to Long Island alone.

The Connie hit a pocket of turbulent air and rattled like a street car crossing points. Gunderson woke in midsnore. He squinted up at my light, unhappily. The rest of the cabin was dark. "Can't sleep?" he asked me.

"Still too nervous about my tie," I said.

He grunted and tried to roll over in his seat. It was a forlorn

170

hope, but that didn't seem to matter. A minute later he was breathing with the timbre of the Atlantic chewing away at the rocky edge of Maine.

26

At Lake Success, Steve finds the headquarters he read about in Paris, the United Nations' home while its Manhattan skyscraper is being built. He makes his way through the bureaucratic maze as far as Franz Wojcik's secretary. That formidable person takes one look at his tired suit and denies him an audience with Wojcik. Steve persuades her to pass on the name he's traveling under, Roland Manet.

While he waits, Steve glances around Wojcik's anteroom. His time there brings home to him how thoroughly his position and Wojcik's have been reversed since their last meeting on the *Joyeuse Ile*. Then Wojcik was the homeless refugee and Steve the prosperous, if amoral, celebrity. Now Steve is a foreigner in his own country, and Wojcik an important member of the establishment. Steve is starting to look toward the exit when Wojcik's shocked secretary returns.

"The undersecretary will see you immediately, Captain," she tells him.

When Steve enters Wojcik's beautifully appointed office, it is clear that more than their social positions have been reversed. Wojcik no longer has the aura of righteousness that seemed to protect him on the old liner. That mantle now belongs to Steve, the casino boss who wanted no part of the world's troubles. Wojcik had been expecting to greet Manet, the jaded captain of the *Joyeuse Ile*, who knew his secret and may have come to trade on that knowledge. Instead, he sees Steven Laird, his great rival and dupe. Wojcik's successive reactions are clearly displayed on his noble face: surprise, panic, and then feigned delight. Steve reads them accurately and his cynical smile returns.

"My dear Mr. Laird," Wojcik says, rising from his seat behind a massive desk and crossing the room to Steve. "I had no idea. The secretary told me Captain Manet …"

"He's dead," Steve says.

Wojcik can barely contain his relief at hearing that welcome news. "But my dear Steve, we thought you were surely dead yourself. That fiend, Professor Benz …"

"Dead, too. I saw to that little job."

Now Wojcik fairly beams. Both his fellow conspirators are dead; his secret is safe. He puts an arm around Steve's shoulder and leads him to a chair near the desk.

Steve remains standing. He understands Wojcik's happiness and cuts it short. "I'm not the only one who made it off the *Joyeuse Ile* alive, Wojcik."

"What do you mean?"

"Tursi did, too."

"Tursi? I'm sorry …"

"That's right, you two never met. You couldn't have. He disembarked before you'd gotten your trunks unpacked. Still, you should remember his name. On your first visit to the casino, you asked for him. Something about some Geneva Exemptions."

Wojcik touches a scar on his cheek while he pretends to think. "Tursi. Yes, I remember him now. But surely he was drowned. Tossed overboard by the Nazis."

"It didn't take. He's alive and well in Paris. And telling some interesting stories about you."

To Steve's surprise, Wojcik breaks down completely. He admits to becoming a pawn of the Germans, after being tortured in their concentration camp. He describes the moment when he awoke in the camp and realized that, for the first time, he was afraid to die. It is a fear that has never left him.

"You will wonder why I would care to go on living a life as

hateful as mine was to me. I've wondered myself. The answer may be that it takes more courage to die well than to live miserably, and I had no courage left. And too, the Nazis made me a bargain more tempting than the one the devil offered Faust."

"What bargain?"

"They offered me the chance to be Franz Wojcik the hero again. To be acclaimed. To be respected. I no longer had my own respect, but I could have the world's. I even had yours for a time. And hers."

Wojcik directs Steve's attention to a framed photograph on his desk. It is a portrait of his wife Maura. He pleads with Steve not to turn him in. He swears that once he and Maura were safe in America he did nothing to further the Nazi cause. Exposing him now would do more than ruin him, he argues. It would also destroy Maura.

While Steve is reacting to this, the woman herself rushes in saying, "Franz, your secretary just told me that Captain ..."

She nearly faints at the sight of Steve. He takes her in his arms to prevent her from falling.

While he is helping Maura to a chair, Steve observes her husband perform an amazing transformation. Wojcik composes himself with an effort, going from the sniveling weakling of his confession to a semblance of his old commanding self. His action answers the question that has been haunting Steve since Paris. Maura is innocent. She doesn't know Wojcik's secret.

Wojcik tells his wife that Steve has just described his miraculous escape from the Nazis. "We're all three safe now," he says.

Wojcik has put his fate in Steve's hands. When Steve hesitates, Wojcik observes that Maura needs fresh air after her shock and suggests that she show their guest the grounds. "We can finish our talk later," he tells Steve.

Dazed himself, Steve walks with Maura along a gravel path that circles a small lake. Maura is dressed in her signature color, white, her simple dress glowing in the sunlight. She asks Steve how he escaped from the *Joyeuse Ile* and Professor Benz's certain revenge. He tells her of the timely aid he received from Roland Manet and how, together, they sailed the ship to England and the Free French Navy.

When he describes Manet's death, Maura bows her head. "He was so full of life."

"He was a sailor," Steve replies. "A sailor who liked long odds."

Steve doesn't tell Maura of Manet's last words or of meeting Tursi in Paris. He has recognized the meaning behind Wojcik's simple suggestion that Steve and Maura go walking together. He has been offered Maura in exchange for his silence.

They sit down on a shaded bench at the edge of the lake. "I'll read your thoughts," Maura tells him, reenacting a game they'd played on the ship.

"Go ahead."

"You're thinking of how old and domesticated I've become."

"Not even close."

"What then?"

"I was thinking of a guy named Faust," Steve says. He is faced with a choice as tantalizing as the one the Nazis made to Wojcik. He has Maura back, for the moment at least, and the chance to have her back for good. The problem, as it was on the *Joyeuse Ile*, is Wojcik. Can Steve expose him without losing Maura forever?

Steve asks Maura about her husband.

"He is a great man," she says. "You were right about that. And about his work being important."

Steve's eyes drift away. In his mind, he hears a ship's foghorn sounding softly.

"I've done my best to keep Franz going," Maura is saying. "To keep his work going. I've tried to be a good soldier, like so many others have been."

"What about now? What about this new job of his?"

174

"Are you asking me if Franz can go on without me? I don't know. I know that his job here is vital, that this place is vital. It's the hope of the world."

"You work here, too, I hear," Steve says.

"Yes, with the lost children. There are so many now. So many mothers dead. So many children lost. I see them sometimes and I think of the children I never had. That's sad and silly, isn't it?"

"No. And it's no reason not to have children of your own."

Maura looks away, embarrassed. "There are other reasons for that."

After a time, she asks, "How about your work, Steven? The dangerous work I couldn't help you with? It is surely done now."

"It isn't, quite," Steve says.

He stands up. "I'm staying at the Club 88 on Lexington Avenue in Harlem."

"Why are you telling me, Steve? Is it so I can come to you tonight as I came to you once before?"

"I'm telling you so you'll know. Eddie and Joe are there, too."

"Eddie and Joe," Maura says, smiling. "I'm glad they're all right. Tell them that."

"I will."

Steve returns to the Club 88. On the street outside, he is confronted by the house detective from the hotel where he and his friends tried to register earlier in the day. The detective, whose name is Jarvis, asks Steve if he remembers him.

Steve takes a long look before replying. "I make it a point to remember cops on the take."

"A former cop, thanks to you," Jarvis says. "I make it a point to remember guys who trip me up. So does Carlo Visconti. He'll remember the editorials you wrote when he tried to take over that little union back in the thirties. And how the publicity stopped him cold. He's sure to remember how you walked off with his girl. What was her name? Maria something, wasn't it?"

"Maria Calabrese."

"Yeah, that's right. One cute tomato. What ever happened to her?"

"Visconti killed her."

"And put a price on your head. I'm surprised you came back, Laird. If someone were to recognize you and pass the word to Visconti, that party would make himself a nice piece of change. So I'm asking myself, how much would you be willing to pay for a case of amnesia?"

Steve smiles slowly and then strikes out at Jarvis, knocking him into an alley next to the club. Lying on his back in the alley, Jarvis goes for his gun. Steve steps on his arm and pulls the gun from its holster. He yanks Jarvis to his feet and then strikes him on the jaw with the gun's barrel.

"I'm sick of dirtying my hands on fascists," Steve says. He pushes the stunned house detective back out into the street. "Go collect your blood money."

The page before me was suddenly shaded as Gunderson reached up for my light. "Excuse me," he said, and switched it off. I sat in the darkness for a time, waiting until his expressive breathing told me it was safe to turn the light back on. I wouldn't be able to sleep until I'd read the end of the story, no matter how long my day had been. Or so I thought. Before I knew what hit me, I was dreaming of being chased by gangsters along a rocky shore.

27

I made it to Manhattan the next morning, as Beaumont had predicted, but not quite as early as he'd guessed. The actor had forgotten to allow for the hours I'd lose traveling east. The good news was that those hours would be waiting for me when I returned to the real scene of the action in Los Angeles. I was ready to start back as soon as I arrived, convinced as I was that I was on a fool's errand. But first I had to go through the motions. I checked into the Hotel Pennsylvania and stayed there long enough to shave and pick up the list of contacts Beaumont had wired ahead for me. Then I was off to earn my good-conduct medal.

It was my second visit to New York City in the span of a few hours, the first having been courtesy of Carl Potts's script as interpreted by my own imagination. The real city made my imaginings seem small and gray. I'd been influenced by too many black-and-white movies shot on too many "authentic" New York sets. I found the original article crowded with more extras than any producer could afford, although calling them extras isn't accurate, as most of them seemed to have speaking parts.

The Technicolor quality of the city was brought home to me when I took a small detour through Times Square. The buildings themselves were stark enough backdrops, but they were daubed with bits of color in the form of awnings and billboards and marquees. The sky above it all was a pale but genuine blue, the same shade as a certain lady publicist's eyes. The square was amazingly clean, given the traffic, and reassuringly intact, given the state of the rest of the world. I felt the same reassurance looking into the ordinary, unconcerned faces of the people I bumped into every few steps. New York was a rare thing in our modern, civilized world, a city that hadn't known a single shell or bomb.

More than one passerby gave my navy-blue suit a second look. It hadn't been an inspired choice. New York was in the midst of a heat wave, according to the cabbie who had driven me in from La Guardia. People were sleeping on rooftops and fire escapes. And visitors from Southern California were wilting faster than Republican presidential campaigns. As fast as my faint hope of accomplishing something useful in New York.

Beaumont's first two contacts weren't worth the shoe leather I wore off tracking them down. The first was a producer who had never heard of Vincent Mediate and seemed only vaguely familiar with the name Torrance Beaumont. My second call was on a retired actress who remembered everybody since John Wilkes Booth and had a story to go with each name. It wasn't much past noon, and she was already working on tomorrow's hangover. She drew a blank on Mediate, too, which almost made her cry. I felt like joining her.

My third appointment was with a theatrical agent named Stanley Wallace. He had an office on West Forty-second Street, with a steamy waiting room that gave the fresh shirt I'd put on back at the hotel the coup de grace. The room was cooled by a single window that opened onto an air shaft. Its ledge was crowded with potted geraniums, bending under the weight of their blooms. I envied them whatever fresh air they were getting. The agency's receptionist was a young woman with the hard edge it took decades to develop anywhere but New York. She also had a way with a wad of gum. The cracking sound she produced as I stepped up to her desk was an abbreviated wolf whistle.

"Nice tan," she said. "What's your secret?"

"Geography." I'd restocked on business cards before leaving California. I handed her one, and received another virtuoso crack in return. She carried my card into Wallace, with me trailing along behind.

"You're late, Mr. Tough-Guy Operative," Wallace said for openers. "Tory said you'd be by this morning." He had the same one-note, side-of-the-mouth way of speaking as Ned Sparks, but he used a higher pitch. Ned Sparks impersonated by a parrot, I decided. "You get lost on the subway or something?"

"I stopped to have a bullet hole sewn up," I said. "I was leaking bourbon."

"Very funny. Alan Ladd should have your delivery. Also

your height. Did you ever notice that about Hollywood tough guys? They're all little fellows." Wallace fit that bill himself. The only good-size thing about him was his head, which lolled at the end of his thin neck like a bloom from one of the waiting-room geraniums. He didn't smile as he talked, but he showed a lot of teeth. Large, mismatched teeth. "Ladd, Cagney, Beaumont. All of them are shrimps. But when they sock some big palooka, he goes down faster than Schmeling did in '38. You have to laugh."

"You do," I said, wondering if the deadpan agent had ever had the knack.

The office was a large filing drawer with a desk in the middle. Every horizontal surface held stacks of paper: correspondence, newspapers, magazines. Wallace sat in the center of the pile like a wartime hoarder who hadn't heard the all clear. To take the chair he offered me, I had to first pick up half-a-dozen copies of *Variety*. There was no place for them on the desk, so I held them in my lap.

Meanwhile, Wallace was discoursing. "When I knew Tory in the old days, he was a pretty boy, a juvenile, a guy in a varsity sweater who sang through a megaphone like Rudy Vallee. That was before *Painted Desert* hit Broadway. Suddenly, there was the college crooner in a dirty shirt, needing a shave, waving a gun at people. It was a sensation. Let me tell you something. If you ever want to win acting awards, spend ten years or so walking on stage with an ingenue in one hand and a ukulele in the other. Then get yourself a part where you shoot people. The critics will treat you like the second coming of John Barrymore."

"I'll remember that," I said.

"Tory's the master of that trick. He's worked it twice now, once here on Broadway and once out in Hollywood. Out there, he spends a few years shooting people in gangster movies, typing himself all over again. Then he kisses the girl and whammo. He's a big romantic star. Tory's changed his skin so many times he probably doesn't know himself who he really is anymore."

"Speaking of knowing people," I said. "I'm hoping you knew a Vincent Mediate when he worked in New York."

Wallace's lolling head almost lolled itself off its stem. "Look, Mr. Operative, if you want to change the subject, just say so. Don't try to finesse me. You don't want to talk about Beaumont? Fine. We'll talk about Vincent Mediate, who, contrary to your fondest hopes, I don't know from Adam."

I started to lift the newspapers off my lap.

"Where are you going?" Wallace asked.

"You just said …"

"I said I never heard of this Mediate character. I didn't say I couldn't help. For an old friend like Tory I can make an effort. I can put in some time."

Wallace waited until I'd dropped the papers back in place. Then he said, "Tory gave me the name of a play Mediate worked on, *Love on the Moon*. From that cockamamie title I could tell it was a thirties production without even looking it up."

"But you did look it up."

"Just get behind me and shove if I'm not moving fast enough for you. You don't have to be so subtle."

"Sorry."

"All right. I looked the show up in our file of old *Playbills*. It opened in '39 and had a nice little run. Vincent Mediate was listed as an assistant to the stage manager. Now, it happens that two of the other names in the program are people I know. People who are still here in New York. They worked backstage on the play, like Mediate, so it has to be they knew him."

He paused to let me prompt him, but I'd learned my lesson by then. After a moment, he nodded his big head with approval. "I've written the names down for you. The first one is Ina Mencher. She's working on a musical over at the Morosco Theater. Tell her I sent you.

"The other name is James Zucco. He's a big-time radio director over at Rockefeller Center. Don't tell him you've been

180

to see me, or he won't talk to you. Zucco and I don't exactly get along. I like to be in the majority, and the majority of people in this town don't get along with James Zucco."

"I see," I said.

"Not yet you don't, but you will. So, was there anything else I could help you with? You need theater tickets? The name of a good restaurant?"

I decided to try a long shot. "Was there a Bert Kramer listed in the *Playbill* for Mediate's old show?"

"No, I don't remember one. You trust my memory or do you want me to look it up?"

"I trust your memory."

"All right, I'll look it up." He opened the center drawer of his desk and produced a yellowed program. On the cover was a drawing of a young couple who were using a sliver of moon for a swing. They were simultaneously gazing into each other's eyes and smiling like jack-o'-lanterns, not the easiest combination to pull off. They'd picked a bad time to fall in love, these two figments of some artist's imagination. I found myself hoping, irrationally, that they'd made it through the war.

"Nope," Wallace said. "Not a Bert Kramer in the bunch. Who is he?"

"A dead writer."

"The only bankable kind. Look at Shakespeare. Look at Eugene O'Neill."

"O'Neill's not dead," I said.

"He will be. Take my word for it. But I'm using up too much of your valuable time. You want my copy of the program? It's the only copy I have, by the way."

"No, thanks."

Wallace nodded his approval again. "Well, enjoy New York. Try not to hit anybody with your brass knuckles while you're here, unless you should get the urge with Jimmy Zucco. Then swing away. And tell Tory his old friends still remember him."

"I'll do that," I said.

28

The Morosco Theater was on Forty-fifth Street, west of Seventh Avenue. Its marquee, which advertised a play called *Dare I Ask?*, was being worked on by three men as I walked up. One man was on a ladder, the second was steadying it, and the third was smoking a cigar. You can spot the supervisors of this world from a long way off if you just learn to look for smoke rings. When I arrived in front of the theater, I could see that the men were posting a notice across the title of the play. *Dare I Ask?* had reached its final week.

I inquired after Ina Mencher at the box office window. The old lady behind the grillwork directed me to an alley that ran up one side of the theater. At the end of the alley and the top of a flight of concrete steps, the stage door was propped open to catch any breeze clever enough to find its way through the maze of the city. No one was standing guard, so I went inside.

I'd seen a lot of Hollywood musicals set in Broadway theaters, but they were no more true to life than a back-lot Times Square. In this case, Hollywood had erred by being too big rather than too small. The theater in a Busby Berkeley picture had a stage the size of a parade ground and seating like the Hollywood Bowl. I wandered onto the edge of the Morosco's stage when I was only a few steps inside the building. The space beyond the dead footlights was dark, but I could clearly see the stacked mezzanines and balconies. They seemed to overhang all but a few rows of the orchestra.

"Looking for someone?" A woman had come up behind me in the wings. She was short and slight and dressed like a teenager in a cotton blouse, a straight skirt, bobby socks, and tennis shoes. Her dark hair was held back on the sides by a pair of bow-shaped barrettes. She was clutching a clipboard to her chest, and her shoulders were rolled forward protectively.

"I was just noticing how close all the seats are to the stage. There's no place to hide from the ticket buyers in this theater."

The woman treated me to a pinched smile. "The ticket buyers have been the ones doing the hiding."

"I saw that you're closing. Sorry."

She relaxed her shoulders long enough to shrug. "A show has to have a real head of steam to survive the dog days in this town. Is there something I can help you with?"

"There is if you're Ina Mencher." Her only answer was to hunch her shoulders still further. "Stanley Wallace sent me."

I handed her a card, but there was no light to read it by in the wings. She led me back toward the open stage door, studying as she went. When she turned back to me in the doorway, I could see that she was older than her outfit had suggested. Her face was drawn downward toward her soft jawline, and her dark eyes floated above dark semicircles.

"You've come all the way from California to see me?" She made it sound as though some inexorable fate had brought us together. An unhappy fate, to judge by her apprehension.

"I've come to ask you some questions about a man you worked with before the war."

"What man?"

"Vincent Mediate. In 1939, you were both part of the production crew for a play here in New York."

"*Love on the Moon*," Mencher said. "A sweet little play. It wouldn't run a week these days."

"Do you remember Mediate?"

"Yes. Why are you asking questions about him?"

"He's involved in some trouble back in California. My agency is looking into it for his studio."

"Trouble?"

"Someone was killed."

"Not Vincent."

"No, a man named Bert Kramer. Know him?"

Mencher shook her head. "We've had so much killing in the

world," she said, "you'd think people would be tired of it. That's what I thought the day the war ended. You should have been here then. In New York. It was like a big party where everyone was welcome. I thought, 'Now things will be different. Now people will be kind to one another.' It didn't happen."

"No," I said. "It didn't."

"What did you want to ask me?"

"How well did you know Mediate?"

She looked past me toward the dark stage. "You've seen for yourself how small a theater is. People are thrown together a lot. That's why there are so many backstage romances. Not that there was anything like that between Vincent and me.

"He was a real hick when I first met him. He'd grown up in some small town in Pennsylvania. Harrisburg was his idea of a big city. It was fun watching him discover the rest of the world. I can remember when he had his first Chinese food and when he took his first ride in a taxi. I was the first Jewish person he'd ever gotten to know. I can still see him drinking it all in, meeting types of people who had only been stereotypes for him before, listening to new ideas."

She paused, giving me the chance to guess what she would say next. I would have needed a year of guessing and a lot of luck. "When you were a kid, did you ever try to see the dandelions grow?"

"Not that I recall," I said.

"I did. They sprang up so fast, I figured you should actually be able to see them growing if you looked hard enough. That's how it was with Vincent. A person should have been able to see him growing back then, he was changing so fast. There used to be a little bar on Eighth Avenue where a bunch of us would go after a show to drink beer and save the world. Vincent would get an earful on those nights. I'd look at him there and think of my old dandelions. You couldn't see the change happening, but every day Vincent was a little different."

"Was Communism one of the new ideas he got with his beer

nuts?"

Mencher took a step away from me without actually moving. "Is that what you came all this way to ask about? Listen, every kind of 'ism' gets chewed over in this town. Anyone could have told you that. You could have dialed any number in the New York book."

"Could anyone in the phone book have told me what 'ism' captured Mediate's heart?"

"I don't think I'm going to answer any more of your questions."

"Mediate's a producer now at Warners. He's got a big car and a big house and a starlet wife."

Mencher made another stab at a smile. "Are you trying to make me jealous? I told you there was nothing romantic between us."

"Then why won't you tell me what you know?"

She looked away from me, out into the alley. It wasn't much of a view, but it evidently had me beat. Even when she finally spoke again, she didn't turn around. "Have you ever seen a short subject called *Death Camp*?"

"Yes," I said. "It was something Mediate put together when he was overseas."

"He filmed it after the liberation of the concentration camp at Buchenwald. We'd heard rumors all through the war about what was happening over there, although a lot of people refused to believe it. Some people still won't believe it. *Death Camp* was the first real view most of us had of that horror, outside of bits of newsreel film. It's too easy to look away during a snippet of newsreel. *Death Camp* made you stare the evil in the face."

"What has that to do with answering my questions?"

Mencher finally turned and looked at me. Her soft face was set in a painful grimace. It was surely the face with which she'd stared at Mediate's record of the death and suffering at Buchenwald. "I wouldn't do anything to hurt a man who had the courage to make that film. Whatever mistakes he made, he paid for them with that."

"What mistakes are you talking about?"

She squeezed past me in the doorway, twisting and drawing herself in so she wouldn't so much as brush my sleeve. "Good-bye," she said. Then she disappeared into the shadows.

29

Compared to the Morosco, Rockefeller Center was one bustling place. It had the advantage of air conditioning, which made bustling in New York in August feasible. I asked for James Zucco twice, first at a lobby information stand and then, after an art deco elevator had carried me up into the RCA Building, at a reception desk behind NBC's plate glass entrance.

"Mr. Zucco is in one of the broadcast studios," the receptionist told me. You would never have guessed there was a heat wave outside by looking at her crisp dress and perfect hair. No stick of gum had made it past her pearly white teeth, either. "Your name is?"

"Scott Elliott." No impression.

"And you are?"

"An investigator." Small impression, negative.

"What kind of investigator?"

"The confidential kind."

"I'll have to call back to see if Mr. Zucco is free." Something about the way she lifted her elegant chin and peered at me down her elegant nose told me not to live in hope.

Nevertheless, she made her call, getting Zucco on the line after a couple of inquiries. "A private investigator named Elliott to see you," she said.

There was a measurable pause, during which the debutante's mouth opened involuntarily. If I'd had a stick of gum ready, I

186

could have slipped it in without a fight. "Mr. Zucco will see you right away," she said. "In Studio C, down that hallway."

The narrow hallway was a one-way street, and I was going the wrong way. The uptown traffic consisted of a half-dozen young men and women loaded down with reams of paper. They were bantering away and jostling one another. They jostled me, too, physically and mentally. They made me think of the young Vincent Mediate and Ina Mencher going off for a beer after working a ten-hour shift on a silly play. That was definitely a new view of Mediate, but not the one I'd come to New York to find.

The door to Studio C stood open. The room beyond was paneled in white acoustical tile, walls and ceiling both. The single deviation in the pattern was a picture window to my left. A long, boardroom table stood in the middle of the wall-to-wall carpeting, with a table microphone for each chair. The only chair occupied was the one at the head of the table. A man sat there, his back to the picture window.

Despite the air conditioning, the man's shirt looked as limp as mine, and his sleeves were rolled up. He had loosened his tie without adjusting the gold clip that held it against his shirt. As a result, the blue silk was accordioned into a series of ripples, each one shining in the light from an overhead fixture. Zucco was my age, but he wasn't sensitive about it. He combed his thinning hair straight back, accentuating his high forehead instead of hiding it. Behind a pair of Fred Wilner–style horn-rims, he had slightly beady blue eyes. They were focused on the table before him, which was covered with sheets of typescript. From where I stood, the pages seemed to have more red on them than black. Zucco was slashing away with a red pencil on a new victim as I watched, striking out line after line and filling the margins with bloody-looking notes.

Instead of interrupting him, I studied the view through the window. Beyond it was a small control room in which a technician stared at a panel of needles and knobs. Through a second window on the opposite side of the control room, I could see another studio. Actors grouped around two standing microphones were acting away, soundlessly.

Instead of clearing my throat to attract Zucco's attention, I asked a question. "Why aren't they dropping the pages of their scripts? I've heard that radio actors drop their pages so they won't make noise shuffling them."

Zucco looked up from the sheet he was editing, swiveled in his chair to follow my gaze, and then turned back to his work. "They're doing a timing rehearsal in there. If you drop your pages during a rehearsal, you just have to pick them up again." He capped his destruction of the sheet before him by drawing a red X from corner to corner. "Got a cigarette?"

I tossed him my pack. He took one out and set the pack on the table near his elbow. "You the P.I.?"

"Actually I'm an operative for a private security company."

Zucco frowned like the original buyer of the original pig in the original poke. "But you're a real detective, right?"

"As opposed to what?"

He gestured toward the bleeding sheets of paper. "Jake Reardon. He's the private investigator on the show I direct."

It dawned on me that I'd been granted an interview because it gave Zucco a chance to do research for his show.

"It's called *Gun for Hire*. Ever listen to it?"

"Sorry. Must be on opposite *Fibber McGee*."

Zucco grimaced. "Is that the best insult you can think up?"

"I wasn't trying to insult you."

The director looked even more insulted. "Jake Reardon mouths off to everybody he meets. But he wouldn't use that line of yours for a warm-up. When's the last time you shot somebody?"

"I'd have to check my diary."

Zucco tossed his red pencil down in disgust. "I'll bet you even drink cocktails."

"Gibsons," I said. I could have used one after a steady diet of

Zucco's double-talk.

"Reardon takes his straight from the bottle."

"With or without a straw?"

"Nuts." Stanley Wallace had mistaken me for a tough customer, but Zucco's eye was better. "I have to tell you, buddy, you're seriously behind the times. Your kind of detective went out of style before the war."

"What kind is that?"

"The urbane man-about-town who sees a crime as a little tear in the fabric of society. A modern detective knows that the fabric is hanging in shreds."

"A modern detective like Jake Reardon?"

"Exactly." Zucco scanned the pages before him and snatched one up. "Here's how this week's show opens. 'I spend my days waist deep in the cesspool of the modern American city, looking for honesty and truth and finding only rot and corruption.'" The director looked up at me for some sign that I'd recognized a kindred spirit.

"Sounds like Jake needs another line of work."

"He can't quit. He's driven by a failure in his past."

"What did he do? Get bounced from a seminary?"

Zucco tried open contempt on me. I stood up under it. "He was a cop. He got his partner killed."

"Tough break." Talking with Zucco was like spending time in a house of mirrors. It wouldn't have surprised me if Jake Reardon had walked in on us, bottle in hand. Worse, I had the feeling that somewhere somebody was busy working over the pages of my script with a red pencil.

"Looks like I'm not going to learn anything from you," Zucco said. "Let's see if I can return the favor. What do you want?"

"Information about a man you used to work with. Vincent Mediate."

"That crumb. He shoot somebody or what?"

"What makes you ask that?"

"Educated guess. His type are big shooters of people."

"What type is that? Ina Mencher didn't seem to think he had one."

"That's Ina all over. Way too soft for her own good. Always was. Still, it's hard to see her shielding Mediate."

"Why?"

Zucco blew some of my own cigarette smoke at me. "Suppose you tell me what kind of information you're after."

"How well did you know Mediate?"

"Better than I wanted to. Not that I ever liked the guy. I remember thinking there was something fishy about him the first time I saw him. I was working on Broadway then, which you seem to already know."

"*Love on the Moon.*"

"A dopey play in a stone-age medium. I can't believe I wasted years of my talent on that dying art form."

"The world's loss," I said.

Zucco smiled, exhaling smoke through the gaps between his teeth. "Not bad for a beginner. Where was I?"

"On Broadway."

"Right. One day just before we opened, the stage manager, whose name was Frank Winslow, announced that he was hiring an assistant. Vince Mediate. This was in the spring of '39. The fishy thing about it was that Mediate didn't know beans about the theater. I mean, he couldn't find a seat without an usher. But there he was, landing a plum job with a play that had a run ahead of it."

"How did he manage that?"

"Drag, buddy. Pure, old-fashioned drag. One of the play's angels was a meat-packing magnate named Miller. He backed Broadway shows, among other eccentric hobbies. Somehow Miller had become Mediate's patron. How, I don't know."

"How is it you know that much?"

"After the play closed and the fighting started, a bunch of us had a send-off party for Frank Winslow. The big sap had enlisted in the Marines. In the wee small hours, after we'd all had too much to drink, Frank told Ina and me how Mediate had landed the job."

"Winslow told you something else, didn't he?"

Zucco brushed cigarette ashes off the table and onto the carpet. "What specifically?"

"Something about Mediate's politics maybe. That maybe he was a Communist."

Zucco laughed. "Or the Prince of Wales, maybe."

"Meaning what?"

Zucco helped himself to another of my Luckies. "I hear Mediate is a big gun these days," he said.

"He's doing okay."

"Plenty of money. Plenty of power. Plenty to lose."

That was the way Bert Kramer had seen it, if I was right about the blackmail angle. I wondered where the director was heading.

"Plenty of lawyers on retainer, probably," Zucco added. "Lawyers with closets full of so-called investigators like you."

"I'm not working for Mediate's lawyers," I said.

"Cross your heart and hope to die? What kind of fool do you take me for? You think I'm going to hand Mediate an engraved invitation to sue me? Go home and tell him his tracks are covered as far as I'm concerned."

"What tracks?"

"Nice try, Philo." He tossed me my cigarettes. "You need help finding the way out?"

"I'm not here to cover Mediate's tracks. I'm here because he's a suspect in a murder investigation."

Zucco was searching the table for more manuscript to maim. "They still use the gas chamber in California, I hope."

"The victim was a screenwriter named Bert Kramer. Ever hear of him?"

"No."

"How about Carl Potts?"

"Another victim? Vince has been a busy boy."

191

"Another screenwriter, a live one with ties to the Communist Party."

"Too bad for him, it being open season on Commies. Funny how fashions change. A few years ago, the fascists had the bull's-eyes on their backs. Now they're sitting pretty. Any that are left, I mean."

"Potts thinks there are plenty left."

"Does he? He'd know better than I. I know we had our share of them in New York before the war. I remember a big rally they held in Madison Square Garden."

He broke off his paper shuffling long enough to picture it. "In '38 or '39, I think. On Washington's birthday no less. It was a big show. Or should I say circus? Stage the size of the Polo Grounds, huge picture of Washington, huge American flags, and giant swastikas on burning globes. That touch, at least, was appropriate."

"Let's get back to the Vincent Mediate story. This Frank Winslow, the stage manager, where can I find him?"

"Nowhere now. He was killed on Okinawa. There's justice for you. Winslow dead and Mediate a big shot in Hollywood. My only consolation is, Mediate's big-shot days are numbered."

"I thought you didn't believe my story."

"About the murder? I don't believe it. I was referring to something they're cooking up in a studio down the hall from here. Something that'll be the end of Vince Mediate and every other fat cat in Hollywood. It's called television."

"I've heard of it," I said.

"Everybody will have, soon. There'll be six licensed stations in New York alone next year. Right now we're broadcasting three hours of programming each and every night. A year from now, we'll be on twelve hours a day."

"Who's we?"

"Me and everyone else who's smart enough to tag along. Television's my next gravy train. It's going to do to radio what radio did to vaudeville. After that, it'll be Hollywood's turn.

Mediate and his brother moguls will be on the breadline or whatever kind of line they have out there. The lotus line, probably. I'm telling you, we're going to give Hollywood a beating it'll never forget."

Zucco's prediction reminded me of another one I'd heard recently, from a man in a black trilby. "You'll have to get in line," I said.

30

By the time I'd finished with James Zucco, I was fed up with Torrance Beaumont and his bright ideas. I called the airline from a booth in the lobby of the RCA Building. There'd been a cancellation on their early evening flight to Los Angeles, and I booked the seat. That left me with an hour and change to kill. I already had a plan in mind for killing it.

I called a man named Merritt Jackson and arranged to meet him in the lounge of the Hotel Pennsylvania. Jackson was there when I arrived. He was seated at the bar holding a tall, frosted glass. A second glass was sweating away at his elbow.

"I took the liberty of ordering you a Tom Collins," Jackson said. "It's too hot to be shaking up any of your damn Gibsons."

"I wasn't planning on doing the shaking myself," I said.

"Are you skipping out on your bill?"

The reference was to my calfskin case, which I'd retrieved on my way to our rendezvous. "I've got a seat on the five o'clock flight out of La Guardia."

"Damn," Jackson said. "That doesn't give us much time for drinking." He raised his glass. "To the 191st."

"To the 191st," I said.

The cocktail was ice cold and tart and all too brief. The bartender had another pair ready when we set our empties

193

down.

"I love New York," Jackson said. "Around here, you only have to remember to say whoa."

He looked as though he'd been forgetting that little step from time to time. His big, square face was redder than I remembered it, but then, almost all his detail work was off. I still pictured him unwashed and unshaven, with a bad haircut and a lived-in uniform. Now his reddish brown hair was carefully trimmed, his fingernails were manicured, and his Palm Beach suit was almost unwrinkled.

Like me, Jackson had been a draftee added to a Tennessee national guard unit to bring it up to wartime strength. It had been natural for the outsiders to band together, and Jackson and I and the other "Yankees" had. In civilian life, he'd been a reporter for the *New York Herald Tribune*. And was again, as I'd discovered when I'd called the paper. Jackson had suggested a drink, by which he'd meant a few.

"So, Elliott, I've been waiting to read in the gossip columns that you'd stolen Betty Grable away from Harry James, but, so far, nothing. What's the holdup?"

"I'm afraid I'll find out her legs aren't really perfect. I couldn't stand that."

Jackson nodded solemnly. "The danger of obtaining one's dream," he said. He then proposed a toast to Grable's legs, and we finished off our second round.

The way I was digging into my maraschino cherries reminded me that I hadn't eaten lunch. As a substitute, I bought a fresh pack of Luckies from the bartender. "Have you gotten your own column yet?" I asked to show that I remembered the old musings, too.

"No. I haven't turned out to be the second coming of H. L. Mencken, that's for sure. To tell you the truth, I'm not even pushing for it as hard as I should be. I haven't gotten my fill of peace and quiet yet. The other day, I was over at Yankee Stadium watching a game and drinking a beer. It must have been a great beer, because I had this euphoric feeling come over me, like I'd conquered every world there was to conquer. I could have died happy just then. You believe that?"

I thought back on a recent cocktail hour I'd spent alone, sitting on a rock on a hill overlooking Los Angeles. "Yes," I said. "I believe it."

We drank again, without speaking the toast aloud. It occurred to me that I was already halfway to drunk, but that didn't seem like such a bad place to be heading.

"So what brings you to New York, Elliott?"

"Business."

"The movie business, I hope."

"Barely. I'm working for Warners as a freelance janitor. Trouble-shooter to you."

"So you're here to shoot some trouble?" Jackson was making designs on the top of the bar with the wet bottom of his glass. Wheels within wheels. "Anything you can talk about with an unambitious journalist?"

"No, sorry."

"Okay, is it something an old army buddy can help you with?"

"Not unless you infiltrated the local Communist Party before the war."

"Sorry. I was strictly a police-beat grade of reporter. International conspiracies were way over my head. I don't even know who would know about that."

"I do," I said. "I mean, I found a guy who could have answered my questions, but he'd been frightened by a lawyer as a child. He blew me a lot of smoke about television and told me a fairy tale about the Nazis renting Madison Square Garden on Washington's birthday."

"That was no fairy tale, brother. He was talking about the big German-American Bund rally. You remember that, don't you? Don't tell me they didn't have newspapers in California back then."

195

"Guess I was too busy chasing Betty Grable to read them."

Jackson was slowing down. He was actually sipping his latest drink. "That was one scary night. February 22, 1939. Twenty thousand people showed up for that rally. Twenty thousand angry, mixed-up people. It was almost ten years after the start of the Depression. Ten years. They say that Roosevelt and the New Deal kept us from sliding into the insanity people like Fritz Kuhn and his German-American Bund were peddling, and old FDR may have, but it was no sure thing as late as 1939."

"Who was this Kuhn?"

"Some auto worker from Detroit with delusions of godliness. He got the Bund organized on a national level. It grew out of some innocent German-American clubs. After Kuhn came along, they kicked out their Jewish members and started dressing up in jackboots and saluting one another."

"Were the real Nazis behind it?"

"They provided some seed money. Kuhn even got his picture snapped with Hitler himself. In '36, I think, during the big Olympic show in Berlin. That raised a few eyebrows over here, but only token opposition."

"They were that powerful?"

"Maybe a hundred thousand members at their peak. They had some influential friends, though. In this town and in Washington. People who'd hate to be reminded of it now. That rally in the Garden was really their high-water mark. The whole scam started unraveling after that. The country was finally wising up to what the Nazis were doing in Germany. Most of the country, anyway. It didn't become more or less unanimous until after the shooting started.

"Around the time you and I were in boot camp, they held some hearings down in Washington on the Bund and other subversive groups. My guess is they wanted all the Bund files collected in one place so no one else could get a look at them. Too many congressmen listed among the sponsors."

Our friend the bartender stopped by again. Jackson watched

him go with undisguised affection. Then he said, "Speaking of congressmen, did you hear about Lieutenant Bass running for the House of Representatives? Remember him? The guy who got the battery lost outside of Schwabhausen."

"I remember," I said.

I did a lot of remembering over the course of the next two rounds. Jackson knew the whereabouts and current occupations of at least half of our old unit. Maybe two-thirds. When I remembered to look at my watch, all my free time and then some was gone.

"Damn," I said. "I'm going to miss my plane."

"Never despair," Jackson said, reaching down to grab my bag. "Wasn't that the motto of the 191st?"

"It was 'never volunteer,'" I said.

Jackson insisted on marching me two blocks to a cab stand he knew. "Gotta have this guy," he said of the cabbie. "He'll give us a break on the fare. Besides which, he was in the tank corps. Good training for this job."

The cabbie's name was Nick, and he was on duty and available. His Coney Island tan made my California version look anemic. Nick watched with too much amusement as Jackson and my bag and I sorted ourselves out in his back seat. Then he requested a destination.

"La Guardia," I said.

"Take no prisoners," Jackson said.

The reporter had his hip flask out before we'd driven our first block. "Join me?" he asked.

"You drink too damn much," I said.

"Look who's talking. You were knocking them back pretty good just now."

"I was thirsty."

"Baloney. Something's eating at you. Something about this Communist business."

"Are you always right?" I asked.

"Just one day a year," Jackson said, sinking a little deeper in his seat. "Today's my day."

I decided to take advantage of the timing. I asked Jackson what he made of the latest Red scare.

He was in the process of tipping his flask toward the roof of the cab, which gave him a chance to think about it. "It's revenge, if you ask me," he finally said. "We sacrificed plenty to keep a gang of thugs from taking over Europe, and what did we end up with? A different gang of thugs in charge."

"They didn't get the whole thing."

"Give 'em time. Right this minute they've got more than they deserve. Remember how far east we got in that last drive?"

"Into Czechoslovakia," I said.

Jackson made an attempt or two to repeat the name and then moved on. "I think a lot about the last little village we reached. About us liberating it and then being ordered to pull back so the Russians could have it. Makes me mad. I think the whole country's mad that way. I think we're looking for scapegoats. I think we're going to take it out on anybody who's been stupid enough to call himself a Communist. That's this man's opinion."

After unburdening himself, Jackson leaned his head back and went to sleep. We were leaving Manhattan by then. On the Queens side of the bridge, Nick ran two of the cab's wheels onto a curb getting around a delivery truck.

The jolt woke Jackson up. "Whatever became of your Silver Star?" he asked me out of the blue.

My answer came from the same place. "I hocked it yesterday."

"If I thought that were true, I'd knock your teeth out."

I had to smile at that threat. "Right now you couldn't knock out my grandmother's dentures."

"Okay, wise guy. So I'll sober up first." He put his head down and got right to it.

31

We made it to La Guardia with five minutes to spare. That was due entirely to Nick, who had raced through Queens the way he and his tank had once rolled across North Africa. I didn't have time to phone ahead to the coast, so I asked Merritt Jackson—back from the grave—to send a telegram for me. To Eloise Englehart, the Publicity Department, Warner Bros. Pictures. "Meet TWA flight. Midnight. Scotty."

Jackson wrote it all down in his official reporter's notebook, steadying it and himself against the side of Nick's cab. "They'll spot you a few more words," he said. "Sure you don't want to say 'Love, Scotty?'"

"You're the writer."

That concession got Jackson's attention. "This Eloise, are you two an item? Off the record."

"Even on the record."

"How are her legs?"

"Grablesque."

"Good for you, buddy. Really. That's great."

We shook hands. "Find yourself a new world to conquer," I said.

"Someday soon," Jackson said.

Our parting scene used up the time I might have spent giving my suit artificial respiration. When I boarded the plane, the well-dressed matron in the seat next to mine gave my general dampness the baleful eye.

"Swam across from Manhattan," I told her.

We flew over that island as we climbed out toward the west. The view should have been spectacular, but the heat had formed a hazy dome over the city. When we leveled off, I looked from the window to the reading material in my lap. It was my faithful traveling companion, the script for *Love Me Again*, which I'd retrieved before surrendering my bag. The script was my reward to myself for having the guts to drop the New York charade and head west. I was now going to find out, finally, how the movie ended.

On my flight east, my private showing of *Love Me Again* had been interrupted at an appropriately climactic moment, just as Steven Laird tossed the blackmailing house detective, Jarvis, into the street outside the Club 88. The sunlit interior of the airliner gave way to the club's smoky darkness, the drone of the engines overlaid by Rawling's little orchestra as it played something fast and hot to accompany Eddie and Joe's dance.

As their number ends, Maura enters the club. Joe spots her and directs her toward the quiet corner where Steve is drinking and brooding. Steve doesn't look up until Maura is standing next to him.

"You knew I'd come," she says.

Steve nods. "We've established a certain pattern, you and I. We fall in love. I drive you away. You come back and we fall in love again. You leave again."

Maura sits beside him and places a white-gloved hand on his arm. "I didn't leave of my own free will, not that last time. You sent me away."

"So I did." Steve looks down into his drink. "I sent you away to be with your lawful husband, a noble man whose work was important. A man who needed you."

"Yes," Maura said.

"Suppose I tell you now that the man I sent you off with wasn't so noble. That his work was important to the wrong people. That he needed you for the wrong reasons."

Maura draws her hand away. "Steve, you're frightening me. What are you trying to say? What are you trying to make of our sacrifice? Of the years we've lost?"

Steve looks into her eyes, searching for an answer. At that moment, two men enter the club. Steve and Maura are too preoccupied to notice them, but Joe is not. He watches the men first scan the room and then approach Steve's table. When one of the men draws a gun, Joe grapples with him, shouting a warning to Steve at the same time. The gun goes off, and Joe falls.

In the pandemonium that follows, the second stranger draws his pistol. Steve pushes Maura down. In his hand is the revolver he took from Jarvis. He and the gunmen exchange fire. They flee with Steve in pursuit. He arrives on the street in front of the club in time to see their car speed away.

When Steve reenters the club, he finds Joe lying in Eddie's arms. He is badly wounded.

Eddie tells Steve to get Maura away from the club before the police arrive. Rawley hands Steve the keys to his car and promises to look after Joe.

Before he passes out, Joe tells Steve, "I'm glad we came home."

Steve drives Maura to the Wojcik mansion on Long Island. In the dark interior of the car, Maura sits with her head on Steve's shoulder. At first he refuses to answer her questions about the shooting. He finally tells her, "It was someone trying to even an old score, one that predates you and me and the *Joyeuse Ile*."

His mention of the ship gives Maura part of the secret. "Did this old business involve a woman?"

"Yes," Steve says. "It got her killed."

They drive for a time without speaking. Maura is lying back in her seat, dazed and distant. Her close-up is alternately brightly lit and dark as they drive beneath a string of streetlights. Then she asks, "What were you trying to tell me back at the club?"

Steve will only say, "I have to talk with Wojcik first."

They find Franz Wojcik at home, waiting for Maura. Steve tells her that he must speak with her husband alone. She reluctantly leaves them.

Wojcik takes Steve into his study, thanking Steve as they go for giving him another chance to argue his innocence. As the study door closes behind them, a third man steps from the shadows, one of the gunmen from the Club 88. Too late, Steve recognizes his mistake. He hasn't been targeted by the mob. The bungled hit was arranged by Franz Wojcik.

Wojcik introduces the gunman as Duncan. "Like me, an employee of a large foreign firm that is no longer in business. We're orphans, Duncan and I. So we look out for one another."

Wojcik laughs at Steve's plan to expose him. "You have no proof for your wild charges. Worse, you have no standing. I suspect you even lack a valid passport.

"You're no threat to me, Steve. I would let you live, were it not for Maura. I felt a change in her from the moment she saw you yesterday. The old spark that refuses to die, threatening to flare again. There is only one way to crush it out forever."

As Duncan takes the disarmed Steve away, Wojcik says, "You should have died a hero's death on the deck of the *Joyeuse Ile*, Steve. I'm sorry I can't provide that blessing for either of us."

Duncan and his partner, a younger man named Kurt, drive Steve back to the city. They end up in a deserted section of the waterfront. The gunmen escort Steve to the end of a pier, intending to shoot him and dispose of his body in the harbor.

Duncan taunts him. "A blindfold for you, Laird? A last cigarette?" Kurt laughs nervously.

"I'll take the cigarette," Steve replies. "You can use the blindfold to gag your hyena."

Duncan hands Steve a cigarette and lights it, stepping close to Steve as he does so. Steve takes one long drag on the cigarette and then flicks it into Duncan's eyes. He tackles Kurt and they go down together. Steve rolls free and escapes into the darkness, Duncan firing after him.

I imagined the set being shot from above, by a camera on a crane. This view would present the dock's random packing cases and bits of machinery as a maze. Through it, the three men race, almost coming together randomly and then randomly moving apart, crossing and recrossing one another's paths. At every twist and turning, Steve is moving closer and closer to freedom. Or so he thinks. From the camera's overhead view, it is clear that he will not make it, that Kurt is moving to cut him off.

Then the second gunman trips over a coil of rope, the noise of his fall alerting Steve that only a stack of cases separates them. Steve scales the pile and waits for his pursuer to pass. A close-up of Steve shows him baring his teeth like a hungry wolf. He is going on the offensive at last.

Kurt circles the cases warily. Back to the close-up of Steve as he jumps. Then in long shot he lands on Kurt, knocking him cold. As Steve retrieves Kurt's fallen gun, his name is called out. He turns and sees Duncan at the end of a long alleyway, his gun drawn and ready. The two men fire together. Steve staggers backward against the pile of cases, the sleeve of his jacket torn by a near miss. Duncan smiles and then pitches forward.

As Duncan falls, Steve says, "That's for Joe."

The action moves to Wojcik's Long Island study. Wojcik is seated at his desk, staring unseeing at some papers spread before him. The room is lit only by a reading lamp on Wojcik's desk. A phonograph is playing the slow movement of a piano concerto, softly.

Maura enters through a curtained door to Wojcik's left. She has traded the gown she wore to the club for a simple white dress.

Maura is surprised to find her husband alone. "Where is Steve?" she asks him.

"Gone," Wojcik says. "He asked me to say good-bye for him."

"Gone?" Maura repeats. "Without seeing me? When will he be back?"

"I don't think he will be back," Wojcik says. "He thought it would be better this way. He was concerned for your safety.

Something that happened tonight. Some danger he put you in."
Wojcik—still seated—turns away from Maura. "You needn't tell me about it if you'd rather not."

"Franz, Franz." Maura steps behind his chair and places her hands on his shoulders. "You have always understood."

Wojcik smiles bitterly to himself. "This danger, did Steve say what it was? Perhaps I can help him."

Maura rests her face against his hair. "Some threat from his past. He told me this afternoon that his work wasn't done."

"The work is never done for a man like Steve," Wojcik says. "The fight is never over. The sacrifice never ends." He reaches up to his shoulder and places a hand on Maura's.

She gently pulls free. "It never ends," she says, nodding in sad agreement. She leaves the study the way she entered it. The camera, taking Wojcik's point of view, lingers on the curtains until they stop swaying.

Wojcik gets up from his desk and crosses the room to a wall of bookshelves. There his eyes fall on a glass case containing a decoration. It is the Legion of Honor, presented to Wojcik by an unsuspecting French government. The background music fades. Its place is taken by the opening notes of the *Heroic Polonaise*. Wojcik's eyes cease to focus on the medal. He is thinking of a moment from the past. Voices can now be heard, calling for silence and attention. Wojcik straightens, holding his head high and raising his hands to an invisible keyboard as he remembers the moment in the lounge of the *Joyeuse Ile* when he played Chopin's hymn to Poland in defiance of his German masters. The music ends, replaced by wild cheering. As the sounds of celebration fade, Wojcik's hands drop, lifeless, to his sides.

Cut to a long shot of the study's paneled door opening. Kurt stands in the dark doorway, hatless, his eyes wide.

Cut to close-up of Wojcik. "Well?" he demands. "Is it done? Where is Duncan?"

Cut to Kurt being pushed into the room, his place taken in the doorway by Steve. Steve's eyes are as dead and black as the automatic in his right hand.

"He's reporting to Professor Benz in hell," Steve says.

Steve informs Wojcik that he now has all the proof he needs of Wojcik's real mission in America. He points to Kurt, who is cowering in a corner of the room. "Your pal there can be identified by witnesses at the Club 88. He'll have to do some serious singing after that if he wants to save his neck. The Feds will roll up you and whatever's left of your stinking organization."

Wojcik staggers over to Steve, almost going down on his knees as he nears him. "Have mercy, Steve. For the love of God." Steve pushes him backward against the desk, but Wojcik continues to plead. "I am a victim, not a monster. I lashed out at you, yes, but it was the only way I could think of to save my life. That was why I worked for the Nazis, to save myself. I never believed in their lies. I haven't believed in anything since the camp. I've only wanted to survive. That's been my only cause. Not fascism. Not democracy. Just Franz Wojcik, living day to day."

During Wojcik's speech, Maura has stepped into the curtained doorway. The look of horror on her face reveals that she has heard her husband's confession.

Steve sees her, but doesn't acknowledge it. He asks Wojcik, "What about Maura?"

Wojcik hides his face in his hands. "She made it possible for me to go on. Not because I love her. I haven't loved anything for years. It was because she loved Franz Wojcik, the hero who believed that ideas were worth dying for. I could see that lost fool through her eyes and play the part again. Without her, I would have forgotten how."

"So she never knew?"

"No. Not the whole truth. She only knows that I'm not the man I once was. She can't love the man I've become, but that hasn't mattered. She holds the lost Franz Wojcik in her heart, and that's what I've needed. I've needed her memories of that dead love."

Maura steps into the room. Wojcik tries to stand, but she brushes past him. He sinks back onto the desk, finished now completely. He has cut himself off from Maura, his last tie to his lost self.

Maura crosses to Steve and stares into his dead eyes. She now has the answer to the question she put to him at the club. Their years of sacrifice have been for nothing.

"Oh, Steven." When he reaches out to her, she steps away. "Let him go, Steven."

"What?"

"Let him go. Please. He can't hurt us anymore. He can't hurt anyone anymore. Let him live with his conscience."

"What about your precious United Nations? What will happen to the dream with scum like him around?"

"I'll resign," Wojcik says. "I'll leave this country. No one will ever hear of me again."

Steve hesitates, and Wojcik plays on his hesitation. He knows that Steve's resolve has weakened because of Maura. "Ask yourself why you are here, Steve. Why you came back to America. Was it to avenge a cause? You, the man who is sick of causes? Was it for the country that turned its back on you? No, Steve. It was for Maura. My wife. You came back for her. That's why I must be destroyed. You must kill me—murder me—so you can have my wife."

Wojcik sees that his speech has confused Steve. As he presses his advantage, Wojcik slides a hand across his desk. "Where is your smug superiority now, Steve? You're just like all the fascists you pretend to despise, murdering to get what you want. You're finishing the Nazis' dirty work for them, killing off the little they left of me."

A close-up follows of Steve's dazed eyes drifting away from Wojcik. Another of Maura watching her husband's hand. A shot of the hand sliding underneath a magazine.

Maura calls out as Wojcik pulls a gun from its hiding place.

Steve raises his automatic and fires. Wojcik topples over behind the desk.

Maura rushes into Steve's arms. Still looking toward Wojcik, Steve holds her for a moment. Then he kisses her.

When the kiss ends, Steve and Maura are standing on a sunlit deck. A peaceful ocean stretches out forever behind them. The camera pulls back, revealing Eddie and the recovered Joe looking on. Steve and Maura are holding champagne glasses, the shot recreating a memory of their last voyage together. They touch glasses as Steve delivers the film's last line.

"Here's to tomorrow."

32

Pidgin was waiting in the terminal when I wandered in with the other survivors of the marathon flight. She was dressed for a nightclub in a silky, rose-colored dress. A matching cape hid the décolletage, which is how fashion-designer types describe the neckline. In place of a hat, she had a gardenia pinned in her hair.

She pretended to powder her deviated septum as I crossed the waiting room to her. I thought I could see her eyes twinkling over the top of her compact, but I wasn't exactly wide awake. To shake off the last of my nap, I kissed her.

"Hope you weren't planning to dance till dawn," I said.

She ran the back of her hand along my stubbly jaw. "I've already had my night on the town, thank you."

"Courtesy of whom?"

"Good. You're jealous. That makes up for the time I spent wondering what you were up to in New York."

"Glad we're starting off even."

"What were you up to, Scotty?"

"My neck in egos and characters. I'll take nice, quiet Los

Angeles any day."

Pidgin slipped her arm through mine. "It's been too quiet lately."

"No big breaks in the case?"

"No. Nobody else murdered, either. That surprises me. In the movies, the murderer always keeps knocking off suspects till he's the only one left. That's usually how they catch him."

"Don't count on that kind of slip from our murderer. It's a safe bet he's seen all those movies."

We joined the crowd waiting for the airline's teamsters to wheel their baggage carts into the terminal. The society matron who'd been my neighbor on the plane was standing next to an equally stodgy gentleman. She was looking from Pidgin to me as though our association had her flummoxed. Hoot Gibson meets Greer Garson. To flummox her some more, I leaned over and kissed Greer again.

I expected a question from Pidgin after that, but not the question I got. "What's the deal with your Silver Star?"

"Excuse me?"

"Your telegram. The message said I should meet you here and ask about your Silver Star. Was that some kind of code?"

"Yes. It means the guy I asked to send the telegram still had a drink left in his hip flask."

"You didn't write the part about the medal?"

"No."

"How about the 'Love, Scotty'?"

"Let's say I initialed the change."

That bit of honesty cost me. "Next time you need a ride," Pidgin said, "call a cab."

"I didn't need a ride. My car's outside. I needed to see a friendly face when I got back."

She thought that over while the bags were distributed. When we'd collected mine, I led us toward a pay phone. "Time I was reporting in," I said.

"If you're thinking of spoiling your boss's sleep, you're out of luck. He's not at home."

"How would you know?"

"Because he was my date this evening." My reaction to that squared things between us again. Pidgin smiled. "I left him just now at the Mocambo, drinking with Tory Beaumont."

We walked out into the night, Pidgin rubbing a little salt in my wound to pass the time. "Mr. Maguire isn't the gangster I took him for. He's kind of a teddy bear."

"A married teddy bear," I said.

"Relax. His motive tonight was strictly research."

"On nightclubs?"

"Paddy calls them hot-cha parlors."

"How endearing. What was he really after?"

"He wanted to question me about people at the studio. Background. Social life."

"Vincent Mediate, for example?"

We paused to avoid a pair of cabs racing for the same fare. "His name came up," Pidgin said.

"Why ask you?"

"Maybe because he wanted the gossip, and I work in the gossip department. Maybe because he also wanted some background on me."

"Did you tell him you had a good alibi for the night Kramer caught it?"

"He seemed to know all about that. About you and me, I mean. He said he'd been talking to Fred Wilner, so Freddy might have mentioned it. Anyway, I think your boss wanted to make sure it was okay for you and me to be holding hands. He's pretty fond of you, Scotty."

Just then, the feeling wasn't mutual. "I hope you spit in his eye."

"No, I didn't. I'm fond of you, too. I can understand why someone would want to adopt you."

"Paddy thinks he already has." We arrived at Pidgin's coupé. "My car's on the other side of the lot. How about a lift?"

"Leave it here for tonight," Pidgin said. "You look too bushed to drive."

"Okay."

When we were settled in and moving, she asked, "Where to?"

"A hot-cha parlor."

The Mocambo was the cream of the Hollywood nightclubs. It was on Sunset, in a building I remembered as the home of the old Club Versailles. The outside was nothing to look at: a half-block of stucco and tile with the club's name done in stylized script. The exterior was a physical representation of Hollywood's basic lesson: what you see is not what you get.

Just inside the door, I surrendered my hat and helped Pidgin out of her cape. I understood then why she had needed one on such a warm night. Her evening gown was strapless and low cut. The cape had saved her from being arrested for defying the law of gravity.

Subtle though I was, Pidgin noted my inspection. "Hold that thought," she said.

We paused at the entrance to the main room to drink it all in. The Mocambo was perhaps the only Hollywood night spot that lived up to the average tourist's image of one. I'd heard the club's decor described as Salvador Dalí on a bender, and that came close to nailing it. Red, green, and yellow stripes were everywhere: on the curtains surrounding the bandstand, on the wallpaper, around the pillars that held up the ceiling. In addition to the ceiling, the pillars supported stylized treetops from which were suspended giant fringe balls in all the colors of a madman's palette. The overall effect might have been called Hollywood baroque, a school of decorating in which too much was barely enough.

Pidgin led me to a more muted corner of the club, where upholstered booths were backed by diamond-paned mirrors with a smoky finish. The booths were lit by cast-iron female figurines bolted to the mirrored wall. Each figure held an electric candelabra and each was dressed the way peasant women would dress if they had plenty of money and no modesty whatsoever.

We arrived at a booth that contained Tory Beaumont and a couple of other men. But no Paddy Maguire.

"You just missed your boss," Beaumont said. "He was called away."

"By whom?"

"He didn't say. He also didn't tell me you were back in town."

"He doesn't know."

The actor grinned and scratched the side of his nose. "In that case, I'm sorry you missed him. Tonight's been too damn dull."

He introduced his two companions as Mr. Shaw, a producer from RKO, and Mr. Maxwell, an out-of-town friend of Shaw's. If the evening had been dull for Maxwell, it had perked up considerably with the arrival of Pidgin Englehart. As he looked her over, he all but howled at the moon. He was a big man going to fat, with a short, black moustache whose hairs were stiff and spaced out along his lip like the bristles of an old brush.

Maxwell had been drinking. It made him poetic. "Warm it, baby," he said, patting the seat beside him.

"What Charles Boyer wouldn't give for a line like that," Pidgin said.

"Come on. I'll keep my hands in my lap till we're better acquainted, if that's what you'd prefer."

"It's what you'd prefer, from the look of you," Pidgin said, sweetly.

"Excuse him, please," Shaw said. "He's had a snootful."

"Not enough to affect my performance," Maxwell assured Pidgin. "If you know what I mean."

We all knew. I was too tired to insult Maxwell or even threaten him. That left planting a fist in his fat maw.

I took a step his way, but Pidgin grabbed my arm. "Excuse me," she said. Then she left us.

As she went, Maxwell called out, "Don't be long, sugar."

"How about you and me stepping out for some fresh air?" I said.

"When you go away, the air will be fresh enough for me," he said back.

"Shut up, Maxie, can't you?" Shaw pleaded. His bald head was shining in the candelabra light like a waxed apple. To me, he said, "He doesn't mean anything."

"That's right, Elliott," Beaumont said. "You and Mr. Maxwell here should be pals. He's an ex-serviceman, too. Isn't that right, Maxwell?"

"Damn right," Maxwell said.

"Saw some real fighting, too," Beaumont added.

"I never said that."

"Oh that's right," the actor said, his voice casual and friendly and yet loud enough to reach all the tables around us. "You were stationed stateside. You still did some dangerous work though, right? Tested hand grenades or trained paratroopers or something, wasn't it?"

I recognized Beaumont's ribbing routine. Maxwell did not, but he was still uncomfortable with all the attention he was getting.

"No," he said.

"Damn," Beaumont said. "Where is my mind tonight? Must be the hootch. I remember now. You were stationed in Miami."

"Skip it," Maxwell said.

"It's all coming back to me. Your daddy got you posted there, didn't he? He was some kind of big-shot supplier. Had connections with the top brass. What was it he supplied again? Something that starts with a C. Carbines? Cartridge belts? C-47s?"

"I said skip it."

"Condoms! That was it. Talk about your vital defense industries." The tittering in the neighboring booths burgeoned into laughter. Maxwell's face was dark with trapped blood and his big hands had gathered into fists on the table before him. By my calculation, it was the moment for Beaumont to back away, to say something polite and drop the subject, leaving Maxwell to simmer in his own juice.

Beaumont thought differently. "What's the matter, Maxie? Where's your sense of humor? When you told us about it just now you were damn near rolling on the floor. Turned my stomach just listening to it. Partying all the time. Chasing a different skirt every night. The war was one long binge for you. All the time better men were dying or being crippled or just plain living in the dirt."

The laughter around us had died away, leaving some serious quiet. Beaumont let Maxwell enjoy a full minute of it. Then he said, "Hit the bricks, you bum."

Maxwell bolted from the booth, the only deviation in his straight line for the door a respectful detour around me. Shaw followed him, after apologizing again to everyone within earshot.

I took the producer's place next to Beaumont. "You were really asking for it that time," I said.

Beaumont shrugged. "I figured I was safe enough with you standing there. You wanted to slug that creep so bad it was making your eyes cross. Besides which, a genius like Maxwell is pretty likely to swallow whole what he sees in the movies. To him, I'm a guy you don't want to fool with. He'd be happier going up against you."

"Thanks for showing him up."

"I hate a phony, so it was my pleasure. And speaking of my pleasure." He waved a pet waiter over and ordered another double. I'd put a safe three-thousand miles between me and Jake Reardon, gun for hire, so I ordered my usual.

"How was New York?" Beaumont asked.

"Hot."

"Did you learn anything interesting?"

"Nobody would come out and say that Mediate is a

Communist, if that's what you mean."

"What did I tell you? A big mouth, a know-it-all, a pretentious phony he may be. But not a Red. Do you know what really burns me about that guy? He bought himself this big, new motor cruiser and he can't even run the damn thing. It's not even a sailboat for Christ's sake. It's a floating bus. Every time Mediate wants to play sailor, he has to rent himself a captain. That spells 'phony' in electric lights, as far as I'm concerned. I hate phonies."

"So you said." It was a common Hollywood prejudice, but an odd one given that the local export was hooey. Or maybe not so odd. For some reason, I thought of the agent I'd met in New York, Stanley Wallace. I passed on his greeting to Beaumont.

"Nice guy, Stan," Beaumont said. "Did you get a word in edgewise with him?"

"Not many." Our drinks arrived. In keeping with the Mocambo's understand elegance, mine was in a green cocktail glass whose stem was shaped like a cactus. I drank it anyway. "He said he knew you when you were wearing a raccoon coat and singing through a megaphone."

"Yeah, we go way back. I was a Handsome Harry myself back then, believe it or not. At least enough of one to fool the old ladies in the balcony."

"Wallace said you've shed your skin a couple of times since."

"What if I have?" Beaumont asked his drink. "It's my skin."

"Which one are we talking about?"

"You giving me the needle now, Elliott? Don't let's forget who bought this round."

"I was just wondering what makes an actor hate phonies so much. Could it be the way an actor makes his living? Pretending to be something he's not?"

Beaumont surprised me by smiling his toothy smile. "Of course that's it, Einstein. You've been out of the acting game too long if you have to ask that. Only you're wrong to pin the rap on actors. An actor isn't a phony; he's a craftsman. He's doing a job, like a plumber or a mechanic. A movie star is a different animal. The stars aren't paid to act. If we suddenly were, the banks around here would be repossessing some choice real estate. A star is paid to be something on the screen. A man-about-town. The girl you left behind. The perfect lover, wife, cowboy, take your pick."

He lit a cigarette and pushed his pack across to me. "That's still no big problem. The star has just become an actor with a limited range. With the really big stars, though, it goes beyond that. The star stops representing a type and starts standing for a quality. Honesty. Sophistication. Fidelity. Courage. Disillusionment. Or some patented combination of the above.

"Now the problems start. How can anyone stand being integrity personified? Or grace and beauty? You can't for long. It isn't human. It's something higher than human, which means it's no damn good. That's my take on this whole dizzy century. Try to perfect man, and you get something you wouldn't want living next door. Try to make your living pretending to be some unattainable ideal, and you end up a drunk who calls everybody else in the world a phony."

"What's the answer?"

"Lose all your hair and become a character actor. That's my plan."

33

Beaumont and I sat for a time watching the place empty. Then I said, "Pidgin must not know the coast is clear."

My host chuckled. "Maguire's got his work cut out for him if he's hoping to turn you into a detective."

"Meaning what?"

"Miss Englehart is long gone."

"Gone? Why would she leave?"

Beaumont always looked a little tired, but as he shook his head now he seemed positively weary. "Try to follow the bouncing ball. She left because she couldn't stay. That creep Maxwell embarrassed the hell out of her, treating her like a good-time girl in front of you. No matter how savvy a woman is or how many times she's been around the block, there's always one goof she'd like to play Mary Pickford for. It's you for Pidgin. Don't ask me why. Anyway, it tied her hands. She would have watered Maxwell with his own drink, if you hadn't been around."

"But I was around."

"So she could either stand there and be talked to like a tough customer or prove to the world she was one by handing Maxwell his head. She was damned either way she played it. Elementary, as that guy on the radio likes to say."

I scanned the club for Pidgin on my way to the coat check. The girl behind the counter confirmed that the lady with the rose-colored cape had gone. As a consolation prize, the girl gave me back my hat. A slip of paper was tucked inside the ribbon. It was a note from Pidgin and it read: "Scotty, come by for a drink if you're not too tired." There was an address below that and a P for the signature. It wasn't preceded by "love," but then Merritt Jackson hadn't been around to handle the rewrite.

I stepped out onto the street, wondering what the chances were of finding a cab. The club's doorman might have been off chasing one. Or maybe he'd just gone home. Either way, I had the sidewalk to myself. I considered going back inside to roust Beaumont, but he already knew too much about my social life. More than I did, it seemed. West seemed to be the appropriate direction to take on a street named Sunset, so I headed west.

I didn't get very far. I'd just passed a narrow alleyway that separated the Mocambo from its neighbor when something cracked me on the back of the head. I hit the concrete hard with both knees. My face would have been next, if some helpful soul hadn't grabbed me by the collar. This Good Samaritan pulled my suit jacket off my shoulders and down around my arms, pinning them to my sides. Then I was sailing into the dark alley, my chin leading the way while my feet scrambled to catch up.

They never quite made it. I landed square on my chest on the dirt floor of the alley, losing the wind I might have used to holler uncle. A kick to my ribs landed solidly, but a second one aimed at my head almost missed. I rolled away from the blow and kept rolling, until I hit the rough stucco exterior of the club. Using the wall as a support, I pushed myself up into a kneeling position, my back to my ballet instructor. He aimed a knee at my left kidney, missing high, but driving me into the stucco just the same. The kick had another, unintended effect: it sprang the buttons holding my straitjacket together. I was able to roll across the wall and raise my arms as the next blow landed. I grabbed a fistful of someone else's sleeve, and, when the arm it contained drew away, it pulled me to my feet.

I shook my left arm free of my suit jacket as I came up. It was too late to block the next punch, but I batted away the two after that. Then I threw my right, flailing suit coat and all, and felt a very satisfying crack.

The proceedings developed a definite rhythm after that, a groggy memory of army boxing matches. I feinted left, feinted left, then leaned into a right, repeating the sequence again and again until the dark shape I was hitting arrived at the alley's opposite wall. When I heard him sliding down it, I backed away.

I was still seeing stars from the sapping I'd taken on the back of my skull and I was breathing like a man a year or two out of training. When the fireworks in my head dimmed a little, I lit a match and bent down to see who my dancing partner had been. Vincent Mediate came to mind, but he wasn't my first guess or even my second. In my punchy state, I was expecting Duncan, Franz Wojcik's fictional henchman, or his dopey assistant, Kurt.

The match revealed Maxwell, the condom heir, with blood in his bristly moustache. I hadn't been able to insult him when it counted, but the old Elliott charm must have made an impression on him. Or maybe Beaumont had been right, and Maxwell had considered me a safer recipient of the beating the actor had earned. However it had come about, I was grateful.

I shook out my match and dropped it on Maxwell's shirt front. "Thanks for waiting up for me, pal," I said.

The Mocambo's doorman was back at his station, complete with a cab. Unfortunately, he also had customers for it, a white-haired old goat who was leading an ingenue to the slaughter. Or maybe it was the other way around. The young lady took one look at me as I bent to retrieve my hat from the sidewalk and gasped.

"May I?" I asked as I stumbled past them and through the open door of the cab. Good manners carried the day once again. The doorman shut me in, and the cabbie asked which hospital I preferred. I gave him Pidgin's address in Burbank.

"Okay, bub," he said. "It's a nice night for a drive."

The apartment building waiting at the end of our drive was brand new. So new that its twin was still under construction next door, across the rough outlines of a courtyard. The ironwork of the new building looked like the bombed-out shell of an old one, shipped over from Europe or Japan for the viewing pleasure of the locals. There was a single light burning in the completed building. I was so certain it was burning for me, that I sent the cab away.

Pidgin's intake of breath when she opened her door for me was a muted reprise of the gasp I'd produced from the lady whose cab I'd swiped.

"You should see the other guy," I said.

Her rose evening gown had been replaced by a burgundy robe. "I saw Maxwell earlier. He wasn't worth getting your face banged up over."

Pidgin's parlor was decorated in severely modern pieces: tall

218

metal lamps with dark conical shades that hoarded their light, razor-thin tables on wire legs, a sofa and a couple of chairs designed by a geometry teacher.

I selected an isosceles triangle and dropped into it, heavily. "What makes you so sure it was Maxwell? How do you know it wasn't the murderer, panicking because I'm closing in?"

"Because this isn't a movie, Scotty. You said as much yourself, not too long ago."

It seemed like a long time to me. "Where's that drink you promised me?"

"Later." Pidgin left me alone with the indirect lighting. Before my eyes had closed completely, she returned carrying a dish of water and some linen. She knelt by my chair, wet a wash cloth, and started dabbing at my cheek.

"What made these scratches, sandpaper?"

"Stucco. I'm going to lead a crusade against that stuff."

"You've got a bruise on your jaw and there's a nice lump over your right eye."

"If you think that lump's nice, you should see the one on the back of my head."

Pidgin made me lean over so she could examine that wonder. I rested my forehead on her shoulder and breathed in her perfume. The fragrance or the poking around she was doing had me seeing stars again.

"You may have a concussion," she finally said. "I'd tell you to have your head examined, but you probably hear that all the time."

I raised my damaged head, and she kissed me. "Good thing he missed your lips."

"Damn good," I said.

Her pale eyes blinked once. "My virtue isn't worth fighting for, Scotty."

"I get to decide what I'm willing to fight for," I said. "That's how it works."

"Don't you have your hands full, defending Hollywood

against the goons in Washington?"

"I'm not defending anything."

"The hell you're not. I've been thinking about it ever since you phoned last night. I think I've figured out why you're still here in Hollywood and why you're doing the work you're doing."

"Then you're two up on me."

"Shut up and listen. I think you're acting out your unrequited love for this town, Scotty. I think you're fighting a rearguard action against anything threatening your lost love."

"Sounds noble," I said.

"It's not," Pidgin said. "It's stupid. You can't even save one little movie. How are you going to protect a whole town? You'll spend your life trying and not get it done. That sounds like a waste to me."

I ran a hand along the lapel of her silken robe. "It sounds like job security to me."

Pidgin brushed the hair back from my forehead. "You must have a concussion."

"Be gentle then."

We tried another kiss. During the course of it, Pidgin moved from the floor beside my triangular chair and up onto my lap. The movement reminded me that I'd also banged up my knees in the fight, but I kept it to myself.

Pidgin was after another secret anyway. "How come you never told me you'd been decorated?"

"How does one work that into a conversation?"

"Around this town, one probably hires a press agent and has it worked into the newspapers."

We kissed again. "Interested in the job?" I asked.

"Not at the moment. Right now we have to figure out what we're going to do with you. If you've got a concussion, you can't go to sleep. You might never wake up."

"Who's thinking about sleep?"

"You're not up to any wrestling either."

"Bet me," I said.

Pidgin didn't take the bet, which was just as well, as I would have lost. Not that I didn't give it the old college try. We made it as far as her ultramodern bed before the throbbing in my head overcame what was left of my ego. While we rested up from the attempt, I tried to find a comfortable way to lean against the bed's headboard. It resembled the grillwork of my LaSalle, executed in lacquered wood, so there wasn't a comfortable way to be found.

"For God's sake, Scotty," Pidgin said. "Stop squirming around and have a cigarette. That's probably what you're thinking about."

It must have been. Once I'd lit a Lucky—the only intact passenger in the crushed pack I found in my suit-coat pocket— the corrugated headboard felt like home.

When I'd settled down, Pidgin started questioning me again. "You've never told me what you found out in New York."

"Because I don't want to lower your opinion of me."

"Tell me about your Silver Star, then."

My Hoosier grandmother would have called it choosing between a rock and a hard place. I chose the hard place.

"There's not much to that story. We'd been shifted north to relieve Bastogne. Damn near every unit in France had been. I was attached to a squad of infantry as a forward observer for my battery. Everything was being improvised in that mess. The infantry guys and I improvised our way into a column of retreating German armor. They were lost, too. Luckily for me, my radio was working that day. I called in a barrage that caught the tanks in the open. The battery fired for a solid two hours. They earned the medal. I got it. That's all there was to it."

"Not in the version I heard," Pidgin said. "The way I heard it, the infantry squad you were with was wiped out. You were the only one left and you were right in the middle of the German tanks. You called in the artillery barrage on your own position.

It was just dumb luck you weren't killed."

It didn't take me long to figure out where Pidgin had gotten her information. She'd had dinner with Paddy Maguire, and she'd been armed by then with Merritt Jackson's boozy telegram.

Pidgin sat up and faced the room's only window, her back to me. Through the window, I could see the faint black skeleton of the ironwork across the courtyard.

"My brother Bill stepped on a land mine," she said. "That's what the letter my folks got said. I like to think he never knew what hit him."

I would have told Pidgin that he surely hadn't known, but I wasn't slipping much past her just then.

I'd forgotten about my cigarette. Pidgin lifted it from my hand and took a long drag. As she exhaled the smoke, she asked, "Why didn't you want to tell me about the war?"

"Remembering bothers me. I like to pretend the whole thing never happened."

"I know the feeling. What a screwy time that was. Everything turned around somehow. It was Hollywood loose over the whole world. Everyone wearing costumes, playing parts, knowing that one way or another it was never going to last. Ordinary joes like you and Billy trying to be Errol Flynn and the real Flynn drinking himself sick because he wasn't an ordinary joe in a uniform.

"Then the war ended, and we were all back to the day before Pearl Harbor, shaking our heads and rubbing our eyes. Those of us who were lucky enough to get back."

I thought of Fred Wilner, another ordinary joe, and his idea that the country had been changed forever. "None of us got back to that day," I said.

Pidgin ground out the cigarette. "So, are you going to tell me about New York?"

"Right after you tell me how well you knew Errol Flynn."

"Someday when you're stronger."

34

My nurse fought the good fight, but slipped off to dreamland around two. I was in no danger of following her there. I'd done too much napping on the flight west, and my souvenirs from Maxwell's upper-body massage made even sitting still for very long impossible. So I smoked and paced and put my thumb marks on Pidgin's glossy magazines. Just after four, I got undressed as quietly as I could and spent some time in Pidgin's shower, finishing up with a blast of cold water to shock myself fully awake. I could have skipped that step. When I wiped the steam from the bathroom mirror, I got all the shocking I needed.

The tracts gouged by the Mocambo's wall along my left cheekbone were browning nicely, while the territory around my right eye had taken on a bluish cast. Above that eye, my brow was still fat and yellow with the last of its swelling. The lump on my jaw had gone down, but it had left a purple smear behind for me to remember it by. All in all, it was a face that black-and-white film could never do justice to.

Pidgin had thoughtfully brought my suitcase in from her car sometime before my arrival. I dug out my shaving kit and worked around the damage. Then I dressed in the last change I'd packed for New York. Pidgin was almost stirring by then, which is to say she'd rolled over onto her back. I sat down next to her, and the movement of the bed woke her.

She opened one eye. "You really look like hell in the morning, Scotty," she murmured. "That could be a problem for us."

"You, on the other hand, look great," I said.

She reached down and pulled the sheet up as far as her chin. "Where are you off to so early?"

"Work."

"I won't tell you to be careful; it might hurt you to laugh."

"Thanks for thinking of me." I leaned over and kissed her.

She closed her open eye. "That was nice."

"You know what we Elliotts say: If you don't have a good kisser, be one."

"Plagiarist."

"I'll call you later."

"If you can," she said.

While the subject of calling was fresh in my mind, I used Pidgin's parlor phone to ring the Maguire residence. The lady of the house answered.

"For crying out loud, Scotty," Peggy said. "Do you know how early it is out here? You should remember to figure the time difference when you call from New York."

"What's the time difference from Burbank? I got back last night. Sorry to wake you."

"Wake me again, you mean. You're the second caller this morning. What's the emergency?"

"I have to talk with Paddy."

"He was the first joker who woke me up. He didn't make it home last night. Business, he said. He told me to meet him at the office with a clean shirt at eight. The almighty crust of the man."

"Hold on to him till I get there."

"Don't worry about that," Peggy said. "He'll be moving a lot slower when I get through with him."

I phoned for a cab and then went down to the street to wait for it. Thanks to the relief map on the back of my skull, my hat felt a size too small, so I wore it pushed way back, like a movie reporter. I could have used my sunglasses, both to hide a few bruises and to dim down the morning, but I'd found them in pieces in my suit coat pocket, one last present from Maxwell.

While I waited, I paced a brand-new concrete walk. I was looking for something to show up besides the cab. I also needed a plan of action. I'd discovered why Bert Kramer had been murdered, thanks to his dying clue, the script he hadn't really written. But I still didn't know who had done it. Instead of

224

finding out, I was dithering around like Nigel Bruce on happy pills.

I might have been stalling because I lacked a little thing called evidence. All I had was the possibility that Carl Potts had authored the script for *Love Me Again* and the certainty that he'd met with Vincent Mediate. As Paddy had pointed out, that meeting didn't even prove that Mediate had been in on the arrangement between Kramer and Potts. Nor could I prove that Vincent Mediate was a former or current Communist. Even James Zucco, a man who clearly hated Mediate, hadn't been willing to confirm that.

There was also a large, messy, loose thread in the form of the anonymous note. Who had sent it and why? Sometime during my restless time in Pidgin's modernist apartment, I'd hatched a cute idea about that. When I made up my mind to visit Mediate, I told myself I was going in search of my missing evidence and maybe even to give the producer a chance to clear himself, nice guy that I was. But as much as anything else, I was after the truth about that note.

But I wasn't going anywhere without a cab. So I paced on, smoking the broken pieces of a couple of Luckies in place of breakfast. Lighting half a cigarette without burning my nose was a knack I'd picked up in the army, where there had always been someone around to ask for a share of a smoke, usually Merritt Jackson.

I was feeling sorry for Jackson that morning, and the feeling came as a little bit of a shock. It had been a long time since I'd had any sympathy left over for other people. Seeing Jackson again had had some kind of therapeutic effect on me. Or talking to Pidgin had. As I paced the virgin concrete along her street, the fighting had never seemed so far away. It might just have been a happy side effect of my concussion, but I had the feeling that if I tried hard enough I could start forgetting the war.

It certainly wasn't the morning making me feel lighter in spirit. The day was already warm, and there was an acrid bite to the air. I thought of autumns in Indiana when the smoke from burning leaves had lingered forever in the still sky. The smoke had seemed symbolic to me, I remembered, a visible sign of an emotion hanging in the motionless air, the tension of waiting for winter to arrive.

Lately I'd been getting my weather information from cab drivers, and the one who finally picked me up in front of Pidgin's didn't disappoint. After he'd inquired about the truck that had run over my face, the cabbie moved directly to the subject of the brown air.

"They're calling it a thermal inversion," he said. "Usually, the air gets cooler as you go up into the sky, but the last day or so there's been a layer of warmer air up there fritzing the works."

"Warmer than what?" I asked.

"The air down here. The stuff at ground level can't rise, 'cause it's cooler than the air above it. You following any of this?"

"Intently."

"In addition to plain stale air, the crud from the oil refineries and every other kind of smoke this city puts out is also trapped. Not a great spot to be in."

"There ought to be a law," I said.

"So, how about those Dodgers? What's their lead now, ten games?"

"At least."

While my driver delivered the rest of the sportscast, I cooked up an alternative explanation for the trapped air choking greater Hollywood. The whole city was in a state of suspended animation, I decided, awaiting the solution of Bert Kramer's murder. Hollywood had somehow sensed that this was no ordinary killing, that it was tangled up with congressional hearings and the threat of twelve hours of television each and every day. What we were tasting with every breath wasn't the trapped smoke of oil refineries and barbecue pits. It was the smoldering suspense of a city anxious to know if it had a future.

If Pidgin's theorizing was correct, the city had someone looking after its future. A champion. It was just too bad for all concerned that the champion happened to be me.

35

The LaSalle was waiting patiently for me in the airport lot. I climbed in on the passenger side and opened the glove compartment. Paddy's standard-issue automatic was still there, bundled inside its canvas sack. I took the gun out of the bag and the holster and verified that there were bullets in its magazine. Then I slipped out of my suit jacket and into the holster, an operation that brought Maxwell to mind more than once. The holster was brand new, and its straps were stiff and uncooperative. They lay a lot better when I added the weight of the gun. When I'd finished dressing I slid over behind the familiar steering wheel—the color of old piano keys—pressed the starter, and pointed the car toward Beverly Hills.

There wasn't much stirring at the Stratford Hotel. I parked a block away and slipped inside while the doorman was staring up at the crusty sky. The elevator was manned by a bellhop who had misplaced his hat. His professional demeanor broke down when he got a good look at his passenger's face.

"What happened to you?" he asked.

"Damned thermal inversion," I said.

The Mediates' hallway was so quiet it got on my nerves. Ringing the bell next to their door was a relief. So much so that I went on ringing it, just to have something to listen to.

The concert ended when Vincent Mediate yanked the door open. He was wearing yellow pajamas and a black robe. His temper matched the robe, but the sight of my friendly face settled him down immediately.

"Don't tell me you actually got him," Mediate said.

"Got who?"

"Kramer's murderer. Who else would you be boxing with?"

I scratched at my swollen brow. "I've been making do with strangers. Let me in, and I'll tell you about it."

"It's damned early, Elliott."

"It's later than you think."

Mediate turned on his heel and led the way into the suite. Instead of a right into the piano-laden living room where I'd interviewed his wife, he made a left into what must once have been a spare bedroom. It was currently serving as an office. There was a desk the size of Paddy Maguire's for Mediate to sit behind and just enough space around it for visitors to stand in awe. Tacked to one wall was a three-foot-by-five sheet of paper. It was a rough sketch of a poster for *Love Me Again*. In it, Beaumont, wearing his trademark tuxedo, held Ella Larsen protectively in his arms. She was also dressed as she had been in their last scene from *Passage to Lisbon*, in a broad-brimmed hat and trench coat. They were both staring out over my right shoulder, Larsen frightened by what she saw and Beaumont grimly resolute.

"So who gave you the facial?" Mediate asked after he'd settled himself behind his desk.

"Nobody you'd know. It took me a while to recognize the guy myself. I thought for a round or two that it might even have been you."

"Me?" Mediate asked, surprised, but only mildly so. "I've heard a rumor that you knew my wife before the war, but I didn't take it that seriously. Should I have?"

"You should have taken me that seriously," I said. "I'm the one who's figured out why Bert Kramer was killed. It was because he was blackmailing a certain wonder-boy producer."

Mediate started moving, but not much faster than the hands of my watch. First he rose slightly in his swivel chair, and his noble head thrust itself forward. Then he planted his hands palms downward on the desktop as a preliminary to launching himself across it. He never made the trip.

"Don't try any sucker plays, Mediate, or you're through. You've got exactly one chance to convince me that you didn't kill Kramer. One dumb move, and you'll be doing your explaining to Sergeant Dempsey."

Mediate settled back into his chair, but his eyes never left mine.

"That's better. Keep your hands where I can see them and pay attention. I know that the real author of *Love Me Again* is an unhappy guy named Carl Potts. We both know why he's unhappy. I was there when you met him at the Cove Inn. Bert Kramer was earning extra money by fronting for Potts. But that wasn't enough extra money for old Bert. He had another deal going at the same time. He was blackmailing you."

"Blackmailing me over what?"

"Don't waste my time. We both know what Kramer had on you. He'd found out that you're a member of the Communist Party or had been, in New York."

Mediate's noble head fell back until it rested on the top of his chair. "If you think that," he asked in a dead calm voice, "why do you care about giving me a break?"

"A lady bought it for you."

"So you did know my wife."

"The lady's name is Ina Mencher."

He snapped to attention without leaving his seat. "Ina? You talked with her? She's out here?"

"No. I talked with her in New York yesterday." Or maybe last week. It felt that long ago.

"How is she? Is she okay?"

"She's getting by."

"Ina Mencher." He proved he remembered more about the lady than her name by adding, "She never told you that I was a Red."

229

"No. She told me you were an impressionable farm boy who was a sucker for every new idea you came across. But she wouldn't say the word Communist. She wouldn't say anything bad about the guy who made *Death Camp*."

Mediate's eyes weren't focused on me or anything else in the room. "Ina saw my film?"

"Too many times for her own good. She wouldn't even tell me how you got your big break on Broadway courtesy of your pal Miller. I had to hear that gossip elsewhere."

"Herman Miller was a friend of my father's, not mine. And he owed me that break."

"How so?"

The producer surprised me by answering the question. "I grew up in York, Pennsylvania. My father was a lawyer. A small-town lawyer, but he had bigger ideas. They did him in. In '28, he and some local money men went in together on a land deal. They were going to turn some old farms into a housing development. Dad was supposed to be a front man for the money, but he couldn't resist sinking what little he had into it, too.

"Then the crash came. It wiped out the development and the Mediates along with it. My father struggled on for a few years, trying to pay off his debts. The strain finally killed him."

"Miller was one of the money men on that deal?"

"Yes. The crash was only an off year for him. I think he had a guilty conscience after my dad died. He got me a job in New York with a Broadway show he was backing. That's where I met Ina, which I guess you know.

"That's all there was to it. After Pearl Harbor, I joined up. I was lucky enough to get posted to a combat film crew."

"Miller's wangling again?"

"No, my own. I learned a lot about working angles in the army. I found out it was my real talent."

"So I've heard. Fred Wilner told me how you put together your first film after Normandy."

"Wilner probably thinks I was working some kind of scam. I'm no gentleman by his Confederate standards."

"Tell me about *Death Camp*."

"After the Normandy film, I had a little more clout. I parleyed it into a bigger outfit and more independence. I was able to slip my crew into Buchenwald with the troops who liberated the camp. Did you see any of the camps while you were over there?"

"Yes," I said. "A small one near Ohrdruf."

"Buchenwald was everything you've heard and worse. Soldiers who thought they'd seen all the horrors of hell got sick at the sight of that place. I did myself. Filming under fire at Normandy had been easy compared to that, but I stuck to it. I made the film."

We both thought about the film he'd made for a time. I was thinking of bodies laid out in a long row. Uniform in their emaciation, the corpses had looked like ties waiting for the track to be laid, a direct line to a maniac's Valhalla.

"Got a cigarette?" Mediate asked.

"Only the makings."

"Do you mind, then?" He pointed to a burled walnut box on his desk. "You can check it first if you're afraid there might be a gun inside."

I pushed the box across to him and tried one of Jake Reardon's lines. "Guns that small don't worry me."

He dug out a cigarette, and I tossed him a pack of matches as I'd done at his cocktail party. This time, he fumbled the catch. When he finally got the cigarette going, he drew on it deeply.

"That one movie cleaned the slate for me," Mediate said through a cloud of spent smoke. "Whatever sins I had on my conscience, *Death Camp* washed away."

"Ina Mencher believes that, but you don't. You let yourself be blackmailed by Bert Kramer. Why didn't you just tell him to take a hike?"

"That's easy enough to say. Kramer wouldn't believe I

hadn't been a Communist. Or if he did believe it, he didn't give a damn. He knew he could ruin me either way."

"How? You said yourself you'd paid for your sins."

"That's my opinion, but it isn't what the people in this town would think if they knew. If I were established, if I had some hits to my credit, I might be able to ride a scandal out. But I'm a new kid on the block. Warners would dump me without a second thought."

"Did Kramer have any proof you'd been a Party member?"

Mediate's eyes moved from mine to the burning tip of his cigarette. "I told you before, I never was a Party member."

"Then it was his word against yours."

"Hollywood isn't a court of law, Elliott. It's a company town and a small one. As small as the town I came from. Everybody here knows everybody else. The wrong word in the right ear would have been enough to finish me. These days the wrong word is Commie."

"If Kramer didn't have any proof, why did you have his office cleaned out?"

The producer shot me a look of admiration mixed with hate. "I wanted to make sure Kramer hadn't left any mention of Carl Potts."

That brought us to the second item on the program. "If you're not a Red, how did you get involved with Potts and his movie? Was that Kramer's idea?"

"No. Kramer was my idea. The worst one I ever had. I got involved because Carl Potts approached me with the script for *Love Me Again*."

"Why you?"

Mediate waved his cigarette at me. "It's not what you're thinking. Potts picked me because I'm new at Warners. He has a grudge against the studio dating from some labor trouble a couple years back. He didn't want to deal with any of the old hands."

"Go on."

232

"We needed a writer's name on the script. Potts also wanted someone who could front for him on an ongoing basis, in the event the HUAC investigations led to a blacklist. I suggested Bert Kramer. Kramer had no political convictions to haunt us. Plus, his writing style was similar to Potts's, so there was a good chance of passing the script off as his work. And I'd heard that he had money troubles."

"From gambling."

"Yes. I thought that would make him easier to deal with. I was wrong.

"Kramer wasn't the problem at first. Torrance Beaumont was. He'd evidently been planning his own production company for some time. He saw *Love Me Again* as the perfect vehicle to launch it. I almost got squeezed out of the project before it was even off the ground. I was lucky to stay on as coproducer."

"But you stayed on."

"Yes. Everything looked great for a while. Then Bert Kramer let me know that he needed more money."

"That's a polite way of putting it."

Mediate brought a fist down on the desktop hard enough to wake the neighbors. "Put it any way you like. I only know that he demanded money and I paid him. It cost me plenty, but everything was under control. Then that damned note arrived on Jack Warner's desk. Kramer panicked. He thought he was going to lose his big chance to ride Potts's talent into the promised land. He became unstable. Unmanageable."

"Somebody who had to be taken care of," I suggested.

"I did not shoot Bert Kramer."

"The night he died, Kramer came to your cocktail party to threaten you. He was going to take you down with him."

"Of course he was. But that doesn't mean I killed him."

"Who else besides you and Kramer and Potts knew that the three of you were working together?"

"No one."

"Not even your wife?"

"No. What are you getting at now?"

"The anonymous note. Remember me telling you that it was aimed as much at you as at Kramer?"

"Because it was written on stationery from this hotel. I remember."

"I think I know who might have sent it."

"Who?"

"You might have." That was the cute idea I'd had in the wee small hours. "You may want to be exposed and punished. Deep down, you may think you have it coming."

Mediate tried to smile. It may just have been my imagination, but his skin seemed to be picking up more and more of the yellow from his pajamas. "You should leave the psychoanalysis to Freud," he said. "I've told you that I was never a member of the Communist Party. And I don't believe that people who are, like Carl Potts, have anything to be ashamed of. This is still a free country."

I hated to give my theory up. While I was trying to think of a way to save it, Mediate seized the initiative. "Have you discussed any of this with Mr. Maguire?"

"Yes. I don't know if I convinced him."

"Then you should talk to him again before you think about going to the police. He can make the decision. You owe him that much loyalty as an employee. It's his firm's neck you're sticking out."

"If you're thinking that Paddy will be easier to get around than I am, you're counting too much on his shady reputation. That's part of his act, like the gaudy clothes and the big cigars. He thinks it's good for business."

"I'll take my chances with his judgment," Mediate said.

"It's your funeral."

36

Mediate let me show myself out. The elevator operator had likewise lost interest in me. We did our free-fall down to the ground floor of the Stratford in silence. When I stepped into the lobby, I was paged in a quiet, dignified way. The pager was the desk clerk who had guided me to the Mediate suite on my first visit, the no-longer-young man stuck, like me, on the bottom rung of his particular ladder.

He had just enough self-control not to inquire about my recent hit-and-run. "Mrs. Mediate instructed me to tell you that she was breakfasting in the Millar Room," the clerk said. "She wondered if you would care to join her for coffee."

I would have joined Kate Smith in a phone booth for the chance of a cup of coffee. I followed the clerk's directions to the Millar Room, a dining area whose tables sat well apart from one another, the better ones in little alcoves. Each alcove had its own tall window. Carole Mediate's table was lit by sunlight reflecting off the blue water of a pool.

Or maybe the pool was reflecting Carole's light. Her white dress was all but glowing, and it was outdone by her golden hair, worn down this morning and spread out artfully along her shoulders.

She'd accented her outfit with a red beaded necklace and lipstick to match. I watched those red lips almost smile and then part in alarm.

"Scotty. What happened to your face?"

"I fought a duel at dawn. The other party chose blackjacks."

As I sat down across from her, I said, "You must be a quick-change artist. I got the impression just now that I'd gotten your husband out of bed."

"You did. I heard him go out to answer the door. I'd been up for some time. He and I are using separate bedrooms these days."

"Sorry to hear that," I said.

A waiter came and filled the fluted vase at my elbow with coffee. "Leave the pot, please," I said.

When he'd gone off empty-handed, Carole said, "I hurried down here because I wanted to catch you on your way out. We really didn't get to finish our talk the other day."

"You got all the important points in. It would be worth my while to help your husband. What's today's offer? Orange groves? Whitewalls?"

I was trying to get a rise out of her, but my studied rudeness only produced a smile. "Sorry if I offended your professional ethics," she said. "I just hate to see an old friend in a nothing job. Now I'm beginning to wonder if you don't prefer it."

That made two of us. I poured myself a refill. Carole had yet to make the first red smear on the lip of her cup.

She straightened her already straight silverware. "In any case, I wasn't thinking of our talk about Vince. I was thinking of the kiss you stole."

She reached her right hand across and covered my left. Her fingernails were done in the same shade as her lips. I remembered it from the Stratford reception. New wound crimson, I'd dubbed it then.

I slid my hand out from under hers. "That kiss was for old times' sake."

This time I wasn't trying to offend her. So, naturally, I accomplished it effortlessly. She went brittle all over while I watched.

Now I knew what the bribe of the day was. It was as though Maura Wojcik had come to offer herself in exchange for the Geneva Exemptions, only to find Steven Laird in the arms of another woman. Not that my availability mattered one way or the other. I had no magic passports that would carry the Mediates out of trouble.

"Sorry for being so forward," Carole said. "I should have

asked whether that duel you fought was over a woman."

"It was, but I was also thinking about your husband. He wouldn't mind shooting me this morning. I don't want to issue him a license."

"Vince wouldn't shoot anybody."

"Glad to hear it."

"Besides," she said, fingering the red beads at her throat, "I told you that we aren't as close as we had been." I must have been looking sleepy, because she spelled it out for me. "We haven't been intimate for some time."

Instead of blushing on that line—the conventional way to deliver it—Carole had actually grown paler. It was a convincing touch, coming from as bad an actress as she was.

"When did the trouble start?" I asked.

"Only a few weeks ago. Up until then, Vince had shared everything with me. I used to hear every dream he had. Sometimes I think they're what I fell in love with, those dreams.

"Then Vince started working on *Love Me Again*. There was trouble from the beginning, but Vince wouldn't talk about it. Since then, he's shared less and less."

If nothing else, this case was giving me a new slant on married life. Carole's revelation reminded me of the statement Violet Kramer had made to the police. The Kramer marriage had started to die its slow death when they'd stopped sharing dreams. Evidently, the disease was contagious.

"I'm scared, Scotty."

Mrs. Nero had finally begun to smell smoke. Or did she really know everything there was to know about her husband and his secret history? Watching her gaze soulfully into her coffee, I wondered if I'd underestimated her acting ability. Carole might have been one of those people who did just fine when there wasn't a camera around.

Our waiter came back to visit his coffeepot and to ask if we were ready to order. Carole wasn't too lovelorn or frightened to eat. Or at least she wanted to put up a good front. While she gave the waiter a verbal blueprint for her eggs, I thought about a mystery she might clear up for me.

Since meeting Ina Mencher, I'd been wondering how the young Vincent Mediate of her memories had become the man Beaumont had recently dismissed as the archetypal Hollywood phony. In the late thirties in New York, Mediate had been a person blossoming under the light of a thousand new experiences. Now, according to Carole's earlier testimony, it seemed as though he'd grown too tall too fast, tall enough to see his studio coworkers as unnecessary impediments.

When it was my turn to order, I passed, and the waiter left us. I said, "There was a subject we touched on the other day that I'm not clear about. You told me that your husband was impatient with little men and little ideas. I think you said the war had done that to him."

"I wasn't expressing myself well that day," Carole said. "It came out sounding terrible, I know. I made it seem as though Vince looks down on everyone else from above."

"He comes across that way all by himself," I said.

"Is that why you don't want to help him?"

"It's what makes helping him an effort. Right now, though, I'm just trying to understand how he got the way he is."

"I told you before that it was the war."

"That doesn't quite explain it. There's a cop downtown named Dempsey who doesn't believe your husband saw any action. He doesn't believe a person could have been to war and still worship the ground this town's built on."

Carole's blond brows almost knocked heads above her angry eyes. "This Dempsey and Vince should form a club. He sounds like another veteran who's outgrown the petty concerns of us lowly civilians. If he got to know my husband better, he'd realize that Vince only thinks of the ground Hollywood's built on as a starting point. He'd like to tear the place down and start over. I'll bet this Dempsey feels exactly that way himself."

"You may be right," I said.

"I *am* right," Carole said, her Bryn Mawr cum Bronx accent listing a little to starboard. "I could write a book on ex-servicemen who won't settle for normal lives. I'm sick of all of you."

"Of us?"

"Yes. You could be the worst of the bunch." Carole was finally getting some color in her cheeks. It didn't become her. "You're a man who's willing to put a silly job ahead of an old friend."

"That reminds me," I said. "It's time I was clocking in."

I stood up, but Carole wasn't through echoing a certain Miss Englehart. "I'll bet you didn't even try to get your old life back, Scotty. Not really. I bet you set yourself up to fail. Acting isn't important enough for you anymore. You want a job that lets you play God."

"According to your husband, I only work for God. And right now I'm late for an audience."

I got as far as the edge of the lobby before I spotted another old friend, Detective Grove. He was out on the steps of the hotel, talking to the doorman. They both looked at their watches. Then Grove punctuated their conversation by sticking his index finger in the other man's chest. The recipient all but saluted.

I stepped up closer to the doorway as Grove walked away. He crossed the street to an unmarked sedan and got in on the passenger side. There was another cop behind the wheel, trying hard to look like he wasn't watching the hotel.

I pulled my hat brim down and went out through the hotel's revolving door, mourning anew the loss of my sunglasses. When the doorman looked my way, I said, "Cab, please."

He whistled one up for me while I dug out a ten from my New York expense money. When I was seated in the taxi, I held the bill up for the doorman alone to see. "What did that flatfoot want?"

There was never a shortage of handsome people to do menial

239

jobs in Hollywood. The doorman had a square, cleft chin and silvery hair. He looked like a Ruritanian general in his summer-weight coat and leather-billed cap. From the longing glance he gave the ten spot, I knew he was a general on half pay.

"He wants me to tip him off when Mr. Mediate calls for his car."

I handed him the bill and told my driver to take the first right he came to. As we made the turn, the unmarked car pulled out of its parking space a half block behind us. So much for my clever disguise.

I fished out another ten and handed it to the driver, telling him to slow down for a second and then to take the long way back to his stand. I stepped from the cab while it was still rolling and dodged between two parked cars. I was crouched there when Grove and his partner sped by a few seconds later.

Pidgin had been right. It did hurt to laugh.

37

Back at Hollywood Security, God was in and getting an earful from the missus. Peggy must have long since exhausted the subject of her helpmate's night on the town. As I entered the premises, she was blaming him for bringing her to California in the first place. I knew this routine well enough to spot the big finish coming up. So I slipped in next to a five-drawer file cabinet that stood on one side of Paddy's double doors.

The doors flew open as I took cover and Peggy delivered her signature line: "We never should have left Baltimore!" She paused long enough to pick up her hat and bag from her desk. Then she marched the length of the front office and out into an unsuspecting world.

I was surprised to find Paddy's office empty. Even more

surprising was a wet red stain running down the wallpaper near the doorway to the executive washroom. There was a dead body on the carpet beneath the stain, but it was a very small one: a flattened tomato. A carton of next-of-kin stood on the desk. Its paper label featured a smiling sun.

When I cleared my throat, Paddy stuck his head out the washroom door a careful inch at a time. His chins were daubed with lather, and he was holding an old-fashioned straight razor.

"You're a brave man to have a machete around with Peggy on the warpath," I said.

"Are you kidding? I had it out for self-defense." He left off scanning for his wife long enough to give me a good look. "What the hell happened to you?"

I was tired of being witty on the subject. "I got in from New York late last night. Pidgin Englehart and I went by the Mocambo looking for you. Some creep named Maxwell mouthed off to her. He and I talked it out later."

Paddy had resumed his shaving. He addressed his next question to the ceiling as he scraped away above his Adam's apple. "How did you leave Mr. Maxwell?"

"On his back."

"Good. That Miss Englehart is the genuine article. You could do a lot worse."

"She's fond of you, too."

Paddy poked his head out again, checking for spies. "Keep that to yourself, if you don't mind. How is it her nibs missed your entrance?"

"I made myself scarce during her exit. I didn't want the sight of me to give her the vapors."

"That'll be the day. But it was still good thinking. If she'd seen her pride and joy marked up like that, she might have come after me razor or no."

He emerged from the bathroom, toweling his face. He was wearing a sleeveless undershirt and the pants of a checked suit. His red suspenders hung loose on either side.

I was hoping that my employer and I had somehow slipped back into our old, unequal footing, that he'd forgotten how we'd last parted company. So I said in my old, casual way: "Having domestic trouble? The neighbors and I couldn't help overhearing."

Paddy's desk chair was wearing a fresh white shirt. He pulled it from the chair back and climbed into it, his big hands making slow work of the buttons. "What you heard was just a spirited exchange of ideas."

"And vegetables. Did Peggy bring the tomatoes to remind you of your vaudeville days?"

"No. I bought them yesterday for no particular reason. This morning I got the bright idea of using them as a peace offering. Let me tell you, they'll never take the place of roses." He stepped back over to the washroom mirror to tie his tie. It was red and yellow and blue and its pattern reminded me of the dazzle paint the British liked to use on their destroyers. When he asked the big question, he used the same breezy tone I was affecting. "Why didn't you let me know that you were coming back from New York?"

I was still standing by the desk, holding my hat. "I was afraid you'd give me another ultimatum. I didn't want to be fired over the telephone."

Being fired face-to-face didn't sound any better just then. Fortunately, Paddy wasn't in the firing mood. "I'm sorry about sending you off that way," he said without sounding especially worked up. "This Kramer business had me doing pirouettes so long I was dizzy."

He didn't seem dizzy now, or even very concerned. He put the finishing touches on a Windsor knot. Then he secured the tie to his shirt front with a stick pin. The head of the pin was decorated with a pearl too big to be real but big enough not to be insecure about it.

"You haven't asked me what I found out in New York," I said.

"Clean slipped my mind. Have a seat and tell me all about it. Tomato?"

"No, thank you." While I ran through my pointless travelogue for Paddy, he fussed with his breakfast cigar. Instead of biting the end off, he clipped it like a gentleman, using a silver cutter he kept in his desk. The cutter had a single prong designed for boring a little hole into the clipped end of the cigar, but Paddy reverted to type and used a wooden match for that step.

"So," Paddy said when I'd finished, "do you still think Mr. Mediate is a Red?"

"Or someone who played at it as a kid," I said. "He wouldn't admit it, but I think he wanted to."

"Admit it? You've spoken with Mediate on the subject?" I expected another pirouette or two, but he maintained his unnatural calm.

"Yes. I wanted to get his side of it." Paddy's sangfroid was beginning to bother me. "To jog him," I added. "And I thought he might forget himself and draw a certain thirty-eight."

"That was a brilliant plan. I'll have to add it to our training manual under the heading of advanced techniques. 'When in doubt about a murder suspect, encourage him to supply a bullet for ballistic analysis.'" He lit his waiting cigar with none of the earlier ceremony. "Did Mr. Mediate come through for you?"

"No. He still says he didn't shoot Kramer. He also denies joining the Party. He did admit that Carl Potts wrote *Love Me Again*. And that Kramer was a blackmailer. Mediate is the generous soul who paid off Kramer's gambling debts."

"So now I suppose you're sure that Mediate is Kramer's killer. I notice you're finally wearing your gun. Why didn't you use it to haul Mediate down to police headquarters?"

"You still don't think Mediate did it, do you?"

"You're asking my opinion? That's a first on this case. What a time to worry about it. You had Mediate dead to rights and you let him go. For all you know, he's heading for Tijuana right now."

"I don't think Mediate killed Kramer."

"Why? Because he didn't shoot you for asking? What about Kramer's famous dying clue, the script he didn't write?"

"I've been wrong about that before."

"You're telling me."

I didn't think I could sell Paddy on my real reason for trusting Mediate, which was that Ina Mencher believed in him. So I handed my employer a line.

"The cops think Mediate did it, and they're always wrong. When I left the Stratford Hotel I spotted Detective Grove watching the place. According to the doorman, he was keeping an eye on Mediate."

"Things are moving again, then," Paddy said. "Carl Potts has done in his own movie and our gainful employment."

"Potts? Why would he talk to the police?"

"They asked him so nicely, he couldn't refuse. I was called away from the Mocambo last night by a hot tip from a new contact I've developed downtown."

"Named?"

"I've promised to take that with me to my grave. He's a big fan of yours though, Scotty. Seen all your pictures. Or was it both your pictures? This guy told me that the police were on their way to pick up Carl Potts."

"How did they tumble onto him?"

"It was Violet Kramer, bollixing things up for us again. She'd recovered from her grief enough last night to remember a Mr. Potts who phoned the house several times over the past few weeks. Her husband wouldn't tell her about Potts or his business, which naturally made her curious. She thought Potts might have been one of the bookies Dempsey had asked her about, so she called headquarters. Dempsey had Potts hauled in for questioning. I happened by in time to witness the proceedings."

"What did Potts tell them?"

"At first just his name, rank, and his alibi for the night

244

Kramer was shot. He was meeting with some writers who figure to be subpoenaed by the House Un-American Activities Committee. A strategy session, Potts called it. He's one spunky little guy, that Potts. He thinks the whole world's against him, but he seems to like the odds. The HUAC gang are going to have their hands full if they get him to Washington. By dawn, though, the police knew all there was to know about who really wrote *Love Me Again*."

"Did Potts mention Mediate?"

"Not while I was there. When I came away, Potts's lawyer had just gotten him a break from the third degree. From what you've told me, it must have been more like a short recess. Potts must have given up the good fight and handed them Mediate."

"I wonder why he held out at all."

Paddy stood up and retrieved a robin's egg blue vest from a clothes tree that stood behind his desk. "He wanted to see his movie made is why. There may not be much hope with the writer in the hands of the police, but if they add the producer to their collection, the jig will really be up."

"Potts knows that Mediate killed Kramer?"

"Or suspects he did. That has to be why he held his name back. Potts has an alibi, but he wasn't sure about Mediate's."

I was pirouetting now myself. "There's another possibility. Potts must know that Mediate is a Communist. He might have been trying to shield Mediate to keep that from coming out. That kind of publicity could kill the movie as fast as a murder trial."

"Faster," Paddy said. "They're probably screwing that out of the little guy right now. And you're sitting there like the landed gentry."

I stood up. "What am I supposed to be doing?"

"Finding Kramer's murderer, of course. Isn't that what you've been trying to do all along, when our real job has been to save the picture?"

He pulled his desk phone over and started dialing. "Now, as

it happens, the two jobs are coinciding. Our only chance to save *Love Me Again* is to prove that the murderer is not named Vincent Mediate. That should be right up your alley. Unless you've changed your mind about him again."

My reply was drowned out by Paddy's exchange with the phone.

"Hello, Stratford Hotel? Hollywood Security calling. Connect me with Mr. Mediate's suite, please. What? Gone? Thanks."

"Arrested?" I asked.

"Not yet." Paddy grabbed his suit coat on his way to the door. "We've got to see that he's not for the rest of today at least. Get over to the studio and warn Mediate to lie low until tomorrow. I'll try to get an interview with Mr. Potts. He's no cream puff; maybe he can hold out for a day if he knows that help is on the way."

"Ask him to make it a week. I may not be able to deliver your murderer on such short notice."

Paddy paused in the office doorway. "Is that so? Well, if you're still thinking of knocking me out of the top spot around here, you'd better make an effort. Otherwise, this old man will show you how."

Paddy and I hadn't slipped back into our old relationship after all. "Are you challenging me?" I asked.

"Telling you. It's time to put up or shut up."

"I'm not interested in your job," I said.

"How do you feel about keeping your own?"

Paddy wasn't smiling, so I didn't either. It would have wasted valuable time.

38

The name Hollywood Security was still reputable enough to get me past the gatekeeper at the Warners lot. Me, but not my gun. The old geezer at the gate spotted it and politely offered to hold it for me. I handed it over happily enough, stiff holster and all.

Vincent Mediate's private secretary was less polite than the guard had been. She was a gray-haired lady who looked me up and down as though I'd said "Pest Control" after "Hollywood." I decided that Carole Mediate had had a hand in her hiring.

"Mr. Mediate is out on the lot," she finally told me.

"Any idea where?" I asked as pleasantly as I could. Having a black eye made batting my lashes a waste of time. I had the feeling it would have been in any case.

"Soundstage seven," she said to be rid of me.

Her phone rang before I'd gotten through the office door. On the off chance it was Mediate reporting in, I dallied. The secretary looked unhappy. Then she looked unhappier. "Soundstage seven," she said into the phone. When she looked up at me, she'd forgotten who I was.

Before leaving the Administration Building, I asked a friendlier face where I could find the Publicity Department. It turned out to be on my way, more or less.

Miss Englehart was at her desk in an office she shared with a half-dozen aspiring novelists. The sound of her typewriter covered my approach. She was wearing a high-waisted skirt topped by a wide leather belt and a billowing blouse.

Pidgin looked up at me, smiled, and pounded her carriage return, all at the same time. "Ever hear of hell breaking loose?" she asked.

"I think I've seen it happen."

"Well, you're seeing it again, Hollywood style. We just received a call from a certain lady columnist. She wanted to know if Vincent Mediate wished to deny a rumor that he's involved in a certain screenwriter's murder."

Paddy's secret source was working both sides of the street.

"You don't look surprised," Pidgin said.

"What did Mediate tell her?"

"Nothing yet. He was locked in a soundstage watching a production number when the call came in."

"What's the studio's line? Will they stand by him?"

Pidgin cast a guilty glance toward the sheet she'd been typing. "He's going to be given what we in the Publicity Department have come to call the Bert Kramer treatment. That was in the works before the columnist called."

"Why?"

"I'm not sure. But there's no stopping it now."

"Do Warner and Beaumont think they can still save the picture?"

"They're still acting like they can. The new writer, Flo Hanks, has been making a pile of changes."

"Like what?"

"For starters, Franz Wojcik isn't a Nazi spy anymore."

"What is he now, a Shriner?"

"No, a Communist. It's pretty clever the way Flo worked this out. In the new version, the Germans slip Wojcik into America the same way they shipped Lenin to Russia in the First World War. And for the same reason: to destabilize their enemy. Wojcik knows nothing of this. He thinks he really has been escaping by the skin of his teeth all the way across Europe. In reality, the Germans have been looking the other way. The fix was in, as your boss would say."

"That change will mean reshooting."

"The scene between Tory and Fritz Taber in the cabaret dressing room, you mean? They're reshooting it tonight, if Flo can get the dialogue hammered out."

"Why the rush?"

"The dressing room set is scheduled to be taken down

tomorrow."

"Anything else different?"

"Instead of Steven Laird shooting Wojcik at the end of the picture, they're going to have Maura do it. I'm not sure why. Ella Larsen might have asked for the change. As the script's written, she's the only member of the triangle without a big moment."

"Member of the what?"

"The triangle." She drew one for me in the air. "You know, two men after one woman."

Dawn was breaking for the second time that day, and its rosy fingers were poking my sore head. "You said that Paddy was pumping you for social news last night."

"Right."

"Did he ask you about Bert Kramer?"

"Among others."

"What did you tell him?"

"The same thing I told you the night we met, that Bert thought he was a ladies' man. But it was strictly in his own imagination as far as I'd ever heard. To get anywhere with a woman, Bert would have to have had held a gun to her head."

"Exactly," I said and kissed her.

The red warning light was off at soundstage seven, and the door was open. The usual studio guard was standing at his usual post near the door, but he'd acquired a shadow in the form of a uniformed policeman. My Hollywood operative instincts told me that it would be one bad time for me to ask for Vincent Mediate. So I told the guard I had a message for Fred Wilner.

"Inside," the guard said.

The policeman took a professional interest in my bruises. "What happened to you, bub?"

"Jealous husband."

The inside of the stage was unnaturally quiet, and it wasn't because it was empty. The cabaret set was stocked with extras in Parisian evening attire. They'd been shooting the Clausen

Brothers' first dance number, or perhaps the scene in which Steve insults the French countess. Torrance Beaumont was on hand and in costume. He and Max Froy were sharing center stage with another familiar figure, Sergeant Dempsey. Under the klieg lights, the fan-shaped scar on the policeman's face shone like cellophane. The three were speaking earnestly in low tones, which accounted for the unnatural stillness of the set. It was the concentrated quiet of a score of extras and a full crew straining to eavesdrop.

Fred Wilner was standing some way off from Dempsey and his supporting players. Judging by Wilner's hangdog expression, he'd already had his chat with the sergeant.

I took off my hat and suit coat and hung them on a nail near the soundstage door. Then I looked around for a prop and found two beauties: somebody's clipboard—fat with paper—and a pencil.

Some technicians were trying to lay a cable soundlessly just outside of the light of the main set. I circled around behind them, my papers under one arm and my pencil behind my ear. I edged around until I was standing where Wilner would be looking if he decided to raise his eyes off the floor.

Finally, he glanced up. For a while, he did nothing more than see me. Then he slowly began to wonder who I was. After an age had passed, he recognized me. He looked at Dempsey quickly and then back to me. I held out my clipboard and pencil to him.

Wilner was game enough to try it. He walked past Dempsey and Beaumont and Froy, not quite sauntering but not tripping over his own feet, either. I waited for Dempsey to ask him where he thought he was going, but Beaumont had the sergeant's full attention.

When Wilner reached me, I handed him my prop clipboard and he stared woodenly at its top sheet. Out of the side of his mouth, he whispered, "I didn't know you in that disguise. How'd you think of the shiner?"

"It just came to me. What have they done with Mediate?"

"Nothing yet. They haven't been able to find him. That's what all the fuss is about."

"Wasn't he here watching the shooting?"

"Right, he was. We heard a commotion outside during the run through. It was the cops trying to get in and our security guard not letting them. Then the stage door opened and Dempsey marched in, demanding to see the boss. Only Vince was gone. His chair was sitting there warm and empty. Somehow, when the lights were down, he managed to sneak out."

"How?"

"Who knows? That's what I've been trying to tell the sergeant. This stage is a barn, not a bank vault. There are any number of ways in and out for someone who knows the layout. Dempsey thought we were hiding Vince in some secret compartment somewhere. If he hadn't gotten word that Vince's car had left the lot, he'd be taking this place apart right now, stick by stick."

Wilner had relaxed enough to page through the sheets on the clipboard, initialing them randomly. "Now I know how Vince survived Omaha Beach. It's hard to hit a man with that turn of speed. What's happened anyway? Dempsey won't say."

I took back the clipboard. "Don't you recognize it? All hell's breaking loose."

Wilner forced a smile. "I remember hell being a lot noisier."

39

I managed to get out of the soundstage the way I'd gotten in. The security guard and the policeman at the stage door had struck up an acquaintance while I'd been inside. They were discussing Jersey Joe Walcott's chances in an upcoming bout. I didn't offer an opinion.

The front-gate guard had also acquired a policeman to chat with. The guard handed me my gun, then peeked into my glove compartment as I tucked the forty-five away. He had rheumy eyes and false teeth that looked like they'd been made for someone bigger, Johnny Weissmuller maybe. Or perhaps the guard had been a bigger man when he'd bought them. I asked him if he wanted to check the LaSalle's trunk for producers.

"If we're talking about the same producer," the old man said, "he drove himself out of the back-lot construction gate. He's halfway to Mexico by now."

A studio grapevine was a remarkable communication system. It could spread the news that you were an up-and-comer, a star on the rise. The pipeline was even better at getting out the word that your career had developed leprosy. In a pinch, it could even handle police bulletins.

I drove to West Hollywood and the Kramer bungalow. The little house on the unwatered lot looked deserted, but that's the way it had looked on my first visit, when I'd found Bert Kramer at home, alive and full of himself. Today, I was looking for his widow. I was hoping she'd tired of her mother's company or Pasadena and come home to do her mourning.

The tecoma bushes around the front of the house weren't wilting away over the death of their owner. They still made the porch a quiet and cool place to contemplate life. Not that I had time for contemplation. I rang the bell and listened for Violet's trademark shuffle. It was a long while coming.

Widowhood hadn't done a thing for Violet. She still had the look of a lapdog going down for the third time. From the whiff I got when she opened the front door, she was doing her drowning in bourbon. Her big brown eyes had a soft focus and her pinched features were as rosy as they'd probably ever been. They looked especially flushed against her washed-out housedress. It was the same one she'd had on when I'd first stopped by.

Violet was thinking of that visit, too. "You here to drop off more bad luck?"

"I hope not. I just wanted to ask you a few questions, if you have the time."

"I'll make the time."

She led me into the rose garden parlor. It was unchanged, except for the addition of a cardboard packing case. The case was open, and some of its contents—framed photographs, books, loose papers—were spread around on the carpet. They were the remains of Kramer's Warner Bros. office, packed up and delivered to his widow on the orders of the solicitous Vincent Mediate.

Violet sat down in her late husband's chair, using up considerably less of it than he had. On the smoking table at her elbow was a tall brown drink that might have been waiting there for Bert. Violet demonstrated that it wasn't by picking up the glass and drinking from it.

"Care to join me?" she asked. "I don't like to drink alone."

"No, thank you," I said.

"That's right," she growled in her Alice Faye baritone. "You're a gentleman. Too early in the day for you. The sun's not over the yardarm on your yacht."

"Something like that."

"Well, no offense, buddy, but my experience has been that gentlemen are losers. Their fancy facade is a front for nothing in particular."

"Is that why you married Bert?"

"Maybe. Bert was no gentleman. He didn't even pretend to be one, which is only slightly less bad than actually being one." She wiped away a single, large tear with the back of her hand.

The tear surprised me. "I'm sorry to be bothering you like this," I said. "I didn't think …"

"That I'd be upset over a little thing like my husband being murdered? Shows what they're teaching in finishing schools these days."

"At the police station you said that your marriage had been

through for some time."

"Did I? You ever been married?"

"No," I said.

"Well, a bad marriage is still a marriage. If a woman can't cry over a dead husband, she should cry over the years she wasted on him."

Her deep voice had been made husky, either by her crying or her drinking. She was laying as much as sitting in the chair, her legs stretched out before her. They weren't long, willowy legs, but they got the job done. As I watched, she reached down to rearrange her dress. When she'd finished, it wasn't doing a noticeably better job of covering her up.

"Too hot for hose and underthings, don't you think?" she said.

I agreed politely, as I'd been taught to do in finishing school.

"What were we discussing?" Violet asked.

"Your marriage and what killed it. In your statement you said there were money troubles."

"Right. Money troubles. But those might have been going away."

"How so?" I asked.

"This new movie, *Love Me Again*. It's supposed to be good."

"It is." Or was, before Florence Hanks got hold of it.

"It might have made the difference for us, a big hit. We could have moved out of this little dump. Maybe to a place up in the hills. We could have gotten our lives back on track maybe."

"Maybe," I said. "If there weren't other troubles."

Violet's no longer hazy eyes drew a dead bead on me. "Like what?"

"We gentlemen call it infidelity."

"Now what are you after?"

"The real reason your husband was shot. From what I hear, he thought he was a ladies' man. Do you know if he ever tried to prove it?"

"Was Bert stepping out on me, you mean?" She took a

254

substantial drink. "God, it takes a long time for you delicate types to say anything."

"Was there another woman?"

"I'm not sure. I had my suspicions."

"Why?"

The question brought out Violet's own delicacy. "Bert wasn't as interested in me lately as he had been."

"How lately?"

"The last month or so. And he was gone a lot and secretive. But there was nothing you could take to a judge. A little face powder on his lapel maybe. And a blond hair here and there."

"Always blond?"

"Bert's fantasies tended that way. Because I'm a brunette, I guess. The grass is always greener on the other side of the fence. Blonder, I should say."

She stood up and crossed to the cardboard box containing the remains of Kramer's office. "Bert loved to have his picture taken with a star. Nine times out of ten, it was a female star who happened to be hitting the peroxide."

She started holding photographs up for me to see. "Here you go. Bert and Betty Grable. Bert and Ann Sheridan. Bert and Lizabeth Scott."

Violet came to a photo that didn't fit the point she was trying to make. She was setting it aside when it came apart in her hands. The glass fell into the box without breaking, and the frame ended up around Violet's wrist. The picture and its cardboard backing fluttered off in different directions.

I picked up the photograph, recognizing it immediately from my last visit to the Writers Building. Kramer's companion in the shot was neither a star nor a blond. It was Vincent Mediate, looking damned uncomfortable while a jovial Kramer waved his fat palm at the camera.

Violet was examining her wooden bracelet. "Somebody bent back the staples on this," she said. "Why would anyone do a screwy thing like that?"

I almost spoke my answer, "to take the picture apart," aloud. I was stopped at the last second by a corollary to that proposition: someone had been searching for something hidden behind the photograph. I retrieved the cardboard backing and looked it over. It was unmarked, front and back.

"It doesn't matter," Violet said. "Throw the whole thing away. There's another one just like it in Bert's study."

I held the photo up to her. "Another of this pose?"

"Sure. I should know. I'm the one who dusts around here. When I feel like it, that is. Today I feel like drinking."

"I feel like a drink myself all of a sudden, if the offer's still good."

"Now you're talking."

She collected her glass and started the long trek to the kitchen. I went in the opposite direction, into the murder room. There I found the duplicate photograph of Kramer and Mediate. It was hidden in a way Edgar Allan Poe would have liked, on a wall of other photographs, a tree hidden in a forest.

Like the picture from Kramer's office, the backing of the study photo was cardboard, secured by a couple of staples pressed sideways into the wood of the frame. I bent these back and lifted the cardboard out. Between it and the blank back side of the photograph was a folded square of paper, a filler, there to hold the glass, the picture, and the backing tightly in the frame. I was hoping the paper was something more than that.

And it was. Unfolded, the filler turned out to be a photostat, a white on gray copy like a photographic negative. The top of the sheet held an engraving of an eagle above crossed flags, American and German. Below the flags, the words German-American Bund were printed in a strange Gothic lettering. The remainder of the white information on the gray sheet was typed. It was a membership application, submitted in York, Pennsylvania, in October 1938. The applicant's name was Vincent Mediate. His sponsor's name was Herman Miller. Their signatures were side by side at the bottom of the sheet.

I sat down hard on the edge of Kramer's desk, my mind miles away. Three-thousand miles away to be exact, in New York City, in the RCA Building, in the studio where James Zucco had wasted my time with his story of the Bund. Only he hadn't been rambling. He'd been telling me in his subtle, cautious way that Mediate had been as far from a Red as you could get. He'd been a fascist, a Nazi.

The clues all came back to me now, faster than I could file them. Zucco had been surprised that Ina Mencher had protected Mediate. Why? Because she was Jewish. She was the last person who should have shielded a Nazi. Except that this Nazi had made *Death Camp*. She'd told me that Mediate had paid for his past sins with that film. I'd heard Communism when she'd said sins, but Mencher knew better. She knew because Winslow, the stage manager, had told her and Zucco the truth. Their play's backer, Miller, had been a sponsor of the Bund. Zucco had told me of Miller's "eccentric hobbies." Zucco had told me everything and nothing. If I was Mediate's spy, as he'd feared, I knew the secret already. If I wasn't a spy and couldn't make sense of his hints, too bad for me. He'd stick his neck out so far and no farther.

I pictured the Bund rally again as Zucco had drawn it for me. This time, Vincent Mediate was front and center, light from the burning globes that flanked the stage reflecting in the brightwork of his fascist uniform. As I watched, the imaginary Mediate held out his arm in a Nazi salute while the place rocked with choruses of "Sieg Heil!"

Something about the salute prodded another memory, pointing me to another clue I'd overlooked. The clue was literally in my lap, the photograph of Kramer and Mediate. In it, the writer stood with one arm around Mediate's shoulder. With the other, he waved at the camera. But he wasn't waving. The upturned palm was the tip-off. Kramer was doing a parody of the Nazi salute. Maybe he'd sent a copy of the photo to Mediate to let him know he was in on the secret. Maybe Kramer had hung the original in his office to taunt Mediate whenever the producer visited. It hadn't been an inside joke, a secret reminder to Kramer of his own cleverness. When Mediate had come after the blackmail evidence, he'd known right where to look for it. That evidence was now ashes in some grate, lost forever but for Bert Kramer's thoughtfulness. He'd made a second copy for himself. For me.

Violet's footsteps were finally returning, shuffling in time with the ticking of the Kramer clock. I slipped the photostat into my pocket and reassembled the frame. I had it back on the wall when Violet entered the study, carrying our drinks.

Sentimental as she had become over her dead husband, Violet still hadn't complied with his request for ice cubes. Or else the cubes she'd made for him were now too sacred to part with. The glass she handed me contained bourbon, neat.

"Happy days," she said. "Not that I'm expecting to ever see any. First the Depression. Then the war. What's going to hit us next, I wonder?"

Television, according to Zucco. He'd certainly made it sound like an approaching plague. Thinking of him reminded me of a loose end Violet might tie up. Namely, who had tipped Kramer to Mediate's Bund membership in the first place?

"Did your husband know a man back east named James Zucco?"

"Not that I ever heard. And Bert didn't have so many friends that I'd forget one."

Two long shots coming in back to back were more than I could hope for. Violet's expectations were even lower.

"What's going to happen to me now?" she asked the photographs on the wall. "What's going to happen to all of us?"

I took my cue from the frozen smiles on the black and white faces. "We all live happily ever after," I said.

Violet laughed. "You must be a veteran. You all sound alike. You can't have given up years of your life for nothing, can you? The world's just got to be a better place now, doesn't it?"

She patted my arm. "Drink up, soldier. It'll help your dreaming."

40

I'd gotten more in West Hollywood than I'd been after. I'd gone there looking for an insight into Bert Kramer's love life, inspired by Pidgin's remark that *Love Me Again* had a love triangle at its center. That insight had revived my old weakness, the idea that script held a clue to the murder. I'd decided that, by grabbing the script as he died, Kramer had been pointing to a love triangle in which he'd held a place of honor. Based on what Violet had told me, I'd decided that the other members were a blond and the blond's husband. Carole and Vincent Mediate.

That was before I'd discovered that Mediate was a secret Nazi, just like a certain Franz Wojcik. I now had a tie-in to the script that was tighter than any reference to lovers or the mob or trade unions. It was tight enough to hang someone, in fact. Luckily, my two new leads, the one I'd found in West Hollywood and the one that had found me, both pointed me toward the same destination: the Stratford Hotel. I got there in a hurry.

The Stratford desk clerk and I were becoming old pals. So much so, in fact, that he knew what I wanted before I asked for it.

"Mrs. Mediate is not in," he said when I drew close enough to hear his carefully modulated voice.

"Did she leave a forwarding address?"

"She didn't leave a message for you, sir. Sorry."

His tone was just shy of polite. "You seem to have the wrong idea," I said. "Mrs. Mediate and I are just old friends."

"Of course," the clerk said, adding another "sir" after a

minute or two had passed.

I didn't like the insinuation, but I thought I might put it to use. "Did Mrs. Mediate have any other old friends dropping by?"

"I'm sure I wouldn't know." No "sir" now.

I started to reach for my wallet, but thought better of it. I'd begun to identify with the clerk, whom I'd cast as another veteran down on his luck. I decided he'd toss a discreetly folded bill back in my teeth. "Where'd you do your time?" I asked instead.

"The North Atlantic. Destroyer."

"I made the crossing myself," I said.

"On some luxury liner they called a troop ship, right?"

"Right. Other than being packed in so tight we had to sleep in shifts, it was pretty swank."

"If your feet stayed dry, you've got no complaints, Army. What are you after?"

"Information about any regular visitors Mrs. Mediate had. I'm not working a divorce case, if that's what you're worried about."

"I know you're not. The cops have been sniffing around here all morning, and they don't do divorces."

"So how about it?"

The clerk looked around without actually moving his well-trimmed head. "There's a guy who's been coming by, but it has to be some kind of legitimate business."

"Why?"

"Mrs. Mediate is an attractive woman. This guy isn't much taller than he is wide. A sweaty kind of citizen, with weasily little eyes. He'd never get to first base with her."

"You can never tell about that," I said. "Some guys are awfully persuasive. Thanks, Navy."

"Thanks again, you mean," he said.

The Stratford's front steps seemed unusually empty, which is to say that the Ruritanian doorman had found somewhere else to be. The moment reminded me of my departure from the

Mocambo the night before and of the ambush I'd walked into. I made that connection too late to do me any good. Before I'd had another useful thought, I felt a familiar grip clamp down on my left biceps. Then I was looking into the close-set eyes of Detective Grove.

"Everything comes to a guy who waits," he said.

"The Mediates are long gone."

"I know that, hotshot. I've been hoping to see you again." The effort of wrinkling my suit was wearing him out. His bad complexion oozed sweat. "What's the idea of playing hide-and-seek with me this morning?"

I tried to shake Grove off my arm. Shaking my arm off my shoulder would have been easier.

"Don't even try resisting arrest, Elliott, or I'll finish the redesign some lucky guy started on your face."

"What's the charge?"

"Interfering with me. I told you not to follow me around. But everywhere I go, I get the feeling someone's been there first, monkeying things up for me."

"Who's following whom?"

Grove drew me close enough to count the pores on his nose. "Cut the wisecracks and tell me why you tipped Mediate that we were about to pick him up."

"I didn't."

"What were you two talking about at dawn, then?"

"It was a private conversation."

Grove almost laughed. "Let's take a drive downtown. I'd like to hear you tell that to Sergeant Dempsey. He's been in such a swell mood since Mediate skipped out on him."

"Fine. Let's go see Dempsey. I'd like to tell him that somebody on his squad has been selling tips to Paddy Maguire and Hedda Hopper. Or was it Louella Parsons?"

It was my day for picking long shots. Grove's face paled a little beneath the sheen of sweat. "I don't know what you're talking about."

"Maguire doesn't keep any secrets from me," I said.

"To hell with Maguire. He doesn't own me."

"The hell he doesn't. He's just paying for you on the installment plan. Now let go of my arm."

Grove complied, reluctantly. I could see the wheels spinning away behind his black eyes, trying to work out a way he could tear into me and still collect his pension. After a while, the works ground to a halt. "Get out of my sight," he said.

"First you're going to answer some questions for me."

It may have been the moment when Grove realized how much he'd sold to Paddy Maguire. He looked that sick. He pointed to a quiet spot behind one of the Stratford's Grecian columns. "Let's get some privacy."

When we were tucked away and comfortable, Grove said, "What questions?"

To test my source, I started with one whose answer I already knew. "Why is Dempsey after Mediate?"

"That Commie, Carl Potts, worked out a deal with Phillips, the assistant district attorney. Or Potts's lawyer did. He's off the hook as an accessory in the Kramer murder. In exchange for that, he gave Phillips Mediate's name and his motive for shooting Kramer."

"Which was what?"

"Kramer was blackmailing Mediate. So Mediate gave him the big send-off."

"What was the blackmail about?"

"Potts didn't know."

"Did Potts witness the shooting?"

"No."

"Did Mediate tell Potts he did it?"

"No. It's what Potts figures must have happened, which made him very nervous about his little red ass."

"What about Mediate's alibi?"

"What alibi? We can't find a gas station attendant, a highway patrolman, or a neighbor who saw the Mediates driving to, arriving at, or coming from Hobart Lake. Dempsey figures that Mediate is lying and Mrs. Mediate is backing him up.

"The clincher is, when we came for him, he ran. He and his bombshell wife are heading south right now."

"Says who?"

Grove checked for eavesdroppers again. "Mediate kept a thirty-foot cabin cruiser down at Marina Del Rey. It cleared the harbor less than an hour after Dempsey kicked in the stage door at Warners. The boat was last seen heading for Mexican waters, which it'll never make. Not if the Coast Guard has anything to say about it."

"Thanks, detective. You've been a lot of help."

Grove made another pass at my arm, but didn't actually grab it. "Wait a minute. You're forgetting something. I don't give dope away."

"Bill our office."

I should have checked in with Paddy after leaving Grove, but that would have just been aiding the competition. Contrary to what I'd told the plainclothesman, Paddy was keeping secrets from me. Specifically, he hadn't told me why he was still backing Mediate.

I wondered if Paddy had succeeded where the police had failed and somehow verified Mediate's alibi. If Paddy had done it, I could, too. That suggested a drive north to Hobart Lake. I had another reason for heading that way. Everyone and his brother knew that Vincent Mediate was heading south. I no longer trusted Vincent Mediate.

North was the direction to drive if you wanted to leave Los Angeles in a hurry. The city's never-ending sprawl was sprawling more slowly to the north, held back by the mountains in front of me, the San Gabriels. Before too long, I'd driven out from under the worst of the haze. The unfiltered sunlight should have been more intense, but it didn't feel that way. The air coming in through the open windows was almost cool and it was scented every now and then by an orange grove the developers had yet to find.

I stopped at a diner and a couple of gas stations, looking for witnesses to the Mediates' late night drive. All I found was lunch and a fresh pack of Luckies.

The ground was already rising to meet the foothills when I passed a little farm cradled in a bend in the highway. The farmhouse, which looked to be ninety percent front porch, sat on a hill that commanded a view of the road. Down by the roadside was a produce stand shielded by a canopy of war surplus green canvas. Today's special was tomatoes, vine ripened.

I drove on for half a mile or so until I came to a spot where the shoulder of the road was wide and sandy. I turned the LaSalle around and drove back down the hill to the little farm in the crook of the highway. The parking lot next to the produce stand was just big enough to hold a single prewar coupé.

The stand was staffed by a woman who looked only slightly younger than the hills behind her. She had a moon-shaped face and silver hair that was brushed straight back and gathered in a bun. Her eyes were trapped between folds of wrinkled lid and a pair of puffy bags, which didn't leave them much working space. They got even less daylight when she smiled at me.

"Some tomatoes today?"

"Please." I picked out a carton at random and paid her for them. From the carton's paper label, a cartoon sun smiled at me. I smiled back. While the old lady counted out my change from a shoe box, I said, "A friend of mine recommended your tomatoes. He bought some yesterday. You probably remember him: a big man who's always smoking a cigar. He dresses, well, enthusiastically."

"Like a cross between a judge and a ringmaster," the old woman said, her laugh lines threatening to swallow her eyes completely. "I remember him. He was here yesterday morning."

"Did he ask any questions?"

"He asked me how late my stand was open. He made a joke about it being an all-night tomato stand. I said it wasn't. I usually close up around four o'clock.

"Then he asked me about my front porch, whether I ever sat out on an evening. I said, yes, I did. Especially in this hot weather. It's been too hot to sleep, and there hasn't been a ghost of a breeze."

"Did he ask if you'd been sitting out three nights ago?"

"Yes, and if I'd seen a certain big car go by. He showed me a picture of one like it. A Lincoln, he said it was. I did see a car go by that night. I'm pretty certain that it was the car he was asking about. I've seen it before in the daylight, so I know it. And it was moon bright two nights ago."

"What time did it pass by?"

"Your friend asked that, too. I said I thought it was eleven thirty, The 'Hour of Redemption' show was just signing off. I remember thinking that it was awfully late for someone to be driving back into those hills."

Mediate had called for his car a little after eleven. He couldn't have driven to West Hollywood, shot Kramer, and made it this far into the sticks in less than half an hour. That would have meant being in two places at once. Impossible for one person, but not for two.

"Could you see if there were two people in the car?"

"No, it wasn't that bright. Most times there are two people, though. A man and a woman. Today when the car went by, they were both inside."

"You saw the Lincoln today?"

"Yes, a couple of hours ago. Going that way." She pointed toward the foothills. "It hasn't come back yet."

I stayed with her long enough to satisfy my curiosity on a final point. "Have any policemen been asking about that car?"

"Yes, the day before yesterday." The memory sobered her so much that her eyes actually reappeared. "I didn't give them the time of day."

"Why not?"

"They didn't buy any tomatoes."

41

I hadn't driven very far into the foothills before I found Hobart Lake. It was man-made, as the large lakes surrounding Los Angeles tended to be. The road I followed crossed an earthen dam from which I could see several houses, set well apart from one another among the pines. Identifying the Mediates' castle was no challenge. A bronze shield bearing an elaborate M was set in a stone gatepost at the end of their drive.

The drive descended from the road on which the LaSalle and I sat to the house, winding a little bit on the way down. The house was big and modern, a collection of flat-roofed cubes arranged artfully against the slope of the hill. It was built of stone and cedar with a minimum of windows, at least on the front of the house. I wondered if they'd saved their glass ration for the side with the lake view. I couldn't spot the Lincoln from the road, but I could see plenty of places to hide one.

I drove on a little way past the stone gate and parked on a shoulder that was carpeted with brown pine needles. I got the automatic out of the glove compartment, but I didn't bother with its holster. I slipped the gun into the pocket of my jacket as I left the car. The weight of it felt like a hand reaching up out of the pine needle carpet to pull me under.

I stepped into the trees and started down the hill, making so little noise on the soft blanket of needles that the birds in the branches above me never stopped their singing. My line of march was parallel to but straighter than the winding drive. When I reached the level of the house, I stopped.

A big carport stretched out from the side of the house closest to me, looking like a three-car garage open at both ends. Through it, behind a screen of trees, I saw the Lincoln. Beyond the car was the lake, the water dazzling in the afternoon sun. A motorboat passed by while I watched. The noise of its engine came up to me like music from the stage of an amphitheater. Monotonous and ominous music. When it died away, I stood for a time, listening for sounds from the house and hearing none.

I left the trees, moving to the corner of the house and then through the carport toward the back of the lot. I found the builder's scrap pile there: discarded stone and lumber, torn cement bags, and empty drums of roofing tar. Mediate had told Dempsey that the house was still under construction. It might have been his only truthful statement. The stonework on the back of the house was incomplete. In some places, the bare framework was visible, and most of the window openings held plywood instead of glass. I followed a gravel path to a back entrance. There was a door in place, but it had no hardware. I opened it, using the hole cut for the lock as a pull, and stepped inside.

I found myself in a skeleton room of unplastered walls that were open to the house beyond. I stepped through a door—or at least a gap in the wall—and into a long passageway. The first room I came to had been plastered and even furnished, in a manner of speaking. A large, canopied bed stood against one white wall. The bed was made up formally, in white satin bedding, as though awaiting the arrival of Cinderella and Prince Charming.

I continued down the hall, past other half-finished rooms, until I came to a large open space. It was a combination entryway and living room, with a stone fireplace, heavy ceiling beams, and passages going off in all directions.

While I was standing there enjoying the sensation of cold sweat trickling down my back, I heard the sound of something being dropped. It was followed by a man's muffled cursing. Vincent Mediate's.

The sound had come from the lake side of the house. I started down a likely branch of the hallway system. It took me to a large room that had a wall missing. In its place was a spectacular view of the lake, complete with the smells and sounds of the pine forest and even a breeze. Plywood sheets were strewn around the room. I guessed that, until recently, they'd been covering up the opening in the wall, which had to be the future home of a mammoth picture window.

The man who had done the impromptu redecorating was seated before the opening, his back to me. His chair was a folding model borrowed from someone's card table. Beside him on the floor was a fifth of scotch, two-thirds full. A wet spot on the floorboards showed where some had recently been spilled, a remnant of the accident that had guided me to the room.

I took out my gun and used it to knock on the side of the doorway in which I stood. "Mind if I come in?"

Mediate almost fell down getting out of his chair. He definitely spilled the contents of his glass. He held the empty tumbler like a baseball and eyed me the way a pitcher eyes home plate.

I raised the automatic just enough to get his attention. "Put the glass down and step away from the scenery," I said.

Mediate set the tumbler down on his chair and took a few unsteady steps toward me. He was dressed for the heat, in a silk shirt and white flannel trousers. The knees of the trousers were soiled, perhaps as a result of his escape from the Warners soundstage. Or maybe he'd dirtied them chasing his glass across the floor before I'd made my entrance. His wavy hair was standing up in places like the feathers of an angry bird. It was a style that went well with the fury that twisted his face.

"So you sold me out," he said. "Was it your own idea, or did Maguire cook it up to save his crooked business?"

"Neither. The seller was your buddy Potts. The cops picked him up last night. He's been doing a one-man hit parade ever since."

"Carl wouldn't do that to me."

"He would to save his skin. He figures you for Kramer's killer. He doesn't want the seat next to yours in the gas chamber."

Mediate gave me an insight into how his hair had gotten so ruffled, shaking his head until the black waves crested even higher. "That fool."

"He's in good company. Dempsey's of the same mind."

"For the last time, I did not kill Bert Kramer."

"Then why did you run? And why did you call your hired captain and tell him to take your yacht south?"

"To give me time to think, to work out a plan. Beaumont's trying to get me kicked off the picture. *My* picture. I've got to figure out a way to stop him."

Only in Hollywood. Mediate was wanted for murder, and all he could think about was his next career move. "How did you get off the soundstage?"

He shook his head again, this time with impatience. "We all heard the ruckus outside. I knew what was going to happen, or thought I did. I blamed you for it. Sorry. In the darkness and confusion, it was easy to slip out the back as Dempsey came in the front. I got into my car and drove off the lot. Nobody tried to stop me.

"I called the marina from a pay phone. I told them to take the boat to Mexico."

"How did it happen to be ready on such short notice?"

Mediate briefly tried looking me in the eye. It was a sign of how much his persona had crumbled that he couldn't quite do it. "I've had the boat ready since things started to fall apart. Since Kramer was shot, I mean."

"Who else did you call?"

"Carole. I had her meet me on the outskirts of town."

"Where is she now?"

He gestured toward the missing wall behind him. "Down by

the lake."

"Fishing?"

"Crying, last time I saw her. Did you talk to Maguire?"

"Yes."

"What did he say?"

"He wanted you to lie low until we could figure things out. I was on my way over to warn you this morning, but Dempsey moved faster."

"Then you believe I'm not a Communist."

"Do I ever."

I shifted the gun to my left hand and searched my pockets with my right until I found the folded square of paper I'd stolen from Violet Kramer. I shook it open and held it up for Mediate to see. "Recognize this?"

He did. For a moment, I thought he was going to dirty the knees of his trousers again. He steadied himself with an effort. "How could you have that?"

"Kramer was a belt-and-suspenders kind of blackmailer. He kept a spare copy tucked away in his house. If you'd taken a moment to look around after you shot him, you would have spotted it."

Mediate took a step my way but stopped when I raised the gun to the level of his chest.

"You played me for a sucker, Mediate, finessed me with your denials about being a Red, denials you undercut with speeches about youthful mistakes. You had me convinced that your youthful mistake was Communism. Instead, it was fascism. How did Kramer find out about your past?"

Mediate shrugged. "I don't know. What difference does it make? He found out."

"So he started squeezing you for money and just plain squeezing your wife. Was she part of the price Kramer shook out of you? Or did he work that little deal out on the side?"

For a moment, I thought I might have to use the gun. Mediate was looking at me with that kind of irrational hatred. Then his

270

reason got hold of him again, one slow inch at a time.

"What I told you this morning was the truth," he said, his voice a slow, painful rasp. "Except for the part about how I got to New York, I told you the truth."

"Let's see if I've got this straight. Everything you didn't lie about was true."

"Would you admit to *that*?" He started to point to the paper I held and ended up using the hand to cover his face. "I told you how my father went bankrupt. That was true. I told you how Miller befriended me. That was true. Only it happened earlier than I said. And the first job he got me wasn't on any Broadway show. It was with the German-American Bund."

"You left out the part where he twisted your arm."

"He didn't have to. I was so full of hate by then I was the perfect recruit. I hated the whole world for what had happened to my father. Or maybe just over what had happened to me."

"What had happened to you?"

"I'd lost my future. My birthright. I'd had it all laid out ahead of me. A decent place in the world. A better than decent place, an important one. It didn't matter that it was in a small town. That town was the only world I knew. And I was one of its anointed. Then overnight it was all gone. I was cheated out of it all. After that, I was ready to hate anybody—Jews, Democrats, Republicans—anyone I thought I could blame for what had happened to me. I did hate them.

"I was a Nazi before I joined the Bund." He pounded his chest. "In here, I was a Nazi."

"So you got to New York because of the big Bund rally at Madison Square Garden."

"Yes. I would have gone anywhere to get away from the town where I'd lost my birthright. New York was the perfect place to start over, so I jumped at the chance to work at the rally. I was just a dress extra, but I didn't care. I felt like I was on my way back. I was on my way to hell.

"I still have nightmares about that rally. About that hall, a huge black space filled with the noise of people screaming and shouting and cheering. About that con artist Fritz Kuhn, trying to clean himself with the American flag. All the while, he was fouling it and the rest of us with the same kind of filth Hitler was spewing. The whole place was swaying with a hatred that was churning against itself like the ocean at a breakwater. I could feel it surging back and forth, some of the audience hating the people Kuhn was telling them to hate and the rest of them hating us. The undertow almost dragged me off my feet.

"At one point, someone rushed out of the audience and charged the stage, trying to shout Kuhn down. Kuhn's elite guard grabbed the guy. If the New York cops hadn't stepped in, they would have beaten him to death. I knew that for certain. And I was wearing the same uniform."

Mediate looked around the empty room. "I'm getting a drink. If you want to shoot me, fine."

He turned away from me and went after his bottle. I used the time to fold up his enlistment paper and tuck it back in my pocket.

Mediate had the bottle to his lips before he turned to face me. When he came up for air, I said, "Go on with your story."

"I've already told you everything else. Everything after the rally happened just like I told you this morning. Only it was worse than I said. Worse than I can say. I was ashamed of myself after I got to know Ina. She was so nice to me. Every moment I was with her, I hated myself for having anything to do with thugs who wanted to wipe their shoes on her kind of people.

"I told you I was sick inside at Buchenwald. It was worse than a sickness. I died that day."

"You didn't serve at Buchenwald. You were part of the army that shut it down."

Mediate cut his latest drink short without tilting the bottle up. Scotch spilled onto his silken shirt. "That's just the way the cards fell. They could have fallen differently. I could have been one of those butchers." He tapped his wet shirt with the bottle.

"I was one, once.

"Now you know why I want to make *Love Me Again*. Why I have to make it. It's a story that's important to me."

That leap set visions of anonymous notes and dying clues dancing in my head again. "Why is the story so important? Wojcik's not an innocent man. He's not vindicated in the end; he's shot. Is that why you're sitting around here drinking when you should be running? Are you waiting for someone to put you out of your misery? To kill whatever part of you didn't die at Buchenwald?"

Mediate looked down at the gun in my hand. I lowered it. "Anyway," I said, "Wojcik's not a Nazi anymore."

"What are you talking about?"

"They've changed the script. Wojcik's a Red now, like Carl Potts."

The drunken fury Mediate had greeted me with came back tenfold. "Beaumont and Warner sold me out, damn them. Damn all of you. You've all sold me out."

He drew the bottle back and took a step toward me.

I aimed the gun at his right leg. "Relax," I said, "or you'll be limping to the gas chamber." I had more to say than that, but I never got to say it. The roof of the house picked that moment to come down on my head.

42

I came to on my back with a sky of satin spread out above me. It was a white sky, but not a bright one. Its folds and creases were lit by a faint evening light coming from my right.

I raised my head with an effort. I was lying on the Mediates' Cinderella bed. The lady herself was seated beside me. She was still wearing the white dress I'd admired in the Stratford's breakfast room. Like the canopy sky above me, her shoulders reflected the soft light coming in through a window behind her.

"What time is it?" I asked. My voice sounded like someone walking through dead leaves.

"Almost seven," Carole said. "You've been out for hours. I've been so scared, Scotty. I didn't think I hit you that hard."

"You were number two on the bill." I passed a hand over the back of my head. There was more of it than I remembered and it was softer. "Where's Mediate?"

"Gone. He started drinking again after we'd carried you in here. He worked himself into a rage over changes to the picture. I don't know what he was talking about. But he blamed Torrance Beaumont for it."

"Where did he go?"

"He went looking for Beaumont. That's what he said anyway. Scotty, he took your gun."

I would have preferred another love tap on the head to that news. I checked my pockets for Kramer's photostat. It was also gone. I tried to sit up, but that was too ambitious a plan.

Carole lay a cool hand on my forehead. "Take it easy."

"Tell me about the night Kramer was shot."

"I've already told you about that."

"Lately I've had bouts of amnesia. Tell me again."

"After the party, we got in the car and drove up here." She looked around her at the half-finished house as though she were making her first visit. Or she might have been thinking it was her last one.

"You told me you two were up here arranging furniture. Is this bed the furniture?"

"Yes. It was my idea, my surprise for Vince. I thought if we had a night here together it might help undo what's wrong with this place. It didn't work out."

"What is wrong with this house?"

"Bert Kramer is. When he was alive, he sucked up the money we'd set aside to build it. Now that he's dead, he's haunting it."

"You knew that Kramer was blackmailing your husband?"

"Yes."

"Did you know why?"

"Oh yes. Kramer explained it to me in great detail."

"When he started blackmailing you for sex?"

"Yes."

"Did your husband know about that?"

"No. Not until you told him."

I raised myself up on my elbows, trying to read her eyes in the half light. The eyes didn't quite match, I noticed belatedly. The left one was less than fully open, and the skin around it was puffy. I took hold of Carole's chin, gently, and turned her head until the left side of her face was lit by the western window.

"Mediate hit you? That was my fault. Sorry."

"It evened us up," Carole said, running a hand lightly over my hair. "Besides, it wasn't your fault. It was Bert Kramer's. I hope he's burning in hell right now."

"Let's talk about how he got there." I tried sitting up again. This time I actually got both feet planted on the floor.

Carole had an arm around me to keep me from falling backward or pitching forward. "I told you we were on our way up here when he was shot."

"I know your car was. I'm wondering if you were both in it."

"What are you saying, that I drove the car up here alone while Vince stayed in town and shot Kramer?"

"Or he did the driving and you did the shooting. It would have been easy for you to get inside the house. Kramer may even have been expecting you. That may be why he chased his wife out of the place."

"You think I could shoot someone, Scotty?"

"If I'd been in your spot, I could have shot Kramer or knifed him or clubbed him to death."

"I didn't kill him. I wanted to, but I didn't do it. I've never even been to his house. Kramer never made me go there. He called it neutral territory."

I would have asked her where Kramer had made her go and what he had made her do, but I was feeling low enough already. "How big a head start does your husband have?"

"An hour maybe. I don't know exactly."

We stood up together, Carole doing more than her share of the lifting. "Where are you going?" she asked.

"After him."

"Take me with you, Scotty, please." She looked around at the house that was haunted by a man who had never set foot in it. "Don't leave me here."

"Leave you here? You're doing the driving."

We made our exit via the front door, like civilized people. On our way through the living room, I checked the fireplace for the ashes of the photostat. There was no sign that anything had ever been burned there. Or ever would be.

Mediate hadn't taken my keys or paused long enough to disable the LaSalle, things he might reasonably have been expected to do. A fugitive with a difference was Vincent Mediate.

The first leg of our journey was extremely short. We drove a mile or so down the lake road to another house. The lady who answered the door looked like Margaret Dumont dressed up to play a lumberjack. She didn't like her first glimpse of us, and I couldn't blame her. After Carole told her we'd been in an accident, she softened up enough to let us in. She fussed over Carole's eye while I called the "motor club."

Paddy didn't answer his office phone. I tried his home number and got his wife. The sound of Peggy's clipped hello did more to steady me than all of Carole's ministrations.

"I thought you'd be on your way to Baltimore by now," I said.

"Scotty, is that you? What are you babbling about?"

"Forget it. Is the boss there?"

"No. He's over at Warners. At least that's the story he told me."

"Call him there. Tell him that Mediate is still in town and that he's after Beaumont. Tell Paddy to be careful; Mediate has a gun."

"I'm dialing already," Peggy said.

Our hostess had overheard enough of my call to part with us without regret. Carole and I made the drive back to town in silence. Most of it, that is. As we entered the outskirts of the city, I found that my head was bothering me less than a question that was bouncing around inside it.

"Why did you go along with Kramer's blackmail, Carole?"

She tried a flip reply that rang hollow. "I don't think it's fair to expect me to deal with two jealous men on one night, no matter what I've done."

"Pretend it's an old friend asking. Why did you do it?"

"Why didn't I just tell him to go to hell? I couldn't. For Vince's sake."

"I guess what I'm asking is: Why didn't you tell your husband to go to hell?"

"I don't understand."

"You knew what he'd done. What he'd been. Why make that sacrifice for him? Why not hand him over to Kramer tied up in ribbon?"

"I'm sure you've got that all worked out. You gave me the accounting once. What was it again? A Lincoln, a boat, a house on a lake."

"Do me a favor. Forget I said that."

"Let's pretend that we are old friends, Scotty. You'd have to give me the benefit of the doubt then, wouldn't you? You'd know I couldn't love a fascist."

"Yes," I said, "I would."

"What Kramer told me didn't start me questioning my feelings for Vince. Kramer's story answered questions I've had all along. There's a darkness in Vince I've wondered about since I met him, something that haunts him. Sometimes I thought it was a woman from his past and sometimes I thought it was the war. Kramer told me exactly what it was.

"Suddenly I knew why Vince was so driven to prove himself and to be approved of by everybody else. I knew why he was so impatient with second-rate slackers like Kramer. It was the guilt driving him."

"What difference did knowing that make?"

"It made me sure that he was no Nazi. That he wasn't all wrong inside. He couldn't be and feel that kind of guilt."

Carole had never read the script of *Love Me Again*, or she would have known that her husband's brand of guilt was the current fashion for the Franz Wojciks of the world. How had Carl Potts gotten that kind of insight? Was he having his own second thoughts about his past loyalties? Or was there a simpler explanation? My brain had played too much patty cake with my skull recently to work out an answer, even a simple one.

"Do you understand what I've been trying to tell you, Scotty?"

"I should have known the answer without asking. You love the guy."

"Love is always the answer."

I looked over to see if she'd said that with a straight face after all she'd been through and with all the trouble she had ahead of her. Carole's expression was just on the serene side of grim.

She met my gaze. "Love makes things right."

"It's got a busy night ahead of it," I said.

43

Carole pulled over at the first cab stand we came to and got out. I took her place behind the wheel, and she leaned through my open window.

"What do I do now, Scotty?"

It was the standard cue for the comeback "I don't give a damn," but that wasn't how I felt about it.

"Check into any hotel but the Stratford and call my boss for orders." I gave her the Maguires' number.

She promised she would and kissed my fevered brow to seal the bargain.

The Warners lot was quiet but far from sleepy. Two guards were on duty at the front gate, one of them the old-timer who had baby-sat my gun earlier in the day.

He remembered me. "Hand over that shooting iron, pardner."

"Don't have it anymore. A crippled newsy took it away from me." While he satisfied himself that I was telling the truth, I asked, "Have you seen Maguire?"

"He left an hour ago. Before the warning about Mediate came in."

I hurried on to soundstage seven. Then I cooled my heels, waiting for the red warning light to go off, signaling a break in the filming. It was almost fully dark, but the heat had yet to knock off for the day. If anything, the air felt hotter, as hot and stagnant as the breath of a long-shut attic. I used a Lucky to flavor the stale air. The guard stationed at the soundstage door was addressing the same problem with a corona that had a familiar shape. He was yet another vote Paddy could count on when he got around to running for mayor.

When the warning light finally went out, I hurried inside. Beaumont and Fritz Taber were still in position on the dressing room set. Max Froy was pitching something to them in a tone too low for me to hear. When the director had finished, Beaumont nodded no, slowly and very deliberately. Froy's next line came out loud enough to be heard by the guards on the front gate: "That's it for tonight, then. Thank you, everyone."

A smattering of applause from the crew followed Froy's concession speech. It wasn't the spontaneous demonstration I'd heard when Beaumont and Taber had played the original version of the scene earlier in the week. This hand was the token response of tired people grateful to be heading home.

When I stepped up, Beaumont was thanking Taber for his good work. Or Steve Laird was. In his hairpiece and makeup and costume, Beaumont seemed far removed from the aging, cynical actor who had bought me a drink at the Mocambo. Nor did he seem like someone who particularly needed my protection. Quite the opposite. I had the impulse to turn things over to him and go home myself.

The actor gave me a long look while he lit a cigarette. "Your boss told me you'd had a run-in with our friend Maxwell. Sorry if I set you up for that."

"Don't be," I said. "I wouldn't have missed it. Where did Paddy go?"

"I dunno. He breezed through here earlier. Looking for somebody, I thought. Maybe for my coproducer. The studio security boys seem to think Mediate can come and go around here like Lon Chaney at the Paris Opera. We got the word Mediate might be dropping by tonight looking for me. That came from you, I hear."

"Yes."

"Well, the cops are watching my house, and I've got half the Warners payroll keeping an eye on me, so we're covered."

A security guard was hovering at the edge of our conversation. Beaumont waved him over. "Go find yourself a cup of coffee, Sid. I'll be okay with Hawkshaw here around."

When the guard had gone, Beaumont said, "Let's find a drink. I'm all in." We headed for his trailer, the actor addressing me in a hushed tone as we walked. "That Sergeant Dempsey wouldn't give us a straight story, but the gossip columnists seem to know all about Mediate's arrangement with Carl Potts. Do the cops think Mediate is their killer?"

"Yes," I said.

"Damn. Why is Mediate sore at me, though?"

"He thinks you're maneuvering him off the picture. And he's mad about the changes to the script. About Wojcik being a Red now instead of a Nazi. Why didn't Mediate know that was in the works?"

"You said it yourself. He was being maneuvered off the picture. So there was no reason to keep him in the know. Ever since you tailed him to Long Beach, his days on this lot have been numbered. But that was Jack Warner's doing, not mine. So were the changes to the script. Hell, I'm not any happier about those than Mediate is. I don't want people thinking that we caved in to those Red-baiters in Washington. Or that we're doing their dirty work for them. I came close to chucking the whole deal over that."

"Are you sure you're not just disappointed that you won't be the one shooting Franz Wojcik in the last reel?"

Beaumont laughed without removing his cigarette from his lips. Its burning tip bounced up and down in the darkness as he answered me. "That change was my idea. In the original ending, there's that hint that I really want Wojcik dead so I can have his wife. Not so good for my image. Now it'll look like Maura shoots Wojcik to get me." He chuckled again. "Wait and see the mush mail I get after that."

I fell out of step with the actor, slowed down a little by what he'd said. But there wasn't time just then for reflection. Beaumont was already opening the trailer's door.

The inside of the dressing room was dark. "Who turned out the lights?" Beaumont asked. "To coin a cliché."

The real cliché was stepping into the dark room with a killer on the loose. It was the kind of mistake people in the movies made, with half the audience whispering "don't" in spite of themselves. I said it myself, I think. I certainly brushed past Beaumont in the doorway as he fumbled for the light switch.

When the trailer's overhead fixture came on, it revealed the Phantom of Warner Bros., Vincent Mediate. He was standing in one of the trailer's far corners. While we watched, he raised a gun. My gun.

Mediate wasn't as ruffled as he'd been when I last saw him.

His hair was combed, and he was wearing his houndstooth sports coat. It was carefully buttoned and even had a handkerchief in its breast pocket. He'd internalized up all the disorder I'd noted at the lake. I could see it churning around behind his eyes.

"Shut the door," Mediate said. "And lock it."

Beaumont could have made a dive for the stage floor; he was only a step from the open door. Instead, he closed the door softly and turned the lock on the knob.

"Give it up, Mediate," I said. "This place is crawling with witnesses."

"Of course it is," Mediate said. "Mr. Beaumont is a big star. He deserves a big audience for his big scene."

The producer hadn't sobered up, in spite of the hours that had passed since our last chat. The secret of his endurance stood on a makeup table at his elbow: an open bottle of Drambuie.

Beaumont noticed the bottle at the same moment I did. "Have you been drinking my booze?" he demanded. "I like that. Turn your back for a minute around here and you end up buying drinks for every sponger in town."

He took a step toward Mediate. I tried to get between them, but Beaumont straight-armed me back against the trailer's side wall, the movement carrying me a little way toward the man with the gun.

"Stay out of this," Beaumont said. "We can finish our talk after I've bounced this no-talent creep."

Veins were standing out across Mediate's noble brow. With his free hand he tugged at the open collar of his shirt. "What did you call me, Beaumont?"

"What's the matter, did all that high living hurt your eardrums? I said 'creep.' As in something that creeps out of a drain."

Mediate pushed himself out of the corner and started for the actor. "Shut up," he said.

"Come over here and make me, creep. To think of all the hot air I've had to listen to about you. The hero of Normandy. The liberator of Buchenwald. All the time, you're nothing but a major-league phony. I hate phonies."

Beaumont had skipped a beat before saying the last three words, and he'd said them at a dead slow pace. I recognized them from our talk at the Mocambo and knew they were a wake-up call directed at me. Beaumont was playing his ribbing game again, this time for high stakes.

Mediate was staggering toward the actor, his gun hand leading the way. He said, "You little ..." and then choked on the next word, spittle foaming at the corner of his mouth. I was as forgotten as the witnesses out on the soundstage.

Beaumont fell back a step and Mediate closed the gap, coming abreast of me. I used the trailer wall as a springboard and threw myself at Mediate, knocking the automatic away from Beaumont as a first step. While we wrestled for the gun, I tried to push the producer back into his corner, but even a drunken Mediate was more than I could lift and carry. He almost managed to draw a bead on Beaumont again, even with my hand clamped on his wrist.

The producer hadn't landed a punch, but I was already seeing stars. I let go of the shoulder pad I'd grabbed with my left and threw all my weight against his gun arm, driving it into a curtained window. The glass behind the window shattered. Mediate gave a little cry of pain and released his hold on the gun. I ducked under his roundhouse right and stroked his jaw with the automatic. He went down in a heap on the floor.

I almost followed him there. Beaumont was standing behind me, holding a fresh bottle of Drambuie by the neck. He was grinning his wolf's grin, the one I'd imagined him grinning just before he tackled Kurt the Nazi gunman in my production of *Love Me Again*.

"You okay, pal?" he asked. "You look pretty white. I probably do, too. I didn't know if you'd pick up on the gag, but you did swell. I would have crowned him good for you, if you'd gotten out of the way."

"Sorry," I said.

"That's okay, pal, that's okay. I might have broken the bottle. Care to join me?"

"In a minute." Running footsteps were already approaching the trailer. I examined the gun first, slipping the magazine out and then ramming it home. Then I patted down the sleeping producer. I found the photostat he'd taken from me at the lake. It was in his breast pocket, cleverly hidden behind the handkerchief. I had just gotten the paper into my own breast pocket when someone started pounding on the trailer's door.

Beaumont answered the summons with a glass in hand, like the host of a party. There was a party's worth of people outside. Sid, the guard, was the first man through the door, but only because he was too big for Froy and Taber to get around.

"You all right, Mr. Beaumont?" the guard asked.

"Fine, Sid, except for being bushed from doing the cops' work for them. My pal Elliott and I just landed Bert Kramer's killer."

"Mr. Mediate?"

"Hell yes, Mr. Mediate. He tried to add me to his collection. Elliott's got his gun."

I handed Sid the automatic. "It's safe enough now," I said. "I unloaded it."

The scene was poorly constructed. Sid held center stage, but he hadn't been given any decent lines. "Mr. Mediate?" he asked again.

"Don't try to figure it out," Beaumont said, patting him on the shoulder. "Just hold on to Sleeping Beauty there until the cops arrive. I recommend a ball and chain."

Froy then started doing what he did best: barking orders with an accent. He drafted two stagehands to carry Mediate out of the trailer. Sid went with them for appearances' sake.

Beaumont fielded the expressions of concern and the congratulations of Taber and the other hangers-on, but his heart didn't seem to be in it. As soon as he could, he sent them packing and shut the door. Then he poured a drink for me and another for himself. His hands were shaking now. So were mine.

I got in the first question. "Are you sure you want to hand Mediate over to the police? It means the end of *Love Me Again*. The studio isn't going to like that."

"To hell with the movie and to hell with the stinking studio. I've made up my mind. I'm not signing on as mouthpiece for any witch-hunters out of Washington. Let them chase their own bogeymen. Before this picture came along, I'd almost decided to set Siren Productions up at another studio. See if I don't do it now."

He tossed back the Drambuie and poured another one. "Now you answer a question for me. Why did you tell that guard you'd emptied Mediate's forty-five? You know damn well you didn't."

"I said it so he wouldn't be surprised when he checked the bad guy's gun and didn't find any bullets."

"It was never loaded?"

"It was when he took it away from me. The bullets are probably still up at Hobart Lake."

Beaumont found a chair and fell into it. "Mediate didn't want to kill me? Why did he come here then?"

To get himself killed or arrested, if I was guessing right. That would have taken too long to explain, so I said, "He came here to scare you. Mediate wanted to show you up as a phony, a pretend hero. To get a little of his pride back. You surprised him. You didn't give him the satisfaction."

Beaumont wouldn't be bought off with flattery. "You stood there and let me tell everyone that Mediate is the murderer. They're calling the cops right now. What am I supposed to tell them tomorrow?"

"Tell them you were setting the real murderer up. Taking the heat off him so he'd get careless and make a mistake. It's a standard ploy in detective movies."

"You know who really killed Kramer?"

"I think so. I'm going to take him now. Want to come along?"

"No thanks, sweetheart. One gun a night is all I face down,

285

loaded or not."

"Speaking of guns," I said, "you wouldn't have one lying around here, would you? I seem to have given mine away."

"As a matter of fact," Beaumont said, "I do." He rummaged around in a cabinet beneath his dressing table and came out holding another automatic, a small, nickel-plated thirty-two. He handed it over. "Forgot I had that until Vince got the drop on us. Belonged to my first wife. She used to shoot agents with it."

"Thanks," I said.

I started for the door, but the actor blocked my way. "Wait a minute. You let me throw my movie away, knowing all the time that Mediate wasn't the killer. Why?"

I thought about it for a moment, looking at the dark crescents that were working their way through the makeup under Beaumont's eyes. "Steve's story wasn't meant to have a sequel. In a better world, nobody's story would. Every man's life would fade to black after he'd done his noblest deed, like Steve's does at the end of *Passage to Lisbon*."

I was thinking of Vincent Mediate, war hero. Beaumont might have been, too. "It's one long drop after that big moment, isn't it?" he said.

"Let's just say the first step is a killer."

44

I left the lot without making the acquaintance of the policemen who were coming for Vincent Mediate. I drove south out of Burbank, obeying all the traffic signals and matching the posted speed limits exactly on the LaSalle's full-moon speedometer. I had no reason to hurry. A studio grapevine was a remarkable piece of work, but it would still take a while for the word to get around that Mad Dog Mediate had been taken.

I drove to West Hollywood and to a little street off Santa Monica Boulevard. I parked along an unlit stretch of the street, squeezing in between a matched pair of black Fords. My coupé hadn't been designed for blending into the background, but, given the darkness, I thought I'd get by.

My parking spot gave me a view of the Kramer bungalow. Through a gap in the shrubbery, I could see a single front window, its shade lit from behind by a weak light, probably the flowered standing lamp I'd admired so much. Apart from that yellow glow, the house looked as dark and deserted as the street. I settled in to chain-smoke and to think, ducking my aching head whenever a passing car made the street a little less deserted. Luckily, few cars passed by.

I used the time to review what I laughingly called my evidence. As with all my previous theories, the script of *Love Me Again* was the base on which I built. Earlier in the day—before Vincent Mediate had turned into a Nazi—Pidgin had reminded me that the story was a love triangle, and I'd jumped to the conclusion that the dying Bert Kramer had been trying to tip us to another triangle, one whose three sides were Kramer, Carole Mediate, and her husband. They had, in fact, been members of a threesome, although Vincent Mediate had been an unknowing participant. But theirs wasn't the triangle Kramer had been pointing to when he'd grabbed for the script, not if I was finally reading that clue correctly.

Torrance Beaumont had set my foot on the path with his crack about Steven Laird wanting Wojcik out of the way so Laird could have Wojcik's wife. Duplicating that scenario would make Kramer one star in an entirely new constellation. Violet Kramer would be the second point of light, and the third would be the man who wanted her badly enough to kill for her.

Carole Mediate had told me that Bert Kramer never forced her to come to his house. He'd called it "neutral territory," not "enemy territory" or "off-limits" or any other euphemism a cheating husband might use to describe his wife's domain.

"Neutral territory" suggested a common ground where two people living separate lives could continue to act out the sham of a marriage. Violet had pretended not to know about her husband's philandering, and maybe she hadn't known for sure. But Kramer had known about her affair. I remembered one of the taunts I'd overheard through the front door of the bungalow on my first visit, something about Violet spending her afternoons at a motel. I'd passed it off as a bad joke, which was how Kramer had seemed to think of it. That was consistent with his offhand remark to Carole. He knew about his wife's affair but didn't give a damn. Something else had been the catalyst for the shooting. I was guessing that it was the same spark that had set the whole story in motion. The thing that had gotten Hollywood Security involved and had led to the exposure of Carl Potts and the arrest of Vincent Mediate. The anonymous note.

Who had really sent the note and why? I'd given up my fond notion that Mediate had sent it as a screwy way of punishing himself. My new candidate was Violet's lover, the missing side of the Bert and Violet triangle. Violet had given me some clues to his identity when I'd stopped by her house that morning. I'd surely frightened her then with my questions about infidelity. Until she'd realized that I was after Bert's secret and not hers. I hadn't really paid attention to her drunken asides. Now I tried my best to recall them. She'd railed against gentlemen, calling them losers. That fit in with her husband's motel crack, which had had her spending her afternoons with Hollywood's premier gentleman, Ronald Colman. Her parting jibe to me had been about veterans and their rosy hopes for the future. So, if I was right, if Violet's comments were references to her lover and not just potshots at me, I needed a gentleman veteran to fill the role I was casting, one who had no love for Bert Kramer and even less for the other target of the note, Vincent Mediate.

About an hour after I'd taken up my vigil, my missing player made his entrance. He must have parked farther away than I had and on the opposite end of the quiet street. I heard his approaching footsteps and knew by their sound that he was my man. They rang out with a regular rhythm that was an echo of dead parade grounds. There was a street lamp opposite the bungalow and down a house or two. By its light, I saw him. First as a shape in the darkness. Then as a man. Then as a particular man: Fred Wilner.

He ascended the bungalow's front-porch steps with only a token glance behind him. If he knocked on the front door, he did it too softly for me to hear.

I climbed out of the car and ground my latest cigarette under my heel. I didn't tiptoe up the sidewalk or try to avoid the creaking front steps. That wouldn't have made much sense given my next move, which was knocking loudly on the door frame with the butt of the ex–Mrs. Beaumont's ex-automatic.

Violet answered the door. If the Kramer case had been a movie, Violet would have been transformed for this last turn. She would have dropped her disguise of housedresses and frazzled hair and revealed herself as a temptress, able to bend men to her will, or at least as a beauty for whom men would happily shoot one another. But this wasn't a movie, as Pidgin and I had taken turns observing. Violet's eyes were a touch more alive than I remembered them being, but her hair was still a half-built nest and the robe she was clutching tightly to her chest was as shapeless and gray as anything she'd modeled for me. She was wearing the scent I remembered from my morning visit, one that had been bottled in Kentucky.

"What do you want?" she asked in a husky whisper.

"I just stopped by to drop off some more bad luck."

"Take it home with you."

She tried to shut the door on me, but I was already leaning against it. My weight pushed Violet off-balance. She stepped back to catch herself, by which time I was inside and shutting the door behind me.

"I'm going to call the cops," Violet said. She sounded mad

enough to do it.

"Fine. That'll save me a nickel."

"I'm going to scream."

"Allow me." I called out Wilner's name. "I know you're in here. Come out with your hands empty."

Wilner stepped out of the bedroom hallway. He'd made himself at home to the extent of losing his hat and suit coat. His hands, which hung at his sides, held nothing but air.

My right hand held a gun pointed at his stomach, but Wilner chose to ignore that lapse of manners. "Hello, Elliott," he said. "What brings you here?"

"That's my line, I think."

The assistant producer stood a little stiffly, but his drawly voice was calm. "I heard they arrested Vince Mediate."

"I was hoping you had."

"I came by to check on Mrs. Kramer."

"You're dressed a little informally to be using last names," I said.

Wilner's glasses were reflecting the light of the standing lamp, which made it impossible to read his eyes. So I read his smile. It was as sincere as a Hollywood pat on the back.

"You're a regular guy, Elliott, so I might as well tell you the truth. One vet to another."

"One vet to another," I said.

"That night I drove Violet to her mother's, she and I felt a certain attraction to one another. It was understandable, given the circumstances, with me acting as her protector, delivering her from a drunken husband. Of course, we didn't even speak of it that night. Bert was still alive as far as we knew. Afterward, when it turned out that I really had taken Violet to safety, maybe even saved her life, I felt an obligation to check in on her. Since then, we've been moving toward an understanding."

"An understanding," Violet repeated, her disgust with Wilner's delicacy barely under control.

"You've been moving pretty damn fast," I said.

"No faster than you and Miss Englehart," Wilner said.

"Leave her out of this."

"Of course," Violet sneered. "Mustn't drag a lady's name into our sordid business."

"Quiet, Violet, please. There's nothing sordid going on here. I'm sure we can count on Mr. Elliott's discretion."

"If you'll answer a question for me."

"Yes?"

"Why did you send the anonymous note to Jack Warner?"

"That note!" Violet hissed at Wilner. She pushed her hands up through her hair, twisting as she pushed. "That damn note!"

"Hush up, honey." Then he asked me a question made ludicrous by Violet's outburst. "What makes you think I had anything to do with that?"

"You're about the only one who could have. For a while now I've been seeing that note as a billiard shot designed to sink two careers, Kramer's and Mediate's. That's why it was sent to Warner and not Mediate in the first place and why it was written on stationery from the Stratford Hotel, a mysterious little touch intended to hint that Mediate knew more than he was telling."

"What was I supposed to have against Vince? I worked for the guy."

"From what I've seen of his working habits, that might have been enough. There's also your war service, yours and Mediate's." I was borrowing freely from what Pidgin had told me the night Kramer was shot, when she'd given me her own reasons for disliking Mediate. "You slogged around in some forgotten jungle for little thanks, while he was making a name for himself with his camera crew, using the war to build a career. And what a career. You had to resent taking orders from a guy who stole the spot that might have been yours if you'd managed to sidestep the fighting."

"Maybe I did resent him," Wilner said. "What would that prove?"

"I have it diagrammed like this. You and Violet have an

understanding all right, but you reached it weeks ago. Maybe months ago. You might have met her at the studio or while you were running an errand for Mediate or you might have bumped into each other at Schwab's Drugstore. We can find out if we look hard enough."

"Sure you can," Violet said.

"Kramer knew someone was beating his time, but he didn't care. He had his own little love nest set up, never mind with whom. He did care about the anonymous note, though. It threatened his secret deal with Carl Potts, threatened his whole career at Warners. But he couldn't figure out who was trying to ruin him. Not until the night he was killed.

"You overplayed your part that night, Wilner. You called Kramer to tell him about a little party he hadn't been invited to, probably after you'd sent Pidgin and me off for a drink. Did you disguise your voice or use the old gag of talking through a handkerchief?"

Wilner maintained the dignity of silence.

"Somehow, drunk as he was, Bert figured it out. On the drive back here from the Stratford, maybe, or once you got here. Maybe it was a look that passed between you and Violet or a slip of the tongue. Whatever it was, Bert finally realized that he wasn't dealing with two mystery men, one who was stealing his wife and another who was threatening his livelihood. There was only one man, and his affair with Violet explained the note. She gave a man Kramer barely knew a motive for wanting to see him ruined."

"You bastard," Violet hissed at me. She'd gone chalky white and her hands were clenched into fists. Her forgotten robe hung open, and her chest was heaving under a scarlet nightgown. "You bastard!"

"Violet, no! He's just guessing. He doesn't know anything."

It was too late for Wilner's calming words. She was already coming at me, screaming and swinging. I grabbed her wrist with my left hand and held it while she kicked me with her knees.

Then I realized that I was pointing the thirty-two toward the ceiling.

"Just leave it up there," Wilner said, as Violet pulled herself free. He had a gun of his own now. He must have had it all along, tucked in his belt at the small of his back. He held it out with a straight, steady arm, just as he'd been taught to do. It was a thirty-eight-caliber revolver.

Paddy would have another entry for the list I was inspiring, the advanced techniques section of his training manual: how to locate the murder weapon.

"Reach up and take that from him, Violet," Wilner said. "But don't get in between us. Good girl. Bring it here."

"Is this a confession?" I managed to ask.

"Call it whatever you like, pal."

The only play I could think of was to keep Wilner talking. Fortunately, I still had plenty of subject matter. "Why did you try to ruin Kramer with that note? And why did you have to kill the sap? Why didn't you just drive the lady to Reno?"

"The note and the killing are two separate subjects," Wilner said, sounding like the college professor I'd taken him for when I first saw him.

"Give me two separate answers, then. One vet to another."

"All right. One vet to another. The note first. I sent it because the lady wouldn't go to Reno with me. Violet and I met a year ago, when I was working on another project, a B picture her husband actually wrote. We met at a studio party and fell in love. Right from the start. Violet meant home to me. The home I'd been dreaming of back on New Guinea. Do you understand that?"

"Yes," I said.

"When my job on the picture was over, I was picked to be Vince Mediate's assistant, which is to say, the guy who told him which foot was his left and which was his right. He was supposed to be a boy wonder, but he was in way over his head and he knew it. He hated being dependent on me, and I hated

293

having to make him look good."

"Did you steer him to Kramer when he needed a front for Potts?"

"Not knowingly I didn't. Vince didn't trust me enough to let me in on that. But he knew I'd worked with Kramer and he asked me a lot of questions about him. Later, when the script for *Love Me Again* miraculously appeared, I started to work out the truth. I knew from the start that there was a dead rat somewhere under the floorboards, as we used to say back home. Kramer and Mediate let enough slip for me to sniff it out. Bert was a sieve when he'd been drinking, and Vince isn't the genius he thinks he is. Besides, the whole town's been talking about the possibility of a blacklist."

"Why didn't you name Potts in the note?"

"Because I didn't know his name. Not until two days ago when Vince dropped everything and drove off the lot like a chicken who's seen the ax. He was off to meet his fellow conspirator. I don't know where."

"Long Beach," I said. "That was my doing."

Wilner made a little bow to acknowledge the debt. "When he placed that call, Mr. Potts must have violated whatever security procedures Vince had set up. I was able to get Potts's name from the switchboard operator. I did some checking and knew I had my man."

"You handed Potts over to Dempsey by having Violet spin a story about Potts calling Kramer."

"Yes. The police needed a little help, seeing as how they weren't getting much from you and Mr. Maguire. But all that is under the heading of the killing, and we haven't finished with the note yet."

"Sorry."

Wilner was finally feeling the weight of the gun. He drew his arm in to his side but kept the revolver's barrel pointed squarely at my chest. "Violet was ready enough to leave Bert until *Love Me Again* came along. Then overnight his gambling debts disappeared. She began to think in terms of her future security."

Violet laughed at that phrasing. I might have, too, at a lighter moment. "You mean she got wind of the money," I said. "Bert was letting things slip at home the same way he was at the studio. Violet did her own job of putting it all together. She decided it would be bad timing to divorce Bert just when he was starting to turn a profit."

"Are you saying I wasn't entitled?" the lady asked.

"Not me, your boyfriend. He worked it out so Bert would never see his big payday. And he couldn't resist taking a swipe at Vincent Mediate at the same time."

"Vince deserved that and worse," Wilner said.

"Bert thought so, too," I said. "But he knew how to hurt Mediate and help himself at the same time. By erasing his gambling debts, for instance."

"He was smart," Bert's widow said. She looked at his successor. "Not half smart."

"Shut up, Violet. Can't you see what he's trying to do?"

If Wilner knew my plan, he was way ahead of me. "So you wrote the note to nip the Kramers' reconciliation in the bud. Let's get to why you killed him."

"You know that already. Bert figured out that I was the one who'd called him about the party at the Stratford. He worked it all out from a slip I made."

"Tell him what the slip was, big man," Violet said. "He drove Bert here without asking directions. Drove him right to the house. Even a drunk could spot a hint that big."

Wilner smiled a crazy little smile that came and went like a flash of lightning. "Maybe I was trying to nudge things along. Subconsciously."

I nodded toward the gun. "It's the conscious nudging that finished you."

"That was self-defense. Once Bert realized what was going on, he went nuts. He ran to his desk and got this out. I tried to take it away from him, and it went off."

"If you're hoping to sell that self-defense story to Sergeant Dempsey, you'd better work in something about Bert turning the radio up real loud with his feet while he wrestled you for the gun. Otherwise, Dempsey's going to think you just took advantage of a chance to bury your lover's husband."

Wilner's lightning smile flashed again. "Well, it was worth a run-through. Looks like it's Mexico for us, Violet. Are you game?"

She was laying back against the wallpaper roses, looking pale and sick. "What choice do I have?"

Wilner made do with that declaration of devotion and turned his attention back to me. "Any last questions, Elliott?"

I found myself thinking in a dizzy, dreamy way of Steven Laird's escape from Duncan on the New York docks. "How about a cigarette?" I asked, giving the game away with a nervous grin I couldn't quite hold in.

Wilner grinned back just as maniacally. "I think not. I read the script, too, remember." He moved over to the radio cabinet and switched the set on. "Sorry, soldier," he said.

I opened my mouth to second that. Then the door next to me was kicked in. Its place was taken by Paddy Maguire, a cigar in his teeth and the twin of my lost automatic in his right hand. Wilner made the mistake of turning his gun toward the sound of the breaking door. Paddy dropped him with a single shot.

"Scotty, are you all right? Mary, Mother of God!"

"Get an ambulance," I said.

I kicked Wilner's fallen gun into a far corner of the room and knelt down beside him. The circle of blood on his shirt front was already the size of a saucer. The wound at its center was making a sucking sound with every breath he took. I'd seen wounds like that before. So had Wilner. When I held a wadded handkerchief against the spreading blood, he tried to smile.

"Don't bother," he said.

Wilner had lost his glasses when he'd hit the floor. Without them, he should have looked younger. Instead he looked very old. The blood in his chest was making him cough. I cradled his head while we listened to the sound of Paddy calling for an ambulance from the study phone.

"Sorry, soldier," I said.

I had a vision of a snow-covered field, dotted with red. Wilner was staring up toward the ceiling, perhaps at swaying palm fronds.

"Do your best for Violet," he said. "My fault. Tell it that way."

The lady in question was still pressed against the wall. She was crying, maybe for Wilner.

"Loved her," Wilner said. Later on I thought a lot about the tense he'd used, wondering if he'd meant he'd once loved her but didn't anymore. At the time he said it, the past tense seemed natural enough. He died as he spoke the last word.

45

Paddy signaled his return to the front room by placing a hand on my shoulder and shaking me gently. "The ambulance is on its way," he said.

"It's too late."

"I know. It was too late when I picked up the phone. Some things you do just to do them. Anyway, I had to call the police."

Paddy collected Wilner's thirty-eight while I got to my feet. He put the revolver in the left-side pocket of his coat, where it balanced the weight of the automatic in his right-side pocket. Then he glanced around the room, paying particular attention to Violet Kramer.

"Where's your gun, Scotty?" he asked. "I know it's not in your glove compartment. I checked just now on my stroll to the house. They got it away from you, I assume."

Wilner had fallen on the thirty-two. I retrieved it and handed it to Paddy. He held it between his forefinger and thumb.

"This used to be a forty-five," he said. "What happened?"

"I left it out in the rain."

Paddy's answering smile was almost as big a relief as the sight of him kicking down the door had been. I told him how I'd lost my gun to Vincent Mediate, what use he'd put it to, and where it was now. Without knowing why, exactly, I omitted all references to the German-American Bund.

While he listened, Paddy took off his homburg and wiped his face with a pink handkerchief. The cloth was the size of a hotel towel, but the project still required several passes.

"Thanks for the rescue," I said when I'd finished my confession. "How did you happen to pull it off?"

"You can thank Tory Beaumont for that. He tracked me down through Peggy and told me you'd gone off after the killer. For some strange reason, he thought you might need help.

"I hurried over here in time to catch most of Mr. Wilner's confession. Thank God I did. I never would have forgiven myself if anything had happened to you because of the stupid competition I dreamed up. Because of my misbegotten pride, I should say. Her nibs would never have forgiven me, that's for sure."

"But how did you know where to come? I didn't tell Beaumont that part."

Paddy's misbegotten pride came on for a final bow. "You're not the only detective on the staff, you know. I had my eye on these two all along."

"You figured out the clue in the script?"

"The devil I did. I'm an investigator, not a medium. I've been watching this bird," he nodded toward Violet, "because she saw Kramer alive last *and* found the body. Besides those two strikes, she's the widow. When you're handed a married corpse, you can lock up the spouse with a clear conscience nine times out of ten. Then she fingered Mr. Potts, which crystallized my suspicions, so to speak. That move was way too cute.

"The problem was her alibi, provided by the late Mr. Wilner there. It had to be malarkey, which made it better than even money that Wilner was in on it, too. When I quizzed your friend Miss Englehart last night about social life at Warner Bros., she told me that Wilner had been pretty active around the lot until a year or so ago, when he'd suddenly started severing ties."

"But you went to the trouble of verifying the Mediates' alibi," I said. "I talked with the lady who sold you the tomatoes."

"I had to do that because a certain employee of mine kept distracting me with the skeletons he was digging out of the Mediates' flower beds."

My hand moved involuntarily to the pocket where I'd stashed the blackmail photostat, but I stopped short of producing it.

"I'd have wrapped this thing up days ago if I'd given you the week off," Paddy was saying. "First blackmail, then murder. It wouldn't have surprised me if you'd tied Mediate to the Lindbergh kidnapping next. If you have, by the way, don't tell Dempsey. He's confused enough already."

"What are we going to tell him? We've got to get our story down."

"Our story? Don't tell me you want to be less than frank with the police. I thought that kind of finagling was beneath you."

"Wilner asked me to do my best for Violet." I turned to face her. She was still sobbing quietly, which was a healthy sign. I'd have been passed out from shock, if I'd had her week.

Paddy stepped up beside me. "I guess it's true what they say about every man having his price. You wouldn't bend the truth to save *Love Me Again* and, coincidentally, our livelihood. But you'll do it as a favor to a murderer because he once wore the same uniform as you."

I was doing even more for another wearer of my old uniform. My hand threatened to reach for the photostat again. I made a fist of the hand and stuck it behind my back.

"It won't take much bending," I said. "Wilner really was the one calling the shots."

"You're way too soft for this business, Scotty. Or maybe I am. I'll follow your lead on the subject of Mrs. Kramer. We'll do what we can for her."

Violet looked up when he said that. Sirens were finally sounding in the distance as she wiped her eyes. "Men looking out for me," she said. "That's the secret of my happy life."

Violet Kramer ended up doing as much for Hollywood Security as we did for her, if not more. After we'd all been delivered to the Homicide Bureau, she backed up our version of how Fred Wilner came to be dead, a point that troubled Sergeant Dempsey more than somewhat. Her confession stressed the pressure Wilner had exerted on her after he'd shot her husband and the feeling she'd had that she was damned no matter what she did. Violet had a real talent for getting that mood across.

It only took Dempsey a couple of hours to tire of my company. Paddy stayed on to share his personal insight into the case, public-spirited citizen that he was. Just outside of Dempsey's office, my path crossed Carl Potts's for the second and last time. He was seated alone next to an empty desk, looking even more shrunken than I remembered. That was understandable, given his long bout with Dempsey.

Potts was blowing his nose as I walked up. His eyes were bloodshot, and he was blinking away in the bright light of the bullpen like the original Lazarus. A man recalled to life and then forgotten.

"What are you still doing here?" I asked him.

"Filing a complaint of police harassment. Or trying to. The cop filling out the form for me went off somewhere and never came back."

"He's home sleeping," I said. I took the missing man's seat at the desk. There were two cigarettes left in my pack. I passed one to Potts, took the other, and lit them both. Then I dug out the